THE DARKER EYE

An sùilean dorcha

IN 1325, BETHOC, *FIOSAICHE*—BEATRICE, SEER of the MacDuffs—retreated to the island of Iona, seeking a life of prayer and contemplation amongst the sisters of the Augustinian nunnery. On Midsummer's night she dreamt of evil days to come when malice ruled men's hearts and fear stalked the land. It is said that in the dawn she awoke, shaken and fearful of what she had seen *tron shùil dhorcha* —"through the darker eye."

THROUGH A
DARKER EYE

PART ONE
OUTCASTS

CHAPTER ONE

John Wallace saw the smoke rising out of Glen Nevis, and his stomach knotted. In the heat and still air of the summer's day, the grey cloud hung in a boiling mass above the hilltops. Across the glen, at the foot of Ben Nevis, a cottage was burning. It was too far to see clearly, but he knew it was the Cameron cottage.

The redcoats had been camped at Fort William for months, using it as a base to suppress the West Highlands. The smoke could only mean they had entered Glen Nevis. Since the defeat at Culloden in the spring of the year, smoke in large quantities was a cause for alarm in the Highlands. Stories of murder and destruction were common; whole clans were herded onto ships and sent to the Americas, never to return.

John had been on his way across to Loch Eilde Mòr to search for some of his uncle's black cattle that had strayed. Climbing the side of Stob Coire a' Chàirn, on the south side of Glen Nevis, he had taken the track that crossed over to the Loch Eilde Mòr side of the mountain. Had he passed this way a few minutes earlier, he would have missed what was transpiring on the other side of the glen.

The redcoats would push farther into the glen and could not fail to come across his uncle's farm a few miles beyond the Cameron cottage. John's uncle,

Murdoch, away to the upper shieling, would guess what the smoke meant, but his cousin, Maighread, was at the farmhouse. The thought of what would happen if the redcoats found her alone set his heart racing.

"I'll be baking most of the day," she had told him that morning, "making oat cakes. That will please you well enough." She was almost fifteen and used to being left to her own devices. She would be absorbed in her work and unaware of the danger.

John had left the farmhouse just after first light, made his way to the top of the glen, over the ridge and down to the track on this side. If he went back the same way, he would not reach the farmhouse in time. It would be quicker to descend to the floor of Glen Nevis and cross the river. Once on the far side, he could cover the distance to the farm in less than an hour. Two miles to the east a spring cut through the hills, forming a deep corrie. The burn ended at a cliff face and fell to the floor of the glen to join the water of Ness. It was the only place he could get down to the floor of the glen without being seen. John slung his plaid over one shoulder and his hunting bag over the other and set off across the hillside.

When John reached the corrie, he crawled over the top of the ridge on his belly. He could see no sign of movement, and he slid over the edge onto the face of the mountain. He began to slide at an alarming rate and realized he had underestimated the steepness of the slope. He leaned back and dug his heels into the scree, but twice he almost lost his balance and felt the drop sucking at him, filling him with the urge to tumble to the rocks below. Finally, the slope eased, and he came to a stop and sat down on his haunches. The corrie was off to his right; the burn spilled over the edge to the floor of the glen below.

A flash of red at the edge of the forest sent a jolt of alarm through him. It had to be a British patrol, and John leapt to his feet. He thought the redcoats were too far away to see him, but his boots sank ankle deep in the scree, and he felt as if he was running through a nightmare, afraid to look behind him.

By the time he'd covered half the distance, John's legs felt like they were on fire, but the ground became firmer, and he covered the last fifty feet at a dead run. He threw himself down and crawled into the corrie out of sight. The burn had formed a pool in the base of the corrie, and he scooped water into his mouth. The water was cool and carried the peaty tang of the Highlands; he hadn't realized how parched he was and drank deeply.

John rolled onto his back. The sun was high, and he estimated that it must be close to midday. With half the day gone, he hoped the soldiers would not press farther into the glen. He was alarmed to see a small river of stones running down the slope, marking his descent and he skirted the pool and moved to the edge of the corrie.

John searched the far side of the river. A track emerged from the trees where he had seen the flash of red, but nothing moved. The only sound in the glen was the curlew crying high above. As the minutes passed, John's eyes began to sting from concentrating; he realized he was rigid with tension, and he rubbed his eyes with the palms of his hands and rolled his neck.

When he looked back at the floor of the glen, John was startled to see a man standing in the open. He swayed on his feet as if near exhaustion. His clothes were in tatters and he wore the brogans of the Highland crofter on his feet. Farther downstream three soldiers emerged from the woods, their red jackets bright against the green of the forest.

The man started moving towards the river. When he saw the redcoats, he froze for a second, and then started running.

John felt a shock of recognition. It was Alexander Cameron. Years ago a cow had kicked him, breaking his left leg, and leaving him with a permanent limp. He ran with a staggering gait, throwing one leg out to the side, covering as much distance sideways as forward. Instinctively John started to get to his feet, but a musket shot cracked out from below, and he threw himself down again.

The redcoats must have chased Cameron from the far side of the glen. They looked winded, but now that they could see their prey, they bounded forward, whooping and hollering. One soldier dropped to one knee and raised his musket. John saw the smoke from the firing pan, and even as the weapon recoiled, he saw Cameron fall. He cried out in pain and pitched forward clutching his leg. The ball had struck the ankle. He tried to get to his feet, but the leg wouldn't hold him, and he collapsed again.

Cameron crawled to a boulder, pulled himself to his feet, and hopped around on one leg to face the soldiers. The redcoats slowed their pace and spread out, surrounding him like dogs cornering a stag.

The trooper closest to the river came round to Cameron's left side. He was heavily built, and John saw sergeant's stripes on his arm. He ran with a jerky stride, landing heavily, but he covered the ground quickly. He called out to the troopers and they boxed Cameron in. The sergeant ran in and kicked the crofter's left leg out from under him; Cameron fell on his back, and his breath came out in a gasp. The soldiers fell on him with their boots. Cameron rolled himself into a ball, begging for mercy, but they were enjoying themselves and ignored his pleas.

Finally they stopped and two of the soldiers leaned their muskets against the rock and picked Cameron up. His body was limp, and they struggled with the weight. Suddenly Cameron thrust his shoulder into the chest of the soldier to his right, sending him stumbling backwards. He turned and punched the second man in the groin. John heard him scream, and he dropped to the ground. Cameron lunged for the muskets. The sergeant covered the ten feet between them in two strides and struck Cameron on the side of the head with his fist, and he collapsed.

John could hear the sergeant berating the soldiers. One man was still nursing his groin, and the sergeant kicked him in the ribs as he tried to stand. The other soldier dragged Cameron to his feet and twisted his arms behind him. His colleague staggered to his feet and took hold of one of Cameron's arms. The sergeant paced back and forth. John could see him jabbing at Cameron with his finger. He nodded to the soldier on Cameron's right, and he grabbed a handful of his hair and pulled his head back savagely. His back arched, and his hips were thrust forward. The sergeant took a running step and kicked Cameron in the groin. The blow landed with sickening force, lifting him off the ground.

Cameron screamed—a high-pitched female sound that unmanned him. John felt humiliated for him and dreaded what would come next. The soldiers let him slide to his knees, but pulled his arms up between his shoulders so that he stayed upright. The sergeant stepped in and kicked him again. Cameron screamed, but the sound was cut off as he threw up. The sergeant stepped back, and the soldiers tightened their grip as the sergeant started winding up to kick him again. Suddenly a voice rang out across the clearing, and the sergeant stumbled and almost fell on top of Cameron.

John was startled to see a party of soldiers spreading out along the edge of the trees. An officer stood in front of the group. He was dressed in a blue frock coat, white breeches, and black riding boots. John examined him closely. He was about thirty years of age. He had an angular face, sallow skin and a Roman nose, and black hair tied behind his head in a knot. What struck John most was his demeanour—he wore arrogance like a cloak, and his voice rang with contempt.

"Sergeant Crammer, I ordered you to capture that man and bring him to me for questioning." The soldiers watched the captain warily.

"Captain Scott, sir, the man is a lawless brigand. We were attempting to subdue him." Crammer's voice was apologetic, almost whining.

"I will decide who lives and who dies here, Sergeant Crammer, not you! Is that understood?"

"Yes, Captain Scott. Yes, sir." Crammer nodded his head, his voice strained with forced sincerity.

Captain Scott glared at him, and Crammer stood still, his face a mask of humility. Finally the captain turned his attention to Cameron.

"Bring him here."

Sergeant Crammer broke into a run.

"Simms, Busk, bring the prisoner at the double." One of the solders kicked Cameron to get him moving. He tried to roll himself into a ball again but the soldier kicked him on the side of his head, knocking him half-senseless. They pulled him to his feet and dragged him across the clearing. Sergeant Crammer fell in behind, and the group came to a halt in front of the captain. Captain Scott took a step closer to the prisoner. The sergeant grabbed Cameron's hair, and pulled his head back, and Scott studied his face.

John was shocked by the casual brutality of these men. He had heard stories of the redcoats' cruelty when the Jacobite rebellion had been crushed earlier in the year. Every week there were rumours of executions and imprisonments. People were fearful for themselves and their families. John had heard the crofters speak of their hatred for the English, but he had not understood it till now. His anger flared at their treatment of Cameron, but he knew there was nothing he could do, and in his heart he knew this would not end well for Alexander Cameron.

* * *

Scott kept his eyes on Cameron and called out,

"Lieutenant Sackville, report." A young man came forward at the run, stopped in front of the captain, and saluted.

"Sir." The lieutenant looked straight ahead, eyes fixed on a point in the distance. Scott's stomach churned at the sight of him. Lieutenant George Sackville was Scott's nephew and the captain hated everything about him: including his slender frame and delicate features. Even when he stood to attention, he carried himself with a grace more suited to the theatre or the ballroom than the hills of Scotland.

Scott could not suppress a sneer. The lieutenant wore black leggings, fine black leather riding boots, and a bright blue coat, the same colour as Scott's but more elegantly tailored from better cloth. He wore the uniform with the ease of a man long used to the finer things in life. The lieutenant's father was the Duke of Devon and one of the most powerful men in England. This puppy, with his soft hands and genteel manners, would inherit wealth and power beyond anything Scott could hope for in his lifetime.

The duke had arranged for his son to serve under Scott for the purpose of making his time in the army as easy as possible. The duke had promised promotion and rewards in return for his cooperation. Scott had agreed to the arrangement, but that was a year ago in London. Here in the west of Scotland, it was a different world. His nephew's talk of London society, the theatre and the court grated on him, and his attempts to develop a rapport with him only served to increase his contempt for the boy.

Scott raised his right arm and pointed at Cameron.

"Hang that man, Lieutenant." Lieutenant Sackville stepped back as if he'd been struck.

"Captain Scott, Captain Scott," he repeated. The blood had drained from his face, and his voice was barely a whisper. "Captain Scott, there has been no trial!" He looked around in desperation, but the men stared back coldly.

Scott repeated his order.

"Lieutenant Sackville, you will hang this man immediately. We are at war, and there will be no trial." He did not try to hide the contempt in his voice. The lieutenant fell back.

"Captain Scott, this man has not been tried for any crime and cannot be summarily executed."

Scott stepped forward till his face was six inches from the lieutenant's and screamed, "You will obey my order." Flecks of spittle flew from his mouth and landed on the lieutenant's face.

Lieutenant Sackville looked down, swallowing convulsively, and Scott kept on without drawing breath.

"Sergeant Crammer, you will prepare this man for punishment." He glanced at the prisoner. "Lieutenant Sackville will take command of the detail and give the order."

Crammer started barking orders.

"Simms, Busk, bring the prisoner." He set off across the clearing, the two troopers dragging Cameron, half-conscious, behind him.

Scott turned back to his nephew. The lieutenant was pale as a ghost and a tic had started working in the corner of his mouth.

"Lieutenant Sackville, you will take charge of the punishment detail." His voice was calm, but the venom it carried was palpable. As the lieutenant's distress increased, Scott's voice became quieter and more menacing. "You will carry out my orders."

The lieutenant blurted out, "There has been no trial; this man cannot be executed without due process of law." His voice was edging on hysteria.

Scott pressed on relentlessly.

"This man is a rebel. You will obey my orders, or you will be court-martialled and drummed out of the army in disgrace." The lieutenant shuddered at the threat. His head came up, and he met Scott's eye, but he couldn't hold his gaze, and Scott knew he would obey.

Defeated, the lieutenant mumbled under his breath, "Yes, Captain," then turned and walked like a condemned man towards the edge of the clearing.

Scott watched as Sergeant Crammer threw a rope over the branch of a pine and tied the knot. The prisoner stared at it, the reality of what was about to happen dawned on him, and he began to struggle. He was fighting for his life and, even in his weakened state, Simms and Busk had difficulty holding him. The sergeant took a handful of Cameron's hair and pulled his head back until he overbalanced and went down hard. All three men jumped on him, and the fight seemed to go out of him. Sergeant Crammer stepped away.

"Tie him fast and cut the rags off him."

Simms put his knee between Cameron's shoulders, grasped his wrists and wrenched his arms back. Cameron cried out in agony.

"How does that feel, Highlander?" Cameron screamed again, but Simms pushed his face into the dirt and stifled the cry. Busk cut away the remains of Cameron's shirt. He sawed through his belt then ran the knife down to the

9

ankle on both legs, and the cloth fell away leaving Cameron naked. Under Captain Scott's command killing the Highlanders wasn't enough—their dignity had to be taken as well.

Crammer called out to the men. "Bring him."

The troopers dragged Cameron to the tree and lifted him to his feet, and Crammer placed the noose around his neck and pulled it tight.

The troops gathered round. They were seasoned veterans, inured to the sight of death. For them an execution was entertainment to be cheered on by shouts and insults. Now they stood silent. The tension between the two officers was obvious and none dared draw attention to themselves.

"Four men on the rope, smartly now," Crammer shouted. "Jump to it." The four soldiers closest to the tree ran to pick up the rope. Lieutenant Sackville stood ten feet back, his face pale as a corpse. Scott stood behind him, malice in his eyes.

As the noose tightened around his neck Cameron looked about him in confusion and fear, sensing his life was in the lieutenant's hands.

"Please, sir," he pleaded, "I've done nothing wrong, sir." His voice started to rise in desperation, and Crammer smashed his fist into his kidney. Cameron grunted and his legs went out from under him, but Simms and Busk held fast. Lieutenant Sackville stood with his back to his uncle.

Scott spoke again. "You will give the order to carry out the punishment, Lieutenant Sackville."

The lieutenant turned and snapped back in desperation, "This is wrong, Captain—"

Scott cut him off in mid-sentence. "Give the command, Lieutenant. That is a direct order. Now, Lieutenant."

Lieutenant Sackville looked at the prisoner for a moment as if seeking forgiveness then turned to Sergeant Crammer.

"Sergeant Crammer." His voice was little more than a whisper. He started again. "Sergeant Crammer, carry out the execution." He dropped his head, unable to watch.

Crammer stepped forward and saluted. "Yes, Lieutenant, haul away smartly now."

The four men grasped the rope and walked backwards till Cameron's feet came off the ground. Crammer called out to them to make the end fast, and the clearing fell silent except for the sound of Alexander Cameron slowly choking. His body twitched and kicked; then there was a splattering sound and the air filled with the sharp smell of feces as his bowels let loose. Cameron's face was purple, and his tongue protruded from his mouth to an extent that did not seem possible. Finally his struggles ceased, and he hung limp, turning slowly in the breeze.

The air was like the heat before a thunderstorm, and no one made a sound as the moment drew out. Then Scott turned on his heel and walked away. Lieutenant Sackville lifted his head and looked at the horrific figure hanging from the tree.

"My father will hear of this," he burst out. "Do you hear me? My father shall hear of this, and it will cost you dearly, Captain Scott." His voice gradually petered out.

Scott turned towards him, and the lieutenant recoiled when he met his gaze.

"Captain Scott, Captain Scott, I did not mean . . ." he stammered, falling over his own words till he gradually fell silent.

After a moment Scott spoke. "Sergeant Crammer." His voice was matter of fact.

"Yes, Captain." Crammer looked at the top button on Scott's coat.

"Sergeant Crammer, this is the lieutenant's first campaign, is it not?"

"Indeed it is."

"I believe it's his first action of any kind. Sergeant, is it not customary in this regiment for an officer to carry a trophy away from his first action?"

A glimmer of cruelty flashed in the sergeant's eyes, and his lips curled in the beginnings of a smile.

"Yes, Captain, that is the regimental tradition."

Scott looked at the sergeant.

"Sergeant Crammer, you will retrieve the trophy for the lieutenant."

"Yes, Captain." Crammer pulled a dagger from his belt and hefted it in his hand as he approached Cameron's body. The sergeant grasped the dead man's genitals in his left hand and slid the knife underneath them. As Crammer made the first stroke Cameron's body twitched violently. Some of the troopers gasped. One soldier crossed himself then looked around nervously, afraid to betray a Catholic upbringing in this Protestant army.

The sergeant waited till the spasm passed.

"Not dead yet, Highlander? Well, maybe now you wish you were." Crammer laughed at his own joke. The sergeant stood back while the blood splattered on the ground and, with one final stroke, severed the prisoner's manhood from his body.

Crammer marched across the clearing and held the bloody trophy out to Lieutenant Sackville.

"Your first blood, Lieutenant."

Lieutenant Sackville looked in horror at the bloody mess in Crammer's hand, he stepped back and came up against two troopers.

Scott moved closer.

"You must accept your trophy, Lieutenant, or the regiment will be insulted."

"No," the lieutenant blurted out. He reared back, but the troopers grasped his arms and held him fast.

"Let go of me. Let go of me this instant—that's an order." His voice carried across the clearing and echoed back from the mountain, mocking him with its pleading tone.

Scott nodded. "Lieutenant Sackville, you must accept your trophy as is expected of every officer in the regiment."

A moan issued from the lieutenant's throat, and he increased his efforts to escape, but the soldiers trapped him between them.

"If you will not accept it, we must assist you." Scott looked at Crammer. "Sergeant, you will assist the lieutenant."

Sergeant Crammer seized the lieutenant's right hand. The lieutenant clenched his fist, but Crammer forced his hand open easily.

"No, no, stop," the lieutenant screamed in Crammer's face. "This is madness! Stop." Crammer deposited the bloody mass in the lieutenant's palm and forced his hand to close around it. The lieutenant looked at his hand in horror as blood and a grey liquid oozed from between his clasped fingers and dripped onto the ground.

Captain Scott spoke again.

"Sergeant, is it not customary for a new soldier to taste the blood of his enemy?"

"Yes, Captain," Crammer replied. "That is the custom, I believe."

"The lieutenant is not a willing participant. You must assist him." Scott's voice rose in encouragement.

"As the captain orders." Crammer was enjoying himself. His lips were pulled back in a savage grin, revealing blackened teeth and purple gums. He fed on the lieutenant's humiliation as he bent his arm at the elbow, forcing it up towards his face.

Lieutenant Sackville called out in despair, begging Crammer to stop, but the sergeant kept forcing the bloody handful upwards. Suddenly Crammer grabbed the lieutenant's head and pulled it down. He opened his hand and forced the dead man's genitals against the lieutenant's mouth. The lieutenant fought furiously but could not free himself. The sergeant held him in a headlock, and his right hand worked back and forth, rubbing the bloody mess into his mouth.

The lieutenant let out a howl of despair, and his stomach heaved. Crammer and the troopers released him and stepped back as a stream of brown vomit poured from his mouth. The lieutenant fell to his knees, gasping for breath, and a moan of rage and humiliation came out of him. He looked at Cameron's genitals still clutched in his right hand and, with a cry of disgust, shook his hand free of the bloody thing. He got to his feet and lurched away. He careened into several of the soldiers and threw up again. Then he staggered away towards the river.

Captain Scott's face was devoid of emotion as he watched his nephew stumble down the riverbank. He turned to Crammer.

"Sergeant, we will break here for the midday meal."

"Yes, Captain." The remains of a smile still lingered on Crammer's face.

CHAPTER TWO

JOHN WATCHED THE YOUNG OFFICER fall to his knees and plunge his face into the river, coughing and spitting as he washed out his mouth. After a few moments he stumbled away from the water and sat down on a stone, holding his head in his hands. He hugged himself like a child rocking back and forth, and the sound of his sobs carried up to him.

John was confused by the emotions that rose in him. The lieutenant was part of the invader army, but he was also a victim of their cruelty and ruthlessness. He wasn't much older than John, and he couldn't help but feel sympathy for him. He didn't understand how he could feel disgust at the English and, in the same moment, feel compassion for one of them. He buried his head in his hands, sickened by what he'd seen, and a silent rage at injustice and cruelty took root in him. He knew it would stay with him for the rest of his life.

The redcoats sat in groups around the clearing to eat their midday meal, and as the heat of the day increased they lay down in the shade of the forest, and quiet settled over the glen again.

As John watched the clearing his thoughts turned to his family. It had been two months since he'd seen them, and he hoped the terror that was gripping the Highlands had not touched them. His home was in Crieff, a hundred miles to the south. Crieff was the centre of the cattle trade in Scotland, and

John's father was one of the town's principal traders, as his father had been before him. He would be getting ready for the great "tryst" or cattle market held in the third week of August, only a few weeks away.

For most of the summer John worked on his uncle's farm. Murdoch MacRae was his mother's brother. His cousin, Maighread, was an only child, and Uncle Murdoch welcomed his nephew's help with the heavy labour. John's father approved—he said that learning how to care for cattle would stand him in good stead when he entered the family business. John thrived in the mountains and looked forward to each summer. The work was hard, but he enjoyed the freedom to roam the mountains and glens. It was also a welcome break from his studies at the college in Crieff. He had found that he had a talent for languages and, besides English, could speak basic French and a little Spanish, and was fluent in the Gaelic of the West Highlands; but he had little interest in mathematics and other subjects.

He was brought back to the present when he saw the captain emerging from the trees. Suddenly Maighread came into his mind, and he knew he had to reach her before the redcoats advanced farther into the glen. The captain called out, and the big sergeant came running. The captain spoke to him for some minutes, pointing at the river, then to the east, farther into the glen. The sergeant saluted and ran off, shouting the men to their feet.

* * *

Scott composed his features as he walked down the riverbank.

"Lieutenant Sackville." Scott kept his voice quiet, almost soothing. The lieutenant did not respond; his eyes were vacant like an opium addict. "Lieutenant Sackville." Scott raised his voice. "You will come to attention now."

The lieutenant raised his head and looked at him but didn't respond.

Scott's contempt for his nephew rose to the surface. "Lieutenant Sackville, you will obey my instructions immediately."

The lieutenant came to his feet slowly like an old man crippled by age, squared his shoulders, and met the captain's eye.

Scott spoke slowly, each word laden with the contempt he felt for the boy. "Lieutenant Sackville, you will take ten men and patrol farther into this valley. You will bring all livestock to Fort William for the use of the army. You will destroy all standing crops, and dwellings of any kind are to be razed to the ground. "

Scott glanced at Crammer breaking the men into groups. "Any Highlanders you encounter will be taken prisoner and brought to Fort William for questioning. Resistance will be put down ruthlessly. You will report to me this evening and present me with a detailed account of your activities. Do I make myself clear, Lieutenant?"

Lieutenant Sackville responded, but his voice was almost a whisper. "I understand the orders you have given me, Captain."

Scott watched his nephew intently. "Sergeant Crammer will accompany you with ten regulars."

A flicker of emotion flashed in the young man's eyes and Scott pursued it like a hound that smelt blood. "Gathering up a few cows and burning a shanty or two should be within your capabilities. If not, Sergeant Crammer will ensure that my orders are carried out." Scott turned and made his way up the path.

"Sergeant Crammer, have the men fall in. Lieutenant Sackville will lead the patrol." Scott turned away and took the path down the glen.

* * *

John's stomach ached with dread. The patrol couldn't fail to come across his uncle's farm. The need to warn his family gnawed at him. The soldiers moved slowly along the riverbank. John watched impatiently until they disappeared into the trees but he held back. Descending the slope would start a slide in the scree. In the still air the sound would carry a long way.

John tried to gauge the passage of time. He tried counting to a hundred, but his mind was too agitated, and he kept losing his place. He concentrated on breathing steadily and tried to ignore the images that forced their way into his mind. Finally he could contain himself no longer, and he slid out of the corrie.

John came down the slope in a series of long strides, digging his heels into the scree to control his descent. A mound of soil and vegetation rose up from the floor of the glen, and he angled to the right towards it. On solid ground he loped down the hill, grabbing the whin bushes to keep his balance.

On the riverbank he crouched down and closed his eyes to listen. He heard the scree hissing down the hillside behind him, the splash and gurgle of the river, and a curlew crying above the glen, but nothing that signalled danger. He opened his eyes and found himself looking at Alexander Cameron's body turning slowly in the breeze, and he looked away, sickened by the sight of his tortured body.

The river was shallow, and John splashed across quickly, climbed the embankment, and set off upstream. He ran hard across the open ground and breathed a sigh of relief when he reached trees. He followed the path, stopping at every bend to listen. He guessed the redcoats would be half a mile ahead, but it wasn't long before he heard the sound of their voices. He closed the gap until he saw the tail end of the patrol and moved into the trees, matching their pace.

John's mind raced trying to think of a way to get past the patrol. He thought of trying to lead them away from this side of the glen, but there could be other patrols in the area. He could run into a trap. He could get around them to the north, but it would take too long. In the end he was forced to dog their trail and hope an opportunity would present itself.

The woods began to thin out and finally disappeared entirely. Ahead, the glen was open pasture: short grass picked clean by the black cattle and raggedy sheep of the Highlands. John couldn't follow the patrol without being seen. His only option was the riverbed, but he couldn't move until the patrol rounded the bend out of sight. The soldiers were moving at what felt like a snail's pace, and he silently urged them on.

Finally the head of the column moved around the bend, the young lieutenant striding out in front. John ran to the riverbank and slid down to the beach. He waited until the last soldier disappeared and set off. At first John ran half doubled over, but he realized that on the beach he was in plain sight, and he straightened up. He searched the riverbank for movement. If the redcoats spotted him, they would wait until he came within range of their muskets; his stomach churned as he expected a musket ball to slam into his chest at any moment.

John found himself running flat out, feet pounding into the mud, his breath coming in gasps. Fifty feet from the bend in the river he slowed and made for a place where the bank had collapsed. He threw himself down, forcing himself to breathe slowly until the roaring in his ears stopped.

After a few minutes John raised his head over the bank. The patrol had stopped three hundred yards beyond the treeline. He couldn't see the young lieutenant, but he recognized the big sergeant standing head and shoulders above the rest of the group. They had stopped opposite the bridge his Uncle Murdoch had built across the River Nevis. The farmhouse was half a mile farther up the side glen to the south, hidden from view. Apart from the bridge and the path on the far side, the glen looked uninhabited, and John hoped the patrol would pass on by.

Six soldiers broke from the group and set off across the glen to the north, and then John saw the lieutenant step away from the patrol. He shaded his eyes with his hand and looked up at Coire na Gabhalach. John followed the direction of his gaze and his heart sank as he saw the column of smoke rising above the hills.

The lieutenant motioned to the sergeant and the two remaining soldiers. The lieutenant pointed in the direction of the side glen and the sergeant and the two troopers crossed the bridge and took the path up the hillside. The lieutenant followed slowly; he made his way up the track to where a granite boulder lay beside the path. He sat on the rock looking across Glen Nevis.

John slid back into the riverbed; he ran across the stepping stones below the bridge to where the Gabhalach burn joined the River Ness. The burn fell down the side of the glen in a series of steps. John kept his head below the bank and climbed splashing his way up over the stones and gravel. On the glen above, the burn made a loop into the middle of the glen and curved back on itself. John's uncle had built the farmhouse on the flat land inside the loop.

The burn meandered across the floor of the glen, and John pushed hard, keeping his head below the bank. Finally he came to the loop, close to the farmhouse, and he raised his head above the bank. The farmhouse was a hundred yards away, a single-storey building, long and narrow with thick stone walls and a thatched roof. The house stood at right angles to the burn, facing west towards the mouth of the glen. The door faced down the glen, to shield the house from wind and rain in winter and to provide a view of the glen below. A half-finished bridge across the burn stood behind the croft.

All seemed quiet, and John slid back into the bed of the burn and set off. He had taken a dozen steps when he heard Maighread scream, and the sound galvanized him. He leapt out of the burn and ran like a deer for the farmhouse.

The front door was open, and John could see a square of sunlight in the middle of the floor; beyond that the interior was in darkness. He reached the end of the building and pressed himself against the wall. The blood was roaring in his ears, and there was a hard ball of fear in his gut. It would be foolish to rush blindly into the farmhouse but he felt himself being pulled towards the door.

John took a breath, turned the corner and crept along the front of the building, keeping his back against the stone wall. Halfway to the door he heard the sound of voices from inside, but couldn't make out the words. He heard Maighread call again, but she was drowned out by men's voices. Suddenly he was gripped by the sensation that he was being watched. The hackles rose on the back of his neck, and he searched the moorland, fearful that a soldier had been left outside on guard, but there was no sign of movement.

John let his breath out slowly, and as he started to move, a musket discharged inside the farmhouse. The ball struck one of the stone door pillars and whirred away into the distance. John spun around, took three running steps, and threw himself onto the ground and crawled around the corner of the building.

John got to his feet and flattened himself against the wall. His instinct was to get away from the farmhouse, but he forced himself to think. The soldiers couldn't have seen him. The musket must have been fired at someone inside the farmhouse and missed its mark, ricocheting off the doorpost. He realized that if he'd stepped through the door, the soldiers could have shot him at their leisure. It was a sobering thought.

John crept to the corner and looked around. There was no sign of movement. He heard voices raised in anger and Maighread crying out, fear in her voice. He turned and ran to the back of the building. The burn was ten feet from the side of the house, the bridge directly in front of him. He moved along the back of the house, trailing his fingers along the wall as he had when he was a child.

The walls of the farmhouse were three feet thick and built of blue fieldstone. The back door hung on the inner side of the wall, the hinges on the side nearest him. John inched his way forward, placing his feet carefully. He stepped around a stack of firewood, and the rich smell of oak and ash filled his nostrils. As he approached the door he could hear voices from inside, harsh laughter and shouting that urged him to haste. He slid onto his stomach and edged forward.

The door stood open, the sunlight illuminating one half of the room and throwing the other side into shadow. It took a moment for his eyes to adjust, and at first he couldn't make out what he was looking at. The soldiers were standing around the kitchen table swaying back and forth like drunkards. Then one soldier stepped back, and the real picture of what was happening became chillingly clear.

The soldier's breeches were pulled down and his member stood out from his hips swinging back and forth as he rotated his hips luridly. The two other soldiers were holding Maighread down on the kitchen table and he had stepped back to avoid a kick from her right foot.

The tall sergeant stood on the far side of the table; his left arm was around Maighread's neck, pinning her against his chest. Her bodice was open, exposing two plump breasts, and the sergeant kneaded her left breast cruelly. The men were howling with delight, and the more she struggled and cried out, the more they enjoyed it.

The third soldier stood over Maighread, pinning her body to the table; her skirt was pulled up above her waist, revealing long slender legs and narrow hips. A tremor ran through John at the sight the dark triangle of hair at the apex of her thighs. Maighread was his cousin, but he felt a stab of want in his groin at the sight of her naked body; her vulnerability and distress somehow made it more poignant, and he looked away ashamed.

Suddenly Maighread turned and sunk her teeth into the sergeant's arm below the elbow. He let out a bellow of rage and tried to pull away, but she gripped his arm with her hands and hung on, worrying the flesh like a dog with a bone. John saw a flash of red as she drew blood and Maighread screamed through her teeth. It was a harrowing sound, like an animal caught in a trap, tearing its own flesh to be free.

Maighread's scream cut across John's nerves like a blade, and the poisonous brew of guilt and confusion that had paralyzed him turned to anger that swept away all fear and caution. He came to his feet and scooped up one of the ash logs, hefting it in his right hand. Two feet long and three inches in diameter, it made a perfect club. He threw his shoulder against the kitchen door, sending it crashing against the wall, and charged into the kitchen.

"A Wallace, a Wallace!" The battle cry of his clan came to John's lips.

The soldiers froze in shock as John charged into the room, screaming like a madman. The man nearest him stepped back, frantically trying to stuff his manhood into his breeches. John swung the ash log with all his strength, turning his body into it and struck him square on the side of the head. The soldier dropped like a stone, his shrunken manhood spilling out of his breeches as he fell.

The sergeant and the other soldier released Maighread and launched themselves at John. Maighread threw herself up from the table, venting her rage in an ear-piercing screech. She locked her arms around the soldier's neck, and he staggered against the table trying to shake her off.

John swung the club backhanded at his head. The soldier saw it coming and raised his hand to protect himself. The log struck him in on the side of his face, breaking his nose and smashing the teeth on the right side of his jaw. The soldier screamed in pain and collapsed to the floor with his hands over his face, blood pouring through his fingers.

The swing threw John off balance, and the sergeant slammed into him, knocking him off his feet. He crashed to the dirt floor, and Crammer's full weight landed on top of him. John felt as if his chest had been crushed. The breath was knocked out of him and a searing pain shot through his back. His fingers opened on reflex, and the club flew from his hand.

Crammer got his hands around John's neck and started to choke him, grunting with the effort. John was shocked at the strength and viciousness of the man. He couldn't breathe and darkness began to close in on him. In desperation he locked both of his hands around the sergeant's right thumb and put all his strength into one effort to pull it away from his windpipe. There was a crack and John felt something give in Crammer's hand. He cried out in pain, and the pressure eased on his throat.

John gasped half in pain and half in relief as air rushed into his lungs and strength flowed into him. The sergeant leaned back for a moment, and John pushed up hard, trying to throw him off, but Crammer slammed him back to the floor, and drove his fist into John's face.

John landed half on his side; he tucked his chin into his chest and rolled his head to the side. Crammer was punching left-handed, but the force of the blow was stunning. The back of John's head struck the floor. Colours flashed behind his eyelids, and he struggled to stay conscious.

Crammer grunted in frustration and rolled John over on his back, pinning his arms to the floor with his hands. He bent over John and snarled.

"I'll be the end of you, boy, and it won't come easy." He pulled back his lips in a cruel smile as he spat the words at him. John knew that he was looking death in the face, and it terrified him.

Crammer shifted his position, and the weight on his chest eased. John arched his back and a surge of relief ran through him as his hand closed around the hilt of his dirk. He couldn't free it from the scabbard, but his resolve hardened. Fear didn't leave him, but he learned in that moment that if he could fight or take some action, he could control his fear.

Crammer sat up on his chest and pulled his left arm back to strike. John braced himself for the blow, forcing his chin down on his chest. Crammer was too heavy to throw off, but John knew that when he struck him, his weight would be thrown forward, and he might be able to free the dirk. He gathered his legs under him for the effort.

There was a blur of movement behind Crammer that drew John's eye; the sergeant saw it too and glanced over his shoulder. Maighread swung the fire iron at Crammer's head, twisting her body to increase the force. Crammer cried out in anger and threw up his right arm to protect himself. There was a crack as the fire iron glanced off his elbow and struck Crammer on the side of the head. The force of the blow knocked him off John, and he dropped to the floor motionless.

John rolled to his feet, tearing his dirk from its scabbard. The sergeant lay on his back, one leg twisted under him, his right arm thrown across his chest. His left arm lay alongside his body, the hand still closed in a fist. His head lolled to one side and blood flowed freely from a gash on the side of his face where the fire iron had struck.

John's breath was coming in gasps, his mind was screaming with fear and anger, and the need to kill this man consumed him like a hunger. John stooped over Crammer, anticipating the cut and the rush of heat as the blade did its work. A blue vein stood out on Crammer's neck, and he could see the pulse beating slowly. John had never killed a man. Part of him was repelled by the idea and another part of him wanted it. The sound of running footsteps broke the spell, and John turned to see a dark shape fill the doorway.

CHAPTER THREE

"WHAT'S TO DO HERE?" THE young lieutenant thrust the door open and stepped into the cottage holding a sword in his hand. The door crashed against the wall and rebounded, striking his left shoulder, and he turned in alarm.

John reacted instinctively. He came up from the floor, uncoiling like a spring and drove his shoulder into the lieutenant's chest, hurling him back against the door. The impact drove the wind from his lungs and the sword dropped from his hand and clattered to the floor. John drove his fist into the lieutenant's stomach and a shudder ran through him as he realized he still held the dirk in his hand. The rippling sensation as the blade cut through muscle and sinew horrified him, but a darker instinct took hold of him and he drove the blade in to the hilt.

The lieutenant's eyes flew wide with shock.

"No." The word faded from the lieutenant's lips. He looked at John in bewilderment, and his knees buckled.

John stepped back, pulling the dirk free, and the young man slid to the floor. John was astonished at how much blood there was. His hand was deep red in the sunlight, and he felt sickened by what he'd done. A moment earlier he had been filled with the lust to kill the sergeant. Now that feeling of triumph and invulnerability seemed like a distant memory.

John heard a sound behind him. He turned in alarm and froze astonished at what he saw. Maighread was standing over the first soldier John had knocked out. She held the fire iron in her hands. She swung it in a windmilling motion and brought it down on the trooper's head with sickening force. His face was a pulpy mess; the jaw bone protruded through the skin on one side.

Maighread stepped to the right and swung the iron again, aiming for the trooper's groin. Her bodice was torn open exposing milky white breasts. A keening cry came out of her as she swung the iron, a wretched sound that became a scream as the fire iron struck the soldier's groin.

Behind him John heard voices out in the glen, and a jolt of alarm ran through him. He stepped into the doorway to listen. The sound was a long way off but coming closer. He stepped back into the kitchen.

"Maighread," he called. She was gasping with exertion, oblivious to everything around her as she swung the fire iron again. John judged the moment, wrapped his arms around her, and lifted her off her feet.

Maighread screamed in rage and fought furiously, trying to strike him with the fire iron. He was astonished at her strength, and he had to exert himself to hold her.

He put his mouth to her ear and called, "Maighread, Maighread. It's John. Maighread, it's John. Stop now. Stop."

Maighread went limp in his arms, and the fire iron clattered to the floor. John set her back on her feet and released her. She turned and looked at him. Her eyes were wild. She made a mumbling sound, but no words came out. She dropped her eyes for a moment. When she raised them again, they had a haunted look like a frightened animal. Then she burst into tears.

"Oh, John, it was so horrible, so horrible." She threw her arms around his neck and clung so tightly to him that he almost overbalanced. Her body was shuddering with emotion. Each sound wrenched from deep inside of her.

John knew that the voices outside must be the soldiers who had gone to the north side of the glen. They would have heard the musket shot and would be coming to investigate. He eased himself away from Maighread, took her head in his hands and turned her face to his.

"Maighread, we must leave." She didn't seem to hear him at first. Her eyes were awash with tears, unfocused and frightened.

"Maighread, Maighread, there are other soldiers in the glen. We must get away now." He saw a flicker of alarm in her eyes, but she didn't move.

26

He took her by the shoulders.

"We have to get away from the farmhouse, Maighread. Other soldiers will come, and there isn't much time."

A light of recognition dawned in her eyes and she stepped back, pushing her hair out of her eyes with one hand. She became aware of the state of her clothing, let out a shriek of alarm and turned her back on John, desperately pulling her tattered blouse closed. She looked at him over her shoulder.

"What do you think you're looking at, John Wallace? Do you think I'm some trollop that you can stare at naked any time you please?" Her voice was sharp with indignation and outrage.

John was taken aback by her sudden change in demeanour and stung by her tone. She had gone from a state of murderous rage, to hopeless anguish, then to indignation and outrage in the space of a few moments. He'd risked his life to save her, and she had turned on him as if he was to blame for her state of undress. He despaired of ever understanding women, but he remembered the sensation of her breast pressed against him. The colour rose in his cheeks, and he turned away.

The soldier Maighread had struck lay on the kitchen floor like a broken doll. One leg was folded under him in an unnatural position. His face was a mess of torn flesh and blood. His right eye had swollen completely shut, and his left eye had the dull flat stare of the newly dead. John ran to the front door and looked outside. There was nothing moving in the glen, and he breathed a sigh of relief.

Maighread had repaired her torn clothing and stood looking around the kitchen, her face pale. A pool of blood was growing around the body of the trooper she had beaten with the fire iron, and she shuddered at the sight.

"Maighread." John spoke softly. She turned to him, fear and confusion in her eyes again.

"What's happening, John?"

John was thinking quickly. Even though he could see no one in the glen, he knew the soldiers must be close, and they didn't have much time. It was a miracle they had survived the fight; surprise had been on their side and he'd been lucky, but he knew their luck wouldn't hold.

John took Maighread by the hand and led her to the back door. She pulled away, words pouring out of her.

"John, John, what will we do? Father will be angry." She was talking half to herself.

John stopped by the door and motioned her to wait. He crouched down and glanced outside in both directions and waited, listening until he felt satisfied there was no immediate danger.

John turned around, but Maighread was gone, and he rushed back into the kitchen. She was standing over the soldier she had bludgeoned with the fire iron, staring at his battered face in horror. John placed his hands on her shoulders gently, and she turned to face him.

"He's dead, John. I killed him." It seemed she was only just realizing what had happened.

"And the others." John motioned towards the young lieutenant's body. Maighread looked at it for a long moment and turned back to him.

"They will hang us, John." She was trembling and tears started in her eyes again.

John took her face in his hands, smearing her cheek with the lieutenant's blood.

"Maighread, we must get away. Other soldiers are coming." She seemed bewildered.

"How is it that you're here, John? You were over the mountain after the beasts. How did you come to be here?"

"I came on the soldiers farther down the glen and made my way back, but there's no time for that now. We must go." He urged her towards the door.

"John, John, if you hadn't come." Her voice began to rise in anguish.

"There's no time for this now, Maighread. We have to go before it's too late."

John was becoming exasperated. Maighread didn't seem to grasp the danger they were in, and every moment they stood there, the redcoats came closer. He put his arm around her and turned her towards the door.

"Come now, Maighread. We must hurry."

They were almost at the back door when they heard voices in the glen, and they froze. John ran to the front door and looked out, staying back in the shadows. What he saw drove a shaft of alarm through his chest. Two troopers were coming across the glen at a steady run.

John gauged the distance between the soldiers and the farmhouse. They were half a mile away, moving at such speed that he and Maighread couldn't escape without being seen. He turned and ran across the kitchen.

"Soldiers coming fast." Shock registered in Maighread's face. He grabbed her arm and dragged her towards the back door. She resisted.

"What are you doing, John?

"There is no time for talk now, Maighread, we must go." His voice was harsh, and it betrayed an edge of fear beneath the surface. Maighread stopped pulling back and ran with him to the door.

John stopped short. "Wait."

He ran back to the kitchen table. Half of the table had been swept clean in the melee, but a loaf of bread and square of cheese lay at the far end. He swept them into his hunting bag and turned again for the door.

They ran out into the sunshine, and John immediately felt exposed. The farmhouse stood between them and the troopers, but across the burn the ground rose steadily, two miles of open moorland. They would be seen before they could reach the crest of the hill. John was confident that he could outdistance the troopers. Maighread had been born in the Highlands, but she spent most of her time working around the house, and he knew she wouldn't be able to keep up.

The Gabhalach burn was ten feet from the farmhouse door. As they ran across the grass, John saw that Maighread was barefoot, and it confirmed what he must do. He jumped down into the water and turned to catch Maighread. She was light as a feather and landed with almost no splash.

"Come." The water was only a few inches deep. He took Maighread's hand and splashed his way downstream towards the bridge.

Maighread went along, but she was obviously confused.

"John, the burn is shallower farther up. It's easier to cross by the stones." She meant the stepping stones they had set in the burn when they were children.

"You must hide in the old cave." The water was getting deeper now and he was pulling her along.

"What do you mean, *hide*?" Maighread pulled back, stopping them both in the middle of the burn. "What do you mean, hide in the old cave?" She let go of his hand.

John turned to face her.

"Maighread, you will not be able to keep up with me."

Even as he said the words, he knew it was a mistake. Maighread clenched her hands into fists and held them against her stomach. John had seen this before and knew what it meant. She had her mother's temper and didn't take kindly to being told there was something she couldn't do.

"I was born in this glen, and I can outrun any English they send to chase me." The colour rose in her face as her anger came to the surface.

John thought that he would lose his mind at the stubbornness of this girl. They were standing up to their knees in the burn, faces inches apart, glaring at each other. He could feel his own temper rising and struggled to control it. He thought he heard voices on the far side of the farmhouse. He cocked his head to listen, but the sound didn't come again.

Then his anger was gone, and John was overcome with a sense of hopelessness.

"We'll both be killed, Maighread. If we stand here and argue, we'll both die."

"Then let's go, John." She grasped his hand in hers and tried to pull him towards the shore. John didn't move.

"John, we must get away before more soldiers come." She turned him around, almost pulling him off his feet, and he took a step forward to steady himself. Maighread redoubled her efforts, but John leaned back against her.

Maighread was almost screaming with frustration.

"John, come with me now." John didn't move. He was exasperated with her but couldn't help being drawn to her spirit. She was so intense and single-minded that he almost laughed. He gently drew her closer and bent forward to look into her eyes.

"Maighread, you cannot outrun these men. I have spent half of my life on the hunt, and I don't know if I can outdistance them now."

John knew how stubborn Maighread could be, and he knew trying to hold her would only increase her determination.

"They're close, Maighread. You must hide in the old cave, and I will lead them away."

"No, John, no." Maighread's lips trembled but her anger was gone and her face was a mask of pain and anguish. "Come then," she said. She took his hand and waded downstream.

Three arches of the bridge had been finished, reaching the middle of the burn. The second three had never been completed. The burn was high, and the water was waist deep at the bridge. Even in summer it was ice cold, and John was shivering. They stooped under the second arch, and Maighread held on to John's arm to keep her balance. There was a hollow section in the centre of the arch accessed by a small opening. They'd discovered it as children and called it the old cave.

They had built a stone shelf inside that always stayed dry. It was their secret place, and they'd spent many hours there, dreaming of what they would do when they grew up. The entrance to the cave could not be seen even from the floor of the burn. There was little chance it would be found, and if Maighread stayed quiet, she would be safe.

John looked inside.

"It's still dry. Don't come out until after dark." He moved to make room for Maighread to climb inside.

She crouched beside him and looked inside. "I wonder if the candles and the flint and steel are still here."

"Maighread, you mustn't light a candle—they might see the light. No matter what happens, you must stay hidden."

She looked at him sharply.

"What do you mean? You mean if they catch you." John didn't answer.

Maighread started to speak, but John put his fingers to her lips.

"Don't come out even if they burn the farmhouse. Stay hidden until it's dark and make your way to the high shieling. Your father will be there. I will come there when I can."

Maighread clutched John's arm.

"John, they would have used me." Her voice was cracking with emotion, and tears were streaming down her face. John made to speak, but she grasped a handful of his hair and pulled him to her mouth and locked her arms around his neck.

John was startled at the fierceness of her embrace and by her strength. Her mouth tasted of honey and the berries from the mountainside. It drove a feeling of want in him, and he crushed her to him as the burn flowed around them, holding them in its icy embrace. Finally they broke apart, both shivering violently.

"I must go, or it will be too late," John said. She looked at him but didn't speak, fear in her eyes. John helped her climb into the entrance, and she turned and pulled him to her once more and kissed him softly.

"Come back to me, John Wallace," she said. Then she turned and melted into the darkness.

* * *

John watched Maighread's bare feet disappear into the cave. It was completely black inside, and even though she was only a few feet away, it seemed as if she'd vanished from the world. For a moment he thought of climbing into the cave and staying with her, but he dismissed the idea. He wanted to speak, but no words would come, and half in regret, half in relief, he turned and waded out into the burn.

John was overcome with foreboding that he would never see Maighread again and looked back at her hiding place for a moment. Then, angry at his indecision, he struck out upstream. The cold seemed to penetrate to his bones, but with each step, his resolve grew, and he splashed his way across the burn.

On the bank John pulled his boots off and wrung out his socks. The wool would keep him warm even when it was damp, but squelching with water, it would wrinkle and cause blisters. On this day blistered feet could make the difference between life and death. John's hair hung past his shoulders, and he took a cord from his hunting bag and tied it behind his head. He had his mother's auburn hair and green eyes. Her face came into his mind, but he couldn't afford to be distracted, and he forced it away.

John followed the footpath upstream alongside the burn. At seventeen years of age, he was just above middle height. Lean and strong from months spent roaming the hills and mountains, he ran at a steady lope. His uncle's words came back to him from the hunt.

"Only a fool exhausts himself in the first mile. The hunt may be long, and you will need your strength at the kill."

The burn wound back and forth across the floor of the glen for two miles, making its way south to the foothills of Binnein Mòr and Corrie Mòr. There he would leave the path and strike uphill; if he could reach Corrie Mòr, the redcoats would be hard pressed to catch him, and he could be onto the mountain by nightfall.

John held his pace, breathing steadily. His mind was racing with all that had happened and the rhythm helped him concentrate. Some would say he'd acted rashly. Others had been forced to watch their women be used by the English. It was the price of survival, they said, but he knew he couldn't have stood by while Maighread was raped.

John didn't regret what he'd done but had no illusions about the consequences that would follow this day. Two soldiers killed, one of them an officer. The redcoats would find out who owned the land, the farm would be lost, and his uncle's family would become fugitives with a price on their heads.

Another thought struck him: if the soldiers weren't able find him or his uncle's family, they would seek others to hold responsible. The soldier who survived the fight could describe him, and it wouldn't take long to confirm that Murdoch MacRae was his uncle, and he was John Wallace of Crieff. The English would vent their anger on his family. He had to warn them, but even if he could reach them in time, what could they do? His family had been cattle traders in Crieff for generations. They couldn't just leave their home and livelihood to go into hiding.

John's thoughts were interrupted by a shout behind him, then the crack of a musket. He stopped and looked back. Two redcoats were standing behind the farmhouse. One was holding a musket with smoke still coming from the barrel. He started to reload and the other soldier splashed across the ford and broke into a run.

John turned away. The urge to run flat out was almost overwhelming, but he held back, counting his steps, one breath for every four strides.

The burn turned to the right towards the hills, and he could see the corrie over a mile away. John glanced over his shoulder. The redcoat was only a few hundred yards behind him. Panic seized him, and he stumbled and almost fell. The soldier let out a shout. It was both a challenge and a warning.

John picked up his stride and ran on smoothly. He glanced over his shoulder again. He knew this showed fear but couldn't resist. The trooper was about thirty years of age. He looked strong and not overly heavy in the body. He had dropped his musket and was closing the gap between them steadily.

John increased his pace for a moment, but forced himself to slow down. The trooper could run, but he was pushing hard, and John didn't think he could hold the pace. He looked back again, and his instinct was confirmed. The soldier was red in the face and gasping for breath. He had run himself out and was already slowing.

John held steady, looking back once in a while to make sure he kept his lead. The redcoat made another effort to close the gap, but couldn't keep it up and fell back again. John sensed he wouldn't last much longer.

Ahead the footpath turned to the left, following the burn. Corrie Mòr lay straight ahead. The corrie was steep and covered with scree and loose rock. The soldier might do well enough on the flat, but John knew he would be no match for him on the hillside. He would have to leave the smooth ground of the footpath and cross the heather to reach the corrie. It would slow him down, but he had no choice.

Some instinct made John look back, and he was alarmed to see the redcoat closing on him. He was gasping for breath, and near the end of his strength. Then John saw the pistol in his right hand and fear seized him. The soldier wasn't trying to catch him. He was trying to get within pistol range. John swore out loud. He didn't know what the effective range of a pistol was, but the soldier must think he had a chance of bringing him down.

John left the footpath and ran hard for the corrie. The ground was broken and filled with potholes and pools of water. He had to slow his pace for fear of stepping in a hole and breaking a leg. He concentrated on covering the ground and resisted the urge to look back.

Ahead, a burn cut across his path. It was five feet wide, but he couldn't see how deep. John measured the distance, lengthened his stride, and leapt across the gap easily. As he landed, the ground gave way under him, and he threw himself forward, tucking his shoulder under him as he rolled. The momentum carried him forward, and he came to his knees half facing the way he had come.

The crack of the pistol shot was stunning, but even as the sound filled his ears, he knew it had missed. He would have felt the strike before he heard the report. He got to his feet and leapt away, bounding over the heather like a stag; then he heard an English voice calling out behind him.

"You've beaten me, boy."

John felt a thrill of elation. He skidded to a halt and turned to face the soldier. It was a decision that he would never forget, for it almost cost him his life. The soldier was less than fifty paces away. He was standing in the classical shooting position, side on to the target, arm extended. He'd called out to John to make him stop, and he had fallen for it.

As if in a nightmare, John's limbs wouldn't respond to his commands and he moved as if through deep water. He saw the hammer fall and the puff of smoke as the primer fired. Then his hunting bag was thrown backwards with tremendous force. It spun him around as if he'd been kicked by one of the wild Highland cattle; then he heard the crack of the pistol.

John staggered back, struggling to retain his balance. The trooper was carrying a double-barrelled pistol, unheard of for a foot soldier. He must have picked it up on the battlefield and kept it hidden from his officers, who would have confiscated such a valuable weapon.

There was a round hole in his hunting bag where the ball had entered, and the flap was almost torn off where it had exited. A cold sweat broke out on John's forehead as he realized how close he'd come to death, and he turned to face the redcoat, ready to fight or run. The trooper was bent over, resting his hand on his knees. He was done and would run no farther. He stood upright, and they looked at each other. He had plain features and brown eyes, and he brushed his hair out of his eyes with a peculiar backhanded gesture.

The soldier was gasping for breath, but he called out to John. "You'll not escape, boy. I've seen your face, and I'll know you again."

John cursed his own stupidity, but he forced himself to keep his face impassive, and as he turned away the trooper called out again.

"We'll find you, boy. If we can't find you, we'll find your family. We'll hang them naked from the trees and leave them for the crows to pick clean." He was still gasping for breath, but the malice in his voice was palpable, and he wore a smile of satisfaction on his face.

The trooper's words were like nails in John's chest. He knew this day had branded him a killer and an outlaw, but it had also marked his family for persecution. His legs began to tremble, and he thought he would be sick. He had to move, or he was lost. He steeled himself, grinding his teeth until his jaw hurt, and turned away. His first steps were hesitant, but he grew stronger with each stride.

The trooper called again. John couldn't make out the words, but his voice rang with the arrogance the English wore like a badge. John felt the trooper's eyes boring into his back as he climbed, and he resisted the urge to look back and give him the satisfaction of seeing him show fear. He climbed steadily until the corrie turned east and hid him from view; then he crept around the side of the hill where he wouldn't be seen and looked back.

The trooper was five hundred feet below him on the footpath with his companion. There was something disturbing in the way they stood watching, not moving. After a moment John turned away, but farther up the corrie, he looked again and saw both soldiers running back towards the farmhouse.

The day was drawing to a close and the entrance to Maighread's hiding place was in shadow. John thought about going back to lead her to safety, but he dismissed the idea. The redcoats wouldn't give up the hunt, and she would be safer making her way to the summer pasture alone. He slid down into the gut of the corrie and started to climb again.

A mile farther up John emerged onto the shoulder of Binnein Mòr, the mountain that dominated the south side of Glen Nevis. There was smoke in the glen. It rose straight up until it was level with the hilltops; then it was blown away across the mountainside, a black smudge against the darkening sky.

The redcoats had set fire to the farmhouse. John had known it would happen, but it was still a shock. It was part of the price to be paid for coming to Maighread's aid. His only solace was that if the soldiers had vented their rage by burning the farmhouse, they wouldn't stay in the area. If Maighread remained hidden, she could make her escape after dark.

John's heart was heavy as he climbed the shoulder of Binnein Mòr. He could reach the summer shieling quicker if he kept to the shoulder of the mountain, but it was open moor and the risk of being seen was great. He would go around the base of Scor Eilde Beag and Sgurr Eilde Mòr by the shores of Loch Eilde Mòr and climb back into upper Glen Nevis from the northeast. It would take most of the day tomorrow, but it was a surer path.

By the time he'd made his way around the mass of Binnein Mòr, it was almost dark. He needed to keep moving, but only a madman travelled the moors at night. He could slip into a hole and break a leg or walk off a cliff in the dark. He found a hollow and, out of the wind, ate some of the bread and cheese; he lay back in the heather, looking up at the sky.

John's mind was in turmoil. He'd killed one man and caused the death of another. For himself he had no regrets. He would do the same again if he had to, but he knew this day had changed his life forever, and he feared what the future held. Images and sensations flashed through his mind like a dream that he couldn't stop. The taste of Maighread's mouth, the feel of her breast pressed against him, and the look of fear and confusion on the young officer's face as he died, played over and over in his mind until finally he fell into a troubled sleep.

36

CHAPTER FOUR

"DEAD—YOU SAY LIEUTENANT SACKVILLE IS dead . . ." It was neither a question nor a statement, and Scott repeated it again almost to himself. "Dead."

Sergeant Crammer stood in Scott's tent. His right arm was bandaged from wrist to elbow and supported in a sling. A purple bruise discoloured the right side of his face, and a blood-soaked bandage was wound around his head, covering one eye. A trickle of blood seeped from under the cloth and ran in a line down his face as if someone had opened his cheek with a razor.

Two troopers stood behind Crammer, supporting him as he swayed on his feet. They were part of Scott's platoon. Busk's nose was broken, his eyes were swollen almost shut, and his face was purple with bruising. A bandage held his jaw closed, and he seemed oblivious to the blood oozing from his mouth. The second trooper, Simms, was unhurt.

Scott turned back to Crammer.

"Killed by a boy." He leaned back against the table in the middle of the tent.

"We did everything we could, Captain." Only one side of Crammer's mouth moved when he spoke. His words were slurred as he struggled to get them out.

Scott showed no emotion as he absorbed the information and considered the implications. The minutes dragged on and the troopers shifted on their feet, eyes averted.

Scott grasped a candlestick from the table in his right hand and swung it in an arc striking Crammer on the jaw. Scott felt Crammer's teeth crack, but it gave him no satisfaction. The sergeant dropped like a stone and rolled himself into a ball, covering his face with his left hand. Scott kicked him in the ribs; frustrated he was not doing enough damage, he started kicking him in the head.

Scott kicked Crammer till he was gasping for breath and could barely speak.

"You let him be killed, Crammer. You let my nephew be killed." Scott was incoherent with rage, and spittle flew from his lips as he screamed at Crammer.

Scott kicked Crammer in the face, sending a stream of bloody spittle across the floor. As he raised his foot to stamp on his head, one of the soldiers called out.

"Begging your pardon, Captain," Trooper Busk said, "but the boy's still alive." Busk struggled to speak with his mouth bandaged. Scott whirled to face him.

"Where is he?" Scott demanded. A look of distress crossed Busk's face.

"I don't know, Captain. One of the other troopers chased him but he escaped into the hills."

Scott pointed at Busk.

"You're telling me a boy did this, incapacitated Crammer and killed my nephew?"

Trooper Busk shuffled back in alarm and nodded.

"I was taken by surprise and knocked unconscious. When I came to, Lieutenant Sackville was dead and the boy was gone." Scott considered having them all flogged, but there would be time enough for that later. He turned to Simms.

"Get this filth out of here." He kicked Crammer's inert body. The two men started to drag Crammer out of the tent.

"Wait," Scott said, "send the soldier who chased the boy to me, and send Morehouse to me immediately."

"Yes, Captain." They dragged Crammer out of the tent, relieved to escape Scott's presence.

Scott fell into a camp chair and massaged his forehead. He cared not a fig that his nephew was dead, but there would be consequences. Scott had held his nephew in contempt, but his father was another story. Lord Sackville, the Duke of Devon, was a powerful man.

The duke had placed his son under Scott's command to shield him from the more unpleasant aspects of military life. The understanding had been clear. If Scott played his part in safeguarding the boy, he would be rewarded. The duke was one of the prime minister's closest advisors, and his personal wealth was immense. He could have done much to advance Scott's career. Now he would have to send a dispatch telling him his only son had been killed. It was a task he didn't relish.

It was late in the day when a trooper reported to Scott that Daniel Morehouse was asking for him.

"Bring him," Scott barked. A few minutes later Morehouse stepped into his tent.

"Where've you been? I sent for you hours ago."

"I had business down the loch side, Captain, and didn't hear you had requested my presence until recently." Morehouse always had to assert his independence. Scott despised the man, but he had his uses, and he was always willing to betray his countrymen for a moderate consideration.

Scott looked at Morehouse.

"Lieutenant Sackville, who was under my command, was killed earlier today along with another soldier while on patrol in Glen Nevis."

"I heard an officer had been killed—word of these things spreads quickly, Captain."

Morehouse showed no reaction, but Scott was sure he was calculating how to profit from the deaths.

"I want you to find out who owns the farm in Glen Nevis where the lieutenant was killed and the name of the boy who killed him."

Morehouse massaged his jaw. "What happened to the boy?" he asked. Scott could barely contain his agitation.

"He escaped into the mountains to the east of Glen Nevis. The patrol burned the farmhouse, but he must have family. I want to know where he will run to, and I want him apprehended and brought to me. There will be a price on the boy's head by tomorrow."

Scott saw the glint of avarice in Morehouse's eye; money was the only thing that moved the man.

"How much will the reward be, Captain?"

"That remains to be seen, but it will be generous—the murder of a British officer is no small thing." Morehouse nodded, looking at Scott thoughtfully.

"There is talk that the lieutenant is from a wealthy family, Captain." There was an insolent undertone in Morehouse's voice.

Scott's temper flared, and he barked at him, "Find the boy and bring him to me. Now get out."

"Right away, Captain." Morehouse stooped under the entrance to the tent and was gone.

Scott knew he had allowed himself to be provoked. Morehouse had guessed how much he needed to capture the boy. No doubt it would cost him dearly, but that was a lesser concern. The main thing was to find the boy and hang him quickly.

* * *

John came awake, sat upright, and closed his eyes to listen. He heard the sound of the breeze rising up the hillside, bees humming in the heather, and a curlew crying in the glen below. The breeze carried the smell of peat and blooming heather. He heard nothing out of the ordinary, but something had awakened him. Something stirred at the edge of his perception, but he couldn't hold on to it. He opened his mouth and took shallow breaths, concentrating as the minutes passed. Then he heard it, so faint that he doubted his senses, but instinct compelled him to wait, and it came again, a sound that froze his heart. Hounds—it was the sound of hounds baying on the scent.

John slid out of the hollow and crouched in the heather as he tied his plaid across his shoulders. He listened again but heard nothing but the wind and the birds singing in the glen. He wondered if he had imagined the sound of the hounds, but in his heart he knew they were real.

John was well up on the side of Binnein Mòr; to his left stood Sgurr Eilde Mòr, to the right Sgurr Eilde Beag. Coire an Lochain formed the glen between the peaks, with the loch directly below him. A burn rose at the far end of the loch and ran to the southeast before plunging down the mountainside to Loch Eilde Mòr a thousand feet below.

John went downhill in long strides, sliding and grabbing handfuls of heather to keep his balance. A hundred feet above the loch shore he broke into a run. The ground was firm, and he pushed hard for the head of the loch. He felt exposed in the open, and after a few hundred yards he threw himself down in the heather and looked back at the mountain behind him.

Nothing moved on the skyline, and he let out a breath in relief then rolled to his feet and bounded away along the loch side. The loch was half a mile long, and John pushed until his chest burned. As he approached the southern end of the loch the mountains on the far side of Loch Eilde Mòr came into view. He felt as if he was running in a dream, and some invisible force was holding him back.

The ground alongside the burn was soft and broken, making heavy going, but finally it began to fall away. John was thirty feet from the edge of the glen when he heard a shout behind him. A cry of triumph that carried clearly in the still air. Then the hounds started to bay. John threw himself over the edge of the glen, crying out in frustration; a few more paces, and he would have been clear. He crawled back to where he could see the corrie.

The redcoats were coming down the face of Binnein Mòr. The sight of them was a shock. There were at least ten soldiers and two civilians handling the dogs, straining to hold them back on the slope.

John turned and threw himself down the mountainside. The heather was waist deep, and he had to force his way through. He quickly realized that he wouldn't reach the loch shore before the redcoats were on him, and he angled towards the burn. The heather tangled his feet and clutched at his clothes, slowing every step until he finally slid into the bed of the burn.

The burn was steep and treacherous, and John grasped the heather at the side to slow his descent, sliding on his backside for half the distance. At one point the burn went over a cliff, dropping twenty feet to the rocks below. John had to take to the heather to get around it, but below the waterfall the channel was broader, and he made more progress.

Loch Eilde Mòr was two miles long, and five hundred yards across at its widest point. A breeze had sprung up from the south. It sent ripples across the surface of the loch and set the heather in motion as it rose up the mountainside. A river ran out of the south end of the loch that John knew must join the River Leven some miles to the south. It was the only way out of the glen. Open moorland lay in every other direction.

When John reached the loch shore, he turned south and immediately heard a voice cry out above him. He looked up and, to his dismay, saw four soldiers at the top of the slope, pointing down at him and shouting excitedly. One soldier started running along the top of the ridge. John couldn't see his face, but something told him it was the man who had almost shot him the day before.

John ran along the loch shore as if the devil was on his heels. The ground was firm underfoot, and the grass was dry from weeks of no rain, golden brown, like wheat ready to be harvested.

John skidded to a halt.

"Dry grass!" he said to himself. He gathered handfuls of grass and twisted them into bundles. He took the flint and steel from his hunting bag and a pouch of dry moss. He placed the moss on a flat stone and the bundles of grass next to it and set to work. John struck the steel rhythmically, and sparks flew from the flint in tiny streams of light. His spirits rose at the sight, but the moss didn't take. He heard the soldiers calling out above him, and he knew they would start down any minute. John's hands shook. He forced himself to stop, and it took all his resolve not to run.

The moss was packed into one dense lump. John pulled it into a looser consistency and set to work again. Smoke began to rise from the moss immediately. He blew on it gently and let out a bark of satisfaction when it burst into flame. He held a bundle of grass over the flames, and it caught fire immediately. John ran along the shore and started to fire the heather. The weather had been hot for weeks, and the bone-dry heather caught fire easily. He worked his way along the base of the hill, stopping every ten feet to fire the heather.

When all of his grass torches were burned up, John ran out to the shore of the loch to get a better view. The breeze was fanning the flames; they leapt up the hillside, roaring and crackling, and in minutes the fire had become a roaring inferno spreading a mile across the mountain.

John could hear the soldiers' cries of alarm above him. The wind shifted, and for a moment the smoke cleared, and he could see the slope above him. Three troopers were halfway down the mountainside. The flames were only a few hundred feet below them, moving uphill with frightening speed, and they were frantically trying to climb up out of danger. Then the wind changed again, and he lost sight of them. John bounded away along the loch shore. The soldiers were hidden from him, but their screams followed him as he ran.

John knew it would take the redcoats hours to get around the fire, and he needed to be far away by the time they reached the loch shore. Farther along, the mountain came right down to the water, and the path petered out.

John waded along the edge of the loch for a hundred yards to where the path picked up again. On an impulse he stayed in the loch wading waist deep to get around a patch of reeds. It was heavy going. The mud clung to his feet, and the cold drained his strength, but he pushed hard for the river mouth.

Once he entered the river, he made more progress. The riverbed was gravel, and in most places the water was knee-deep. A few times he sank to his chest, and once he had to swim across a pool. John pressed on for a mile downstream to where a burn joined the river from the east. The burn curved to the south across the floor of the glen to the base of the hills. The water was ice cold, and by the time he reached the base of the hills, John was numb and shivering.

The burn climbed steeply up the hillside. The stones were covered in moss and lichen, and after an hour of scrambling over the rocks and waterfalls, John's hands and knees were bruised and bleeding. The cold was draining his strength, and when he reached a place where the burn levelled out, he rolled onto the bank and lay shivering on the grass.

After a few minutes, he sat up and looked around. He was on a step on mountainside covered in grass and heather. At the edge of the clearing he saw a patch of blueberries. The berries wouldn't give him much strength, but they would stop the gnawing in his gut. When he had eaten his fill, he lay back on the grass trying to ease his aching muscles. It was past midday and the sun was directly overhead. As its warmth seeped into him, the shivering gradually slowed, and the tension eased. Exhaustion crept over him and he slept.

CHAPTER FIVE

JOHN STRUGGLED AWAKE AND LOOKED around in alarm. The sun was sinking towards the mountains, and he realized he had slept for hours. He crawled to the edge of the shelf. The mountains to the north were blackened by the fire. It still smouldered in places, but the smoke had cleared. The sunlight reflected off the loch like a huge mirror, making it impossible to see anything to the west. John had no idea what had become of the redcoats, but he knew he shouldn't linger.

John searched the mountains above him. As the sun started to set, it seemed to draw the clouds with it to the west, revealing a pass a thousand feet above him, and he started to climb. Halfway through the climb it started to rain, making the slope treacherous, and he clawed his way up the last hundred feet on hands and knees. The pass ran to the east. It was narrow with almost vertical walls of rock on both sides. Below he caught a glimpse of the river winding its way to the south. Then the clouds closed in around him.

As John made his way into the pass the rain increased until he could only see a few yards ahead. He inched his way forward, till at one point the pass was blocked by a wall of solid rock. It was almost dark, and as he felt his way along the rock he realized it was actually a boulder blocking the pass. After a moment the rain stopped, and he realized he was beneath the overhang left when the boulder rolled away from the hillside.

John crept to the back of the overhang and sat down against the hillside. He was exhausted and knew he couldn't go any farther tonight. He was wet and shivering, but at least he was out of the rain. He wrapped his plaid around his shoulders and rubbed his arms and chest until the chill went out of him. He was trying to form a plan for what he would do next when his head sunk onto his chest and he fell into an uneasy sleep.

John was awakened in the night by the sound of stones falling in the pass, but he drifted off to sleep again quickly. The second time he awoke he sensed something had changed, and after a moment he realized that the rain had stopped. He got to his feet, feeling stiff and sore; he had rolled onto his side in the night and the left side of his body was numb. He felt his way around the boulder, and stepped out into the pass. The clouds were beginning to clear, and dawn was not far away. His stomach was growling, but he felt rested, and he set off, keen to see what lay on the other side of the mountain.

As John moved forward, the light grew around him, the pass began to open up, and he finally emerged at the eastern side. The mountain dropped away below him. The floor of the glen was in darkness, but the morning breeze carried the smell of peat and the gamey smell of cattle up to him. The cattle smell was strong, and John thought that one of the droving roads must pass through the glen. He must be on the side of Meall na Duibhe or Meall na Cruaidhe; the Rannoch Moor would be to the east.

The tryst, the annual cattle sale, at Crieff would begin in a week, and the herds would be making their way to the town. There were no roads in the true sense of the word—the drovers sought out the easiest routes where there was grazing to keep the animals fat and healthy. Cattle would be on the move across the western Highlands, heading for Crieff, where in the course of the week twenty or thirty thousand animals would change hands.

John started down the mountainside, and as the light grew he saw a black river of cattle spread out along the floor of the glen. It was over a mile long and must have contained more than a thousand beasts that would be worth a fortune at Crieff. He could see no sign of the drovers who would be moving the herd, but he knew they would be close by. By the time John reached the floor of the glen his legs were burning, and he stopped for a moment and looked around him.

The glen widened to the south with mountains rising on both sides to form a broad glen. A river ran down the west side of the glen, leaving a narrow strip of land between the river and the mountainside. The cattle were crowded into the gap and stared at him with bovine indifference as he climbed the side of the hill to get around them.

John had to go some distance along the hillside to get past the herd. He came down to the floor of the glen in a hollow in the mountainside. As soon as he reached level ground, he smelt smoke and looked around in alarm. At the back of the hollow three men sat around a fire. Steam was rising from a pot suspended over the flames. The men were wore plaids around their shoulders, ragged breeches on their legs, and brogans on their feet. These would be the drovers moving the herd south.

John started to run out into the glen, and a shout went up behind him. He had only gone five paces when a man stepped out from amongst the cattle. John went left, but the cattle were in his way, and the man moved right to block his path.

"Where are you going in such a hurry, boy?" John heard a whoop and looked around to see the drovers bounding towards him, all armed with clubs. Three or four dogs followed at their heels, their barks and growls adding to the general uproar. Two of them came straight at him. The third ran up the side of the hill to get behind him.

John faced them, and his dirk was in his hand before he realized it. The first man lifted his arm signalling to the others and sneered at John. "No man shows me a naked blade." John realized his mistake. Drovers were renowned for their hard living, hard drinking, and hard fighting, but they would encounter travellers almost daily, and there was no reason to believe they would harm him. Drawing his dirk had insulted them, and their pride wouldn't allow the insult to pass.

John backed away as the four men edged closer.

"What's your name, boy?" the first man said. He was clearly their leader. He was about forty years of age, a head shorter than John and twice as broad. Behind him on the riverbank the herd parted and a man mounted on a pony pushed his way through and urged the animal to a trot.

John watched the drovers nervously. The big man drew a short sword. He lifted his head, and the drovers began to challenge him screaming insults and keeping the noise at fever pitch. The dogs followed their master's lead, snapping at John's heels and growling furiously. John backed up against the herd. The animals were alarmed by the noise and milled about anxiously.

John knew that the big man was the real danger, and he watched him from the corner of his eye as he searched for a way to escape.

John heard the sound of hoofbeats approaching and risked a glance over his shoulder. The man and pony were a hundred feet away.

"Hold hard there. Hold hard," he called out. The big man made a motion with his head, and the drovers backed away and sat down on the side of the hill.

The man brought his pony to a halt.

"MacPherson, what are you about? Who is that now?" He pointed to John. His voice was soft and melodious, but it had an edge of authority all the same. MacPherson looked at John.

"A cattle thief, I think, Mr. Macnab."

"What cattle has he stolen?"

"None yet—we caught him before he had the chance. Then he drew steel on us."

"I am no cattle thief," John called out. "I was simply defending myself."

Macnab urged his pony forward, and John saw he was older than he had first thought, but he looked robust and healthy. His clothes were well-made of good cloth, and his boots were made of expensive leather. The pony was young and carried his weight easily. There was something familiar about him. John was sure he'd seen him before, but he couldn't bring it to mind.

Macnab looked at John.

"What's your name, boy? Where are you from?"

"My name is my own business as is where I'm from." It was hotly said, and he immediately regretted it.

Macnab turned on his pony, keeping his eye on John.

"MacPherson, we have beasts to bring to market, do we not? Time to be up and doing."

MacPherson made to speak, but Macnab pre-empted him. "Be about your business. I'll see to the boy." MacPherson glared at John in silent acknowledgement that it wasn't over between them; then he motioned to the drovers.

"See to the beasts. Get them moving." The drovers went back to the fire and started to pack up their camp.

Macnab dismounted easily in spite of his bulk.

"I'm John Macnab. I am a drover and cattle dealer. You may know my name." The cattle were still agitated and the pony was nervous and Macnab rubbed his ears to calm him. It had been years since he'd seen him, but John recognized him now. John Macnab was highly respected in the cattle trade across the Highlands. He'd done business with his father and had visited his home in Crieff many times.

"Your name is well known in the Highlands. I've heard it often enough," John said.

"You are Alexander Wallace's boy."

There was no telling how Macnab would react if he knew that John was being hunted by the redcoats, but there was no point in denying his identity.

"I am John Wallace. You've done business with my father and have been a guest in my home."

Macnab motioned to the cattle spread along the glen.

"The herd will be delivered to your father this coming week." He looked at John questioningly. "Do you have trouble, John?"

"I have no trouble." John knew he was too quick. Macnab considered him for a moment.

"A curious thing for a man with blood on his dirk to say." John was abashed and quickly sheathed the dirk and slid it around to his back. Since the defeat of Charles Stewart's army at Culloden, Highlanders had been banned from carrying weapons. Because of the need to defend their herds, drovers had been given a dispensation to carry weapons. These days it was unusual for a man to be seen openly carrying a weapon.

Macnab patted the pony's rump and opened the saddlebag.

"When was the last time you ate, John?" Macnab took a cloth from the bag and offered it to him. It contained dried oat cakes. Hunger clutched at John's stomach at the sight of them, and he began to eat ravenously.

"I am grateful." The words were mumbled through mouthfuls of food. John thought the oat cakes were the most delicious things he'd ever eaten. He sat on the side of the hill and ate the four cakes without stopping.

Macnab scratched the pony's ears and watched him for a moment. Then he sat down beside John on the hillside.

"You will be travelling home then. The tryst at Crieff will begin in a week, and your father will want you there." It was more of a statement than a question, and John thought Macnab was trying to put him at ease.

"It's our custom to have the family home for the tryst, and there's always work to be done at that time."

Macnab was watching him, and his eyes were troubled.

"These are difficult times, John. You are welcome to travel with us if you have a mind. We will be at King's House tomorrow, and then perhaps we can talk again."

John nodded. "My thanks, Mr. Macnab; till King's House, then."

* * *

A herd the size of Macnab's only covered ten miles in a day. The slow pace let the animals graze on the rich grass in the glens, putting on weight as they travelled to ensure they arrived at market in peak condition. Macnab had told John he bought the animals in the Western Isles, landed them on the mainland at Kyle Rhea, and brought them south by Glen Garry and Glen Shiel. Tomorrow they would reach the King's House Inn, where they would rest for a day before the final push to Crieff.

The drovers rested the cattle in the middle of the day, and John spread his clothes out in the sun, and by the time they moved on again, they were dry. The herd was spread out across the glen. The drovers stayed around the edges, keeping the animals moving and calling their dogs to bring the stragglers back. John stayed at the back of the herd and helped where he could. Late in the day they came to a low pass that marked the transition from mountains to open moor, and the drovers let the animals spread out to settle for the night.

As John came through the pass, he saw Macnab sitting on his pony, watching the herd. When he caught sight of him, he nudged his pony forward.

"So, lad, dried out and rested by the look of you."

"Yes, thank you, Mr. Macnab."

"You'll be hungry, I'm sure." He handed John another cloth-wrapped package. John unfolded it and found oat cakes, cheese, and a piece of dark bread.

"My thanks again, Mr. Macnab." He wasn't able to resist biting into an oat cake.

Macnab pointed across the darkening moor.

"There is the King's House Inn. We'll rest there a day, and then take the road south to Crieff. You're welcome to travel with us if you have a mind. We can use your help with the herd."

"You're kind, Mr. Macnab, but you have drovers enough for the herd, I think. I'm grateful for your help; as you have said, these are difficult times, and I wonder why you are helping me."

Macnab looked at him curiously.

"I have known your father these many years, and I owe him a great deal. I wouldn't be in business today if it were not for him, so when I come across his son alone in the mountains, it's natural that I would offer my assistance."

John didn't respond, and after a moment Macnab went on.

"I have travelled these drove roads for over thirty years, and I've seen more than is good for one man. Something troubles you, I think, but you're right to be cautious. Know only that you have nothing to fear from me."

John nodded his thanks and Macnab turned his pony away. On the open moor, there was little shelter, but John found a hollow out of the wind. He ate some of the oat cakes and cheese, and tried to make himself comfortable. Macnab had ridden off into the hills. The drovers were nowhere to be seen, and suddenly he felt alone in this vast landscape. He could see the King's House Inn in the distance, a faint beacon of light against the darkening sky, and he gazed at it, lost in thought until sleep took him.

John awakened with a renewed urgency to reach his home. He didn't believe the redcoats would have given up the hunt for him. He knew it was safer to stay with the herd, but he had to force himself to ignore the urge to set off immediately. The drovers had roused the herd at first light, and it was spread out like a dark stain across the moor. It wasn't the drover's habit to start so early, but John was sure that the availability of *uisge-beatha*, the water of life, at the King's House Inn was large in their minds. He ate a little bread and cheese and drank from a burn. He waited until half the animals had passed, then got to his feet and moved with them.

The King's House Inn was a spec of white against the dark of the moor. John watched it all morning, but it seemed to grow no closer. At the midday break, the drovers kept the animals moving, and by mid-afternoon the inn began to take shape. It stood at a crossroads where the drove roads from the north and west joined the road to the south in the centre of a vast landscape of mountains and moorland. To the west lay the entrance to Glen Coe, to the southeast the Rannoch Moor stretched seventy miles in any direction, an empty wasteland of rock and peat bog, and to the north lay Ben Nevis.

The inn was eighty feet long and thirty wide, built of stone with a thatched roof. The main standings were to the southwest of the inn, and John estimated there were three or four thousand animals gathered in the area. The drovers took care that there was no mingling of the herds. Drovers were renowned as a lawless breed, but when they gave their word to bring a herd to market, they would defend the animals with their lives. However, if a few animals were to stray into their own herd, they would feel obligated to take advantage of such good fortune.

Macnab's drovers brought the herd onto a standing to the south of the inn. It took over two hours to bring them all in, and by the time this was accomplished it was late in the afternoon. As soon as the herd was settled the drovers set off for the inn with shouts and whoops of delight.

John had contained himself all day, but the need to reach his home was like an ache that he couldn't ease. He almost left there and then, but felt obligated to thank Mr. Macnab, and he went to find him at the inn. As he made his way across the moor, the sky began to darken and the clouds gathered ominously.

The inn had a weather-worn look about it. The walls were ten feet high, the peak of the roof ten feet above that. There were no windows and the doors at each end were the only openings. To the east of the inn John saw Mr. Macnab's pony tethered with several others. He had almost reached the inn when the rain started to come down in torrents, and he ran for the door.

The inn was filled to bursting with drovers, cattle dealers, and travellers standing in groups, eating and drinking. The noise of men shouting and laughing was deafening, and the air was thick with smoke and the smell of unwashed bodies. It was well known that a state of riotous drinking was maintained at the King's House Inn, day and night during the droving season. This was John's first experience of it in person.

One room took up half the length of the building. An open fire burned in the centre. The smoke was meant to escape through a hole in the thatch, but much of it lingered, forming a thick haze inside the building. A cooking pot was suspended over the fire, giving off an aroma of bad meat. Men sat on the floor around it, drinking and occasionally testing the contents.

At the far end of the room a door opened onto a dark passageway that John knew would give access to rooms set aside for the inn's more affluent patrons. To the left of the door a bar ran along the wall, from behind which the proprietor dispensed various types of ale and whisky. Wooden tables and benches around the other three walls were crowded with men eating and drinking.

John worked his way around the room, but he saw no sign of Macnab. He had almost given up when he caught sight of him and the drovers sitting at a table between the bar and the wall of the inn. Macnab saw him and waved him over. As he approached the table two drovers got to their feet and elbowed their way into the crowd. Macnab sat with his back to the wall, MacPherson across from him. MacPherson slid along the bench to make room for him. John nodded to him but MacPherson ignored him.

Macnab motioned to the platters of food on the table.

"Eat, you must be hungry."

"My thanks." John had to raise his voice to make himself heard. He helped himself to salted beef, cheese, and bread. He ate hungrily, and MacPherson slid a jug of ale across the table. The ale was strong and bitter, tasting vaguely of apples, but it quenched his thirst, and he drank deeply.

John leaned across the table towards Macnab.

"Mr. Macnab, I must be on my way. I need to get home as soon as possible."

"Best wait until the morning," Macnab said. "The rain is on for the night. It won't be easy to find your way in that." He motioned to the door. John turned and looked. The rain was coming down in sheets. He was torn. He knew Macnab was right, but every hour he delayed put his family in greater danger.

MacPherson took a pull from his tankard and looked at Macnab.

"Only a fool goes out on a night like this." John was stung by the rebuke and hot words rose to his lips, but when he met MacPherson's eye, he saw no malice. He was a blunt man, who spoke his mind. He was stating the obvious, and John's anger dissipated as quickly as it had come.

John looked at Macnab. "I've no money, Mr. Macnab. I cannot pay for the food or lodging."

"Your father will make it good. I don't think he would take it kindly if I let his son go hungry and sent him out in a night like this."

"I'm grateful, Mr. Macnab." John looked out at the rain. He would travel faster in daylight and dry clothes.

A short time later the two drovers returned bringing ale and two jugs of *uisge-beatha*, which they distributed around the table. John knew the strength of the Highland *uisge-beatha*. It would have given offense not to accept the offer. He only drank a little of the fiery liquid, but it started a warm glow in his stomach that eased the tension in him.

John feared the drovers would press him to drink more, but they ignored him, drinking steadily and becoming more animated as the night wore on. MacPherson engaged in furious debate with a man at the next table about a cattle sale from the previous year. John thought it would end in violence, but it eventually petered out.

When MacPherson turned back to the table, he grasped John's wrist and motioned with his head over his right shoulder.

"The two men at the table by the door show a great interest in you. Do not seem to be looking now." John turned but didn't look directly at the table. Eight or ten men sat around the table, but none of them seemed to be looking in his direction.

"Which ones?"

"Against the wall."

Both men looked about thirty years of age. One was heavyset with blunt features, red faced from drink. The other one was slightly built. He had a thin sharp face and dark hair hanging to his shoulders. His clothes had been good quality once, but were now worn and shabby. Neither man seemed familiar.

"I don't know them."

"I didn't ask if you knew them; I only say they are watching you."

"Do you know them?"

"They're not drovers. If they're cattle buyers, I haven't seen them before." John turned back to the table. "What do you make of it?"

MacPherson shrugged his shoulders. "They drink little, and their heads are together when they talk."

"I've never seen these men before. What could they want with me?"

"I know nothing of that, but they are about bad business."

MacPherson and Macnab exchanged glances and looked at John, as if expecting him to say something more. Macnab held John's eye for a moment then pursed his lips and looked at MacPherson.

"Keep your wits about you tonight."

MacPherson lifted his chin in acknowledgement, got up, and disappeared into the crowd. Neither John nor Macnab spoke, and after a few minutes Macnab got up.

"Get what sleep you can. We'll speak again in the morning."

"My thanks again, Mr. Macnab." Macnab nodded and disappeared through the door to the other half of the building.

John sat with his back to the wall and sipped his ale. Gradually the uproar died down. Even the drovers' renowned tolerance for *uisge-beatha* had its limits, and one by one they curled up on the floor and went to sleep. John folded his plaid into a pillow and lay down on the bench, trying to make plans for the following day. It was four days' travel to Crieff; he could be there in three if he pushed hard. He was still planning the route in his mind when sleep overcame him.

* * *

The need to relieve himself brought John awake. The fire had died down and gave off barely enough light for him to pick his way across the room. Bodies were strewn about the floor haphazardly. The sound of their snores was startling, and John wondered how he had managed to sleep through it. In the dim light he stepped on a drover's foot. He awoke roaring and lashed out with his fist. John stepped aside and stood still. The man looked around in confusion for a moment then lay down and was snoring again in seconds.

John reached the door without further incident. Outside the rain had eased to a drizzle, but the night was dark and cold. He pulled his plaid around his shoulders and moved along the side of the building, keeping under the thatch.

John was preparing to relieve himself when he heard a sound behind him. It was the sound of leather rubbing on the stone. He whirled around in alarm. A man was moving stealthily along the side of the inn towards him. He took a step back; then something struck him on the side of the head and blackness engulfed him.

CHAPTER SIX

WHEN JOHN REGAINED CONSCIOUSNESS, HE was draped over the back of a pony, his wrists and ankles tied under the animal's belly. The left side of his face was numb, and the eye had swollen shut. His head was pounding, and he felt as if his blood was boiling behind his eyes. He turned his head, trying to ease the pain, and his stomach heaved, and he vomited down the pony's flanks. The pony came to a halt, and a man shouted something. John couldn't make out the words but knew it was an insult. His plaid had fallen over his head, and when he moved his head to try and see, blackness engulfed him again.

When John came to, he was lying on his side on the grass, and his hands and feet were tied. His head was throbbing, and when he tried to sit up the effort made his head swim. He lay on the bank of a river, and from the position of the sun he reasoned it was running to the west. On the other side of the river a range of mountains ran east to west against the sky. It had to be Glen Coe. Whoever had captured him was taking him to Fort William.

Downstream a brown pony stood in the river. When it dropped its head to drink, John saw the man holding the reins. It was the narrow-faced man from the inn that MacPherson had pointed out. A sound behind him made him turn, and he grunted as pain shot through his head. The heavyset man from the inn was standing a few feet away.

"Eh! The young murderer's awake." The man casually kicked John in the stomach. It knocked the wind out of him and sent a spasm of pain through his guts.

"That's to keep you quiet. Give us any trouble and you'll get more of the same."

Morehouse called out to him.

"Let him be, Mullin. He'll get more than a kicking when we get him back to Fort William." Morehouse led the pony up from the river, and they lifted John onto its back and tied his wrists and ankles under its belly. John was still trying to get his breath and couldn't fight back. Hanging upside down made the blood rush to his head, and he had to fight the urge to throw up.

He shouted, "Who are you, and where are you taking me?" Neither man answered. John tried to call out again, but the pony lunged down onto the riverbed and knocked the wind out of him again.

Morehouse led the pony into the river, and as it plodded across, its hooves splashed cold water onto John's face. A few drops touched his lips, and he was seized by a raging thirst that dried up his throat. As the pony climbed out of the riverbed, John craned his neck around. His range of vision was limited, but he saw enough to confirm that they were in Glen Coe.

The river ran against the south side of the glen, and they were travelling on a narrow strip of land between the river and the mountainside. John knew this side of the glen was not well travelled; they wouldn't want to encounter anyone who would question their purposes. There were many who would cut the throats of anyone in the pay of the English, and his captors were taking no chances.

Despite the pain in his throat, John cried out.

"Help, help me. Drovers, come to my aid." His throat was burning, but he gathered himself and shouted again. "Help me, help—" His cry changed to a gasp of pain as Mullin slammed his fist into his kidney. Mullin hit him again and John grunted, paralyzed by pain. Mullin hit him again higher up and John convulsed, biting through his tongue and filling his mouth with blood.

Morehouse called out annoyed. "Let him be. We need him alive."

"His howling will draw attention to us."

"Scott wants him alive, so let him be."

Mullin put his face close to John's ear. "If you call out again, I'll gag your mouth and pound your guts till you choke on your own vomit." Then he led the pony on.

John's head was swimming with nausea, but Morehouse's words jarred him. Scott wanted him alive. Captain Scott, the man who had hanged Alexander Cameron and humiliated the young lieutenant. He despaired of being at the mercy of this man. He prayed that Mr. Macnab and the drovers would come to his aid, but in his heart he knew it was a foolish hope.

His captors kept going all morning. John was lost in a wilderness of pain. His face ached, and he thought his jaw was broken. There was no feeling in his lower back, and he feared that permanent damage had been done to his insides. Hanging upside down made him feel as if the blood would burst from his eyes, and thirst was a raging demon that haunted his every moment.

Sometime in the afternoon they moved into the shade. John opened his eyes and saw they had entered a stand of birch, and a few minutes later they emerged into a small clearing. Morehouse made the pony fast to a tree, and they lifted John down and sat him with his back against the tree. John followed the two men with his one good eye as they went about setting up camp. Finally Morehouse came to John and looked down at him then called to Mullin.

"Give him some water. We need him alive to collect the reward."

Mullin brought a water skin and poured water over John's mouth. The water ran down his face, and John moved his head, trying desperately to get some of the precious liquid into his mouth. Mullin found his antics amusing and poured water in his eyes and on the side of his face, laughing at his distress. John coughed as water went down the wrong way and Mullin squatted down and grabbed him by the hair.

"Had enough, boy?" Hatred flowed out of John and Mullin stopped laughing and sat back on his heels.

"We'll see how long you wear that look with a rope around your neck."

Mullin went back to setting up camp. The men knew their business and quickly got a fire going and bedded the pony down. They ate bread and cheese and passed a stone jug back and forth between them. John's stomach rumbled, but he would die before he asked anything of these men. As it got dark, Mullin came and checked his bonds, pulling the knots tighter. John's hands were numb, and he had long since given up any hope of freeing them.

Morehouse and Mullin lay down by the fire, wrapped themselves in their blankets, and were soon snoring. John was exhausted. His body ached, and he had no recollection of sliding onto the ground and drifting into blackness.

In the morning Mullin kicked John awake. The sun wasn't up, but they had already packed up camp. They lifted him onto the pony and another day of agony began. They followed the same pattern. At midday they fed John a mouthful of bread and allowed him to drink again, but kept him tied.

That night they camped in a forest on the side of a mountain. John saw the sun reflected on a body of water to the west and guessed they were close to Loch Leven or Loch Linnhe, and in the middle of the following morning they entered Fort William. Outside of the fort, Mullin lifted John down from the pony and untied his ankles. He cried out in pain as the blood started to return to his feet, and it was some time before he could stand.

John saw they had brought him to the military camp at Fort William, the main base for the British Army in the west of Scotland. The fort had been built years ago. Over time it had fallen into disrepair and had been hastily reconstructed at the start of the Jacobite rising. The fort was situated on the eastern shore of Loch Linnhe, close to where the River Ness emptied into the loch beneath the shadow of Ben Nevis. The entrance to Glen Nevis was only a mile away and his uncle's farm, a few miles up the glen.

An army camp had been built to the south of the fort. Lines of tents stretched along the shore of the loch. Beyond them was a staging area for the supply system that followed the army. Artillery pieces were lined up in rows next to supply wagons with the horse lines farther back. Foot soldiers made up the bulk of the British Army, but it depended on wagons and pack horses to keep them supplied.

John saw fifty or more cavalry horses tethered to a separate line. They were still saddled and must have recently arrived at the camp. They were sleek animals with shining coats; they were filled with restless energy and pawed the ground impatiently. John knew they were horse guards, and he wondered what was important enough to bring such an elite company to the Highlands.

Mullin took the pony to the horse lines. When he returned, Morehouse gave John a shove between his shoulder blades. Each step sent a jolt of pain through him, but he wiggled his toes and gradually the feeling started to return to his feet. They led him to a large tent at the end of one of the rows.

A soldier stood guard at the entrance, and Morehouse called out to him as they came up.

"Inform Captain Scott that Daniel Morehouse is here."

A moment later Scott stooped under the fly and stood looking at John.

"Bring Crammer," Scott said. Then he went back into the tent.

They waited in silence. John shifted from foot to foot to ease the cramps in his legs and feet. After a few minutes John saw four troopers approaching between the tents. The big man at the front was the sergeant he had fought in his uncle's farmhouse. He was walking slowly and his right arm was in a sling. Crammer's face was black and blue. One eye was swollen shut, and when he saw John his good eye glinted with hatred.

The guard lifted the fly and called out,

"Captain Scott, sir."

Scott stepped out of the tent and pointed at John. "Is this the one?"

"Yes, Captain." Crammer slurred his words. He didn't notice the stream of saliva that ran down the side of his face.

Scott looked at John. His eyes were pale killer blue, and he knew that he was as good as dead.

"Take him. Bring the other one, too," he said and re-entered the tent.

Morehouse and Mullin stepped back, and two troopers took John's arms and marched him towards the south end of the camp. At the horse lines they turned away from the loch, and when John saw where they were taking him his mind quailed.

Six wooden tripods stood at the edge of the forest, some still bloody from the daily floggings, and beside them a gallows had been erected. The troopers halted and waited.

Crammer and the other troopers had followed. Crammer's mouth twisted in a sneer that made his damaged face even more repulsive. John could see he wanted to taunt him, but he struggled to speak through his broken mouth.

The man beside him didn't have the same problem. He wore a broad smile and nodded his head slowly. Recognition must have shown on John's face.

"You outran me once, boy. See how fast you run with a rope around your neck." It was the trooper who had shot at him with the pistol.

The troopers came to attention as Scott came striding across the field. A column of soldiers followed, marching a civilian prisoner between them. Scott stopped in front of John.

"What is your name, boy?" John didn't answer. He knew that he wouldn't live to see another day, but there was no point in letting them persecute his family, a small comfort that he could take to his grave.

Scott swung the riding crop in his hand, striking him on the left side of the face. John cried out in pain and would have fallen, but the troopers held him upright. His face burned with pain and tears poured from his left eye before it swelled shut again.

John turned his head to avoid a second blow and cried out in shock as he recognized the prisoner the soldiers were escorting. It was his uncle, Murdoch. He had aged ten years since John had seen him last, and his clothes hung on his frame like rags. There was blood on his face, and he was holding himself around the middle. He met John's eye and silently mouthed, "Maighread is safe."

Scott motioned to the soldiers.

"Bring him." The troopers dragged Murdoch MacRae to where Scott stood.

"Who else took part in the massacre?" MacRae met Scott's eye silently. Suddenly John understood what was happening. The redcoats thought that others were involved in the fight at the farmhouse. Either the survivors were afraid to admit that he had killed two of them, or a massacre by a band of Highlanders was a more acceptable story for the captain to report to his superiors, and they didn't know Murdoch MacRae was John's uncle.

Scott paced back and forth tapping the riding crop against his boot. Then he turned to the sergeant.

"Hang him," he barked.

"No," John cried. "No."

"Quiet, boy," Murdoch called out, and he hawked and spat at Scott's feet.

John was furious and terrified at the same time and in spite of his uncle's warning he screamed at the top of his voice, "You can't hang him. There's been no trial. There's no justice here."

As the troopers pulled Murdoch towards the gallows, he started to struggle but the troopers held him easily. In moments they had bound his hands behind him, and the rope was around his neck. John heard a shout and the sound of horses' hooves drumming on the ground. Across the field he saw the horse guards coming at the gallop.

"Carry on," Scott said. The troopers walked away with the rope and Murdoch MacRae was lifted off the ground.

John's hands were tied in front of him. He bunched his fists and struck the trooper on his right in the face, sending him staggering back. John launched himself forward trying to reach his uncle.

"No, no," he screamed. The second trooper threw his arm around John's neck, forcing his head down. John fought with all his strength, but the soldier held him, and his companion beat John until he couldn't stand. The troopers lifted him, and held him facing the gallows, so he could see Murdoch swinging on the rope.

Murdoch MacRae's face was purple; his tongue protruded from his mouth, and he was making choking sounds. John realized he was still alive, but a part of him couldn't face the horror of what was happening and wanted it to be over.

A musket shot cracked out behind them, and all heads turned. The horse guards changed formation, spreading out in line abreast, then formed a crescent around the gallows. An officer walked his horse forward. He wore epaulets that John thought signified the rank of major.

He addressed himself to Captain Scott.

"I am Major Anders of His Majesty's Horse Guards. You are Captain Scott. Am I right?"

"What is the meaning of this, Major?" Scott demanded. He pointed to the troopers. Where did you come—?"

The major spoke with a thin nasal drawl. "You will come with me, Captain. Your presence is required in Edinburgh."

"You have no authority here," Scott said and made no attempt to hide his anger at this affront to his dignity in front of the men.

Anders nudged his horse forward.

"You will come with me now, Captain Scott, or I will have you tied across a horse." Anders lifted his hand, and his men drew their muskets and levelled them at the group.

Scott was overcome with rage. "I am a British officer. You will not treat me in this manner."

John saw Scott's neck flush as he barked the words. Anders was unmoved.

"The Duke of Devon has ordered that you attend him in Edinburgh. My orders come directly from the Prince of Wales."

Scott fell silent, and the blood drained from his face. When he had recovered his composure, he pointed at John and spoke to his sergeant. "Hang him."

The sergeant stood looking at Scott dumbfounded. Then he started to give the order.

"Stop!" Anders called out. "Cease this."

"This man killed the duke's son. We have run him to ground, and he must be executed," Scott shouted in frustration.

"Your commission is suspended, effective immediately, Captain Scott. I am to bring you to Edinburgh. You have no authority to order an execution."

Anders glanced behind him. "Sergeant Evans, take charge of the captain."

The sergeant and the two troopers stepped down from their horses. The sergeant took up a position in front of Scott, the troopers behind him, and the horse guards closed the circle tighter around the group.

The soldiers holding John fell back, leaving him swaying on his feet. Freed from their grip he called out. "Major, they have hung my uncle. He's still alive. Let him free, I beg you."

The major looked at John, and then the gallows, and waved to the trooper nearest him. He urged his horse forward and sliced through the rope with his sabre, and Murdoch's body dropped to the ground in an untidy heap.

John rushed to where he lay and threw himself down, desperately trying to remove the rope from around his neck, but it was deeply imbedded in the flesh, and he couldn't free it. He cried out in frustration and anguish, rolled Murdoch onto his stomach, and tried to get a better grip on the knot.

"Help me," he called. "For pity's sake, a knife."

The trooper who had cut the rope was at John's side. "Step back, boy."

He laid the sabre across the rope and cut along its length. The man was an artist with the blade and the rope parted without so much as scratching Murdoch's skin. John rolled his uncle over and put his ear to his mouth. He couldn't hear him breathing, and he heaved him onto his stomach again and pushed down on his back with his full weight. He'd seen this done with a child that had almost drowned, to make its lungs work. He kept pushing and checking to see if his uncle was breathing until he became exhausted.

The trooper put his hand on John's shoulder. "He's dead. Leave him now."

John ignored him and kept working. In his heart he knew it was hopeless, but he couldn't stop. Suddenly John was lifted away from his uncle, and two of the horse guards dragged him back. He looked at the lifeless body of Murdoch MacRae, and he felt as if a piece of his heart had been cut from him.

Major Anders spoke again. "Captain Scott." He gestured to a spare horse held by one of the troopers.

Scott's face was working with rage and frustration. Then he made a cutting motion with his hand and walked towards the horse.

The sergeant called out, "Major, what about the boy?"

"Leave him."

"Major, they will hang him when we leave."

"Bring him," Anders said and pulled his horse around.

John's mind was numb. He couldn't grasp that his Uncle Murdoch was dead, but as the guards started to lead him away, the spell broke. He broke free of the horse guards and charged at Scott, but the guards recovered quickly and held him. John twisted in their grip and called out.

"It's not over, Scott. I will see you again."

Scott didn't react as the horse guards trotted off across the field. John looked at his uncle's lifeless body, and tears of grief and anger rolled down his face.

The troopers prodded John along with their carbines, leading their horses behind them. At the fort there was some confusion about what to do with him. The horse guards sought out the sergeant at arms, but the sergeant was adamant there was no room at the fort for more prisoners. The troopers argued they had been ordered to bring John to the camp and to follow on with all haste.

"I will speak with my officer. Wait," the sergeant said.

John slumped to the ground and the troopers let him be. He couldn't get the image of his uncle choking to death out of his mind. He had killed the young lieutenant and had been the cause of this. He sat consumed by guilt, and darkness settled on his mind.

CHAPTER SEVEN

IT WAS SOME TIME BEFORE the sergeant returned with two redcoats in tow.

"These men will take the prisoner." The redcoats lifted John to his feet.

"He's not to be killed. Our major was clear."

"He'll not be hanged, although he may wish he had been." The horse guards mounted up and galloped away across the field.

One of the redcoats checked John's bonds, and they led him around the perimeter of the camp. They made their way to Loch Linnhe and turned south along the shore. Both soldiers were veterans. One was in his forties, and John was sure the other was over fifty, old to be on active duty.

"Where are you taking me?" John said.

"You'll see soon enough," the older man said.

The loch was two miles across at this point and broadened to the south. Hills rose steeply from the loch shore treed with birch and larch. The footpath was well beaten, with the tracks of cart wheels and footprints imbedded in the mud.

They walked for an hour; then the path turned away from the loch shore into the woods. Ahead of them, a rocky point ran out into the loch for a quarter of a mile. The path ran up the side of the hill, cutting across the base of the point. As they came to the top of the hill, John saw the masts of a ship through the trees, and he began to hear voices calling out on the other side of the point. He looked at the guards expectantly. Neither spoke but the older man prodded him on with his musket.

As they started to descend, the view opened up and John saw the ship anchored off the beach. John had never seen a seagoing ship this close, and it looked huge. He guessed it was over two hundred feet long, with the main deck twenty feet above the waterline. The hull was painted black with the piping around the deck and forecastle picked out in white. The rigging was a spider's web of ropes running in every direction, and the sails were tied to the underside of the spars in evenly spaced bundles like the muscles of a sleeping giant. John could see men on the deck and lower parts of the rigging moving with a purpose that he found oddly compelling.

Two boats were drawn up on the beach, and men and women were being boarded in groups, soldiers urging them on. As soon as each boat was loaded, it pushed off. John could hear the cries of the women as they pulled for the ship. As they came down to the beach, a sergeant called out to them.

"Who do you have there, Trooper Williams? Another stinking wretch to be sure."

"Orders from the captain. This one goes with the rest." He pointed to the ship.

"It makes no difference to me. Put him on board."

"You're putting me on that ship? Where is it bound?" John said. Neither man answered as they pushed him towards the last boat, already fully loaded.

As they came to the boat John dug his heels in. "Tell me where you're taking me."

One of the other soldiers drove the stock of his musket into John's stomach. The force of it knocked him backwards over the gunnels. The second man lifted his legs and tumbled him into the bottom of the boat, and in moments the sailors were pulling for the ship. With his hands tied John couldn't get to his feet. Two men took him by the arms and lifted him onto the bench along the gunnels.

"Thank you." Neither man spoke. Their eyes were fixed on the ship.

John examined the ship. *Orion* was painted in white letters on her bow. It loomed above them, solid and menacing like a dark monster from a dream, but John was fascinated by it. As soon as they were alongside, the people were urged to climb the ladder to the deck, twenty feet above them. Some of the women cried out at the prospect of the climb, and the soldiers threatened to throw them overboard if they didn't try.

John was near the bow, and they came to him last.

"I can't climb with my hands tied," he said. One of the soldiers untied his hands and pushed him towards the ladder.

"No tricks now, boy." John's hands were numb, and he rubbed them together, trying to get the feeling back. He was afraid that he wouldn't be able to hold on to the ladder, but once he started to climb, his strength came back, and he went up the side of the ship easily.

John stepped onto the deck and followed the others to the bow. There were sixty or seventy people standing against the rail, and John didn't think he'd seen a more forlorn-looking group in his life. It was obvious that many of them were related and from the same clan. Even their clothes were made from similar cloth.

John was thinking quickly—when the soldiers put him in the longboat, they hadn't said he was a prisoner, and the boat had returned to the beach immediately, so as far as the ship's crew knew he was a member of the same clan.

There was tremendous activity on the ship. The longboat was hauled on board and made fast to the deck. A dozen sailors walked the windlass around, and John felt the moment when the anchor broke free. Sailors swarmed up the rigging and broke out the sails, and he watched in amazement as the canvas billowed out in white clouds high above the deck. The ship came alive under his feet. She came on the wind and bore away from the shore.

The ship eased out of the cove, heeled to port and surged forward. The clanspeople howled in fear and clutched the ship's rail, and the sailors urged them towards the bow, to a hatch leading below decks. There was some pushing and shouted threats from the clansmen, but they were out of their element, and in the end they went below meekly.

John followed, not wishing to draw attention to himself and climbed down the ladder into the hold. The "tween decks," as it was called, had been set up to accommodate large numbers of passengers. There was less than six feet of headroom between the decks. Bunk beds had been built along the sides of the hull, and these were assigned to families with children. The centre area was open, and hammocks hung from the roof and bulkheads for the single men.

The hold was filled with noise as men claimed bunks for their families or a hammock for themselves. The sounds of retching and wailing added to the uproar as the motion of the ship started to affect the clanspeople's stomachs. John found a spot near the front of the hold and sat down with his back against the bulkhead.

He had no idea where the ship was heading, likely Glasgow or some other port in the Lowlands. It didn't matter. He was a strong swimmer, and once they reached port, he would slip over the side. He must bide his time until the opportunity presented itself, and he settled down to rest and recover his strength.

John's hammock was on the port side of the hold. The man next to him had tried repeatedly to climb into his hammock, but found himself sitting on the deck after each attempt. With a sigh he slid across beside John.

"I think you have the right of it, lad. It's safer down here." He had a weather-beaten face that could have been thirty or sixty years of age.

John nodded agreement.

"What's your name?" he said.

"I am Ewan MacLeod. We're all MacLeods from Skye." He lifted his chin towards the other clanspeople.

"Why did the English put you on this ship?"

MacLeod shook his head. "No, lad, it was our own laird put us on this ship. We've been on the land as long as our people can remember, and he drove us out as if we were dogs. He said we were no good to him any longer, and he sent the redcoats to bring us here and put us on this ship." MacLeod looked down for a moment, and when he looked up, his eyes were wet.

John waited till he composed himself.

"Where are they taking you? Where is the ship bound for?" MacLeod frowned.

"You don't know, lad?"

John felt unease stirring in him. MacLeod's eyes held a sadness that seemed to have no end.

"America, lad. This ship is bound for Massachusetts, wherever that might be. We are to become indentured servants, bound to serve a master for seven years. I fear that none of us will see our homeland again."

John felt as if the air had been driven from his lungs and couldn't find his voice. He took MacLeod by the shoulder.

"There must be a mistake. It cannot be true." MacLeod looked back at him steadily, and he knew he was telling the truth. John leapt to his feet and rushed across the deck, knocking a clansman to the floor, ignoring the shouts that followed him up the ladder. He came out onto the deck and rushed to the lee rail.

The ship was under full sail and a stiff breeze was pushing her down Loch Linnhe on the falling tide. They'd passed the narrows between Inchree and Caran and were into the lower half of the loch. The water was rough, a hint of what awaited them in the Irish Sea. He recognized the entrance to Loch Leven off the port bow, and he knew it was true. This ship wouldn't touch land again on this continent.

The shore was more than two miles. He didn't know if he could swim that far, but it didn't matter. He pulled his boots off and grasped the rail gathering himself for the leap. Something struck him on the side of the head, and he staggered across the deck. Loch Leven glowed in the evening sunshine, but his vision blurred, and the green of the hills started to bleed into the grey of the ocean. John couldn't tell if it was sea spray or tears that filled his eyes; then he saw no more.

CHAPTER EIGHT

EDINBURGH SPREAD OUT ALONG THE banks of the River Forth. The town was dark, but the smell of it was thick on the wind, a pungent mixture of chimney smoke, fish guts, and raw sewage. Edinburgh Castle, built on a granite outcrop, sat like a brooding menace over the town.

The troop had ridden from Crieff the previous day with only two stops to rest. Scott had spoken with Major Anders only once. He asked him why he was being taken to Edinburgh when his command post was Fort William. Anders had answered that his orders had come from the Prince of Wales and would say no more. Scott had protested, but the major made it clear he would restrain him, if necessary, and Scott had no choice but to go along.

The troop followed the road around the base of the castle, Major Anders riding in front; Scott was two rows back, flanked by two sergeants. The horses made a tremendous racket as they moved through the town. Their steel shoes threw sparks from the cobbles, making them seem like mounted demons in the rain-streaked night. The men called to each other, their voices harsh and guttural, and people rushed inside and shuttered their windows as they passed.

In the centre of the town they climbed uphill for some distance and emerged into a square directly below the castle. Anders dismounted in front of a four-storey stone building. He signalled for Scott to do the same, and a trooper took their horses and led them off into the darkness. Light was spilling from the doorway of a tavern across the square. Two young women stood in the doorway calling out to the men, and several of the troopers made haste to join them.

Major Anders motioned to Scott.

"Come with me, Captain." Anders climbed an outside staircase to a door on the second floor. He waited for Scott on the landing and entered the building without knocking. The sergeants followed at a respectful distance. Anders took a flight of stairs to a broad landing and went to a door on the left and knocked. He motioned for Scott to stop and stepped inside, and Scott's anger flared at being made to wait outside with the sergeants. A moment later the door opened and Anders stood to the side.

"Captain Scott." He motioned for Scott to enter. He followed him inside and closed the door.

Scott found himself in a long narrow room. The windows at one end looked onto the square. A fire burned in a fireplace in the wall opposite the door. Scott could feel the heat across the room. Bookshelves lined the walls on both sides of the fireplace, and a desk stood to one side.

The room was lit by a candelabra in the middle of the room and candles fixed around the walls. It was a world apart from the cold rainy night outside, but Scott took no comfort from it.

Robert Sackville, the Duke of Devon, stood with his back to the fire, looking at Scott. He was in his mid-fifties; he was lean as a whippet and wore his thinning hair tied behind his head. He had the same delicate features as his son, but there was a firm set to his jaw. He was dressed in a black frock coat and breeches, and Scott guessed his polished riding boots had never seen the back of a horse.

Scott walked across the room and stopped ten feet from the duke. Lord Sackville stared at him with pale grey eyes; his face was blank, and he barely seemed to draw breath. Scott felt humiliated being treated like this. He could feel Anders's eyes burning into his back, and the colour rose in his face. Finally he could not tolerate the indignity any further.

"My lord—"

"Silence. Silence, I say." The duke barked the words. His voice was high-pitched, almost feminine, but it carried an edge of authority.

The duke stood motionless, but tension emanated from him, and he watched Scott with fierce concentration, struggling with some powerful emotion. Scott knew the stakes were high for him, and he kept his temper in check. The clock ticking on the desk seemed to fill the room, and a log cracked in the fire and made Scott start.

Finally the duke spoke.

"My son is dead." He cast his eyes down for a moment, and when he raised them they were wet with tears. The duke was finely drawn and Scott felt a twinge of unease in his gut.

"My son was entrusted to your care and now he is dead. How do you explain that?"

"My lord, Duke—"

"Silence!" the duke screamed. He stepped close to Scott, and spittle flew from his mouth as he spoke. "You will speak when I say you may speak." He stepped back, wiping his mouth with his sleeve.

Scott blinked at the intensity of the man. He hadn't seen this side of him, and was alarmed that he had so badly misread him.

"You are a ruthless and vicious man, Captain Scott, despised and shunned by your colleagues and fellow officers. A talented officer whose excesses of vindictiveness and cruelty have caused you to be passed over for promotion on more than one occasion, a man destined for mediocrity and to decline into obscurity."

Scott bridled at the insults and struggled to hold his temper. The duke made a gesture with his hand.

"I believed these qualities would serve to protect my son from the more unsavoury aspects of military service. This was the nature of our agreement, was it not, Captain?" The duke shouted the words in Scott's face. Scott was no coward, but he knew he faced danger here that he was not equipped to confront.

The duke put his hands behind his back. "Some months ago I began to receive disturbing reports of how you were treating my son."

Scott blinked in surprise and the duke went on.

"Do you think me a fool, Captain? Do you think I would not take steps to watch over my only son and heir? I've been aware of your behaviour for some time, but I took no action. I hoped that George would mature and learn to stand up for himself."

The duke turned away and warmed his hands at the fire. When he turned back, the tension had gone out of him.

"It appears I was at fault, Captain." He wrung his hands together and spoke softly.

"You should be court-martialled and drummed out of the army. Transportation to Van Diemen's Land would be a fitting end to your career."

Scott felt the blood drain from his face. He'd faced death many times, but the thought of losing his commission made his guts churn. For Van Diemen's Land he didn't give a damn, but the army was his life.

The duke watched him, almost detached. "Such would have been your fate, Captain, were it not for the wishes of my wife, your older sister."

Scott drew a sharp breath at the mention of his sister. He wanted neither help nor pity from her.

"I don't know why she would intercede on your behalf, given the malice you have directed towards her over the years. However, against my better judgment, I have acceded to her wishes, and you will be neither court-martialled nor transported."

The duke looked away for a moment.

"You will be transferred to Massachusetts. You will retain your rank and will be assigned to a regiment engaged in protecting His Majesty's American Colonies." The duke paused for a moment and went on. "You will never set foot in this country again. If you do, you will be arrested and court-martialled, and you may expect to be subjected to the sanctions I have previously described. Do we understand each other, Captain? A simple yes or no will suffice."

Scott was stunned—he would retain his commission, but he was banished to the ends of the earth.

"We understand each other, my lord," Scott said. The duke held his gaze for a moment longer, cold hatred in his eyes; then he nodded to Major Anders. Scott suddenly realized that the duke had been trying to provoke him. Anders stood ready to act.

Abruptly the duke turned back to the fire and spoke over his shoulder. "Major."

"Come with me, Captain." Scott realized it was over. Anders held the door and followed him out. Scott made his way down to the square and stood on the outside landing, breathing in the cold evening air.

Anders came down the steps behind him.

"Captain Scott, you will be billeted in the inn for the night. My two sergeants will accompany you."

"I don't need your puppies to sit on my doorstop, Major."

Anders continued as if he hadn't spoken. "Tomorrow we ride for Greenock on the Clyde, where the brig *Raven* is provisioning. She will sail for Boston within the week. Till tomorrow then, Captain." Anders turned and walked away across the square.

* * *

The troop rode into Greenock two days later. Scott found his chest waiting for him at the dock along with Sergeant Crammer and his men. It seemed they were to share his fate. Scott was confined to the ship and Anders and the two sergeants remained on board. Shortly before the ship cast off, Anders spoke to Scott.

"Captain Harbin, the master of the *Raven*, has your orders. He will deliver them to you when the ship has sailed." Anders turned and went down the gangplank without speaking further.

An hour later the *Raven* caught the evening tide, and Scott heard the mate call out, "Bring her onto the port tack. The wind is fair for America."

Scott stood on the deck and watched the green hills of Scotland slip past. He couldn't resign himself to this fate, and resentment and acrimony consumed his mind like a cancer that grew stronger with every moment that passed.

CHAPTER NINE

JOHN AWOKE IN DARKNESS. ALL around him he heard voices and the snores of many people sleeping. He was lying on his back on a wooden floor, and the room was moving as if he'd drunk too much *uisge-beatha*. Above him he heard a man calling out orders, but the sound faded as if blown away on the wind. The man called out again and his memory came flooding back. When he sat up, a searing pain pierced his head, and he lay back nauseated and dizzy. He touched the left side of his head, and his fingers came away sticky with blood. A wave of pain swept over him again, and he swallowed, trying not to throw up.

John closed his eyes and began to gather his thoughts. He remembered attempting to jump overboard, but after that everything was dark. He could make out the shape of the hammocks swinging back and forth above him, and then he heard someone speak to him.

"They cracked your head open, lad, but you'll live." John winced as he turned his head. Ewan MacLeod was sitting against the bulkhead, watching him. "I have your boots," he said.

John leaned on his elbow and looked at MacLeod. "What happened?"

"They dragged you down here. Said you tried to go over the side."

"The ship is bound for America. I'm not of your clan. I do not belong . . ."

"It makes no difference, lad. They are paid to bring us to the Americas, and they don't care who belongs and who doesn't." MacLeod slid his boots across the floor. "They're grand boots, lad. Best put them on before someone takes a shine to them."

A lantern hung by the ladder casting the hold in a dim light, and John looked around him. The hold was thirty feet long and ran the full width of the ship, narrowing towards the bow, and it was packed with clanspeople. Many lay moaning in their bunks or throwing up in the slop buckets. The smell of vomit and human waste was overwhelming.

"Are you injured?" MacLeod asked.

"I have bruises enough, but there are no bones broken, unless you count my head. How long was I unconscious?"

"Two or three hours, I think."

John felt the ship begin to turn. A voice called out on the deck above, and a wave of sadness washed over him. He was being carried away from his homeland and everything he knew, and he was seized with the need to get off the ship again. He pushed himself to his feet, but he had to grasp the hammock to steady himself.

"The weather is rough and they've locked the hatches down. We can't get out, lad." John felt the world begin to spin; then strong hands took hold of him.

"Rest now. There's nothing to be done."

John remembered climbing into the hammock, and then nothing till he was awakened by the sound of shouting and feet stamping on the deck above. He opened his eyes and felt disorientated until he realized the hammock was swinging with the motion of ship. He lay still for a moment and looked around him. The hatch was open and daylight was streaming into the hold. It was cold, but his plaid was wrapped around him, and he whispered a word of thanks to MacLeod. People were pressing forward, trying to get onto the ladder. When John heard a sailor shouting at the clansmen to get in line for food and water rations, his stomach growled and he was seized with a raging thirst. He rolled out of the hammock and held on to the rope as dizziness washed over him again. When it passed, he staggered across the deck to the ladder.

When John stepped on deck, he had to grab hold of the hatch combing to stop himself being blown off his feet. The day was bleak and overcast, and dark clouds hung low over the horizon. The sea was flat grey and the waves ran forty feet in height, three times that distance between their peaks. The masts swung wildly across the sky, but the crew worked the sails a hundred feet above the deck, seemingly unconcerned.

The clanspeople were gathered round the deckhouse behind the mainmast, lining up to enter the galley. Seawater streamed over the decks, and a rope had been strung from the hatch to the deckhouse. John clung to it as he made his way aft. He felt the clanspeople watching him, curiosity and hostility in their eyes.

Four paces from the deckhouse John had to let go of the rope. He had almost reached the deckhouse when the ship rolled to port, and his feet went out from under him. He slid down the deck and came up hard against the port rail. He grabbed the mainmast shrouds, and for a moment he hung over the rail looking down at the green water surging past. Then the ship righted itself, and he regained his balance. The clanspeople's faces wore expressions of alarm or indifference, and one girl seemed to find the whole thing amusing.

She looked a few years older than John. She was small and slender, but she held on to the deckhouse rail easily. She wore a shapeless grey dress with black boots peeping out from under it and a shawl around her shoulders. John saw a sparkle of amusement in her eyes and felt vaguely foolish. The man behind her nudged her, and she moved around the corner of the deckhouse. He looked at John suspiciously then followed her. Judging by his age, John thought he must be the girl's father.

John's thirst had returned with a vengeance as he waited in line, and when he turned the corner of the deckhouse, he was relieved to see only a few people ahead of him. A seaman stood inside the door, belaying pin in hand to keep order. John rubbed the side of his head, wondering if he was the one who had knocked him out the previous day.

The seaman motioned for John to enter. It was dark inside and it took a moment for his eyes to adjust. An iron stove stood against the wall to his left. Down the right side of the galley six tables were fastened to the deck. The table tops were divided into squares with raised edges to keep the plates from sliding off.

The cook stood by the stove, beside him a sailor with a belaying pin in his hand. There was one man ahead of him, and John watched as the cook scooped a ladleful of biscuits into his hands.

"Is that all? That wouldn't feed a child." The sailor tapped him with his belaying pin.

"If you don't like it, others will eat it." The man gave him an appraising look then turned away.

John stepped up as the cook scooped more biscuits out of the bucket. John held his plaid open and the man dropped them into the cloth. It looked like dried doe and lard, but to John it seemed like manna from heaven. A wooden cask was fixed to the wall beside the table; the cook picked up a mug and held it under the spigot. John could hardly contain himself when he saw the water, and he had to restrain himself from grabbing the mug out of the cook's hand.

As the cook handed him the mug, John lifted it to his mouth and drank greedily. The water was bitter, but he gulped it down, spilling some down his chin.

"Go easy, boy. That's all you'll get today." The words had a sobering effect on him, and John lowered the mug and caught his breath.

"Drink it slowly. No one will take it from you." John nodded his thanks.

John moved to the nearest table trying not to spill his water. The man at the end of the bench slid along to make room for him. John sat down and put the mug on the table and kept his hand on it. The biscuits were rock hard, and he gnawed a piece off of one and chewed it slowly washing it down with a little water. It tasted like wood chips, but he hadn't eaten in days, and he didn't complain.

The man beside him looked at him.

"Where are you from, boy?" John resented the demanding tone, and he didn't like being called boy.

"Where are you from?" he barked in return.

"We're all from Skye." His answer was straightforward, and John regretted his harsh words. He didn't know how long he would be on this ship, and it occurred to him that it would be best not to antagonize these people.

"I'm from Glen Nevis."

The man nodded.

"Aye, they took some of our people from there as well." John wondered if this man was connected to someone he knew in Glen Nevis, but he didn't think this was the time to ask.

John ate the biscuit, hardtack the sailors called it, and washed it down with what was left of his water. Hungry as he was, he couldn't eat all of the hardtack and put what was left in his hunting bag. He returned the mug to the cook. He almost asked for more water but thought better of it.

"Is there more food later in the day?"

"That'll be all you'll get today. Once a week you'll get meat if we can light the stove, otherwise hardtack is all you get."

"How long will the voyage be?"

"Ask the captain." The cook busied himself securing the lid on the barrel and ignored John.

Shortly after, the sailor guarding the door banged his belaying pin on the stove.

"Clear the galley. Everyone out." He moved along tapping the tables with the belaying pin. People were reluctant to leave the warmth of the galley, but the seaman herded them out.

As John stepped on deck, the wind bit into him. He pulled his plaid around his shoulders and made his way down to the hold. Old MacLeod was sitting against the bulkhead, and he sat beside him.

"Is this what we're to eat the whole voyage?" John held up a piece of hardtack.

"Best not to let people see it. There will be little enough left before this journey's over."

John put the hardtack in his bag.

"How long will it take to reach America?"

"They say two months if the weather holds, three if it doesn't."

"Two months on this ship. I don't know if I can endure it."

"There's nothing to be done, lad. There's no way back."

As John listened to the sounds of the ship—the creaking of the rigging, sailors calling out orders—his mind wandered to his home and family. They would hear of Uncle Murdoch's death, but would have no way of knowing what had happened to him. He determined that if he survived this journey, he would find some way to send word back to his family. It was only midday, but the pain in his head had returned, and his eyes were becoming heavy. He climbed into his hammock and wrapped himself in his plaid. The motion of the ship eased the pain and after a while he slept.

* * *

John was awakened by someone shaking his shoulder, and he opened his eyes to find MacLeod standing beside his hammock.

"Time to eat."

"Aye." John swung out of the hammock and held on as his head spun for a moment; then he followed MacLeod up on deck. The weather was the same, but the ship was heading more directly into the swells, and there was less rolling motion.

The ship's bell sounded the change of watch, and John determined he would learn how the system worked and what each bell meant. The bell was the signal to eat, but as they only ate once a day, it didn't make sense. Then he realized that he must have slept for a whole day.

He looked at MacLeod.

"Did I sleep a day and a night?"

"That you did, lad. A blow to the head is dangerous. I've seen the like before." John touched the side of his head. It was stiff with dried blood, but the pain was only a dull ache now, and his vision was clear.

MacLeod touched his shoulder.

"We must get in line."

It was a long wait, but finally they were given their ration. John sat by MacLeod and examined the clanspeople as they ate. There were men and women of all ages. It was plain to see that many were related. John remembered MacLeod telling him how they had come to be on board but couldn't recall the details.

John turned to MacLeod.

"How is it these people are here?" MacLeod looked at him sharply, and John thought that he had offended him, but his voice betrayed no anger.

"It was in the spring we first heard of the clearing. My brother came back from Fort William with news that the MacDonalds from Loch Leven had been forced off their land, and the redcoats had burned their crofts. My brother said we should be prepared lest the same thing happened to us, but I said the laird wouldn't allow it."

"What did you do?"

"There was nothing we could do. We planted the spring crops and went about our business. We heard nothing more of the MacDonalds or their fate.

Then in the second week of August the laird sent word that he would speak to us on the Sunday. He said to bring clothes and food for three days. We didn't know what to make of it, but we gathered at the kirk on the Sunday morning."

MacLeod rubbed his eyes.

"What happened?"

MacLeod shook his head. "The laird didn't come until midday. Then one of my brother's lads came running, calling out that a company of redcoats was marching up the glen."

MacLeod shifted on the bench as if he was in pain and then went on. "The laird went up on the steps of the kirk to speak. He said the Jacobite rising was over. The cause was lost, and there was no longer a place for us on Skye. He said that we were to leave that very day, to be sent to America to a new life. Lachlan MacLeod shouted that he wouldn't go and started to walk away. The redcoats shot him dead on the spot, and after that no one resisted."

MacLeod looked down at the table.

"How did you come to be on this ship? What will become of you in America?" John said.

When MacLeod looked up there were tears in his eyes. "The redcoats drove us out of the village and burned our homes as we walked away, three days' march to Fort William, sleeping in the open. A British officer told us we were to be sent to a place called Massachusetts. He said that we were to be indentured servants, and that after seven years of work we would be free, and that we would be given land and tools to farm and have a better life."

John was astonished at MacLeod's tale. He'd heard rumours of such things but hadn't believed them until now.

"What is an indentured servant?"

"I don't know, lad, but it sounds like slavery to me. I'm too old. I won't live to see it through." MacLeod leaned on the table and held his head in his hands.

The galley had gone quiet, and all eyes were on old MacLeod as if he had spoken what they were feeling. John saw terrible sadness in those eyes, and he felt as if he was intruding on their grief and looked away.

MacLeod gathered himself and turned to John. "What about you, lad? How do you find yourself on this ship?"

"The redcoats came to my uncle's farm in Glen Nevis. They burned the croft and took us to Fort William. Uncle Murdoch resisted, and they hung him." John didn't think it wise to let it be known he had killed a British officer.

The clanspeople were watching him, some with sympathy in their eyes, others with suspicion. The girl who had found him so amusing the day before looked at him sadly. A sailor banged his belaying pin on the stove and called out.

"Outside with you now. Make room for the crew."

The galley filled with sound as people got up to leave, bickering about being pushed out onto the cold deck. John drank the last of his water, and got up from the table. The girl was ahead of him at the door. She looked back and giggled as she stepped out onto the deck, and the man behind her scowled. He was about twenty-five years old, burly and thickening around the middle. He had a mean look about him and John wondered if he was the girl's brother. She looked old enough to be married, but she didn't act as if she was. On deck, the clanspeople looked fearfully at the huge swells and hurried back to the shelter of the hold.

John stayed on deck. He was fascinated by the ship and its workings. He studied the raised section at the bow where the sailors slept. This was the forecastle—the fo'c'sle, they called it. The entrance to the forward hold was just astern of this. The galley deckhouse behind the mainmast was the only structure on the deck. The bridge deck stood ten feet above the main deck with the ship's wheel and binnacle in the centre. John watched the sailor making adjustments to the wheel, constantly looking at the horizon then up at the rigging. He understood the basics of navigation, but he was fascinated by the idea that one man was able to steer this huge vessel, and he stayed on deck until the rain drove him below.

* * *

The weather was rough for the next few days, and they ate hardtack and water. John stayed on deck when he could, preferring the wind and rain to the noise and stench of the hold. He watched the sailors work and tried to learn what he could about how they sailed the ship. The captain was called Abercrombie, and there were three other officers, Lockman, Kerr, and Grant, as well as twenty deckhands. The crew kept themselves apart from the clanspeople and treated them as if they were cattle being carried to market. In spite of their attitude, John admired the sailors' ability to handle the ship, and just watching as they climbed the rigging made him dizzy.

The weather worsened, and the decks were awash. The first mate ordered the clanspeople below and closed the hatch, leaving only a small opening to admit fresh air. Many clanspeople were sick. The slop buckets were over-flowing, and by the third day, the stench was almost unbearable. John was blessed with a strong stomach, and he lay in his hammock praying for a break in the weather.

On the sixth day when John awoke, the ship's motion was easier, and he knew the weather had broken. When he came on deck, the waves were ten feet at the peak, and the ship was riding the swells easily. John caught the smell of cooking meat on the wind and joined the line at the galley door. The clanspeople seemed to have more energy; better weather and the prospect of warm food could work wonders. John was almost last in line and hoped there would be some left.

When he entered the galley, it was full of noise. People were shouting and laughing, and John's stomach growled at the prospect of hot food. The cook was stirring a large pot, and when his turn came the cook handed him a wooden bowl, ladled stew into it and handed him his ration of hardtack. John's hands were full, and he looked at the water barrel in confusion.

"Come back for your water." All the tables were jammed with people eating hungrily, and those who had finished sat and watched every spoonful their friends ate.

John went to the forward bulkhead where he could sit against the wall, and as he passed the end table, the girl spoke to him.

"There's room here." She pushed along the bench. Her brother looked annoyed but moved to make room.

"Thank you," John said and turned his attention to the food. He dipped the hardtack in the stew and bit into it. It was beef stew, heavily salted and bitter, but it tasted like the best meal of his life, and he moaned in pleasure as he ate, much to the girl's amusement.

When he finished the hardtack, the bowl was still half-full and John realized he didn't have a spoon. The clanspeople each had a spoon of bone or wood. As he lifted the bowl to his lips, the girl placed a wooden spoon in front of him.

"You may use this, but you should try to find a spoon of your own." She had the lilting accent of the islands that made her sound as if she was singing the words.

"Thank you." As he picked up the spoon, her brother glared at him then got up and left the galley.

The girl turned towards John and her leg rested against his.

"I'm Katy MacLeod. How's the stew?" She was nineteen or twenty years old. She had an engaging smile, and a sense of humour that always seemed just below the surface. She had clear skin, dark brown hair, and a gold fleck in her left eye, a flaw that somehow made her more appealing.

John looked up.

"The stew is good. I'm John Wallace."

"Where are you from?"

"My uncle has . . . had a farm in Glen Nevis." Speaking his name brought back the image of his uncle's dead face, and he looked down. The girl acted as if she hadn't noticed.

"What will you do in America?"

"I don't know. I admit I haven't thought on it a great deal."

"We are to be indentured servants. I don't know what that means, indentured. Does it mean that we will be separated from our families and sent far away?" She went quiet, and he thought she might cry, but his mind was on the warmth of her leg pressed against his.

The girl's father, sitting across the table, got up to leave.

"Come, girl." He wiped his spoon on his sleeve and put it in his pocket and left the galley.

Katy picked up her bowl and her father's and held out her hand for the spoon.

"Thanks for the use of it."

"You have to find your own spoon. Our people are superstitious about sharing such things." She put the spoon in her pocket.

"I'll find my own, if I can."

The girl took the bowls and her father's tankard and put them in the box at the end of the galley. The sight of the tankard brought John's mind back to water. He fetched his ration, and when he came back to the table the girl was gone.

John drank slowly, making it last, and returned the tankard to the box and nodded to the cook.

When John stepped out on deck, the day had brightened. A watery sun shone through the clouds, and his spirits lightened. He watched the crew set more canvas, and when he brought his eyes back to the deck, Katy's brother was standing in front of him.

"Stay away from Katy." His voice was thick with menace as he leaned close, trying to intimidate John with his size. "Leave her be, boy, or I'll make you regret it."

John's temper stirred. "I'll speak with whoever I wish, and it's no business of yours."

John took a step away from the deckhouse, keeping a hand on the rail. MacLeod was the same height as him but older and heavier. He grabbed at John's jerkin with his right hand, and John struck his arm away. It wasn't a hard blow, but it knocked MacLeod off balance, and the roll of the ship sent him stumbling backwards.

MacLeod grabbed the handrail, slammed against the deckhouse and his feet went out from under him. He grunted at the impact, but rolled to his feet immediately. He waited for the ship to roll to port and launched himself at John. John stayed on the balls of his feet and held on to the rail. He couldn't let MacLeod get close where he could use his weight and strength, and he readied himself to move.

A voice bellowed from the bridge. "Belay that!"

John looked around. Lockman, the first mate, was standing by the bridge rail. "Belay that, or I'll flog the flesh off your backs."

The mate's voice carried authority, and John froze on the spot. MacLeod grabbed the galley door to stop himself and glared at John as if he would kill him. Then he pulled his way along the rail and around the corner of the deckhouse.

The next day as John sat on deck waiting for the ship's bell, old MacLeod came and sat with him.

"Be careful of Malcolm MacLeod."

"He started it. Is he Katy's brother?"

"He says he's to marry her, although I don't know if her father has agreed to it."

"What does Katy have to say about it?"

"You would have to ask her that, lad, but Malcolm MacLeod won't forget, and he has an evil reputation."

"I'll watch myself."

John didn't see Malcolm MacLeod for some time, but he was sitting at the table when he entered the galley a few days later. John sat at the far end of the galley, and MacLeod left as soon as he'd finished eating. A few minutes later John was surprised when Katy sat down beside him.

"Malcolm didn't knock your brains out, then." She had a mischievous grin on her lips.

"He didn't, but I'm sure he would if he had the opportunity." He bit off a piece of hardtack and went on talking. "They tell me you're to be married, yourself and Malcolm."

Katy's lips formed a tight line.

John motioned with the hand holding the hardtack. "Are you to be married in America, then?"

"Malcolm MacLeod is my cousin, my second cousin to be precise." Her face fell into a frown. "Malcolm has it in his head that we're to be wed, but I have no intention of marrying him. He tries to bully any man who speaks to me, and it's gotten worse since we've been on the ship. There's no getting away from him."

John watched her out of the corner of his eye. "What does your father have to say about it?"

"My father says nothing, and he does nothing. Malcolm's family had good land on Skye. Before we were put off our land he said that Malcolm would be a good man for me. I think he and Malcolm's father had some kind of agreement about land, but he wouldn't speak about it. Since we've been on the ship my father doesn't speak of Skye and doesn't seem to care what Malcolm says about me."

John couldn't tell if the brittle edge in her voice was from anger or distress. Before he could say any more she gathered up her things and left, but as she stepped through the door, she looked back and the sparkle had returned to her eye.

"Goodbye for now, John Wallace," she said.

* * *

They'd be on board for six weeks and conditions were steadily getting worse. For three days the clanspeople were confined below decks. Trapped in the hold John couldn't help but notice that many of the MacLeods looked gaunt and sickly; even the children were subdued. Few of the clanspeople came on deck now, even when the weather was fair, and he realized that some never left the hold except to eat. He hoped for their sake and his own that the voyage would be over soon.

When John awoke on the fourth morning, the hold was unnaturally quiet. As his eyes adjusted to the light coming in through the hatch, his eye was drawn to the corner of the hold. A man sat against the bulkhead and a woman lay beside him on the deck with a child on her lap and two more on the bunk behind her. They were very still. Some of the clanspeople had never found their sea legs and would lie in their bunks for hours, but John hadn't thought anything of it.

Hunger intruded on his thoughts, and he rolled out of his hammock. When he made his way to the galley, he was surprised to find himself near the front of the line. As he waited for his ration, the image of the family in the hold came back to him. Something was not right about them, but he couldn't say what it was. He was still mulling it over when his turn came to enter the galley. As he stepped inside he came face-to-face with Malcolm MacLeod. MacLeod was holding his hardtack and water, struggling to keep his balance. He stopped when he saw John, staring at him with open hostility. John was irritated by his arrogance and stared back.

The galley went quiet and the seconds ticked by. MacLeod had light brown eyes, and the whites had a yellowish tinge that made his stare all the more malevolent. John knew MacLeod had friends on board, but dangerous or not he wouldn't tolerate being bullied.

Katy stepped up beside MacLeod. "Let me help you with that, Malcolm. It wouldn't do to spill any of that precious water." She laid a hand on MacLeod's arm and took the tankard in her other hand.

MacLeod glanced at her, her face tight with strain, and his lip curled in a smile. "As you ask so kindly, Katy, nothing will be spilled today."

MacLeod stared at John with sneering self-satisfaction. John started to speak, but the cook interrupted him. "Keep moving."

The cook's mate stepped between John and MacLeod. "On with you, lad. Get your food now." The mate was forty years old. His face was weather-beaten and wrinkled, but his eyes sparkled with amusement. John felt the heat go out of him and moved along.

MacLeod sat with Katy at the far end of the galley. The clanspeople made room for John at the other end of the table, and the hum of conversation started again. John ate in silence and left as soon as he was finished. MacLeod didn't look up as he replaced his tankard, but John knew it wasn't over between them.

That night, John awoke to the sound of a woman crying in anguish. It was completely dark in the hold, and he looked around, trying to understand what was happening. The woman's voice was shrill and John grasped that she was lamenting the death of her husband and child.

John pulled his boots on and rolled out of his hammock, and the hold filled with the sound of men shouting and stumbling into one another. Scuffles broke out and blows were traded. All John could see were vague shapes moving about like shadows, but he could feel the fear rising in the hold. John's face felt hot and panic started to rise in him. Then he felt a hand on his shoulder.

"Easy, lad." Old MacLeod squeezed John's shoulder. "Wait it out."

John took a breath, glad MacLeod was there.

"A man and a child are dead. What does it mean?" He heard the tension in his own voice, but speaking his fears out loud seemed to ease them.

"There is sickness onboard," MacLeod said.

John remembered the people he'd seen sitting so still the previous day. "What kind of sickness?"

"I don't know, lad, but whatever it is, on board ship there's no way to escape it." John heard the horror in MacLeod's voice, and fear began to creep into his mind.

A few minutes later the hatch was thrown open and the second officer, Kerr, descended the top steps of the ladder. He held a lantern in one hand and held fast to the ladder with his other as he looked around.

"What's happening here?" he called, and all eyes turned to him.

"A man and a child are dead," a man called out. A woman began to wail that they would all die, and an uproar broke out again.

"Quiet." Kerr's voice was shrill, but it cut through the fear. "How many are dead, and where do they lie?"

Kerr came down the ladder. John thought he looked ready to take flight at any moment.

"Here." A man called from the back of the hold. A woman broke into the circle of light around the stairs. She held a girl in her arms, the child's head rolling lifelessly against her breast.

She sank to the deck and cried out. "My child is dead and my man." She looked up at Kerr as if pleading for him to restore them to life.

John saw Kerr's eyes go wide, and he took hold of the ladder. The woman clutched the girl to her, burying her face in her hair, and a wail of such wrenching desperation came out of her that John thought his heart would stop.

"Mother of God, look at her neck," MacLeod whispered. The girl's hair was pulled back and her neck was covered with tiny red spots.

The sight sent a shiver of fear through John. "What is it?"

MacLeod put his mouth to John's ear. "Smallpox. We're all as good as dead."

CHAPTER TEN

SCOTT WAS ASSIGNED A CABIN on the port side of the ship. It was little more than a box six feet long and five feet wide. A bunk took up half the space, and Scott's chest stood against the forward bulkhead, leaving a four-foot square of deck for the door to swing open. He had to stoop under the door casing to enter and could barely stand upright inside. The walls were bare planks and a single oil lamp hung in the middle of the ceiling.

Scott sat on the bunk and stared at the wall, his mind reeling from the events of the past few days. Hot bile rose in his throat when he thought of how he'd been dragged across the country to be humiliated by Lord Sackville and then banished to the colonies like a common criminal. He cursed Sackville, and he cursed his sister for her meddling. He would rather face a firing squad than be beholden to her.

Scott's thoughts were interrupted by a knock on the cabin door.

"Come." The door opened to reveal one of the ship's boys. He was dressed in breeches and a brown shirt, shiny with dirt, a mop of dark hair hanging in his thin face.

"Begging your pardon, sir. Captain Harbin requests you attend him in his cabin."

Scott nodded and stepped into the passageway, pulling the door closed behind him. The officer and passenger cabins were in the stern of the vessel below the bridge deck. The cabins were arranged in a U-shape along the sides and stern of the vessel. The open space in the centre formed a day cabin. A dining table was fixed to the deck and benches were arranged around the table and against the walls. A skylight in the deck above allowed light to enter; the officers and passengers took their meals there and spent much of their time there when the weather was inclement.

Scott followed the boy through the day cabin. A dozen people stood around the table talking animatedly. As Scott entered, the level of sound dropped as all eyes turned to this new face. Scott took in the group at a glance. There were eight men ranging in age from thirty to sixty, three of them ship's officers. The men were well dressed. Scott guessed they were merchants of some sort. Several inclined their heads in greeting, and Scott nodded in response.

Two women sat at the far end of the table, one in her twenties, strikingly attractive. She had fair hair tied up in a scarf and wore a light brown dress that matched her hair. She seemed to mock Scott as their eyes met. The other woman was perhaps just over thirty years of age. She had a not unpleasant face, but she was plain in comparison to her companion. Her hair was pulled back from her face, and her skin was pale as if she hadn't fully recovered from an illness. Two women stood behind them, neither more than twenty years of age. From their dress Scott concluded they were serving maids.

Scott followed the boy through the day cabin and the sound picked up again. The boy knocked on a door in the centre of the aft bulkhead and put his ear against the wood. After a moment, he pushed the door open and stood to the side to let Scott enter.

The captain's cabin was twenty feet deep from the bulkhead to sternpost and ran the width of the ship. Windows were fitted across the transom flooding the cabin with light. The port side was given over to the captain's personal effects: a bunk and two sea chests were fixed to the deck. The starboard side was taken up with storage for charts and navigation instruments. A table, littered with charts and navigation instruments, was fixed to the deck beneath the stern windows.

Scott entered the cabin and the captain got to his feet and stepped around the table. He stooped to avoid touching the ceiling. He was broad shouldered and his stomach bulged under his jacket. He had blue eyes set in a weather-beaten face that was framed by greying hair hanging loose to his shoulders.

"I am Augustus Harbin, captain of the *Raven*. Welcome aboard." Harbin offered his hand. It was calloused and hard, a workman's hand. Scott took a firm grip and inclined his head in response.

"Take a seat, Captain." He gestured to a chair at the side of the table.

Scott dropped into the chair and rested his hands on the arms. He had wondered why all the chairs on the ship had arms; now he realized they were to brace against the roll of the ship.

"I will come directly to the point, Captain Scott. I was advised of your circumstances prior to your coming aboard." He made no attempt to hide the censure in his voice. Scott's temper began to stir, but he held his tongue.

After a moment Harbin went on.

"Major Anders left orders for you in my care, to be presented to you once we were underway." He opened a drawer, removed a slim package, and slid it across the table to Scott.

"You are to open the package in my presence and confirm you have read and understood the orders."

Scott scooped up the package, got to his feet, and strode towards the door.

"Captain Scott. You must open these documents in my presence." He spoke in a quarterdeck voice that filled the room. The tone of command was a challenge that Scott couldn't ignore, and he turned to face Harbin.

"The devil I will, sir."

As he pulled the door open, Harbin bellowed, "This is my ship, Captain Scott. You would do well to remember it"

Scott slammed the door behind him, and the passengers in the day cabin fell silent, staring at him in shock. He ignored them as he strode back to his cabin; then the passengers all started to speak at once.

* * *

Scott dropped the package onto the bunk and sat down seething with indignation. Harbin's arrogance was insufferable. Scott knew his claim to wield total power on board the ship was no idle jest and that made it all the more difficult to bear.

Scott snatched up the package and tore it open. The light was poor in the cabin, and he opened the door and read by the light filtering down the passageway. The orders were from Colonel James Anthony Surrey. He'd never heard of the man, but the document bore the seal of the regiment. He was ordered to proceed to the town of Boston in His Majesty's territory known as Massachusetts on the Eastern Seaboard of the Americas where he was to report to a Major Coxe. Scott's posting was permanent, and under no circumstances was he to return to Britain under pain of court-martial.

Scott clenched his hands convulsively, and a throbbing pain started behind his eyes. He lay down on the bunk and stared wide-eyed, wondering if his sanity was slipping away. He'd barely slept since the dragoons had taken him from Fort William three days ago, and despite the turmoil in his mind, the motion of the ship gradually lulled him into an exhausted sleep.

Scott awoke disorientated, staring at the ceiling. A bell rang, and he realized that was what had woken him. He swung his legs over the side of the bunk and sat up but a wave of dizziness swept over him, and he had to hold on to the bunk until it passed.

"Two bells." Two bells were rung after the first hour of a watch but he didn't know which watch it was. He got to his feet and immediately sat down again as the ship heaved to port. He stretched his back and rubbed the tension out of his neck. He brushed the wrinkles out of his jacket and retied his hair behind his head, a well-practiced routine from years of living in military camps.

As Scott stepped into the passageway his senses were struck by the sound of voices raised in conversation and the smell of meat stew. It must be two bells in the first dog watch, which meant he had slept the whole day. The smell of cooking meat reminded him that he hadn't eaten since yesterday, and he pulled the cabin door closed and hurried along the passageway.

The room fell silent when Scott entered the day cabin, and all eyes turned to him. Fifteen people sat around the table. He recognized the two women from earlier and several of the men. Harbin sat at the head of the table. His expression was blank but his eyes were hostile. Scott stared back and after a moment Harbin broke off.

"Ladies and gentlemen, this is Captain Scott, who is travelling to Massachusetts to take up a military post. Join us, Captain." Harbin gestured to a seat at the far end of the table.

Scott inclined his head and took a seat on the port bench. The benches were fixed to the floor. The only chair was reserved for Harbin at the head of the table.

The man to Scott's right introduced himself. "Henry Meriton. I am travelling to Boston to join my brother in a business venture."

Scott shook his hand. "Captain Scott. As Captain Harbin said, I will be taking up a post in Massachusetts."

Meriton nodded, humming under his breath. He took on the role of self-appointed host and introduced the other passengers and ship's officers. .

"Of course you have met Captain Harbin." He looked at Scott with an expectant expression on his face, and the level of conversation dropped. Scott felt the other passengers' eyes on him. He had no intention of providing them with amusement and was about to say so when a boy placed a pewter plate in front of him and laid a fork, knife, and spoon beside it.

"Would you like some bread, sir?" He held out a wooden bowl containing dark bread. Scott took two pieces and nodded his thanks.

Meriton carried on working his way around the table, naming the passengers and providing a biography of each. Given the time they'd been on board, Mr. Meriton had accumulated a great deal of knowledge about the lives of the other passengers.

When Meriton came to the two women, he leaned forward and gestured with his left hand. The younger woman was Miss Elizabeth Williams from Penrith. She was travelling to Boston and was to marry a military officer there. Meriton waxed lyrical with regard to the glorious estate of marriage and the virtues of seeding the new world with the qualities of the old. His enthusiasm for her anticipated nuptials was met with a blank stare from Miss Williams, but he was in his element and oblivious to everything except the sound of his own voice.

Mr. Meriton turned his attention to the other woman opposite Scott. "Let me introduce Mrs. Lockhart of Boston."

Meriton made a small bow and glanced sideways at Scott. Scott nodded and she inclined her head in reply. Meriton moved on to describe the commercial adventures of the middle-aged man with the heavy jowls sitting to the captain's left. While Meriton provided tidbits of information to illustrate each diner's place in society, Scott noted that he'd made an exception in Mrs. Lockhart's case. He glanced at her curiously but his attention was drawn away by the beef stew.

Meriton's narrative finally ended and the passengers peppered the captain with questions about the voyage. Harbin responded to each in turn. They would be at sea for approximately eight weeks. The weather in the Atlantic Ocean was difficult to predict, and they should be prepared for changes as winter came on. The questions gradually decreased, and the hum of conversation continued as normal.

Scott noticed that Mr. Meriton had fallen silent. He glanced at him out of the corner of his eye, not wishing to encourage further conversation. He sat very still, his gaze fixed on the other side of the table. His face was ashen and every few seconds he swallowed convulsively. Without warning he leapt to his feet and staggered along the passage, crashing against the bulkhead as the ship rolled, and disappeared through the door to the main deck.

Scott saw worried looks around the table. The ship's officers continued as if nothing unusual had happened, but the passengers seemed to have lost their appetites.

"I believe Mr. Meriton is taken ill—" Harbin was interrupted when Miss Williams rushed to her cabin and slammed the door behind her. Her maid followed and slipped quietly inside.

Scott took the opportunity to help himself to more beef stew. He noticed that Mrs. Lockhart was also unaffected by either the motion of the ship or the sudden departure of their two companions. She glanced at Scott, but the man beside her drew her into conversation.

When Scott had finished, he nodded to Harbin and rose from the table. Harbin nodded in return, but his jaw was set. Scott cared little for what Harbin thought of him, but good manners overcame his disdain for the man.

"Excuse me, ladies and gentlemen."

As he moved towards his cabin, the ship's bell sounded, and Scott glanced at the skylight. It would be dark in less than an hour, and he decided to go on deck while it was still light.

Scott's cabin was in darkness, and he felt his way to his chest. His belongings had been stuffed into the chest randomly, and he had to remove half of the contents before he found his greatcoat. He put everything back into the chest and shrugged on the greatcoat. He would organize his belongings in the morning.

Scott made his way along the passage to the main deck. He waited till the ship was level then stepped through the door and pushed it closed before the wind could take it. The bridge deck was ten feet above the main deck and jutted out six feet, forming a sheltered space beneath. Scott stood under the overhang and looked at the sea, astonished at the change that had taken place. The ship was riding waves forty feet in height. The wind was driving hard, blowing the tops off the waves and filling the air with foam.

Seamen were working to secure the ship's boats and other equipment, and men were crawling along the yards seventy feet above his head. They looked like insects clinging to the spars, pulling the sails in hand over hand. He could see their lips move as they called out to each other, but the wind carried the words away. Scott climbed the stairs to the bridge. The French called it the poop deck, and the British had adopted the custom.

The poop deck covered the stern of the ship forming the roof of the cabins beneath. The deck planks were polished white and shone in the darkening sky. Ten feet from the stern bulwark stood an apparatus that looked like two wagon wheels mounted upside down on a central base. This was the wheel steering mechanism that was revolutionizing shipping. A dome of leaded glass was mounted in the centre to house the ship's compass. A seaman stood at the wheel, his eyes moving between the sails, the ocean, and the compass. The skylight that let light into the day cabin was forward of the steering wheel. The helmsman and two officers were on deck: Willis, the first officer, and a junior Scott didn't know.

Scott went to the starboard side and wedged himself against the stern bulwarks. From here he could see the whole ship. She was two hundred feet long and fifty feet wide. He knew little of ships, but the hull looked solid and the sails, ropes and tackle were well maintained. In spite of his attitude it seemed that Harbin kept the ship in good working condition.

Scott was glad of the chance to be alone, and as he ran over the previous few days in his mind, his hands clenched in frustration. He wanted to lash out at something, but there was nothing he could do. He stayed on deck as the night came in from the east, and the wind and the motion of the ship finally bled the tension out of him. He went below and undressed quickly. His cabin was cold and damp, and he wrapped himself in his blankets and tried to stay warm. The last thing he remembered before sleep took him was the ship's bell ringing the change of the watch.

* * *

The weather was bad for the first week of the voyage, and most of the passengers kept to their cabins. The exception was Mrs. Lockhart. She walked on the main deck for an hour every day, unconcerned by the motion of the ship. She nodded to Scott but didn't seek to engage him in conversation.

By the end of the first week, Scott had fallen into the ship's routine, which revolved around the changes of the watch and mealtimes. Harbin ignored him, and most of the passengers kept their distance. The *Raven* plowed her way westward, and as the weeks passed, relations between Scott and Harbin settled into an uneasy truce. The captain avoided speaking with Scott. The ship's officers followed his lead. The passengers for the most part remained polite but distant.

Mr. Meriton continued to engage Scott in conversation, seeking to pry details from him about his posting to Boston. Scott found him irritating, but Mr. Meriton was not discouraged by his reticence and persisted regardless of Scott's rebuffs. Mr. Meriton's passion for gossip was matched only by his need to share his wisdom, and he offered up nuggets of information on the passengers and crew in the hope of drawing Scott into conversation.

Annoying as Meriton was, Scott learned a good deal from his ramblings. He intimated to Scott that this was Captain Harbin's last voyage as captain, and he would be taking a position on the company executive when they arrived in Boston. The next captain of the *Raven* would be one of the senior officers, and Harbin would have a say in the decision. Willis and Reeve were competitors for the position and both sought Harbin's support.

Meriton also confessed that he had made even less progress with Mrs. Lockhart than with Scott. She responded to Mr. Meriton's advances civilly, leaving him feeling charmed though none the wiser, but what he did know he shared freely. Mrs. Lockhart had been widowed a year earlier. Her husband had died while on business in Jamaica the year before, taken by one of the fevers that plagued the Caribbean. Her husband had extensive business interests in Boston and throughout New England. He also had property in London and the north of England. The purpose of Mrs. Lockhart's trip to Britain had been to dispose of these assets.

* * *

One morning in the fourth week of the voyage, Scott was awakened by banging on his cabin door, and he threw off his blanket and rolled to his feet. The banging came again and someone called his name.

"Hold hard." Scott wrapped the blanket around his shoulders and opened the door.

Reeve, the third officer, stood in the passageway. Scott guessed he was in his late twenties, but his weather-beaten face made him look ten years older.

"Captain Harbin requires your presence on the main deck immediately." Scott bristled at his tone.

"What's to do, man, that you must wake me from my sleep?"

"There's an issue with some of your men."

Scott frowned. "I'll come presently."

Scott dressed quickly. He slipped on his only clean shirt and his captain's tunic and pulled his greatcoat on. It was still dim in the day cabin, and he guessed that it was less than an hour past first light. He could hear raised voices from the main deck as he made his way down the passage, and he was astonished at what he saw when he stepped through the door. Ten seamen were holding Sergeant Crammer and two other troopers against the starboard rail. Crammer was struggling and shouting abuse, but the seamen held him fast.

Scott stood to one side of the bridge stairway, Harbin and Willis stood on the other side, and Reeve was close behind. Crammer spotted Scott and called out to him.

"Captain Scott, sir, tell these weevil eaters to take their hands off me." All eyes turned to Scott, and he looked at Harbin.

"Captain, what's going on? Why are they holding my men?" Harbin pitched his voice to carry across the deck.

"Your men instigated a fight in the seamen's quarters, Captain Scott. He pointed at Crammer. That man beat one of my seamen half to death. The cook is tending to him now. He may be crippled."

Crammer called out again,

"It's a lie, Captain Scott. I was set upon by the crew and only defended—"

"Shut your mouth, Crammer," Scott barked. He made a cutting motion with his hand. "You will speak when I tell you to speak."

Scott motioned to one of the troopers close to him and pitched his voice so only he could hear him.

"Get the rest of the men on deck and tell them to wait for my order."

"Yes, Captain." The trooper hurried away and disappeared into the fo'c'sle.

Scott knew Crammer's nature and doubted he was as innocent as he claimed, but he wouldn't let Harbin have the upper hand. He faced Harbin and kept his voice calm.

"These men are under my command. If necessary, I will see to it that they are punished."

"This man almost killed one of my sailors, and he will face punishment immediately." He pointed to where two seamen were lashing a grating to the mainmast shrouds.

Scott stepped around the stairs directly in front of Harbin.

"You will not flog my men, Captain, not without my permission." The colour rose in Harbin's neck.

"I command this ship, and I shall dispense justice as I see fit. You will step back, sir, or I will have you removed from this deck." Harbin's clenched fists looked more like knots on an oak tree than hands.

Scott glanced over his shoulder; the other troopers were coming on deck and lining up along the port rail. Scott counted eleven; each was armed with a belaying pin or club.

Harbin burst out, his voice brittle with anger.

"Captain Scott, what's this? Do you mean to challenge my authority on my ship? That is mutiny, sir. That is a capital offense."

Harbin's arrogance galled Scott, and his temper slipped. "Mutiny be damned. Only men under your command can mutiny and you do not command me, Captain Harbin."

Harbin took a step towards Scott. "I command this ship and any challenge to my authority is mutiny."

"I am not subject to your authority, Captain, nor will you flog my men." Scott raised his arm and the troopers stepped forward and formed a line from the bridge deck stairs to the mainmast.

Scott looked around the deck. The sailors outnumbered them, but his troopers were veteran fighters, bored from weeks of idleness and spoiling for a fight. Scott called his men.

"Four of you relieve the seamen of Sergeant Crammer and confine him below decks until I decide what to do with him." Scott's men stepped up to the seamen and waited. Harbin's face was a mask of fury, but there was doubt in his eyes, and the two other officers looked around them uneasily.

Scott inclined his head to Harbin. "Captain?" he said.

Harbin glared at him in silent fury, but Scott didn't blink. Finally Harbin signalled to his men. They released Crammer and the troopers led him away.

"Report to me in my cabin when Crammer is secure," Scott called out.

He turned back to Harbin. "Captain, if you will excuse me."

He nodded to Willis and Reeve, and turned on his heel. As he crossed the deck he saw some of the passengers watching from the bridge deck, Mrs. Lockhart amongst them. He nodded politely to her and stepped into the companionway.

Scott sat on his bunk, jaw set in anger; Harbin knew his background and would not fail to condemn him to his commanding officer in Boston. He was furious with Crammer and would make him rue the day he was born, but that didn't change the fact that he would be on this ship for another two months. His thoughts were interrupted by a knock on the door, and he sat up. "Come." The door opened to reveal Reeve standing in the passage.

"Captain Scott"—Reeve's voice was cold and formal—"Captain Harbin requests you attend him in his cabin."

"What does he want?"

"The captain did not inform me of that, Captain Scott."

"I'll be there shortly."

"I am instructed to wait for you, Captain."

"Get out." Scott kicked the door and Reeve had to step back smartly to avoid being hit. Scott ground his fist into his palm, speechless with anger for a moment, then threw the door open.

"Lead on."

Harbin was sitting at the table beneath the stern window, Willis stood on the right and Reeve took up a position beside him. Harbin stared at Scott but didn't speak, and Scott came forward and took the chair opposite him. Harbin seemed nonplussed by this, and his jaw tightened, but Scott had no intention of standing to be dressed down like a subordinate.

"Captain Scott, I must advise you that I take the confrontation you precipitated today very seriously. Not only did you defy my authority as captain, you threatened to use violence against my officers and crew. That, sir, is mutiny, and I assure you I will be making a full report to the authorities in Boston."

Scott glanced at Willis and Reeve.

"Is that all you have to say, Captain, or do you have further actions you wish to threaten me with?" Scott knew this incident wouldn't sit well with his superiors, but he wouldn't tolerate being threatened.

Harbin's face flushed, and he made a gurgling sound in his throat.

"These are not idle threats, Captain. Mutiny is a capital offense, and you will face the consequences of your actions when we arrive in Boston," Scott spat back at him.

"You're exaggerating, Captain. There was no conflict, and no one was injured. It's unfortunate if your pride has been wounded, but I will not allow you to abuse the men under my command."

Harbin gripped the table and thrust his face at Scott.

"You will give me your undertaking that there will be no more such incidents." Harbin's eyes bulged from his head as he glared at Scott.

"I don't take orders from you, Captain—"

Harbin lumbered to his feet and leaned across the table, his right hand clenched into a fist. "You will comply with my wishes, or I will have you confined to your cabin for the remainder of the voyage."

Scott came out of his chair and leaned over the table.

"Attempt that, sir, and you shall have your mutiny." Harbin's face was red. The veins in his neck stood out like purple snakes swelling under his collar. Willis stepped around the table and Scott stood and faced him, cold challenge in his eyes, and after a moment Willis stepped back. Reeve's eyes followed Scott with silent fury, and Scott marked him as the more dangerous of the two.

Scott took a step back.

"I have no patience for your threats. Have done now." As Scott reached the door Harbin found his voice.

"I warn you, Captain Scott—" Scott pulled the door shut cutting him off in mid-sentence.

Several passengers in the day cabin stood looking at Scott with astonishment on their faces. Then they all found reason to examine the deck planks or to scrutinize the condition of their fingernails. The exception was Mrs. Lockhart. She inclined her head politely, and Scott nodded in return and passed on to his cabin.

Trooper Busk was waiting outside Scott's cabin. He drew himself up to his full height and saluted.

"Reporting as ordered, sir." Scott threw the door open.

"You have Crammer confined?"

"Aye, sir. He's in the lower hold."

"Keep him confined until eight bells in the morning watch tomorrow then let him out. Tell Sergeant Crammer I do not wish to see his face on deck for the remainder of the voyage, and if he causes me any further embarrassment, I will have him flogged myself. Now get out."

Scott wondered what the consequences of this day would be when he reached Boston. He had no knowledge of the Americas, but the army wouldn't be much different. It might have been better to let Harbin flog Crammer, but there was nothing to be done about it now.

At two bells Scott made his way to the day cabin. Harbin and most of the passengers were already seated. Conversation stopped as he took his place at the table, and the passengers glanced at him nervously. Mr. Meriton was to Scott's right.

"Captain Scott, how are you enjoying the voyage so far?" he said. Scott wouldn't take the bait.

"Mr. Meriton. From my perspective the voyage is progressing satisfactorily."

"Delighted to hear it, Captain Scott." He turned his attention to the beef platter and the hum of conversation picked up again.

After dinner Scott went out on deck and stood under the bridge deck overhang. He watched the sea run past and went over the events of the day in his mind. His thoughts were interrupted when the main deck door opened, and Mrs. Lockhart stepped on deck. She walked to the port side and followed the rail forward. The deck canted ten degrees and rose and fell as the bow plowed into each wave, but she seemed unconcerned by the motion.

At the fo'c'sle hatch Mrs. Lockhart crossed the deck to the starboard side. As she turned along the starboard side, she caught sight of Scott. She made her way aft and stepped beneath the bridge deck beside Scott.

"We are the only two who dare the weather, Captain Scott. I believe our fellow passengers do themselves a disservice. I find the ocean compelling when it is so animated, would you not agree?"

"I, too, find the sea invigorating, Mrs. Lockhart, but I fear our fellow passengers are not blessed with the robustness of constitution necessary to appreciate its splendour"

"I believe you have the right of it, Captain Scott."

Mrs. Lockhart leaned against the bulkhead. She was younger than he had originally thought, no more than thirty years of age, he guessed. She was slender, and she moved with an easy grace on the rolling deck. She looked away to the horizon and pulled her coat around her shoulders.

After a moment she looked at Scott.

"You are to take up a post in Boston, Captain Scott?" Her voice was low and melodic and had a hint of an accent that Scott couldn't identify.

"I am posted to the Americas, Mrs. Lockhart, but I have not yet been advised of the precise location. I'm not familiar with the American Colonies. I am told the territories are extensive, and I imagine there are a number of possibilities."

Mrs. Lockhart smiled.

"Extensive is something of an understatement, Captain Scott. The Americas are larger and more diverse than you can imagine. I don't know your reason for choosing a posting to Massachusetts, but I do not believe you will be disappointed, both in the splendour of the country and in the opportunities it presents."

Scott felt a spark of irritation at the reference to his seeking an assignment to the Americas. He didn't know what Harbin had told the officers or the passengers, but he was sure they knew his posting wasn't voluntary. A stinging reply rose to his lips, but he looked away at the horizon and took a breath.

"Mrs. Lockhart, I'm sure it's common knowledge on board that my posting to the Americas was not of my choosing, so it's hardly likely that I see it as an opportunity."

"Indeed, Captain Scott, it's understood amongst the passengers that an assignment to Boston was not your personal choice. However, I maintain that you will not be disappointed in what you find there."

Scott was still smarting, and his response was pricklier than he intended. "What other details of my personal life has Captain Harbin chosen to share with our fellow passengers?"

Mrs. Lockhart seemed unaffected by the edge in his voice, and she took a step closer as if to speak more intimately.

"With regard to your background, Captain Harbin has been tight-lipped. The passengers know only that your posting to Boston is a mystery." Her mouth turned up in a smile revealing even white teeth. "This has become a source of profound frustration for Mr. Meriton."

Mrs. Lockhart looked at Scott and under her cool unwavering gaze he found that he couldn't maintain his irritation. The temperature was dropping, and he thrust his hands into the pockets of his greatcoat.

"I care little for Mr. Meriton's frustrations, but it seems I am indebted to Captain Harbin for his discretion."

Mrs. Lockhart lifted her chin.

"Clearly you and Captain Harbin are not in accord, given the drama earlier today, but with regard to your personal situation he has remained discreet." The smile creased her lips again, and Scott felt a surge of irritation.

"The situation was unnecessary. Harbin should have spoken to me before he acted. He placed me in an untenable situation."

"I think you acted admirably, Captain Scott, in standing up for one of your men, and Captain Harbin plays the bully too easily for my taste."

"Don't mistake me, Mrs. Lockhart. Under different circumstances I would have ordered the sergeant flogged myself."

"I understand that the seaman is badly injured, but I don't believe that two wrongs make a right, Captain."

Mrs. Lockhart turned up the collar of her coat. "The wind grows cold, Captain, and I must wish you a good night." She looked at him directly as seemed to be her fashion.

"Good night, Mrs. Lockhart."

CHAPTER ELEVEN

THE LANTERN CREATED A POOL of light around the bottom of the hold ladder, and the clanspeople stood in a circle around it, grim-faced and fearful. Kerr, the second mate, looked at the men and women standing around him for a long moment; then he let out an incoherent cry and started up the ladder. In his haste he missed a rung and almost dropped the lantern, but he recovered quickly, scrambled up to the deck, and slammed the hatch shut, leaving the hold in darkness.

There was silence for a moment; then a man's voice wailed, "Plague, there's plague on this ship."

Pandemonium broke out in the hold and MacLeod pulled John back against the bulkhead. "Stay back. They'll kill in their madness."

John stood with his fists clenched. Men were pounding on the hatch with their bare hands, and John heard the crunch of bone breaking as a body crashed to the deck. People were tearing at each other to get to the ladder, and he lashed out twice as men crashed into him, sending them reeling back.

John heard the sound of feet on deck above; then the hatch was thrown back and light flooded the hold. The clanspeople froze, blinking in the light, and John was shocked at the carnage around him. Men and women lay strewn across the hold in bloody disarray. One man sat against the bulkhead, blood flowing from his mouth, and the woman whose child had died knelt beside him, clutching the girl to her breast.

A woman rushed the ladder pushing her daughter ahead of her. The girl had only climbed four rungs when she was dragged from the ladder and fell to the deck. She rolled herself into a ball, blood pouring from her mouth and nose, and her mother screamed and gathered her in her arms. John gritted his teeth in anger. It was Malcolm MacLeod who had pulled the girl from the ladder. He swarmed up the ladder with surprising agility for his size, but a boat hook thrust down from the deck above, struck him in the chest and he crashed to the deck, shouting in anger and pain.

Lockman, the first mate, climbed down the top four rungs of the ladder.

"Back, back." His voice cut through the chaos, and he waved a belaying pin menacingly. "How many dead?"

The clanspeople looked around in confusion.

"How many are sick?"

No one answered.

"Bring the dead on deck." Lockman pointed to two men at the bottom of the ladder. "You two, start with the girl. Hand her up." He pointed the belaying pin at the dead girl clutched in her mother's arms.

One of the men took the girl from her mother and started up the ladder, and Lockman backed up ahead of him. A moment later he came back down.

"Get moving, all of you."

The clanspeople began to examine the bodies scattered around the hold. It was a grizzly task but John thought they were relieved someone had taken charge.

Lockman pounded the belaying pin against the ladder. "Jump to it."

Men brought the bodies to the ladder; John counted eight dead, but he couldn't say which had died from disease or which had died in the panic. He saw a clansman struggling to drag a body across the deck.

"Help me here."

John took a step towards him, but MacLeod pulled him back. "Don't touch the dead, and don't go near those who are sick."

"Give a hand here, boy." The man called again but John ignored him.

John turned to MacLeod. "What must we do?"

"Don't touch the dead or the things they own and pray you don't get the fever. On a ship there is no escape, and many will die."

John felt a tremendous need to get out of the hold, but he heeded MacLeod's words and held back until the crowd came down before he climbed to the main deck. Many stayed in the hold, fearful of going on deck, and others were too exhausted to leave their bunks.

The passengers gathered beneath the bridge as the first hint of dawn lit the sky, and John and MacLeod stood against the port rail. The dead were laid out on the deck by the mainmast. The ship's officers gathered on the bridge and presently Captain Abercrombie came on deck.

"We must take precautions to ensure that the sickness does not spread. The dead will be buried immediately; their blankets, hammocks, and personal effects will be thrown overboard. The bunks must be washed down with sea water." He nodded to Lockman then opened the Bible and started to read the prayer for the dead.

Lockman came down to the main deck. Four sailors stood ready with sheets and rope. "Get on with it."

The sailors were reluctant to touch the bodies but Lockman hefted the belaying pin, and they went to work. They wound each body in a cotton sheet with a ballast stone at the feet. As soon as the captain finished the service the seamen dropped the bodies over the side and Abercrombie slammed the book shut.

"Be about your business now. Bring the clothes and bedding on deck."

The clanspeople went below decks, and MacLeod went with them, complaining that his bones couldn't stand the cold. John sat beneath the bridge deck stairs out of the wind and tried to make sense of what was happening.

Later, when the daily rations were distributed, the clanspeople were subdued. The sailors kept apart from them, and talked in hushed voices. The tension in the galley was palpable, and John felt a slow tightening in his guts that made him want to run far away.

Then a woman at the end of the table burst out, "The dead are buried. There's no danger now." She looked around at blank stares. "One of the crew told me we'll be in port soon. The danger's past." There were murmurs of agreement, and later John would remember how the people had grasped at that hope.

John stayed on deck through the afternoon, watching the ocean. He had come to love the sea in all its moods and colours. It soothed his mind and eased the ache in his gut. As it began to get dark he resolved to sleep on deck. He settled in the corner of the deck and wrapped his plaid around his shoulders. A few minutes later a seaman came hurrying around the deckhouse. Something about his manner drew John's attention. He stopped by the bridge deck stairs, but he was looking up, and he didn't see John.

"Bridge," he called. His voice was strained with fear.

A moment later Kerr responded. "What is it?"

"Twelve more sick in the forward hold, and two in the fo'c'sle have the fever."

"Confine the Scots below. God damn them for their filth. No one gets out unless I give the order."

"Aye, Mr. Kerr." The sailor hurried forward into the growing dark, and a moment later Kerr came down the stairs and went below.

If MacLeod was right and touching the sick was dangerous, then he was safer on deck. John moved into the shadows against the port rail and pulled his plaid over his head, trying to stay out of sight. The ship was quiet. The only sounds were the creaking of the rigging and the pounding of the bow into the waves. Images of the carnage in the hold intruded on John's thoughts, but he was drained physically and emotionally, and even the hard deck planks couldn't keep him from a dreamless sleep.

* * *

John was awakened by the sound of voices close by. He was sore from lying on the deck but felt refreshed. The sun was well up, and he sat up and stretched the aches out of his body. The ship had changed course in the night and was on the starboard tack. The port rail was close to the water, and he could see the ocean surging past below him.

Two bodies lay on the deck by the mainmast, and four sailors were binding them in white sheets. Lockman was reading from a Bible, and John didn't have to hear the words to understand what was happening. When Lockman finished, the sailors carried the bodies to the lee rail, and heaved them over the side.

John stayed on deck all morning, keeping out of the wind and trying to stay dry. He dreaded the thought of going below; the deck was uncomfortable but the air was clean, and he was as far from the sick as he could get. Later, when he lined up for his ration, the cook's mate dished out the hardtack and water.

"Where's the cook?" he said. The mate sneered at him.

"He's sick with the fever you filthy Scots brought on board." John was stung by his reply, but he kept his mouth shut and went to a table to eat.

John had seen MacLeod behind him in the line and a few minutes later he came and sat by him.

"You didn't come back to your hammock last night."

"I slept on deck."

"You may have the right of it, lad. There are twenty sick now; half of them won't live out the day."

"How does it spread? How can people become sick so quickly?"

"No one knows, lad. It kills the strong along with the weak, and they all die as quickly."

MacLeod bit into his hardtack and talked as he chewed. "Stay away from the hold if you can, and maybe you'll live."

MacLeod got up and left. John had the sense he had resigned himself to death. He determined that he wouldn't give in so easily.

John spent the day under the bridge deck stairs. The clanspeople stayed below, except for two men who came up to empty the slop buckets, and at dusk they brought up seven more dead. They laid the bodies on the deck, and a few minutes later Kerr appeared and ordered the seamen to wrap them. John wondered why Kerr hadn't started the prayer for the dead, when a party of sailors came around the deckhouse carrying four bodies already wrapped in sheets. He was shocked. Death amongst the crew made things worse. Kerr hurried through the service and the bodies were dropped unceremoniously over the side.

John passed a second night on deck. The weather was rough, and when the ship changed tack, he moved to the starboard side to stay out of the wind. He slept for a few hours, but by morning he was cold and miserable. There was no movement on deck and a sense of melancholy hung over the ship.

John was first in line for his food ration. The mate glared at him, but John ignored him and took his food to the far end of the galley. He'd become accustomed to the hardtack, but the water was foul, and it was all he could do to force it down. There were no more than twenty-five clanspeople in the galley. He started to ask the man at the next table what had happened to the others but thought better of it.

John was preparing to leave when Katy MacLeod entered the galley. He was shocked at her appearance. Her face was drawn, and she looked as if she hadn't slept for days. When she saw him, she brought her food and sat across from him. She ate hungrily, swallowing the hardtack convulsively.

"Katy . . ."

"My mother's dead." She spoke in a monotone voice, as if the words had no meaning for her. "My little brother's gone, too."

"I'm sorry for your loss, Katy."

She carried on as if she hadn't heard him. "I had the fever, but I'm still alive. One in a hundred lives, they say, so I'm to be considered fortunate."

Katy looked at him with empty eyes.

"What's it like?" John said.

"First there's the headache then cramps in my bowels that made me cry out for God to take my life." She ate her last piece of hardtack and gulped her water. "My little brother was the same. On the third day the cramps passed, and he was fine." She looked at John as if trying to remember who he was. "But it wasn't true. The next day the fever came and the rosy blush, and he was dead by nightfall."

Katy drank the last of her water and placed the tankard on the table.

"What of your father?"

"He has the fever. I think he'll die." As she rose from the table John saw the spots on her neck. They were the same as the girl in the hold but faded to pink. He found himself shifting uncomfortably, and he got up and left the galley.

* * *

John slept on deck for four days. He was cold, but couldn't face going below. He lost count of how many died, but each day the service for the dead became shorter. By the fourth day the sailors didn't bother wrapping the dead. They waited until the prayer was said and dropped the bodies over the side.

A week after the first deaths, the weather moderated enough for the cook to light the stove, and John eagerly anticipated hot stew. The galley was half-full when he entered; the people looked pale and afraid, and to his surprise he saw MacLeod sitting at the one of the tables. Katy MacLeod was next to him. MacLeod motioned for him to join them; Katy looked pale and sickly, but she smiled and waved him over.

The mate doled out the food. The stew smelt wonderful. John put the hardtack in the stew, took his tankard of water and sat opposite Katy.

"How are you, lad?" MacLeod said.

"I'm well enough."

"You don't come below decks. Is it that we smell too bad for you?" Katy said and smiled weakly. "You're well enough where you are. Every day more sicken below decks."

John concentrated on eating his stew, savouring the heat as it burned its way down to his stomach. A few minutes later Malcolm MacLeod entered the galley. He sat at the end of the table to John's right across from Katy. He'd lost weight, and his skin was oily and hung loosely from his jowls. His face was dark with anger.

"You've been told to keep away from Katy." MacLeod's eyes bored into John, and his temper flared.

"Who I speak to is none of your business."

"Malcolm, let him be," Katy said.

Malcolm glared at her and sneered at John. "I thought the fever had killed you, but I hear you were hiding on deck, licking the arses of your English friends."

"You have a foul mouth, MacLeod, but I would expect no less from a craven coward." Malcolm stiffened, but John went on. "We all saw you tear the girl from the ladder in the hold, shaming yourself in front of your clan."

Malcolm leaned over, hawked and spat into John's stew, his eyes shining with malicious glee. John threw the stew in Malcolm's face. It was hot enough to burn, and he staggered to his feet, crying out in alarm. John was on his feet in a second, he slammed his right fist into Malcolm's face, and he fell back, clutching at the table. John's arm was jarred to the shoulder, and he thought his hand was broken.

Malcolm spat out a mouthful of blood and charged at John roaring with rage. He swung right-handed, but John stepped inside his guard and grasped his arm throwing his weight backwards and sent Malcolm reeling across the galley. He slammed into the bulkhead and crashed to the deck.

Someone grabbed John from behind, pinning his arms at his sides, and Malcolm called out, "Hold him for me."

John pushed backwards until they crashed against the galley table; then he kicked the clansman's shin with the heel of his boot. The man howled in pain but held him fast. John twisted to one side, kicking at him again, but another man punched him behind the ear and his head spun.

Malcolm called out again. "Back, back, let me at him."

Two clansmen held John's arms and Malcolm hit him in the face with his right hand. Blood spurted into John's mouth, and it felt as if his jaw was broken; he tried to roll his head but another blow struck him on the temple, and he felt his grip on consciousness begin to slip.

Malcolm grabbed John's hair with his left hand and threw his right fist back. John spat a mouthful of blood in his face, and he reeled back, crying out in disgust. John lunged forward, dragging the two men with him, and kicked Malcolm in the groin. His foot connected with satisfying force and Malcolm collapsed to the deck howling.

John threw his weight against the man on his left, driving him back until his knees caught on one of the benches, and he went over, sending the three of them crashing to the deck. John twisted hard, landing on the man's chest. The impact knocked the wind out of him, and he let go of his arm. The second man went reeling across the deck.

John heard shouts from the doorway and four seamen burst into the galley. The bosun, Ellis, was in front. As Malcolm started to rise Ellis slammed a belaying pin into his ribs. He doubled over, grunting in pain, and Ellis kicked his feet from under him. He tapped Malcolm behind the ear with the belaying pin, and he dropped to the deck.

John held up his hands. "Don't hit me, Mr. Ellis."

Ellis nodded and stepped back. "Pick them up."

The seamen lifted John to his feet and dragged him to the far end of the galley. John sat on one of the benches and held his jaw, trying to tell if it was broken. When he moved it, it made a clicking sound and pain shot through his face.

A moment later Lockman stepped into the galley. "Who started this?" he barked, and glared at the men in the galley.

Malcolm was sitting against the wall, holding his head in his hands. He lifted his head and pointed at John.

"The boy attacked me. The girl and I are to be married, and he won't stay away from her."

"That's not true," Katy called out in frustration. "I won't marry this man."

"Quiet, girl," Malcolm shouted. He started to get to his feet, but Ellis pushed him down.

John looked up at Lockman. "He's lying. He spat in my food. That started the fight, and his clansmen joined in."

Malcolm started to swear at John and pandemonium broke out as everyone shouted at once.

The bosun banged his belaying pin on a galley table. "Quiet, quiet, I say." He glared at the MacLeods.

Lockman looked at John. "You're not one of them?"

"No, I am John Wallace, these"—he motioned around the galley —"are all MacLeods."

"He has done—" Katy started to speak, but Lockman barked at her.

"Quiet." Lockman looked at Malcolm nursing his face then back at John. "There will be no fighting on this ship. I don't care who the girl belongs to or how it started. I will flog the flesh off the back of the next man who causes trouble."

He looked at John. "I knew you were trouble from the start, boy."

He motioned to the bosun. "Put him in the fo'c'sle hold. That'll take the fight out of him." Ellis nodded and two seamen pulled John to his feet.

John pulled back and called out to Lockman. "Mr. Mate, four of them set on me. It's not right."

"I don't give a damn if it's right or not." Lockman nodded to the seamen.

They started to pull John away, but he tensed his shoulders and pushed back. Ellis tapped him on the side of the head with the belaying pin.

"No more nonsense now, or I'll crack your skull."

John saw that Ellis was serious and stopped struggling. As the seamen pulled him to the door Malcolm hawked and spat, John pulled back, and the gob of bloody phlegm landed on a seaman's arm. The bosun stepped close and brought the belaying pin down on Malcolm's shoulder and John heard a bone crack as Malcolm fell to the deck, screaming in pain.

"Get him out of here." Ellis pointed the belaying pin at John.

The seamen dragged John out of the galley.

"Come along easy now, boy, or you'll get the same." They led him to the fo'c'sle hatch and pushed him onto the ladder.

"Stand to below," one of them called. "Hold the boy fast." The fo'c'sle was a triangular space formed by the forward bulkhead, and the sides of the ship as they curved towards the bow. A forward bulkhead separated the fo'c'sle from the chain locker, and the seamen's hammocks were slung against the hull on both sides.

The seamen dropped into the fo'c'sle and one man lifted a hatch cover in the deck.

"Bring him." They pushed John onto a ladder that led down into darkness. He could hear water sloshing below, and the smell made his stomach churn.

One of the seamen prodded him. "Down you go."

John tried to step back, but they held him fast. One man grabbed his hair and pulled his head back. "You can climb down, or we can drop you through the hatch."

John knew the seamen would beat him senseless if he resisted. He stepped onto the ladder and climbed down until only his head was above the deck.

"How long will you keep me here?"

"Till you rot, for all we know." The seaman slammed the hatch cover down, and John had to duck as it crashed into place. The bolt slid home, leaving him in darkness.

CHAPTER TWELVE

BY THE MIDDLE OF THE second month the *Raven* was deep into the Atlantic Ocean. It was Captain Harbin's habit to advise the passengers of the ship's position and progress each day before dinner. On the Monday, he was finishing his report on the ship's position, when Scott entered the day cabin. He waited until Scott was seated and then went on.

"Ladies and gentlemen, as you may have noted, the weather has been worsening over the last few days. It's normal to expect storms at this time of year; however, if the weather doesn't ease in the next twenty-four hours, we will be compelled to turn south."

There was silence around the table, and then several people spoke at once.

Mr. Meriton raised his hand. "Captain Harbin, does this mean our arrival in Boston will be delayed?"

"That is possible, Mr. Meriton."

"Captain Harbin, this is distressing news. I have urgent business that I must attend to in Boston, and a delay will be to my serious disadvantage."

Harbin raised his hand for silence. "We will make every effort to ensure you reach your destination on schedule. However, it's late in the season for an Atlantic crossing, and the safety of the ship, its passengers, and crew is my first priority."

"Are we in some danger, Captain Harbin?" Meriton's voice took on a shrill tone.

"Our arrival may be delayed, but I assure you we will reach Boston safely."

Discussion was interrupted by the arrival of dinner. The smell of hot food seemed to allay the passenger's fears. Even Mr. Meriton held his peace while he concentrated on his salted fish and bread.

After dinner Scott went on deck as was his habit. He was fascinated by the changing colours of the sea and sky, and he found the sea invigorating. The weather was worsening, but they held their course to the northwest for the rest of the day and were still on the same heading when he retired for the night.

The following morning after breakfast Scott went up to the bridge. The wind had strengthened, and the ship's motion was more pronounced. He nodded to Reeve who was the officer of the watch. The wind started to gust, but the rain held off, and he settled himself in the starboard corner of the bridge.

By now Scott was familiar with the workings of the ship. He noted that the crew had put two reefs in the mainsails and taken down the main- and fore-topsails. Even on reduced sail the rigging was creaking with tension, and the *Raven* was surging along. A gust struck her, heeling her to port, and Scott grasped the rail as the deck canted under his feet.

Reeve bellowed at the helmsman, "Ease her off, you fool, or you'll have the spars off her."

Reeve heaved on the wheel and the bow came around to port and the ship righted herself.

"Let her come up like that again and I'll have the flesh off your back."

"Aye, Mr. Reeve. Sorry, sir."

Scott turned his attention to the ocean. To the north the sky was almost black. He wondered if they would be forced to turn south, but his thoughts were interrupted by Captain Harbin's arrival on the bridge.

"What happened?" Harbin barked.

"Heavy gust, Captain, and she rounded up."

"You're officer of the watch, Mr. Reeve. It's your duty to ensure that does not happen. I don't have to tell you the consequences of losing a spar in this weather." Reeve nodded but didn't reply. Harbin looked up at the rigging for a few minutes. Then, satisfied no damage had been done, he nodded to Reeve.

"Carry on, Mr. Reeve."

Harbin stood against the stern rail, legs spread, hands clasped behind his back, his eyes roaming from the sea to the sails and back to the deck. He couldn't have missed Scott standing at the starboard rail, but he didn't acknowledge him. The wind increased to the where Scott was forced to retreat beneath the bridge deck overhang. The swells were twenty feet from peak to trough now, and the *Raven* shuddered as she plowed into each wave. Scott was sure Harbin would alter course before nightfall.

The other passengers stayed below in this type of weather, and Scott was surprised when the bulkhead door swung open, and Mrs. Lockhart stepped on deck. She was wearing a blue coat and a woolen scarf wrapped around her neck. She waved to Scott and went forward along the port rail. Scott watched her make her way around the deck apparently undisturbed by the ship's motion. She was on her fourth circuit of the deck, passing the mainmast when Scott felt the ship come hard to starboard.

There was a cry of alarm from the bridge and a tremendous cracking sound from overhead. Scott looked up and threw himself to starboard as a section of the topmast crashed to the deck, broken spars, shredded canvas and torn rigging piled on top of it. The *Raven* came around broadside to the wind and heeled thirty degrees. Scott grabbed hold of the starboard rail as the topmast and shattered rigging slid down the deck and crashed through the port rail leaving a ten-foot gap.

Scott caught sight of Mrs. Lockhart against the port rail holding fast to the mainmast shrouds. He was relieved that she hadn't been killed by the falling rigging, but she was still in danger of being injured by the debris sliding around the deck. Scott called out to her, but a wave struck them broadside on, and the ship lurched to port. The deck canted sixty degrees. Scott's feet went out from under him, and he grabbed the rail to stop himself sliding down the deck.

The *Raven* slid into the bottom of the trough, the port side rail went under and a green wall of water surged aboard. The wave swept all before it, and Scott watched in alarm as it tore Mrs. Lockhart away from the mainmast shrouds and swept her along the deck.

The *Raven* wallowed in the bottom of the trough. Scott thought they would be driven under, but slowly the ship began to right itself. Scott searched for Mrs. Lockhart, fearful she had been dashed to pieces by the maelstrom. He let go of the rail and slid down the deck, coming up against bridge stairs. He saw her immediately. The wave had her in its grip, carrying her across the deck.

Scott swung himself around to the port side of the stairs and called out to her. It seemed futile in the chaos that surrounded them, but to his amazement she looked at him and called out. Her words were blown away in the wind, but he saw the fear in her eyes. The *Raven* rolled free of the trough, and the wave surged back across the deck as the ship shed tons of water. Scott watched in dismay as Mrs. Lockhart grasped frantically at what remained of the port rail, but the torrent swept her through the gap, and she disappeared in an instant.

Scott cried out involuntarily and launched himself down the sloping deck coming up hard against the port side rail. The scuppers were jammed with rope and broken rigging, and he fought his way over the debris and leaned over the side of the ship, searching for Mrs. Lockhart. The sea was a mass of breaking waves and foam and he had almost despaired of finding her, when a movement close in to the hull caught his eye.

Mrs. Lockhart's blue coat stood out in the white foam; her coat and dress were pulling her down, and she was struggling to keep her head above water. She was ten feet from the side of the ship, but the *Raven* was still moving forward, and she would quickly be left behind.

Scott shrugged off his coat, grabbed up the end of a one-inch line and pulled it in hand over hand. He had freed twenty feet when it went taut. He threw it aside and heaved a large tackle block out of the way, and managed to pull a hundred feet of rope free. Scott wrapped the rope around his right arm. There was no time to find the other end and secure it. He would have to trust that it was tangled in the wreckage and would hold fast. He leaned over the rail and searched for Mrs. Lockhart. It had taken him less than a minute to free the rope, but in that time she'd been swept astern and was almost below him.

Scott climbed onto the rail. He leapt out as far as he could and threw his arms above his head to keep his body upright. He struck the water on his side and was driven deep beneath the surface. The impact knocked the wind out of him, and the cold closed around him, numbing his body and mind as he clawed his way upward.

Scott broke the surface, gasping for air, but another wave drove him under. The rope became tangled around his legs, and his chest started to heave. Panic gripped him, and he fought it down as he worked to free himself. When he surfaced again, the *Raven* had already moved past and the wake pulled him under the stern.

The sea under the stern was less turbulent, and Scott trod water. He turned in a circle, but couldn't see Mrs. Lockhart. The wake was pulling him across the stern of the ship, and he resisted holding his position. He was despairing of finding Mrs. Lockhart when it struck him that she would've been pulled by the same current, and he turned and swam for the starboard side.

The *Raven* was moving away quickly, and Scott knew he would soon be out of the lee of the ship. He trod water, and as he started to turn, he saw a flash of blue. Mrs. Lockhart was twenty feet from him, drifting away from the stern. She was struggling to keep her head above water, and he could see that she was almost exhausted.

Scott struck out hard and fell into a sidestroke, pulling with his left arm, dragging the rope behind him. His boots were filled with water and felt like weights on his feet, and the rope was becoming heavier with every moment. He knew he was nearing the limit of his strength and feared he wouldn't reach her in time.

Scott was less than six feet from Mrs. Lockhart when she disappeared beneath the surface. He let out a cry of despair and called on every reserve of strength he possessed to drive him the last few feet. He trod water, pulling on the rope until he had enough slack; then he rolled over and dove beneath the surface. He could see less than an arm's length in front of him, and the cold closed around him like a tomb, drawing the strength out of him. His hand brushed against something soft, and even numbed with cold, he knew it was Mrs. Lockhart's coat. He took hold of it and kicked for the surface with all his strength.

Scott came up roaring and drew one gasping breath then another. He grasped Mrs. Lockhart's collar with both hands and pulled her head above water, kicking hard to keep them afloat. Her eyes were closed and she wasn't breathing, and he put his face close to her and screamed her name. The effect was astonishing. Mrs. Lockhart opened her eyes and coughed up a mouthful of water. She drew a rattling breath, coughing and spitting up water, and Scott felt a wave of relief wash over him. Mrs. Lockhart's face was only a few inches from his, and she looked into his eyes with a mixture of fear and incredulity.

Scott held her at arm's length to give her room to swim and made several attempts to speak, but his throat was on fire. Finally he managed to croak out, "When I say . . . you're . . . around my neck." The effort left him coughing and gasping for breath. Mrs. Lockhart shook her head, confusion and fear in her eyes.

The peaks of the waves towered fifteen feet above them, and Scott trod water, turning them in the direction of the ship. As they rose to the crest of the next wave, he caught a glimpse of the *Raven* two hundred feet away, and he felt a tug on the rope. Scott lifted the rope above the surface, and her eyes went wide as she recognized what it meant.

". . . around . . . neck," Scott shouted.

Mrs. Lockhart swam close and slipped her right arm around his neck treading water. Suddenly the rope went taut, and they were pulled across the face of the wave and down into the trough. Mrs. Lockhart locked her other arm around Scott's neck and held on fiercely. They were pulled up the face of the next wave, and as they reached the peak, the rope disappeared into the wave dragging them through the crest.

Scott felt as if his right arm was being torn from its socket, and he clung on grimly. They emerged on the back of the wave and slid into the trough. As the rope went slack Scott pulled hard, rolling onto his right side, and managed to get a grip on the rope with his left hand. He groaned in relief as the strain on his right shoulder was relieved. Mrs. Lockhart tightened her arms around his neck and pressed her face into his neck. Scott rolled his head, and she lifted her chin and looked at him. Her face was strained, but now her eyes burned with fierce courage.

The rope went taut, and Mrs. Lockhart ducked her head down as they were dragged under. They surfaced close to the crest of the wave, and the rope went slack tumbling them down the back of the wave into the trough. Scott trod water hard, keeping them both afloat.

"Hold fast." Scott feared that Mrs. Lockhart could lose her grip if she tried to assist him, but the rope went tight and they were dragged under again before she could answer.

They were pulled forward in a series of surges, and Mrs. Lockhart locked her arms tighter around his neck. He knew she understood and was responding the only way she could. As they crested the next wave, Scott caught sight of the *Raven;* she had turned into the wind and was hove to a hundred feet ahead. Her rigging was a shambles, and most of the sails had been torn away. They were being pulled to the starboard side, and Scott realized the crew must have pulled the rope across the deck as they turned into the wind.

As they crested the next wave Scott realized the water was less turbulent, and they were in the lee of the ship. The *Raven* was less than fifty feet away now, but the cold had numbed his hands to the point that he could feel his grip begin to loosen. Scott closed his eyes and concentrated his whole being on holding fast to the rope. His head was pounding. He began to see flashing colours behind his eyelids, and he bit into the inside of his mouth to stop himself passing out.

Scott was slammed against something solid and opened his eyes to see the *Raven* towering above them. The rope went up the side of the ship. As she rolled they were lifted half out of the water, and Mrs. Lockhart hung on grimly. The ship rolled to starboard, and they were dropped into the water again. Even after a few moments out of the water the cold struck Scott like a blow, and he heard Mrs. Lockhart moan in misery.

A moment later a rope ladder rolled down the side of the ship and splashed into the water to their left. Scott heard his name called out, and he looked up and saw two seamen sliding down the side of the ship on bosun's chairs. They splashed into the water on either side of them.

The seaman to Scott's right called out to him,

"Hold fast, sir, just a few seconds." The seaman thrust his hand between them and pulled a line around Mrs. Lockhart's waist then fastened it expertly with one hand. He leaned back and signalled the deck, and they took up the slack. The seaman locked his arms around Mrs. Lockhart's waist and called out, "I have you; let go now." Mrs. Lockhart held fast to Scott, and the seaman cried out again, "I have you Missus, let loose now."

He signalled to the deck and the rope tightened, pulling Mrs. Lockhart and the seaman up the side of the ship. The ship rolled, and they swung free, but the sailor broke the impact with his legs as they swung back against the hull.

Scott was too numb to think as he watched them move up the side of the ship. He felt the other seaman pass a line under his arms and make it fast. Then he wrapped his arms around Scott and braced his feet against the hull.

"Hold fast, sir, and we'll have you out in a moment." Scott felt himself being lifted out of the water. The rope bit into his flesh, but he was barely aware of the pain.

A section of the rail had been removed, and Scott was swung through the gap onto the deck. His legs went out from under him, and the seaman and Willis caught him.

"Let go now, sir," the seaman said.

Scott tried to open his hands, but they were too cold, and he shook his head, unable to speak. The sailor pried his fingers open.

"Get him to his cabin and get him some dry clothes before he freezes to death," Willis said.

Two seamen supported Scott, swaying back and forth like drunkards till they reached the companionway entrance. Scott was shivering so hard that he had to clamp his jaw shut to stop his teeth from hammering together. As they passed through the day cabin, several passengers spoke to him, but he couldn't understand what they were saying, and the seamen almost carried him to his cabin.

Another seaman was waiting at the cabin door.

"All right, Thomas, I'll see to him. You've been in the drink as well, so get yourself warm." The man stepped close to Scott.

"I'm the cook. Daniel Brown, sir. We must get your clothes off, or you'll freeze to death." He took hold of Scott's left arm.

"Help me now, Harry boy."

The cook and Harry pulled Scott's boots and socks off and stripped off his breeches, then his jacket and shirt, leaving him naked. Scott's mind was working slowly. He was barely aware that his clothes had been removed. He felt the cold air on his skin, but it didn't trouble him. He had an overwhelming urge to lie down and sleep, and he sank back towards his bunk.

Daniel Brown called out, "Hold him up, Harry. Don't let him fall asleep." Harry slipped his arms around Scott's chest and held him fast.

"Don't drop him, Harry."

Scott's head fell forward onto his chest. His eyes began to close, and he was sinking down into a warm welcoming place.

Daniel Brown shouted into his face. "Don't fall asleep, sir. You'll die if you fall asleep."

Scott felt something rough rubbing his chest, burning his skin, and he fought his way up from a great depth and opened his eyes. Daniel Brown was rubbing his chest with a ship's blanket.

"Keep your head up, sir."

Scott felt his eyes begin to close against his will, beckoning him back to that warmth. Then something struck him, knocking his head to the side. His face stung and a wave of anger rose up in him. He tried to speak, but another blow struck him, making his whole face tingle with pain.

"Keep your head up, sir. You'll die if you sleep."

Scott drew a shuddering breath and clenched his fists and set his feet on the deck, trying to take his own weight. Daniel Brown kept rubbing his arms and legs until it hurt. Slowly his mind began to clear, and then the pain started. He was frozen, but as the blood began to return to his limbs he felt as if his whole body was on fire. It spread through his arms and legs, carrying agony to his fingers and toes, and he cried out at the cruelty of it.

The cook held a bottle to his lips.

"You must drink, sir, to warm your insides." Daniel Brown was insistent. "You must drink, sir." He barked the words into Scott's face.

Scott's anger flared at his insolence, but he took the bottle in both hands and drank. The brandy burned its way down his throat into his stomach and started him coughing, and he gasped for breath, but the fiery liquid seemed to put life back into him.

The cook and seaman Harry kept working on Scott until he could think and speak again. Finally Daniel Brown stood back.

"I think you're through it, sir, but you must rest now." He motioned to Harry, and stepped out of the cabin.

"Begging your pardon, sir. No offense intended with the rough treatment, but it's what needs doing when a man is frozen."

"You have my thanks, Daniel Brown. I take no offense," Scott said.

Brown nodded and closed cabin door, and Scott lay back on the bunk and closed his eyes. He didn't know how much time had passed since Mrs. Lockhart had gone overboard. It didn't seem to matter as exhaustion dragged him down into sleep.

* * *

Scott awoke to the sound of the ship's bell, but he had no idea which watch was changing. He'd rolled out of the blankets as he slept, and he was shivering. He pulled a blanket around him and rubbed his arms until he started to warm up. His stomach growled. He sat up, but the cabin swayed around him, and he held on to the bunk until it passed. Then he dressed as quickly as he could.

When Scott entered the day cabin, he was still feeling light-headed but he could tell that the weather had moderated. There were three people in the day cabin: Mr. Meriton, Willis, and a passenger named Sloan that Scott had barely spoken to. They were finishing breakfast, and Scott realized he must have slept the previous day and through the night. Mr. Meriton leapt to his feet and rushed forward to greet him.

"Captain Scott, my good fellow. Let me assist you." Meriton took his arm and conducted him to the end of the table. Scott resented the familiarity, but he was still uncertain of his balance and held his peace.

Scott tore off a piece of bread and took a bite. It was hard and almost stale, but it was food.

"You must be starved, Captain Scott. There is still some hot porridge. Let me help you." Meriton spooned porridge into a bowl and placed it in front of him, and he nodded his thanks. The porridge was lukewarm, but he ate it hungrily and refilled his bowl twice more.

Willis had left the day cabin when Scott entered. Scott's mind had been on his stomach, and he hadn't paid attention. The door to the captain's cabin opened, and Willis and Harbin emerged. Harbin slid into his chair, and Willis sat across from Scott. Neither spoke until he finished eating.

Harbin leaned on the table. "Captain Scott, yesterday I was able to observe your actions from the bridge. I must tell you that it was the most courageous act that I have ever witnessed."

Scott looked at Harbin. "May I enquire as to Mrs. Lockhart's health?"

"She is recovering well. Miss Williams and her maid spent the night with her, and I am assured that she will be on her feet again in a day or two."

"I am gratified to hear that, Captain."

Scott looked up at the skylight.

"The ship's motion is easier. Has the weather moderated?" Scott was looking at Willis, but Harbin answered.

"We have altered course to the southwest, away from the storm."

"Thank you for your consideration, Captain. If you don't mind, I would like to take a turn on deck."

Scott took a piece of bread and slid out of the bench. He leaned on the table to steady himself as the ship rolled. Harbin leaned forward, anxious to speak.

"Captain Scott, I realize that we haven't seen eye to eye, but I have to tell you, sir, that I am compelled to modify my opinion of your character. Your actions yesterday were exemplary and—"

Scott barked at him. "I care little for your opinion of my character, sir, and you'll not lecture me on it, exemplary or other."

Harbin came to his feet. "Good God, man! Are you not capable of civil behaviour?" The colour was rising in his face.

"Civil behaviour, Captain, is not well served by arrogance and conceit. These things alone you have shown me since I stepped aboard this ship." Scott strode away, leaving Harbin stuttering, and made his way to his cabin.

Scott ate the bread while he selected clothes from his sea chest. The clothes he had worn yesterday would be useless until they could be washed in fresh water, but his greatcoat hung behind the cabin door and he pulled it on, thankful for its warmth.

When Scott came on deck, the damaged rigging had been cleared away, and a rudimentary repair had been made to the breach in the rail. The top thirty feet of the mainmast had been broken off, and it had been stripped of its sails and yards, and the deck planks had been repaired where the fallen rigging had landed. The fore- and mizzenmasts were intact, and the ship was making good headway under a jury rig.

Scott climbed to the bridge deck. Reeve was on duty, and he uncharacteristically lifted his hand to his cap. Scott took up his accustomed position in the corner of the bridge and scanned the ocean and the sky. After a few minutes he went to the binnacle and looked at the compass.

"The course is south. Southwest and a half south, sir." The helmsman sung out the words.

Scott nodded and returned to the rail. To the north the sky was dark and clouds hung low over the ocean. To the southwest the sky was grey but the clouds were trailing white streamers across it. The air was refreshing, but Scott was still weak, and after an hour he sought the comfort of his bunk.

The next morning Scott was back on deck, but a squall came out of the southwest, and the rain drove him under the bridge deck. He held out his hands and washed his face in the rain. It felt clean and refreshing. When he took his hands down from his face, Mrs. Lockhart was standing a few feet from him. He blinked in surprise and she laughed.

Mrs. Lockhart wore a cream-coloured dress and a sea-green coat. She'd let her hair down, and it fell past her shoulders in thick curling waves. The wind whipped it into her eyes. She pushed it out of her face, and it streamed away behind her as if straining to take flight. Mrs. Lockhart was transformed from the conservative widow of yesterday to a young woman sparkling with life and vitality.

Scott was lost for words, but he quickly regained his composure.

"Mrs. Lockhart, I had not . . . are you well?"

"I am very well, Captain Scott, thanks to you."

"You are recovered from your ordeal, the cold . . . ?"

"I am very well recovered, Captain Scott. I trust that you have not sustained any injuries as a result of our adventures?"

"No, Mrs. Lockhart, not at all."

Mrs. Lockhart laughed, a soft lilting sound that was as natural as it was appealing. She stepped closer and her expression became somber.

"I was drowning, Captain Scott. If you hadn't come to my aid, I would have died. When I felt your hand grasp me in the ocean, I thought it was the angel Gabriel sent to bring me to judgment. I owe you my life, Captain Scott." She put her hand on his arm. "And I owe you a debt of gratitude that I will never be able to repay." She smiled again, and her eyes searched his face as if seeking something that eluded her.

There was a shout from above. Someone came clattering down the stairs from the bridge, and Mrs. Lockhart stepped back.

"The voyage is less than half over, Captain. There will be time enough for us to become better acquainted."

"I will look forward to it, Mrs. Lockhart."

"Now I must take a turn around the deck and walk the cold out of my bones." She stepped out onto the main deck and looked at the sky.

"The weather is fine, Captain. I hope you will be spared the necessity of coming to my rescue again today." Her eyes flashed with humour as she turned away.

CHAPTER THIRTEEN

JOHN FELT HIS WAY DOWN the ladder, counting ten rungs to the bottom. The hull shuddered each time the bow took a wave, and in the confined space the sound was deafening. The air was dank with moisture. There was water sloshing around in the bilge beneath him, and the stench that rose from it made his stomach turn. He was in total darkness. The motion of the ship made him feel as if he were falling into a black void, and he held on to the ladder as he tried to get his bearings.

John stretched out his left hand, trying to get a sense of how large the space was. He let go of the ladder, and as he stepped forward the deck plunged beneath him, and he was thrown against the forward bulkhead and crashed to the deck. The deck was slimy with moisture, and he slid across the deck, feeling his way back to the ladder.

John hooked his foot around the base of the ladder and stretched out, exploring the deck around him with his hand. Four feet from the ladder his hand dropped into space, and he pulled back in alarm. Cautiously he stretched out again and started to explore the rest of the space. The hold was the same triangular shape as the fo'c'sle. It was fifteen feet from forward bulkhead to the bow. In the middle of the deck there was a square hole three feet across. The edges were squared like a hatch, but there was no cover or ladder, and the water in the bilge sounded deep enough to drown in.

John climbed the ladder and pushed against the hatch and banged on it with his fist.

"Let me out of here." The hatch cover was solid wood, and he was doubtful anyone could even hear him. The ship's motion made it difficult to hold on, and he retreated to the deck. He sat with his back against the forward bulkhead and braced his feet against the ladder. The damp seeped through his clothes, and he sat on his hunting bag and put his plaid between his back and the bulkhead.

John rebuked himself for losing his temper in the galley. The image of Malcolm spitting into his stew came back to him, but he dismissed it. There was no point using up his strength in pointless frustration. The sound of the bow pounding filled his ears, and he pulled his plaid over his head and tried to block it out. He braced himself against the bulkhead and moved with the ship as it met each wave. He had no way to measure the passage of time and finally his head dropped onto his chest, and he drifted in and out of sleep.

John came awake disorientated, and the sound of the bow pounding into the waves brought him back to where he was. Once he awoke to find something pulling on his sleeve and something wet brushed against his skin. He lashed out, and his hand struck something heavy. It screeched in alarm and scuttled away. John wiped his hand on his plaid in disgust. The rat's fur was cold and damp, and he had the sense that it was bigger than his hand. He listened, straining his ears for the sound of its claws on the deck, and his imagination conjured images of the vile creatures swarming over him.

John was awakened by the sound of the hatch opening above him. He was stiff and sore, but he leapt to his feet and onto the ladder. The light in the fo'c'sle hurt his eyes, and he squinted at the sliver of daylight from the deck above. He started to climb out of the hatch, but a sailor put his foot on his shoulder.

"No, you don't." John held on to the ladder.

"Let me out."

"You better get used to it, boy. You'll be there till we reach port."

"No, no, you can't do that. Let me speak to the captain." John tried to force his way up the ladder again but the seaman held him down.

"Do you want to eat, boy, or not?" He had something wrapped in a cloth in his left hand and a clay jug in the other.

John hadn't had anything to drink in almost two days, and he focused all his attention on the jug.

"Give me the water." He reached up and the sailor handed it down to him. It was a half-gallon jug, and by the weight he guessed that it was almost full. He gripped the handle firmly and swung down into the hold again, completely focused on the jug's contents. The cloth bundle dropped on the deck beside him, and he snatched it up. The hatch began to close, and John looked up in panic.

"A hammock, give me a hammock."

John worked the cork out of the jug and lifted it to his mouth. The water had a burnt taste, but he swallowed it, and stopped for a moment gasping for breath then drank again. The jug was half-empty, and his stomach felt bloated and swollen. He knew that they wouldn't bring water again till the next day, and he should ration it. The cloth contained half a dozen hardtack biscuits. He ate two right away and put the rest in his hunting bag, and then he sat against the bulkhead to wait.

The next day a crewman called Waters brought him food and water. John didn't try to climb out of the hold. Waters handed him a water jug, took the empty one, and gave him another bundle of hardtack.

"I would like to speak to the captain."

"The captain has the fever. They don't think he'll live."

"How long till we reach port?"

"I don't know, boy. Some say a week, some say a month. What does it matter? The fever will kill us all before we reach land."

"Have many more died, then?"

"Enough questions now." Waters stepped back and appeared again a moment later.

"Here, lad." John was startled when a bundle of canvas landed next to him on the deck. He looked at it for a moment bewildered, and then realized that it was a hammock.

"Thank you," he called out, but the hatch had closed, leaving him in darkness again.

The ropes felt solid and the canvas was in good condition. John tied one end to the ladder four feet above the deck and felt his way around the bulkhead looking for a place to fix the other end. The bulkhead was smooth, but where it met the ship's side, there was space between one of the braces where he could feed the rope through. The brace was close to the upper deck, and he repositioned the other end close to the top of the ladder, so it would hang level.

John climbed into the hammock. It felt wonderful to be able to relax his body, and before he realized it he fell asleep. He was awakened by the sound of squealing and scratching below him, and he rolled out of the hammock, landed on all fours and felt his way to the ladder. He swept his hand around the deck searching. He could hear the rats trying to tear his hunting bag open.

John hooked his foot around the base of the ladder and threw himself towards the opening in the deck. He landed on his left side crushing one rat and trapping another. A third scampered away squealing in fright. His hand brushed against the hunting bag but it started to slide towards the opening in the deck. He lunged forward desperately and felt a surge of relief when his hand closed around the strap.

John felt a sharp pain in the back of his hand. He cried out in alarm. He pulled back against the ladder and kicked out with his right foot, sending the rat squealing across the deck, and a moment later he heard it splash into the bilges. He wedged himself against the ladder and opened the bag, relieved to find nothing had been damaged. He ate three hardtack biscuits and drank some water then climbed into the hammock, nursing his hand and hoping it wasn't poisoned. In minutes he was asleep.

John was awakened by a crack like cannon fire and then a crash on the deck above. The ship rolled to port, and he was thrown around wildly in his hammock. He swung out of the hammock and wedged himself against the bulkhead. Above something heavy was scraping across the deck, and he guessed part of the rigging had been carried away and was dragging in the ocean, causing the ship to list. He stared up as if he could see through the deck planks and imagined the crew working to cut away the rigging.

John had a strong stomach, but even he was beginning to feel ill when at last the ship righted itself and took on a more natural motion.

"Thank God for that," he said. He sat for a long time, listening, but he could hear nothing from the deck above, and finally he climbed into his hammock and lay listening to the sound of the waves and the water sloshing in the bilge.

Since the storm he had eaten all of his food and drunk all the water. He had slept three times, but he had no idea how much time had passed. He was trying to think of some way to mark the passage of time when the hatch above him was thrown open.

"Come on, boy, if you want to eat." It was Waters. John pulled himself up the ladder.

"What happened?"

"Give me your water jug." He dropped to the deck and grabbed the jug and was back on the ladder in seconds. He handed the jug to Waters and took the full one in return.

"What happened? There was a storm—was there damage?"

"The foremast was carried away." Waters looked around guiltily. "The mainmast topsails and top gallants were carried away, and the mizzen is damaged beyond repair."

John was stunned—over half the ship's sails were damaged or destroyed.

"Was it in the day or night?" Waters looked at him as if he were mad.

"It was during the second dog watch. The foremast was carried away and put a list on her; I thought she would go under." Before he could go on, John cut in.

"The crew must be exhausted. Ask the captain to let me out, and I'll work."

"The captain's dead. We buried him today. Lockman won't let you out." He started to close the hatch.

"Wait, how long to port?"

"I don't know, lad, but it won't be soon." He closed the hatch and John clung to the ladder, reluctant to go back down into the dark.

* * *

John resigned himself to enduring the rest of the voyage in the hold. Counting the times food was brought to him was the only way he could track the passage of time. The stale air and dampness were taking their toll on him too. His gums were inflamed, and his teeth felt loose in their sockets, and the muscles on his legs felt soft and pulpy. He knew these were signs of scurvy. No one knew the cause of scurvy, but he knew it wouldn't get better until he was on land.

It was becoming colder, and even though he was wrapped in his plaid, John shivered constantly. He asked Waters where they were heading, but he said he couldn't tell him. John suspected he didn't know.

"Lockman's in charge, and he says nothing, though we must trust our lives to him." The scowl on his face told him there was no love lost for the first mate by the crew.

When Waters brought him food, John continued trying to glean more information from him.

"It gets colder all the time."

"Aye, lad, we're well to the north." He glanced over his shoulder and John saw the rash on his neck.

"What of the fever?" Waters looked down at him.

"No deaths for eight days. The mate says it's over."

"What do you think?"

"Many have died, and more will die before we reach land, I think" He stood and closed the hatch down.

The next day John had a fever. He'd been shivering the previous day and now lay sweating in his hammock. He gulped water and lay half-conscious as tremors wracked his body. There was an itch under his arms, and he scratched till it bled. The itch stopped, but his armpits ached inside. Then it moved to his chest, and it took all his willpower not to scratch it.

The next time Waters opened the hatch John was delirious and couldn't climb out of his hammock. He heard Waters suck his breath in. A moment later he felt the water jug touch his chest, and he grasped it instinctively. Waters had lowered the jug on a rope and as soon as John had it in his grasp he pulled the rope up. A moment later a package of hardtack dropped onto his stomach, and the hatch slammed shut again.

For John the days passed in a haze. He ate and drank and was aware of the hatch opening and closing, but he had no memory of seeing Waters or speaking to him. He drifted in and out of sleep until he couldn't tell dreaming from waking. He knew he had smallpox, and that he must fight it, but he was powerless against the exhaustion that overwhelmed him. The next time John woke he was shivering. He pulled his plaid around him and curled into a ball. Hunger gnawed at his gut, and he bit off a piece of hardtack and held it in his mouth till it was soft enough to swallow. There was more hardtack left, and he wondered how many days he had been delirious.

John felt his armpit. It was tender to touch, but the swelling had gone down, and the ache was less. He knew he would live. He let a long breath out slowly, and the tension went out of him. It was said that if you survived the smallpox, you wouldn't get it again. He should be thankful, but he wouldn't feel grateful until he was free of this hold.

The next time the hatch opened, John saw a different seaman looking down at him.

"Where's Waters?" he said.

"Waters is dead from the pox you brought aboard," the seaman stepped back from the hatch. "Come up, so I can see your face, boy." John came up the ladder slowly. When his head was above the deck, the seaman put a boat hook on his shoulder.

John recognized the man. Higgs, he thought.

"What is happening to the ship?"

"Let me see your neck," Higgs said.

"What're you doing?"

Higgs tapped John on the side of the head with the boat hook.

"Show me your neck." John pulled his collar down, and Higgs put the boat hook against his face and turned his head to the other side.

Higgs stood up and laid the boathook against the bulkhead.

"You'll live. There's not many that do." Higgs handed John a jug of water and a package of hardtack and motioned for him to get back down into the hold.

"What is happening on board? Are we near to port?" Higgs started to swing the hatch cover down and John called out again. "For pity's sake, tell me something to keep me from going mad."

Higgs held the hatch cover and looked down at John.

"I've lost count of how many of your mangy countrymen we've thrown overboard. Half the crew are dead, and the ship's crippled. Lockman tells us we'll make landfall any day, if we live to see it." He slammed the hatch cover down and shot the bolts home.

* * *

Six days later John felt a change in the ship's motion. The pounding at the bow faded and the ship eased to a gentle roll. He lay in his hammock, listening intently. Even deep in the hold he had been able to hear the wind howling in the rigging. Now there was nothing. It could only mean they were hove to somewhere. Land—they had to be near land.

John climbed the ladder and pounded on the hatch with his hand.

"Land, are we near land?" There was no response from above, and reluctantly he climbed back down and swung into his hammock. He didn't know what would happen next, but whatever it was, it had to be better than this stinking dungeon.

Later that day the ship moved on the starboard tack, barely heeling. John felt her come around; then there was a clang on the deck above and the anchor chain rattled on the other side of the bulkhead, followed by a splash as the anchor struck the water.

John let out a yell of triumph. He rolled out of the hammock and stood looking up at the hatch, willing it to open. Without the sound of the bow pounding he could hear the crew moving about the deck, and he stood impatiently waiting. The hatch didn't open and finally John climbed into the hammock in despair, wondering if the crew had forgotten about him.

Another day and night passed, and John was asleep when the hatch cover was lifted. He rolled onto the deck and rushed up the ladder.

"Not so fast, boy." Higgs stood to the side of the hatch. John looked up at him as if he was mad.

"We are in port. Let me out."

"The first mate has said you're to remain below decks for the present."

"No, that's not fair. I've been in this hole for weeks."

"I can't help it." Higgs face softened. "I don't know what's to become of you, lad, but they won't keep you here forever." Higgs handed him a jug of water and a package of hardtack.

John wanted to fight his way out of the hold, but he knew it was hopeless and he climbed down again.

"At least let me out for a while."

Higgs shook his head and closed the hatch.

CHAPTER FOURTEEN

THE RAVEN MADE LANDFALL SOUTH of Boston on the morning of September 1, 1746. She pushed up the coast against a northerly wind, and sighted Boston mid-afternoon. Scott watched the coastline move past. The land was flat with broad marshes running down to the sea, dark sand and black rock on the beaches, and forested hills in the background. On an overcast day, it didn't look so different from Britain or any more inviting.

All hands were on deck to handle the ship, and the passengers lined the rail, eager for the first sight of Boston. The *Raven* entered a wide bay and Scott climbed to the bridge to get a better look. Headlands to the north and south formed a large protected anchorage with a dozen islands scattered across the bay. A lighthouse stood on an island on the north side, and a river estuary formed an inner harbour.

The tide was ebbing as the *Raven* beat its way into the bay and tacked back and forth, working her way between the islands. Scott had learned enough during the voyage to know that without the mainmast topsails, their ability to manoeuvre was limited. His suspicions were confirmed when he heard Harbin give the order to heave to and anchor. The *Raven* came about to the northeast and hove to a mile offshore, and there were exclamations of dismay from the passengers when the anchor let go.

Scott went to the bow and examined Boston more closely. The centre of the town stood on a peninsula connected to the mainland by a narrow neck of land, and houses and other buildings spread out around the harbour on both sides of the river. From the centre of the town a pier ran out into the harbour for a quarter of a mile or more. Scott had never seen anything like it. He estimated more than a hundred ships were anchored in the outer harbour or tied up at the wharves along the shore. There was a great deal of small boat traffic back and forth to the beach and, as he watched, a cutter put out from the pier, heading towards the *Raven*.

Scott heard Captain Harbin call out to the passengers, and they gathered around the bridge deck stairs.

"Ladies and gentlemen, as you have seen, we were not able to make the tide. We'll lie at anchor and enter Boston on the next tide."

Scott saw the looks of disappointment on the faces of the passengers, and there was a good deal of grumbling. Mr. Meriton stepped forward.

"Captain Harbin, the tide is on the ebb. It won't turn for six hours, by which time it will be dark. Must we spend another night on board?"

A collective sigh rose from the passengers as they realized what Meriton was getting at.

Harbin nodded. "You're correct, Mr. Meriton. We won't be able to make the harbour until high tide tomorrow, mid-morning, if I'm not mistaken."

Meriton looked at the captain in consternation. "That won't do, Captain. I have business of the most urgent nature, and I must get ashore at the earliest opportunity." He looked around seeking support from his fellow passengers.

"I 'm afraid there's nothing else for it, Mr. Meriton. I've no control over wind or the tide. We will have you safely ashore tomorrow in the forenoon. You have my assurance on that."

Scott was surprised when Mrs. Lockhart stepped forward. "Mr. Meriton, if I may?"

Meriton dropped his hand and nodded.

"My company has offices in the harbour. My manager will have seen the *Raven* drop anchor, and, if I am not mistaken, he has dispatched a cutter to bring me to shore. I'm sure there will be room onboard for more than myself and my maid. I'm happy to extend an invitation to as many passengers as can be accommodated."

They all started talking at once; a passenger called out that he'd spotted the cutter and several rushed to the port side to see for themselves. Harbin climbed back to the bridge and called out to the bosun to prepare to receive the cutter.

Mrs. Lockhart came to where Scott stood by the mainmast.

"Captain Scott, will you be coming ashore with us?"

"Much as I would like to Mrs. Lockhart, I must see that my men are billeted properly. I'm afraid I must resign myself to another night on board the *Raven*."

Mrs. Lockhart looked around the deck as if gathering her thoughts, then turned back to Scott.

"I owe you my life, Captain Scott. That is a debt I will not soon forget."

"I assure you, Mrs. Lockhart, you need not feel obliged to me."

"I always pay my debts, Captain Scott, but don't mistake me, this is not a burden of guilt or gratitude that I assume reluctantly. This voyage has changed me, and I am stronger for it."

Mrs. Lockhart searched Scott's face. He found it disconcerting to be the object of such scrutiny. There was strength in her eyes and also vulnerability, a combination of qualities he found both disarming and compelling, and he returned her gaze, aware that the passengers were watching.

Mrs. Lockhart smiled and extended her hand to him. "I trust this won't be our last meeting, Captain Scott."

Scott inclined his head and took her hand. "That would be my wish, Mrs. Lockhart."

She looked over her shoulder. "The cutter awaits, so for now, Captain Scott, I will say farewell."

Scott watched as she climbed onto the ladder and disappeared below the level of the deck. He went to the rail and looked over the side. Mrs. Lockhart was seated in the stern of the cutter with several other passengers. The descent down the side of the ship was daunting for many of them, and the bosun's chair had been rigged to lower them to the boat. As soon as the last passenger was on board, the cutter cast off and Scott watched it move across the bay until it was lost in the bustle of the harbour.

* * *

Scott was on deck next morning as the anchor was hauled. Captain Harbin kept her beating back and forth across the bay until the tide started to flood then rode it into the harbour. As soon as the *Raven* was made fast to the pier, the deck became a hive of activity as a stream of dock workers, merchants, and clerks poured off the gangplank onto the ship.

Scott saw a young lieutenant step on deck, followed by a grizzled sergeant twice his age. He wore a wool greatcoat over a dark blue uniform, and his boots were polished to a high shine. He saw Scott and came directly to him and saluted.

"'I'm Lieutenant Paine, liaison for Major Coxe. I am assigned to meet each ship to provide support to officers arriving in port. Welcome to Boston, sir."

"I am Captain Scott. My orders are to report to the military commander in Boston."

"That would be Major Coxe, sir. I will convey you to his offices."

Scott pointed to his troops gathered against the ship's rail. "I have twelve troopers that accompanied me—see that they're found billets."

"My sergeant will bring them to the barracks on Deacon Street for the present, sir."

Paine turned to the sergeant. "Sergeant Evans, see to it please and have the captain's luggage transported to the officers' quarters."

The lieutenant turned towards the gangplank. "If you would follow me, sir."

As Scott stepped onto the gangplank he saw Captain Harbin standing on the bridge. Harbin raised his hand in salute, and Scott nodded in reply.

When he stepped onto the dock, the ground seemed to move under his feet, and he grabbed the rail to steady himself.

"It's not uncommon to be unsteady on your feet after a long voyage. It will pass, sir."

"I don't require instruction on the effects of sea travel, Lieutenant Paine," Scott barked in reply.

"No, sir. Of course, sir." The lieutenant looked down, stung by Scott's retort.

Paine led Scott along the dock past a row of warehouses bustling with activity and into a narrow street lined on both sides with bakeries, butchers, and haberdasheries. Every second establishment was a tavern that would've looked the same in London or Liverpool.

They emerged onto King Street, a broad thoroughfare running away from the river, and the lieutenant turned left. He kept a few paces ahead of Scott until they came to where a soldier stood guarding a gig. Paine motioned for Scott to climb aboard, and the lieutenant took the reins.

As they drove, Scott looked around him in surprise. He had conjured an image of the Americas as a rude backwater outpost. There were many buildings—the governor's palace, a library, and a theatre—that would not have been out of place in London or Paris. Booksellers were clustered along one street and what looked like a printing house stood close by. As first glance Boston had a refined feel about it, and Scott wondered what other notions he had about the colonies would prove false.

The barracks were located two miles from the town along the banks of the river. Lieutenant Paine led Scott to a plain-looking building on the west side of a central square.

"This is the officers' quarters, sir. There are several rooms available on the second floor that you may choose from."

"How many officers are billeted here?"

"Ten, sir, and the food is passing good."

They entered a large hallway with doors opening on both sides. It was warm enough that Scott pulled off his gloves and unbuttoned his coat.

"This is the officers' mess." Paine pointed to a door to the right and continued to a set of stairs at the back of the building. Scott was still unsteady on his feet and held fast to the banister.

At the top of the stairs they took a corridor to the right.

"There are three rooms vacant, sir." The lieutenant showed Scott two rooms at the front overlooking the parade ground, and a third looking east towards the woods. The room had two large windows that gave it a light airy feel. The furniture was basic, and there was a fireplace on the south wall. It was far from palatial, but it was a step up from his last posting.

"I'll take this room," Scott said. "Have my chest and other belongings sent up."

"Yes, sir, I expect that they'll arrive shortly, and I will enquire as to when Major Coxe will see you, sir."

"Please do. What time is the evening meal served? I haven't eaten since yesterday."

"At seven o'clock sharp, sir. In the meantime I'll arrange for the cook to prepare some cold cuts and broth, if that would be acceptable."

"That will do admirably."

The officers' mess was a large room furnished with easy chairs, a card table and several well-stocked bookshelves. Scott made himself comfortable by the fire while Paine went about his business.

The lieutenant returned ten minutes later, entering from a door at the back of the room.

"Captain Scott, your belongings have arrived, and the cook will have beef stew and cold cuts for you shortly, sir." Scott nodded.

"Very well, Lieutenant. Carry on." The lieutenant saluted and strode from the room.

A short while later the cook, a harried looking man in his fifties, informed Scott that his food was ready in the dining room. He ate beef stew with fresh bread, both of which were excellent, and began to feel warmer and more comfortable than since he'd set foot on the *Raven*. When he returned to his room, his chest and other belongings were sitting in the middle of the floor. A fire had been set in the grate, warming the room nicely.

Scott threw his coat on the bed and started to unpack. He had only half completed the task when there was a knock at the door.

"Come." Lieutenant Paine entered and saluted.

"Major Coxe sends his regards, sir. He'll see you at four o'clock today." Paine consulted his pocket watch. "I will return to show you to his office in one hour, sir."

"Very well, Lieutenant. Carry on."

An hour later Paine led Scott to the main administrative building. The troopers at the door came to attention and one held the door open and they entered a large square foyer. The ceiling was open to the second floor, and windows above the door flooded the space with light. Half a dozen offices opened off the foyer, and a corridor ran along the centre of the building in both directions.

The lieutenant led Scott to a staircase at the back of the foyer and up to the second floor. Coxe's office was on the right.

"Captain Scott to see Major Coxe." A clerk got to his feet, knocked on the door and held it open.

"Captain Scott, sir." Scott entered the office and the door closed behind him. The office took up the entire east side of the building. It had a high ceiling, and windows on three sides filled it with light. The room was furnished lavishly. Two walls were given over to bookcases, and a fireplace in the east wall kept the room at a comfortable temperature.

Coxe sat behind a desk at the window overlooking the parade ground. He was in his mid-fifties, portly, and had drinker's nose. His thinning white hair was pulled behind his head, and he wore the kind of waxed moustache that had long gone out of style. He wore a dark blue uniform with gold braid at the collar and cuffs, over a white linen shirt.

Scott stepped up to the desk and saluted.

"Captain Scott reporting for duty, Major." Coxe extended his hand, and Scott was surprised at the strength of his grip.

"Take a seat, Captain." He had a deep baritone voice and enunciated each word carefully. "Welcome to Boston, Captain Scott."

Coxe picked up a document from the desk.

"This dispatch was delivered to me an hour ago. It comes from the *Raven* and is signed by the secretary to the minister of war of His Majesty's government and provides specific instructions with regard to your career in Massachusetts."

Scott started to speak, but Coxe held up a hand.

"I am also in receipt of a report from Captain Harbin of the *Raven*. The report makes reference to an incident that took place during the voyage and charges you with serious misconduct. I must tell you, Captain, that if these allegations were proven to be true, your tenure as an officer with this command would be short-lived. "

"If I may speak, sir?"

Coxe waved him to silence.

"I am further astonished by the second part of Captain Harbin's report. He describes your actions in the rescue of a Mrs. Lockhart from certain death. Harbin notes that as the captain he is compelled to record and report all incidents that take place on board ship. Further he asserts that the gravity of the incident documented in the first part of his report is outweighed by your actions as described in the second part."

Coxe fixed Scott with a withering look.

"What am I to do with you?" He threw the report down on the desk, heaved himself to his feet, and paced over to the window.

Scott felt the heat rising in his neck, but he forced himself to keep his voice calm.

"If I may speak, sir?" Coxe came back and motioned for Scott to proceed as he sank into the chair.

"I haven't had the opportunity to read the accusations Captain Harbin has levelled against me, but I presume it pertains to an incident with one of my men. Captain Harbin proposed to flog one of the troopers under my command without my approval. I acted to protect the integrity of military—"

Coxe exploded at Scott.

"Good God, man! You instigated mutiny on a commercial sailing vessel. That's a hanging offense." Coxe slumped back into the chair and stabbed the air with his finger. "The flogging of one miserable trooper is not sufficient grounds to challenge the authority of a ship's captain at sea."

Scott's temper flared.

"I demand the right to confront Harbin—" Coxe slammed his fist down on the table.

"You will do nothing of the sort, sir." Coxe took a breath. "Your conduct on the *Raven* is grounds for a court-martial. However, as you were responsible for saving the life of one of the most prominent citizens of Boston, Captain Harbin has requested that no action be taken against you." Coxe shook his head. "Captain, I suggest that you get settled in the officers' mess. Lieutenant Paine will see you have everything you need, and we will speak again in a few days."

"Thank you, sir," Scott said. He could feel Coxe's eyes boring into his back as he made his way to the door.

* * *

In the hallway Lieutenant Paine and the clerk were standing with their heads together. They stopped talking when Scott emerged, and the lieutenant stepped back looking guilty.

"Lieutenant Paine, you will accompany me."

"Yes, sir." Scott stepped out around the parade ground and the lieutenant had to hustle to keep up with him.

"Lieutenant, there's a bathhouse in the officers' quarters, I presume. Also, I will need to have my clothes cleaned and pressed. "

"I will instruct the orderly to prepare the bath immediately, sir. A woman from the town comes twice a week to do laundry. The orderly will see to it, sir."

Scott stopped in the foyer of the officers' quarters.

"Tomorrow I wish to see the rest of the facilities, also the town of Boston. Please arrange a mount for me. You will accompany me. I presume that you are familiar with Boston."

"I'll notify the stable master, sir. I'm sure you will be pleased with the mounts, and the stable master will also provide you with a saddle and tack."

Scott spent an hour in the bath, scrubbing until his skin was red, washing the smell of the *Raven* out of him. He donned the cleanest garments in his chest and took dinner in the mess. The meal was plain—beef steaks, potatoes, and bread with wine, but in comparison to the food on the *Raven*, it was a feast. The fire had been going in Scott's room all day, and it was warm and comfortable. He undressed and climbed into bed. He had barely pulled the blankets over him before he drifted into a dreamless sleep.

Scott ate breakfast early and met Lieutenant Paine in the foyer at eight o'clock sharp. The morning was cold, and it had rained, but the sky was clearing. The stables lay on the north side of the soldier's barracks and could accommodate over a hundred animals. Master Sergeant Harper was in charge of the stables. Scott selected a three-year-old grey gelding called King. Sergeant Harper had the lieutenant's mare brought out. They walked the horses around the base for half an hour while the lieutenant described the buildings and their functions.

There were currently two hundred common soldiers in the barracks and twelve officers.

Scott had learned from the orderly that only the junior officers lived on the base, and the senior officers stayed in lodgings in the town.

"Lieutenant, I understand some officers take rooms in the town. What can you tell me of this?" Scott said.

"Many of the senior officers live in one of the rooming houses in Boston. Those who are married keep a house if they can afford it. I can acquaint you with some of the better locations if you so wish."

Scott looked at the sky.

"I would like to tour the town this afternoon. Let's take advantage of the weather while it holds."

"If I might suggest, Captain, there's a path along the river leading to Boston that may provide an interesting perspective."

"Lead on, Lieutenant," Scott said.

* * *

Scott was called to Major Coxe's office the following Thursday morning.

"Captain, what do you know of the political and military events that have taken place in the region over the last year?"

"We are at war with France in Europe, sir. My understanding of how that has been translated to the American Colonies is limited," Scott said.

Coxe fetched a map and spread it across the desk. It showed the Eastern Seaboard of North America from the Caribbean Sea to the French Colonies. He tapped Boston, and then pointed along the coast to the northeast.

"This region is known as Acadia by the French. A year ago it was annexed by Britain. The locations that are key to holding the region are Louisburg in the north and Annapolis Royal in the south."

Coxe put his finger on the northeastern shore of a large island north of Acadia.

"This is Louisburg. An expeditionary force out of Boston captured it just over a year ago. The town has a good harbour that services the fisheries along the Eastern Seaboard. More importantly, it guards the entrance to the St. Lawrence River, the main entryway into the French Colonies. The French population has been deported, and the town is garrisoned with British troops."

Coxe ran his finger over on an area to the northeast of Boston.

"This is the Bay of Fundy. Here is Annapolis Royal. The French call it Port Royal. Annapolis Royal is crucial to securing this whole peninsula." Coxe outlined a long finger of land to the east of the Bay of Fundy.

Coxe sat down again.

"Some months ago we received information that the French had gathered a fleet of between fifty and sixty ships in ports along the Normandy Coast. Over ten thousand soldiers embarked for the French Colonies in the late spring.

"Ten thousand, you say?"

Coxe went on. "Earlier in the summer a French force of several thousand approached Annapolis Royal from the northwest. There was a standoff. We sent ships to reinforce Annapolis, but by the time they arrived the French had withdrawn."

Scott blinked in surprise.

"We don't know the whereabouts of these troops or of the remainder of the ten thousand. Our guess is that they are likely at Quebec or Mont-Royal on the St. Lawrence."

Scott leaned on the desk.

"What defenses are at Annapolis Royal?"

"There's an earthen fort reported to be in a poor condition. Repairs are being expedited. There are three hundred troops stationed at the fort. You can expect that number to increase."

Scott was astonished. He'd heard nothing of this. The attack on Annapolis Royal would have taken place when he was at sea.

"What of the settlers in the area?"

"I believe there are between two and three thousand settlers in the area. They are of French origin and steadfastly refuse to take an oath of allegiance to the crown. They cooperate with the administration at the fort, but I believe they're playing a waiting game, hoping the French recapture Acadia."

Coxe tapped two towns on the map in the northwest.

"This is Quebec, and this is Mont-Royal on the St. Lawrence River. The French fur trade is centred here. This is the heart of French wealth and power; the danger will come from there."

Coxe sat back.

"You can expect further activity this year, and we must be prepared for all eventualities. My instructions to you, Captain, are to familiarize yourself with the regiment and prepare to see action. We will discuss further developments as they come up."

Scott found the discussion fascinating and he didn't feel the same hostility from Coxe as he had in their last meeting.

"You'll be assigned an infantry platoon. The men that came with you from Britain will be included," Coxe said. He got to his feet and Scott followed suit.

"Briefings are at eight o'clock each Monday morning. You'll meet the other officers at that time, and you will be included in the regular patrol roster. That will be all, Captain."

* * *

Over the next few days Scott explored Boston and the surrounding area. Boston was larger than he'd first thought. The heart of the town lay between the harbour and the Charles River. The streets were laid out in a geometric pattern. There were a number of parks in the centre of the town, and many stone houses built around squares similar to the more elegant parts of London. Scott was forced to admit there was much about Boston that was pleasing.

Scott made several forays into the countryside following the Charles River. There were farms along the riverbanks growing vegetables and grain crops, and cattle were to be found grazing wherever he went. After a few miles the farms and homesteads petered out giving way to forests of oak, birch, elm and other species that he didn't recognize. There was prosperity and plenty wherever he went; also opportunity, he thought.

The following Monday morning Scott attended his first briefing. Fourteen officers were present, including himself. Six were captains, the rest junior officers, most barely twenty years of age. Coxe introduced Scott to the group. A few welcomed him, but most were standoffish.

Coxe reviewed the Annapolis Royal situation and asked each officer to report on the readiness of their troopers and how quickly they could be put into the field. All reported they could move at a few days' notice, although Scott sensed many were less than enthusiastic at the prospect of being posted to Annapolis Royal. The meeting lasted a little under an hour; then Coxe dismissed the group.

As the meeting broke up, Major Coxe took Scott aside.

"Captain, several incidents of fighting have been reported to me involving the men that came with you from Britain. A sergeant seems to be the main instigator. See that it's stopped, Captain."

"I'll see to it immediately, sir."

"Very well, Captain." Coxe nodded and moved away calling for his adjutant.

The next day Scott sent for Sergeant Crammer.

"Sergeant, I've received a complaint that you are the instigator of fighting amongst the troopers in the company."

"I beg your pardon, sir. They are rough soldiers, rowdy by nature."

"Rough soldiers or not, Sergeant, there will be no more fighting. Do I make myself clear?"

"Yes, Captain."

"Dismissed." Scott knew Crammer's nature. It had its uses, but if he became a problem, he would have to do something permanent about him.

The following day Scott visited a rooming house Lieutenant Paine had recommended. The establishment was run by a Mrs. Broadhurst, a widow in her fifties. She welcomed Scott as if he were a long-lost son, and led him to a set of rooms on the south side of the building, overlooking the garden with a view of the river. The price was reasonable and included three meals per day and laundry services.

Scott agreed to take the rooms, and Mrs. Broadhurst said she would make arrangements for Scott's luggage to be brought from the army base. She also directed him to a stable close by where his horse could be cared for.

It was still early, and Scott decided to walk around Boston. He had been planning to visit the library and found it in a square close to the commercial centre of the town. It was a stone building that took up half a city block. He stepped into the foyer and the hush that inhabits all libraries settled around him. The ceiling soared thirty feet above his head. The floors were laid in polished stone and hardwood, and rows of bookshelves ran the length of the building. The library had a good selection of maps, and Scott spent an hour studying the Eastern Seaboard of North America.

It was late, and the sky was darkening as Scott left the library. He walked out the front entrance and came face-to-face with Mrs. Lockhart. He was startled and stopped abruptly. A shadow clouded her eyes for a moment, and then she flashed the same enigmatic smile he had seen on the *Raven*. She spoke to her two companions then came to Scott and held out her hand.

"Captain Scott, how good to see you."

Scott took her hand. Her grip was firm, and he felt her focus that intense gaze on him once again.

"I hope you are fully recovered from the voyage," he said.

"I've been back in Boston for a week and already the voyage and the storm seem like a long time ago. But what of you, Captain? Have you joined your new regiment? Where are you to be posted?"

"I have joined my regiment, and it seems that for the present I am to remain in Boston."

Mrs. Lockhart gestured to the couple standing behind her. "Captain Scott, may I introduce my uncle and aunt, Mr. and Mrs. Stanley Atkinson."

Mr. Atkinson shook hands with Scott. "I am pleased to meet you, Captain. Our family owes you a debt of gratitude."

Mrs. Atkinson took Scott's hand. "Captain Scott, I've heard a great deal about you. I must tell you that you are not what I expected, but I am not disappointed."

Mrs. Lockhart held up her hand. "You must forgive my aunt, Captain Scott. Directness is a trait that runs deep in the female side of our family."

Mrs. Atkinson made to speak again, but Mrs. Lockhart pre-empted her.

"Captain, you have been here but a short time, but you must tell us your impressions. Do you find Boston to your liking?"

"I do, Mrs. Lockhart. I find it most pleasing. It's larger and more elegant than I had been led to believe."

Mrs. Lockhart smiled. "What did you expect to find, Captain Scott?"

"In truth I don't know. This is my first visit to the Americas, and I had little to inform my expectations."

Mr. Atkinson put his hand on Mrs. Lockhart's arm. "I hate to interrupt my dear, but I'm afraid we must go. We're already late."

Mrs. Lockhart nodded.

"It's good to see you, Captain Scott. I hope that we shall meet again soon."

"It would be my pleasure, Mrs. Lockhart," Scott said.

Halfway down the steps Mrs. Lockhart turned.

"You must come to the governor's ball at the end of the month, Captain Scott."

"I'm afraid that I am not familiar with the event, Mrs. Lockhart."

"You must come, Captain. I'll see that you're invited. Good day, Captain."

CHAPTER FIFTEEN

SCOTT MOVED INTO MRS. BROADHURST'S house the next day. Mrs. Broadhurst took pride in her establishment and made every effort to ensure her guests felt at home. Scott's rooms were comfortable and the food excellent. There were three other gentlemen guests in the house. One was engaged in the sugar trade, the other was a lawyer new to Boston, and the third a principal in one of Boston's smaller banks. Two elderly sisters shared rooms at the back of the house. Scott encountered his fellow guests at meal times. He was polite and courteous but didn't engage them.

Scott attended the briefing the following Monday, and when he returned to Mrs. Broadhurst's, he found a note awaiting him. It was written on embossed paper and bore the seal of the governor of Massachusetts. The note formally invited Scott to attend the governor's ball on September 28, 1746, at the governor's mansion in Boston. The note was signed by the governor's private secretary.

* * *

Mrs. Broadhurst arranged to have Scott's best uniform cleaned and pressed. She also recommended a haberdashery where he purchased three white linen shirts, a neckerchief, and pair of black shoes with silver buckles. The ball was held on a Saturday evening at the governor's mansion, and guests were requested to arrive by eight o'clock. It rained throughout the day, but it let up in the evening. Scott walked the two miles to the governor's mansion, wearing his greatcoat in case the weather changed again.

As Scott approached the building, a steady stream of coaches arrived at the entrance, and footmen rushed forward to open the doors and hand the guests down safely. The foyer blazed with light and colour. It was eighty feet across. The ceiling rose fifty feet over Scott's head, and the floors were paved in polished stone. The foyer was lit by six chandeliers augmented by candelabras mounted on the walls. Scott estimated there were over a hundred people in the foyer, and the babble of conversation was almost deafening.

A servant relieved Scott of his greatcoat and directed him to the main ballroom. He followed an elderly couple as they weaved their way through the crowd; the men were elegantly dressed and the women sparkled with jewels. In the main ballroom a hundred men and women danced. A floating tide of silk and linen moving around the floor. Two hundred guests stood around the sides of the dance floor and against the walls.

The couple stepped inside and the man handed a footman a card and he formally announced them. Scott caught only the last half of his name, which sounded like Whitten. He waved the footman away and moved to the side of the door where he could observe the room.

Scott accepted a glass of what he thought was wine but turned out to be port. It was excellent, and he sipped it slowly. More people were coming into the ballroom crowding around the sides of the room and spilling onto the dance floor, and he moved back between two pillars to get out of the crush. The room was becoming uncomfortably hot, and he decided he had fulfilled his obligation to attend, and it was time to leave.

Scott finished his port and was making his way to the door when he saw Mrs. Lockhart on the dance floor. She was gliding along in the arms of a dark-haired man of about fifty, laughing and full of life, moving with the same easy grace she'd shown on the deck of the *Raven*.

Scott hadn't expected to see her, and he wasn't sure how it made him feel, but he turned and made his way to the food tables at the end of the ballroom. He took a pastry and bit into it. It was sweet and pleasant. He hadn't eaten since lunchtime, and filled a plate with sweetmeats and pastries. There was a constant press of people trying to get to the table, so he took another glass of port and stood back against the wall.

He ate most of what was on his plate and washed it down with the port. He felt better for having eaten but started to feel foolish, and he couldn't imagine what had prompted him to stay. The dance finished, and he thought it an opportune time to leave, but the press of people at the food table was intense, and it took him some minutes to work his way around it.

Scott set his plate down, and when he turned towards the door Mrs. Lockhart was standing behind him. She wore a gown of dark blue silk cut off the shoulder and low in the back. Her hair was pinned on top of her head, revealing a long slender neck and pale shoulders. She wore a necklace of rubies that blazed in the candlelight, scarlet against the whiteness of her breast.

Mrs. Lockhart extended her hand. "Captain Scott, I am so glad you could come."

Scott took her hand and inclined his head. "I must thank you for your invitation, Mrs. Lockhart."

"You must thank Governor Shirley for the invitation." She gestured to a man to her left. "May I introduce William Shirley, Governor of Massachusetts?"

Governor Shirley extended his hand. "Captain Scott, I owe you a debt of gratitude for saving the life of Mrs. Lockhart, one of Boston's most important merchants and a personal friend."

"Thank you, Governor. I am pleased to have been able to render assistance."

"If I have the right of it, Captain Scott, you did more than render assistance. Your actions were extraordinary."

Scott didn't doubt that the governor was aware of his background. His orders had been signed by the secretary to the prime minister of Britain, and documents from that office would be brought to his attention.

"You're too kind, Governor. In retrospect such events often seem more dramatic than in reality."

"Perhaps so, but we are in your debt. If I can ever be of assistance to you, Captain, you have only to ask."

Shirley smiled at Mrs. Lockhart. "I must take my leave, duties of office you understand." She smiled at him indulgently and patted his arm like a favourite uncle.

"Captain Scott." Shirley nodded and was swallowed up by the crowd.

Mrs. Lockhart smiled at Scott.

"It's strange, don't you not think, Captain? When you look around at this glittering ballroom, how far removed it seems from the deck of the *Raven*. Doesn't it make you feel that life is precious and that we shouldn't waste a moment of it?" She directed her gaze at him and in the midst of the revelry around them she seemed almost sad.

Scott held her gaze aware that people were watching them.

"It's been my experience, Mrs. Lockhart, that when one is confronted by death, life tastes all the sweeter if you have the courage to seize it."

"Do you seize life, Captain Scott? As to your courage I have no doubt."

"I've seen death many times, Mrs. Lockhart, and the saying holds true, but with time the feeling fades, and we fall back on complacency."

"Should we confront death, then, Captain, in order to appreciate life more fully?"

"It's a philosophy that some embrace. I have known soldiers who seek out danger as if it were a drug only grave peril can satisfy."

Mrs. Lockhart laughed, a soft melodic sound that welled up from inside her. "Do you think we shall find such menace lurking in the governor's palace? Do you dance, Captain?"

Scott was caught off guard by her sudden change of demeanour, and he hesitated. Mrs. Lockhart kept her gaze fixed on him, challenge in her eyes.

"I can dance, Mrs. Lockhart, although I confess it's not an activity in which I take great pleasure."

"Will you not overcome your reluctance this once, Captain? The minuet and the gavotte may present their challenges, but I doubt that we shall encounter deadly peril on the dance floor."

Scott felt the eyes of the guests on them, and he was grieved that he had let her entrap him so easily. He forced his features to show no emotion and inclined his head.

"How can I refuse, Mrs. Lockhart?"

Scott offered her his arm, and Mrs. Lockhart smiled. They walked onto the dance floor and waited for the orchestra to start. When Scott had first met Mrs. Lockhart on the *Raven*, he had thought her plain. Here in this ballroom she shone with health and vitality and exuded intelligence and strength of character. He was forced to admit that, perplexing as she was, he was strongly drawn to her.

The orchestra played the first bars of a piece Scott recognized as German. Mrs. Lockhart stepped close and put her hand on his shoulder. Scott took her right hand in his left and swept her into the dance. Scott had not spoken falsely when he said he could dance. Dancing had been drilled into him in the seven years he had spent at Dr. Lawrence's boarding school in Berwick-upon-Tweed. He had little taste for the activity but could accomplish it with panache when it suited him.

Mrs. Lockhart looked startled at first as Scott steered her effortlessly around the ballroom. Then she threw back her head and laughed with pleasure.

"Captain Scott, you never cease to surprise me."

"As I said, Mrs. Lockhart, I have mastered the art, but I am not possessed of the motivation to practice it habitually."

"We shall have to change that, Captain. Such a talent is not to be wasted."

The floor opened before them, and Scott was aware of the crowd staring. Mrs. Lockhart anticipated each turn and pause as if they had danced together all their lives. Scott was conscious of her closeness. She wore a perfume of rosemary and citrus, and beneath it he caught the musky scent of her skin. His senses flared as she brushed against him, and he drove forward recklessly. Finally the dance ended and Mrs. Lockhart laughed and clapped her hands.

"Captain Scott, I am breathless. I would not have dreamed such talent lay hidden in you." Scott inclined his head.

"You're too kind, Mrs. Lockhart."

They had no sooner stepped off the dance floor than Governor Shirley appeared out of the crowd.

"Captain Scott, Elisabeth my dear. You are to be congratulated. I believe you have caught the imagination of the room."

The governor took Mrs. Lockhart by the arm. "If I may, my dear, there is a matter of some urgency that I must speak with you on."

"Of course."

She looked at Scott, and her mood turned serious. "Thank you, Captain Scott. I can't recall when I danced as we did this evening, but I am afraid this business will not wait. Will you excuse me?"

"Of course, Mrs. Lockhart."

Mrs. Lockhart took the governor's arm.

"Captain, will you take tea with me this coming week?"

"I would be pleased to, Mrs. Lockhart," Scott said.

"I will send a note to your quarters. Until then, Captain." She grasped the governor's arm with both hands, and they disappeared into the crowd.

Scott took a glass of port and sipped it slowly, and a number of the other guests smiled and nodded. He found it hypocritical that a few minutes ago these people wouldn't give him the time of day, but a few words with Governor Shirley and Mrs. Lockhart made him acceptable. It was time to leave. He finished his port and exited the ballroom. As he waited for the footman to retrieve his coat, Major Coxe came up the stairs. He was accompanied by a woman with a large florid face, wearing a red dress and an excess of jewellery, whom Scott took to be his wife. Coxe looked startled when he saw Scott, but he recovered quickly, nodded, and led his wife into foyer.

As he walked home, Scott replayed the evening in his mind. He hadn't expected to meet Governor Shirley. The governor had been polite but reserved. Scott knew his opinion could have an influence on his career. He wouldn't curry favour and despised those who did. Nevertheless it did no harm to have made the governor's acquaintance.

Mrs. Lockhart was uppermost in his mind. He didn't understand her purpose in inviting him tonight, but he had enjoyed the evening and being close to her. The scent of her skin came back to him, and a ripple of anticipation ran through him as he thought of her invitation, but the rain came on and he hurried on towards Mrs. Broadhurst's house and a blazing fire.

* * *

At the briefing the following Monday morning Scott was assigned a troop of infantry. He was to be responsible for their well-being and discipline, and he would lead them in the field. Major Coxe indicated there had been no change in the situation at Annapolis Royal, but that they should stand ready should events move quickly. Coxe dismissed the group and drew Scott aside.

"Captain Scott, I suggest you become acquainted with your men and see to their training. It's my expectation that you will see action this year."

"What type of action, Major?"

"All in good time, Captain," Cox said, "which means when our masters in the governor's office decide to advise us." Scott started to speak again, but Coxe waved him off. "All in good time, Captain."

Scott followed the river path to Boston. It was threatening rain, and he pushed King into a gallop. He reached Mrs. Broadhurst's just ahead of a downpour to find a note waiting for him. It was sealed in a velum envelope and closed with a company seal. It contained a single page, written in an elegant hand, and he knew it was from Mrs. Lockhart before he read it. She invited Scott to take tea with her the following Thursday at 2:00 p.m. at her residence. An address in Garden Court Street was listed, and the note was signed by Mrs. Lockhart.

Scott sought out Mrs. Broadhurst in the kitchen.

"Might I have a word with you, Mrs. Broadhurst?"

"Of course, Captain Scott. Let's go into the parlour." Scott followed her to the front of the house. They took chairs on either side of the fireplace, and Scott held up the note.

"I'm invited to visit a residence in Boston, and I was wondering if you might be able to provide me with directions. The address is in the North Square area on Garden Court Street."

Mrs. Broadhurst raised an eyebrow.

"I can certainly direct you, Captain Scott. Garden Court Street is one of the more elegant neighborhoods in Boston. Might I enquire who you will be visiting?"

"I am invited to take tea with a Mrs. Lockhart. I made her acquaintance on the *Raven* during the voyage from Britain."

Mrs. Broadhurst's eyes widened.

"Mrs. Lockhart is a prominent citizen in Boston and, as I understand it, one of the richest."

"I'm afraid I have little understanding of Mrs. Lockhart's personal circumstances."

Mrs. Broadhurst smiled, and her eyes crinkled with pleasure in anticipation of an opportunity to gossip.

"Everyone knew of Mr. and Mrs. Lockhart. Mr. Lockhart was one of the most successful merchants in Boston. Mrs. Lockhart is an Atkinson, one of Boston's oldest families, also very well-to-do. They were a well-known couple and moved in the highest circles."

Mrs. Broadhurst sat up and clasped her hands together, gathering her thoughts, and after a moment she went on.

"It was very sad when Mr. Lockhart died. He was taken by some awful disease in the tropics, or so it was reported in his obituary." Mrs. Broadhurst shook her head sadly. "Such a handsome man. I saw him from time to time in the town, you know, going about his business."

Scott made to speak, but Mrs. Broadhurst was in her element.

"There were rumours, though, that all was not well." She nodded her head sagely as she parsed her knowledge out in small portions, the better to savour it. "They were married eight years, but there were no children. There was talk that Mr. Lockhart had a wandering eye, but that's not unusual when men have wealth and power."

Scott interrupted her. "When did Mr. Lockhart die precisely?"

Mrs. Broadhurst cocked her head to the side. "I believe it was a year ago now. Yes, I think it was late last fall or early winter." She smoothed her dress. "The strangest thing of all, Captain, is that after Mr. Lockhart died Mrs. Lockhart announced her intention to take over the running of his business."

Mrs. Broadhurst sat forward. "It was almost a scandal, Captain. Whoever heard of a woman taking charge of such an enterprise?"

"It's indeed unusual, Mrs. Broadhurst, but what was the upshot?"

Mrs. Broadhurst clapped her hands in delight. "That's the most astonishing thing, Captain. There was talk of ruin at first, but the enterprise has grown and prospered under her guidance."

Scott nodded. "Based on the little I know of Mrs. Lockhart that would not surprise me."

A light came into Mrs. Broadhurst's eyes, and she dropped her voice to a whisper. "If I might be so bold, Captain. It's the talk of the town that you acted to save Mrs. Lockhart's life on board the *Raven*."

She looked at him appreciatively. "The officers of the *Raven* refuse to discuss the voyage, but the common seamen speak your name with respect and admiration, I am told."

Scott demurred. "I'm sure that the events that took place on board the *Raven* are subject to exaggeration, Mrs. Broadhurst, and I don't seek to further such embellishments."

Mrs. Broadhurst smiled knowingly, nodding her head in satisfaction.

"Of course, Captain, as you wish." Mrs. Broadhurst not only accepted his reticence to speak about the voyage of the Raven, but she seemed genuinely pleased by it. "I'll be happy to direct you to Garden Court Street."

162

* * *

Mrs. Lockhart's house was a three-storey red brick townhouse at the west end of Garden Court Street, looking out onto the park. The front door was in the centre of the house with windows on either side. The door and window frames were painted black in striking contrast to the red brick. The front door was accessed by a short flight of steps, and as he approached, Scott saw there was also a basement below the main floor.

Scott pulled the chain at the side of the door and a bell sounded in the depths of the house. A moment later the door was opened by a girl dressed in a maid's uniform.

"Captain Scott to see Mrs. Lockhart."

"Yes, sir. Please step inside, sir." Scott stepped into the hallway, and the girl closed the door softly behind him.

"Let me take your coat, sir. If you'll wait a moment, I'll let Mrs. Lockhart know you're here." The girl folded his coat over her arm and disappeared into the back of the house.

The hallway was wide, the ceiling was open to the second floor and a window above the front door filled the space with light. A staircase led up to the first floor. The floors were laid in polished red oak. Oil and watercolour paintings decorated the hallway and staircase. Scott knew little of art, but the paintings were beautiful and tastefully arranged, creating a sense of warmth and comfort.

Scott heard footsteps behind him, and he saw the maid who had accompanied Mrs. Lockhart on the *Raven* coming along the hallway. She stopped and curtsied.

"Good day, Captain Scott. Mrs. Lockhart will see you in the upstairs parlour, if you would follow me, sir."

Scott followed her up to the first floor and then towards the front of the house. She knocked on a door on the right, and held it open for him.

"Thank you," Scott said.

"Yes, sir."

As the door closed behind him Scott's eyes went wide with astonishment. He was standing in a bedroom. Across the room Mrs. Lockhart stood beside the bed. She was wearing a red silk dressing gown that clung to the contours of her body. Her hair fell past her shoulders in dark waves and cast half her face in shadow. He glimpsed white teeth between her red lips. She brushed her hair back from her face and looked at Scott, then loosened the sash and let the gown slide to the floor. Her body was slender and pale in the firelight. The flare of her hips flowed smoothly into slender legs, and Scott's eye was drawn to the dark triangle at the base of her belly.

Scott stopped breathing as she stretched out her hand to him.

"Come, Captain Scott, let us see what there is to be between us?" She turned to the bed, revealing a smooth back and round bottom, and slid beneath the covers, propping herself up on one elbow.

Scott went to the bed and looked down at her.

"This is unexpected, Mrs. Lockhart."

"Yes, Captain, but I suspect it is not unwelcome." Mrs. Lockhart watched him silently as he undressed. She examined his body closely, lingering over the scars on his chest and shoulder. Scott stepped closer to the bed, and she hooded her eyes as she looked at him for a long moment; then she lifted them to meet his. She pulled the sheets back and reached out to him as he slid beneath the covers.

Mrs. Lockhart put her hand on his chest and pressed him down onto the bed. She slid on top of him and put her mouth on his. Scott ran his hands over her body, kneading her flesh, and she pressed herself against him, moaning softly. He rolled on top of her, and she wrapped her legs around him and let her breath out in a sigh as she drew him to her. He was astonished at her strength and the intensity of her want; the taste of her mouth and the smell of her skin were intoxicating and he sank into the heat of her with unbridled lust.

Scott awoke as the afternoon sun was sinking, and the room was almost dark. The sheets were crumpled where she had lain. The scent of her hair lingered on the pillow, and a shiver ran through him as he breathed it in. Scott slipped out of bed and walked to the toilet, filled the wash basin and sponged his body, and towelled himself dry. He dressed and made his way downstairs.

The maid was standing at the foot of the stairs.

"Mrs. Lockhart is waiting for you in the parlour, sir." Scott nodded and she held the door for him.

"Thank you . . ." He raised his voice to form a question.

"Mary, sir."

"Thank you, Mary."

Scott stepped into the parlour, and Mary closed the door behind him. The parlour was to the right of the front door looking out onto the park. It was richly furnished with leather sofas and chairs. A writing table stood by the window, and bookshelves lined the wall opposite. A fireplace in the wall opposite the door heated the room. A table and two chairs had been placed to the right of the fireplace, with a tea service and plates of toast and jam. A feather of steam was rising from the spout of the teapot.

Mrs. Lockhart sat facing the window. She wore a blue velvet dress over a white lace blouse. Her hair was loose and brushed forward over one shoulder. It shone in the candlelight, reflecting the colour of her eyes as she smiled at Scott.

"Will you join me for tea, Captain Scott?"

Scott crossed the room keeping his eyes on her and took the chair opposite her, and she poured tea into a china cup.

She set the cup down. "Milk, Captain Scott?"

"Thank you."

"Please help yourself to toast, Captain. The jam is excellent." She added milk to her tea and took a sip.

Mrs. Lockhart set her cup down and looked at him. "I trust you are not disappointed in me, Captain Scott?"

"Indeed, madam, far from it."

"Do you think me a harlot, Captain?"

Scott shook his head. "In truth, Mrs. Lockhart, I don't know what to think of you. I don't' believe I have encountered anyone like you before."

She laughed. Her voice had the same lyrical quality he'd found so appealing on the *Raven,* and her eyes sparkled with mischief. "Nor I you, Captain."

Scott smiled in spite of himself. "I must admit that I had not anticipated such generous hospitality, Mrs. Lockhart."

"It was hospitality well met, Captain, and I think that under the circumstances you may call me Elisabeth."

Scott smiled. "My given names are Frederick Arthur. You may use whichever pleases you."

"I think I like Captain best."

Scott was hungry, and he helped himself to toast, and the jam was indeed excellent.

"Mrs. Lockhart—Elisabeth, you are aware that my posting to Boston was not of my choosing, and you saw the conflict on board ship?"

"I'm aware of your history, Captain."

"And yet you befriended me on the *Raven* and have now extended your . . . generosity to me. I admit that I find it both refreshing and perplexing."

Mrs. Lockhart placed an elbow on the table and rested her chin on her hand.

"On the *Raven* I saw you stand up to Captain Harbin and his whole crew. If I am to be honest, I don't think you had the right of the matter, but that is neither here nor there. You stood your ground, and that strength is rare, Captain."

Scott started to speak, but she held up her hand to silence him.

"And in the sea, Captain, we learned something of each other, and I am changed since that day in a way I do not yet fully understand."

Scott cupped her face in his right hand and smiled with such warmth and tenderness that he felt his throat constrict. She leaned across the table and kissed him, and the taste of her mouth made his head spin. They both sat back, but Mrs. Lockhart held fast to his right hand.

"Will you dine with me here on Saturday evening, Captain?"

"I would be delighted to."

"Then it's agreed, seven o'clock sharp."

Mrs. Lockhart walked with him to the door, and Mary brought his coat and helped him into it. Mrs. Lockhart put her hands on his chest, stood on her toes and kissed him, and he crushed her mouth with his. After a moment they broke off, and she stepped back holding him at arm's length.

"Until Saturday, Captain. Now leave before I change my mind." She let him out the door, and it closed silently behind him.

* * *

Scott had known many women—they had loved or hated him, but none had held him. All seemed shallow in comparison to Elisabeth Lockhart. Images of her filled his mind: the colour of her eyes when she laughed, the feel of her skin against his, and her intensity when she was aroused. She occupied his thoughts as no woman had before.

On the Saturday evening Scott felt the tension between them from the moment he saw her. The food was delicious, and the wine was excellent. He watched her as she ate. She cut her food into small pieces and placed each piece in her mouth without touching her lips. He was captivated by her beauty and her grace, and by the refined sensuality she lavished on him.

In the weeks that followed, Scott took tea with Mrs. Lockhart on Wednesday afternoons and dined with her on Saturday evenings. She invited him to attend social events and introduced him to Boston society. Scott had little appetite for social mingling, and didn't suffer fools gladly, but it seemed important to her that he accompany her, so he held his tongue and played the part.

PART TWO:
A SAVAGE HEART

CHAPTER SIXTEEN

THE SHIP SWUNG AT ANCHOR. John could hear hammering on the deck above, and now he could hear the ship's bell, so he knew the time of day. The rest of the day and the night passed slowly. The cold was biting, and he stayed in his hammock, wrapped in his plaid and waited.

The next morning, at two bells in the forenoon watch, the hatch opened. "Up you come, lad."

John gathered up his hunting bag and plaid and climbed the ladder eagerly.

Higgs closed the hatch and nodded to the ladder to the main deck. "Up you go."

John climbed the ladder quickly, but by the time he got to the top he was breathing hard. Three months on board ship, smallpox, bad food, and being confined to the hold had taken their toll on him.

As John stepped out onto the main deck, he cried out in pain and put his hands over his eyes. After weeks of darkness the sunlight was agony, but after a few minutes the pain eased, and he looked around him in shock. The ship looked as if it had been torn apart by a giant. The foremast was broken off ten feet above the deck, and the top half of the mainmast was missing. The starboard rail was missing from the bow to amidships, the galley was crushed flat on one side, and holes in the main deck big enough for a man to fall through had been covered over. What astonished John the most was that the entire ship was covered in several inches of snow.

Some instinct made him look to the port side.

Land.

"Where are we? What place is this?" John said.

"The storm blew us far to the north, and we have put in here to repair the ship."

"What town is that?"

"Louisburg. They say it's a French town the British captured a year ago."

"How long—?" John started to speak but Ellis pulled him forward.

"Move along, boy." Two soldiers stood by the mainmast rubbing their hands and stamping their feet. They were dressed in the red coats of the British Army but they wore knee-length boots instead of shoes.

A line of clanspeople stood at the deckhouse waiting for their rations, and John saw Katy MacLeod and her father amongst them.

"John," she called out. Her father spoke angrily.

"Quiet, girl. You've caused enough trouble." Katy covered her mouth with her hand.

Malcolm MacLeod was standing behind her in the line, watching John intently, and when their eyes met, his mouth twisted into a sneer. He had a scar over his left eye, and John hoped he was responsible for giving it to him.

The bosun pulled John along, and he struggled to keep his feet on the slippery deck. Ellis led him to the port side where a ladder had been rigged down the ship's side.

"Where are you taking me?" He started to pull back.

Lockman, the first mate, was standing by the bridge stairs, and he called out, "We've no time to be guarding you. You can rot in the prison on the mainland till we leave."

Ellis pulled John to the rail and leaned close.

"You'll be better off ashore, lad." It was kindly said, and John looked at him in surprise.

"You could be confined below for months. Now, go when you have the chance." John nodded his thanks.

The longboat bobbed in the water at the bottom of the ladder. There were six sailors at the oars and two soldiers in the stern. John slung his hunting bag and plaid around his neck and climbed onto the ladder. By the time he was halfway down, his legs were shaking, and he tightened his grip and went down slowly. One of the soldiers took his arm as he stepped down into the boat, and he sat down thankfully on the gunnels. It was bitterly cold, and he wrapped his plaid around his shoulders and turned his back to the wind.

"Give way," The soldier next to him called, and as the boat pulled away John looked back. The damage to the ship was extensive. It would take weeks if not months to repair, and he shuddered at the thought of being confined in the hold all that time. Katy MacLeod waved cheerily, but Malcolm stepped up behind her, and she turned away.

* * *

Ten or twelve ships lay at anchor, and on the north side of the harbour, two ships were careened on the beach and men were working on the hulls. Along the northwest shore, dozens of fishing boats were pulled up on the beach, and men were offloading their catch. Wooden buildings were strung out along the shore for a mile or more; behind them, row upon row of drying racks had been set up, filled with fish. John couldn't estimate how much fish the boats brought in each day, but it had to be hundreds of tons.

John turned to the soldier next to him. "What kind of fish are these?"

"Cod, boy. Cod is the reason this town is here." The soldier to his left spoke to him. He was the oldest and seemed to be in charge.

"You're to go to the prison in the barracks."

"How long will you keep me there?"

"Till your ship is repaired."

"What will—?"

"Enough talk now," he said.

They were making for a gate in the stone wall that surrounded the town, and as the boat ran up the beach two men stepped ashore and held it fast.

"Come on, boy." The older soldier climbed onto the beach. John followed. He marvelled at the feel of dry land, but he had to set his feet apart to keep from falling over. One of the soldiers took his arm.

"Move along now." John had difficulty walking, and two soldiers held his arms, laughing at his antics as they pulled him along.

"Don't have your land legs yet, boy," the older soldier said. "It'll take a day or two." John was relieved that it wasn't caused by the smallpox or scurvy.

They made their way up the beach, and as he passed through the gate, John couldn't help but notice that the wall was covered in wooden planks. He'd never seen anything like it before.

"Why is the wall covered in wood?" he asked the older soldier, who only shook his head.

One of the younger soldiers answered. "The sea water and the rain leach the mortar out of the wall. The wood protects it. I work as a mason on my free days." He seemed proud of the opportunity to show off his knowledge.

John was overwhelmed by the sights and sounds of the town, and he looked around trying to take it all in. Inside the wall a row of buildings followed the curve of the shore for a mile; they were built of blue-grey stone and wood with wooden tiles on the roofs. Most buildings had two floors with private dwellings, taverns, and warehouses, standing side by side. It was obvious that the town had been under siege. Many buildings had been damaged. Some had holes in the walls and roofs, and a few had been entirely demolished.

They led John into a narrow street running uphill away from the harbour. The houses were separated by wooden fences enclosing gardens and livestock pens. He struggled on the snow-covered cobbles, making heavy going of the hill. Near the top they passed three houses with red crosses painted on their doors. John caught up with the old soldier.

"Is there plague in the town?"

The man shook his head. "There was smallpox weeks ago, but they say it has run its course."

He frowned, and John thought that he might have lost family or friends and didn't press him. He wondered if the townspeople knew there was smallpox on the *Orion,* but he thought it wouldn't be wise to mention it.

A large red stone building dominated the top of the hill. John had seen it from the harbour, but close up it was more impressive. It was solidly built with glazed windows, but it had an austere look about it. It was surrounded by a wide ditch, and the front gate was accessed via a stone bridge. Two soldiers stood guard at the entrance, and John guessed this must be a military barracks of some kind.

The old soldier led them across the bridge.

"Who goes there?" the guard called out. Both guards looked cold and bored and the challenge was only a formality.

"Patrol bringing a prisoner from the ship *Orion*."

"Enter."

They passed into a tunnel that ran right through the building. To the right a door opened into a large high-ceilinged room with bunks ranged around the walls. Half a dozen soldiers sat at a table eating. The wave of heat from the open door and the smell of cooking fish made John realize how cold and hungry he was. They emerged into a triangular enclosure formed by the barracks and the outer wall of the town. A parapet ran around the top of the wall with cannons spaced every hundred feet. The north side of the enclosure was formed by an extension running at right angles from the main building like a bridge with three arches thirty feet high. The ends of the arches had been walled in stone, and each had a wooden door in the centre and a barred window to one side. There was a smaller arch built into the outside wall, and soldiers were passing back and forth into the dark interior.

The soldiers led John to the first arch. The door was secured by an iron bar mounted on a pin on the right-hand door that dropped into a slot on the left door. The old soldier lifted the bar and pulled the door open, and the other soldiers pushed John towards the door.

"What is this place?"

"No more talk now." They pushed him inside and pulled the door shut behind him.

* * *

John found himself in a large square room with a round ceiling formed by the arch. Three steps led down to a dirt floor. A barred window to the right of the door let in daylight, and he was astonished to see a fireplace in the west wall with a fire burning in the grate.

The room had gone quiet, and a dozen men stared at him with a mixture of curiosity and hostility. Most were between thirty and forty years of age. Six men sitting to the left of the fire wore military uniforms. Two men on the right were dressed in what had once been good quality clothes though they were now no more than rags, and John took them to be merchants of some kind.

Two men stood out from the rest; although he had never seen one before, John knew immediately that these men were native Indians. They were not much older than he was. They had strong open faces, clean features, and light brown skin. They wore their hair in long braids and dressed in a combination of animal skins and brightly coloured cloth garments. One of them was big with a barrel chest and powerful arms. The other was lean and bony, but despite the differences, John was sure they were brothers. He was fascinated by them. They didn't seem to take offense, and studied him in return.

One of the men to the right of the fire spoke to John in French. "Who are you? We have not seen you before."

John was out of practice speaking French and struggled with the words. "I am John Wallace. I was brought here from the ship *Orion*, which lies in the harbour."

"Another mouth to feed," one of the soldiers chimed in, in English.

"Pay no heed to them. They're English and don't like anybody."

John was shivering violently, and he moved towards the fire. One of the Indians moved and made space for him. John sat on his heels, holding his hands to the fire, and almost cried out in pain as the heat began to seep into his bones. The young Indian sat cross-legged on the floor beside him. He was lean and muscular with an angular face and deep brown eyes. He seemed to find everything amusing, and when John looked at him he couldn't help but smile.

"Thank you," he said.

The Indian spoke good French, but his accent made some words difficult to understand.

"The French don't like you because they think you're British. The British captured Louisburg a year ago, and the French hate them. The British don't like you because they think you're French. The British also don't like you because another prisoner means less food, but there's always enough food."

His face broke into a grin. "I am Louis Pictou. This is my brother Mathieu Pictou. We are Mi'kmaq." To John's surprise, Louis now spoke in English.

"I am John Wallace." They shook hands, and John liked him immediately. Mathieu nodded at John but didn't speak.

Louis produced a loaf of bread from a bag at this side and offered it to John. John looked at him in surprise and Louis nodded.

"Eat. You look like your starving."

"Thank you again." The bread was heavy and almost black, and when he broke it open, it was still moist inside. He took a bite, and he could taste fat, salt, and grains of some sort that he crunched with his teeth. He ate the whole loaf without stopping, much to Louis's amusement.

When he finished, he looked at Louis.

"Thank you for the food. I've not eaten well of late."

"Where have you come from?"

"I came from Scotland."

"I don't know this place Scotland. Is it in the land of the British?"

"It was conquered by the British a year ago. They killed some of my family and forced me onto the ship."

"Why have they brought you to this place?"

"The ship was damaged in a storm. It lies in the harbour being repaired."

"Why are you a prisoner?"

"I got into a fight with a man on the ship, and they imprisoned me in the hold. Whatever happens now, I'm glad to be off the ship."

John looked at Mathieu and back to Louis. "Why are you and your brother prisoners, and where did you learn to speak English?"

"Our home is to the south in the place the French call Acadia. I learned the French language there and English when I was small. A year ago a sickness came to our village." As he spoke a change came over him, and the laughter left his eyes.

"The British brought the sickness to our village and to other villages. Many died. They burned with fever and their lungs filled with water till they choked. The British wanted revenge on us because we fought against them with the French. They wanted us all to die, but we didn't die." Anger burned in his eyes as he spoke.

Louis went quiet. John waited for a moment then asked, "How did you come to be in this place?"

"We came north to trade with the French. Furs for weapons and tools. We were trapped in the town when the British attacked, and when the town surrendered, they locked us in this prison with the French and the English dogs."

Louis looked at the British soldiers, and his face broke into a grin again.

"Our home is many days journey to the south, across the salt water to the mainland."

John looked at him in surprise. "Are we on an island here?"

"The island is large, and it is an easy crossing to the mainland if the weather is good. Our home is on the bay where the ocean races. The British call it

Fundy. They have a fort to the south of our village that has changed hands between the British and the French many times. My father traded with the British, and from the children of the soldiers I learned to speak their language."

They were interrupted by sound of the bar being lifted. The door swung open, and three soldiers entered. Two stayed by the door. Two soldiers carried an iron pot. The steam leaking from the lid filled the cell with the smell of cooked fish. The third man carried a basket of loaves like the bread Louis had given John. John's mouth watered at the smell of hot food, and in spite of eating the bread, his stomach growled. The soldiers set the pot and the bread on the floor and left the cell.

The prisoners gathered round, and one of the men John had taken for a merchant took charge of the food. He stirred the contents of the pot with a ladle, and John thought he had never smelt anything so good in his life. A prisoner produced a basket of wooden bowls and handed one to the merchant and he filled it with soup and handed it to the first man in line. The other merchant handed him a loaf of bread, and he retreated to his place by the fire to eat.

When all the other prisoners had received their ration, the merchant turned to where John, Louis, and Mathieu were sitting, and held out a bowl of soup to John. "Eat. You look like you need it."

John lifted the bowl to his mouth. The soup burned his lips, but he ignored it. It was codfish soup; it was more like stew than soup and heavily salted. The other merchant handed him a loaf of bread. He broke a piece off, dipped it in the soup and ate, relishing every bite. He knew that he should save some bread for later, but he couldn't help himself and ate the soup and the loaf at one sitting.

When he finished, he sat back against the wall and looked around. There was no talk as the prisoners ate. Louis sat next to him, and John waited until he'd finished.

"How long have you been here?"

"The town surrendered in summer last year. Many ships came and took the French people away. They told us they were sent to their own country across the big sea. The British said we weren't to be trusted and put us here."

"You've been here for over a year?"

"We have been here too long."

John motioned to the men who had distributed the food. "What of these men?"

"They're the last of the French. They will be sent to their own country when a ship comes to take them."

"What will they do with you? They can't keep you here forever."

"We are not French. They'll not send us on ships. Perhaps they'll kill us. The British kill many prisoners."

"I know that well enough."

John lifted his chin to the soldiers.

"Why're they here?"

"They stole food, wine or tobacco, and they are put here as punishment." Louis's face broke into a grin. "The French and the English hate each other. The soldiers think they're too good to be in the same prison with the French and with us."

They sat for a while without talking, and John leaned his head back against the wall. The heat from the fire seeped into him and with food in his belly he began to feel drowsy. He tried to stay alert. He knew he had to have his wits about him if he was to survive, but in spite of himself he curled up on the floor and slept.

* * *

John awoke as the cell door opened. Every muscle in his body hurt and his hip and back were numb. He saw daylight through the door and realized that he must have slept the rest of the previous day and through the night. No wonder his back ached, but he felt rested and stronger than he had in a long time.

Louis sat close by.

"You slept as if you were dead, but I'm glad you're not dead. We would have to bury you, and it's difficult to dig in the frozen ground." Louis was grinning, and John grinned with him.

Two soldiers stood outside the door muskets resting against the wall. They seemed little concerned the prisoners would try to escape. A third soldier stepped into the cell. He was in his thirties, unshaven and running to fat. From the surly expression on his face John guessed he wasn't fond of guard duty.

"Latrine detail, get moving." None of the prisoners moved, and the man walked into the cell and pointed at Louis and Mathieu.

"You two and you, boy." He pointed at John, and Louis grinned as he got to his feet.

Louis nudged John. "Come. At least we get out of the cell for a while."

John got to his feet, but it took an effort to walk straight. There were four latrine buckets in the cell. Louis picked one up, and John did the same. The bucket was heavy, and he took care not to spill the contents on his boots. Mathieu took one bucket in each hand, holding them out from his body as if they weighed nothing.

Louis turned right outside the door and entered the small archway John had seen the day before. John stopped inside to let his eyes get used to the dark.

"Get a move on, boy." One of the soldiers pushed him, and he stumbled, spilling the some of the contents of the bucket on the floor. When his eyes became accustomed to the dim light, he realized that the chamber was a toilet built into the outer wall of the town. The floor sloped down to the northwest where a pool of stagnant water covered the corner of the chamber. An arched passageway in the north wall was half-submerged in the pool, and an iron grill blocked the opening. This must be the outflow. John guessed it ran under the wall and exited outside the town.

They emptied their buckets in the pool and the guard left the chamber.

"Get the rest done," he said over his shoulder.

"It's our task to clean the mess every day." Mathieu's eyes were laughing. It was the first time that John had heard him speak, and he had a deep voice that filled the chamber.

Louis and Mathieu filled their buckets from the pool and started to wash down the floor, flushing the accumulated waste into the pool, and John followed their lead. It was an unpleasant task, and they worked hard, wanting it done quickly.

"Do the prisoners take turns doing this?"

Mathieu looked up. "No, it's a pleasure reserved for us alone."

Louis laughed. "The British must dislike you as much as us to honour you with this job." His laughter was so infectious that John couldn't help but join in.

When they were done, John went to the pool and crouched down, looking along the passageway. The passageway ran under the wall, to the north. He could see the sun reflecting off the water at the far end. Louis crouched down beside him.

"Where does it go?"

"It connects to a swamp on the outside of the wall."

"Is it deep?"

"Why don't you take a swim and see for yourself? You'll smell so bad the British will be forced to set you free." Louis seemed delighted at the idea and grinned from ear to ear.

"Come, enough foolishness now." Mathieu's voice boomed out behind them. They picked up their buckets, and the guard escorted them back to the cell.

John sat beside Louis, warming himself by the fire, Mathieu close by. Neither one seemed bothered by the cold. He thought that growing up in this land, they had become inured to it. They also looked healthier than the other prisoners. They had strong white teeth, smooth skin, and an appearance of well-being. Most of the men in the cell were missing half their teeth. The ones they had left were rotting, and they looked pale and unhealthy.

John's thoughts were interrupted by the sound of the bar being lifted as the soldiers brought the food. They followed the same routine. The merchants ladled out the soup and distributed the bread. It was the same fish stew with fish heads floating in it. The bread was freshly baked, and John sat with Louis and Mathieu and ate without speaking. With a stomach full of hot food and well rested, he felt stronger than he had in months.

CHAPTER SEVENTEEN

THE DAYS FOLLOWED THE SAME pattern. Each morning John, Louis, and Mathieu would clean the toilets, a task that took an hour to complete. Food was brought at midday, and they were locked in the cell for the rest of the day. Some of the English prisoners worked repairing the town walls; others cut firewood for the barracks and the prison. At first John was content to be warm and have a full belly, but as his strength returned, he started to gather more information about his surroundings.

At the end of his first week he approached the French merchant who dished out the soup each day.

"I'm John Wallace, could I speak with you?"

"Of course. I am Justinien de La Tour, and this is my friend Pierre Le Blanc." La Tour was in his forties, tall and lean. His face was deeply lined, and he had dark thinning hair and grey eyes. Le Blanc was younger, no more than thirty, big boned and inclined to fat, but his flesh hung loosely on his bones as if he'd been starved. He had a round face and a turned-down mouth that gave him a sour look. Despite his appearance, John found he had a lively intelligence and a dark sense of humour.

John sat against the wall. "Do you know what the date is?"

They both laughed and de La Tour responded, "It is October 12, if I am not mistaken."

John thought about that. Somehow it didn't seem right. He'd left Scotland three months before, but it felt as if years had passed.

"You lose track of time in prison. One day blends into another."

"How long have you been here?"

"Since the town fell to the British. Over a year."

John struggled to find the right words in French, but they didn't seem to mind, and they corrected his grammar and pronunciation.

John spoke with them over the following days, and he gradually developed a picture of what had happened in Louisburg. Louisburg was the centre of the French fishing industry here in Ile Royale, as they called it. France was a Catholic country as were Spain and Italy. Catholics don't eat meat on Fridays, and the traditional substitute was fish. This created a huge demand for fish that couldn't be met by the European fishing fleets.

John tried to remember his geography lessons from the academy in Crieff. He had learned little about the colonies, and he struggled to understand where Louisburg was. De La Tour did his best to explain.

"Louisburg is on the island the French call Ile Royale." He used a stick to draw a rough map of North America on the floor. John recognized the main features of the Eastern Seaboard and a few of the larger communities like Boston.

De La Tour drew a more detailed map and pointed out the important towns and fortresses in French Canada—Quebec and Mont-Royal, Louisburg, Port Royal, and the Bay of Fundy in Acadia to the south. He also indicated Boston, from where the British had launched their attack on Louisburg.

John brought the discussion back to Louisburg.

"Why do the British want Louisburg?"

"The St. Lawrence is the main entry into the French territories. The British are afraid France will use Louisburg as a base to recapture Acadia and Port Royal. I fear they have ambitions to rule all the French territories one day."

John was struggling to understand all that de La Tour told him. "What happened when the British captured the town?"

"The siege went on for months. The town has strong defenses against a sea attack, but the British landed down the coast and approached overland, attacking where the defenses are weakest. They captured the north fort and turned the guns on the town; after that it was only a matter of time until the town capitulated."

John shook his head.

"What happened to the French who lived in Louisburg?"

"The British put them on ships and sent them back to France."

"How many people?"

"Almost five thousand in all. Some had been here all of their lives and will be destitute in France."

"Why didn't they put you and Pierre on a ship?"

"Pierre and I protested the way that the British treated the residents, stripping them of their belongings and treating them like criminals. The commander said we were inciting unrest and locked us up in here."

"What will happen to you?"

"I do not know. I think when it suits them, they will send us back to France."

De La Tour didn't seem concerned about what would happen to him.

"What will you do in France?"

"I've been trading with France for over ten years. I have property in Bordeaux, and I can carry on my business from there."

"When will they send you back?"

"They don't tell us such things, but soon the ice will block the passage, and we will be here until spring."

His talks with de La Tour helped John understand where Louisburg was located and something of the conflict with the British. He knew that if he was to survive, he must learn everything he could about this land and its people.

* * *

On the fourth day, John was sitting with the Frenchmen when the door opened and discussion stopped as two guards entered. Both men were in their twenties. Both had the ruddy complexions of drinkers and the arrogant swagger of bullies.

"Shit detail. Get moving, you savages." The elder of the two men looked at Louis and Mathieu. His voice was surly and antagonistic. Louis and Mathieu got to their feet and John rose along with them. The soldier looked at John.

"This must be the convict." He spoke over his shoulder to his comrade. "What do we do with this one, Harry?" John bristled at being called a convict but held his tongue.

"Three shit cleaners are better than two, and we can get back to the guard-house and a mug of ale all the sooner."

As they started towards the door, the second soldier, Harry, drove the butt of his musket into Mathieu's back.

"Faster, you savages," he shouted. Mathieu turned to face him. His eyes glinting with hatred. Louis put his hand on his shoulder and said something to him in the Mi'kmaq language. Harry hawked and spat in Mathieu's face and stood back hefting his musket. Mathieu let out a cry of rage and lunged for him, but Louis grabbed his arm and shouted something in Mi'kmaq that made him stop.

Harry sneered.

"Come and get me, you stinking savage." He balanced on the balls of his feet musket at the ready. Louis was talking to Mathieu and trying to pull him away, but Mathieu stared at Harry, unblinking.

John put his hand on Mathieu's shoulder. "Stop, Mathieu." John spoke in French. "This isn't the time."

Mathieu looked at John, and there was murderous rage in his eyes.

"There will be another time, my friend." He pushed him gently.

Something struck John between the shoulder blades, sending him stumbling forward, grunting in pain.

"The boy's an Indian lover, so he should be treated like an Indian." The second guard called out. Mathieu caught John's arm to stop him falling. It felt as if his arm was being crushed in a mangle.

"Enough, Mathieu." Mathieu let go and John's arm tingled as the blood rushed back.

"There will be another day," Mathieu said, and wiped the spittle from his face with his sleeve.

The soldiers followed them out of the cell, muskets at the ready. The other guards watched with blank faces, and John sensed they were afraid of Harry and his friend.

As they entered the toilet, John spoke quietly to Louis. "Who are these men?"

"Their names are Daniel Brown and Harry Pitt. They've tried to make us fight before. It gets worse as time goes on."

Mathieu looked up from his work. "When it's time, I will kill them both." He spoke quietly, but the resolve in his voice was chilling

The guards rotated every four days, changing between patrolling the outer wall, gate duty, and guarding the prisoners. It was eight days before John saw Brown and Pitt again. They brought the food at midday and immediately started to provoke the brothers. They kept up a constant barrage of insults and jibes, pushing and prodding them with their muskets. Pitt was the leader. He seemed to hate the brothers or Indians in general, and lost no opportunity to insult them, particularly Mathieu. Neither Mathieu nor Louis reacted, and that seemed to infuriate them more, and John was relieved when the guard changed.

The next day the level of the pool had risen till it flooded most of the chamber. They looked at each other in surprise, and Louis asked John, "What does it mean?"

"Something must be blocking the outflow outside the wall."

John went to the entrance. "Guard, guard."

"What do you want? Get on with your work."

"The toilet's flooded. Come and look." Two soldiers came to the door, and one peered inside wrinkling his nose at the smell.

He called to his comrade at the door. "Get the sergeant, quick." The soldier waved and hurried off along the back of the building.

The guard walked a few paces from the toilet door and leaned on his musket.

"What now," John said.

"We wait. We always need to have orders, even when it has to do with a flood of shit."

A few minutes later the sergeant came hurrying along the path.

"Out of my way," He pushed his way past John into the toilet and emerged a minute later. John was standing in the entrance, and the sergeant grabbed him by his lapels and put his face close to him.

"I told you to stay out of my way." The sergeant's breath stunk of ale, and his face was flushed with anger. John's eyes flew wide with shock, and the sergeant pushed him back against the wall.

The sergeant stepped away from the door.

"Ice has built up outside the wall. It needs to be cleared away or the whole place will stink of shit." He pointed to John and the brothers. "Take these jailbirds and break up the ice and be quick about it." Then he strode away towards the guardhouse.

They waited while the guards discussed what they were to do next.

"You look as if you have seen a ghost." Louis laughed. "The sergeant is a dog that barks but doesn't bite."

"He has a rash on his neck. He has a drinker's face that hides it, but when I was close to him, I saw it. I think the sergeant has smallpox"

"Are you sure?" Louis looked alarmed.

"I've seen the marks before."

Louis started to speak, but the guards led them out of the barracks and across the bridge. The weather was cold and clear, and John had a good view of the town and the ships in the harbour. He searched for the *Orion* and finally found her anchored on the far side of the harbour. He couldn't tell what condition she was in, but her masts had been replaced, and a barge or water boat was tied alongside. John wondered how things were for Katy and Old MacLeod, and it occurred to him that he hadn't thought about them since he'd been in the prison.

His thoughts were interrupted by the guard. "Move. Let's get this over with."

One soldier led them down towards the harbour with the second guard trailing behind. They made their way through the streets for ten minutes, and emerged onto the clear ground between the houses and the harbour wall, and turned towards the north bastion. The bastion was a massive stone construction with gun apertures every twenty feet, and John could see the muzzle of a cannon peeking out from every one.

The north gate ran between the bastion and the harbour wall. It was twelve feet high, built of wood reinforced with iron braces. The gatehouse was built into the seawall, and there was a guard at the door.

"Wait here." The guard disappeared into the gatehouse. He emerged a few minutes later carrying two shovels and a pickaxe and handed them to John and the brothers.

"Open up," he called. The guard pulled the gate back, and they filed out. The gate swung shut behind them, and John heard the bar slide into place. On the outside the gate was still pitted and fire-blackened from the siege.

The lead guard barked an order. "This way." He turned left along the town wall.

John followed and as soon as he stepped off the track he sank knee-deep in snow. It was a mile to where the toilet drain came through the wall. In places, they had to dig their way through snowdrifts that reached the top of the wall, and it took an hour to reach the drain. It was almost completely blocked with snow.

"Get it cleared," the lead guard barked.

John and Louis shovelled snow away from the entrance, and Mathieu used the pickaxe to break up the ice inside the tunnel. He swung the pickaxe as if it was a child's toy, throwing out stones and frozen dirt so quickly that John and Louis had to scramble to keep up with him. It was hard work, but after weeks of captivity it felt good to move, and John began to warm up.

They cleared the ice and snow away until they reached an iron grating similar to the one inside the toilet and found the mouth of the tunnel frozen solid with ice. The tunnel had been damaged by cannon fire and one side had collapsed, adding to the blockage.

"We have to break the ice dam," John said.

"I'll do it," Mathieu said.

Mathieu held onto the grating while he hacked at the ice with the pick. With four strokes he cut out a large chunk and water started to flow over the top of the ice, carrying the latrine stench with it. The ice was thick, but once the surface was broken, it came away easily. Mathieu drove the pickaxe into the ice around the grating and pulled back with all his weight. There was a loud crack and the grating broke away from the wall on one side. The ice sheet shattered, and water surged out of the tunnel.

Mathieu sank chest deep in the water. He dropped the pickaxe and grabbed the grating and pulled himself towards the side of the tunnel. John leaned into the tunnel and Mathieu grasped his hand and heaved himself out of water. The ice blockage was broken, and the volume of water coming out of the tunnel was diminishing, but the smell of sewage was still overwhelming. The senior guard glanced into the tunnel.

"Good enough. Now back to the barracks with you." The stench had driven the guards back, and John realized they hadn't seen the damage to the grating.

As they headed back John looked at the landscape around the town. The area around the toilet outlet was swampy. Beyond that the snow had been blown into drifts like frozen waves rolling away to the treeline.

"No one could survive out there." He spoke his thoughts out loud without realizing it.

Louis looked at him sharply. "The British cannot leave their towns in winter. It's not so for the Mi'kmaq."

"What do you mean?"

"This is our land, and we travel it as we wish." John started to speak, but the guard called out. "Get a move on, boy." He gave John a push, and he fell in behind Mathieu.

They hurried back to the barracks, and the guards went straight to guard-room fire. Three other soldiers led them back to the toilet.

"Get it cleaned."

"Can we eat first?"

"You can eat when the work's done. Now, get on with it."

The water in the toilet had dropped to its normal level, and the three of them set to work. On impulse John went to the grating and examined it closely. The ends of the grating were anchored in the walls and ceiling, and the stonework and mortar were in good condition.

Louis squatted beside him.

"The bars are strong. It took cannon fire to break the outer grating."

"There will be no cannon fire in here, I think," John said.

"If you want to escape, you could crawl under the bars." Louis got to his feet and threw a bucket of water onto the floor, laughing as Mathieu jumped back in alarm.

John laughed with him, but he returned to the grating. As far as he could see, the grating wasn't fixed to the floor of the tunnel. An iron bar ran along the bottom of the grating, but there was a six inch gap between the bar and the floor stones. The floor stones were set less tightly than the walls. He picked at the mortar with his finger, and it came away easily. Then he crouched down and looked through the bars. The light was poor, but he saw enough to pique his interest.

"Bring the mop."

"Are we cleaning inside the tunnel now too?" Louis said. "Maybe we should ask the guards' permission."

John ignored him and slid the mop handle through the grating and prodded the floor. The floor stones only extended a foot past the grating. Beyond that the handle sank into mud.

John sat back on his haunches.

"If we had a tool, we could dig out the stones and slide under the grating. The grating at the far end is loose, and we could pass through."

"We don't have a tool, and the soldiers wouldn't let us dig out the stones."
Louis was enjoying himself.

John marvelled at Louis's ability to find amusement in this situation, but
it brought him back to reality and his enthusiasm evaporated.

"You're right, Louis. Where would we go? How would we survive in this
frozen land?"

"We would go to my people."

John looked at him in surprise. "How could you survive out there? I've
never known such cold."

"The winter is deadly, but if you know its ways, you needn't fear it."

"How far is it to your village?"

"It is many days' travel. We have made this journey before."

John looked at the grate. "First we'd have to get out of this prison, but
for now we have to clean the shit or the guards will wonder what we've
been up to."

When they entered the cell, John was shivering uncontrollably. He sat
by the fire and pulled his plaid around him. Louis and Mathieu sat close by.
Steam was coming from Mathieu's clothes, but he showed no discomfort
from having been up to his chest in icy water. John would have asked Louis
about it, but he was too tired to speak. The warmth from the fire crept into
him, and he drifted off to sleep.

John awakened when the food arrived, and he got to his feet still groggy
from sleep and stood in line with Louis and Mathieu. The fish stew burned
its way down into his belly, putting warmth back into him, and he ate half
his bread and put the rest in his hunting bag for later.

When de La Tour had finished, he brought his food and sat beside John.

"I heard you were outside the barracks today?"

"We cleared a blockage from the toilet drain, and almost froze to death,
so the shit can flow freely."

De La Tour flashed a smile then became serious. "Did you see any sign
of sickness in the town?"

John looked at him sharply. "Why do you ask?"

"I overheard the guards speaking of it fearfully."

John remembered the panic on the *Orion* when sickness broke out. He
was reluctant to speak of it, but it would make itself plain soon enough.

"There are houses with red crosses on the doors."

De La Tour swore under his breath.

"There's more. I saw the marks of smallpox on the sergeant's neck this morning."

"How do you know it's smallpox?"

"My father described the symptoms to me, and there was smallpox on the *Orion*, the ship that brought me here."

De La Tour sucked in his breath.

"There were deaths on the ship?"

"Half the crew and many passengers. I had it, but I got better. They say if you survive, it doesn't come again."

De La Tour looked around the cell. "If there's plague in the town, the ship that will take us to France won't enter the harbour. If we do not die from smallpox, we'll be trapped here until next year's sailing season."

"If it's the same sickness, many will die."

De La Tour started to get to his feet. "It would be best not to speak of this."

John nodded and de La Tour made his way back to his place on the other side of the fire.

* * *

The next morning when they were called to do latrine duty, John was dismayed to see Brown and Pitt waiting for them. Pitt was surly as ever, but Brown was quiet and withdrawn. The latrine was in poor condition, and it took over an hour to clean.

Brown and Pitt stood by the entrance, and when they were finished John started to walk back to the cell.

"Where do you think you are going?" Brown stepped in front of him. "I didn't say you were done." John stopped and Brown's face twisted into a sneer. "I need to inspect the latrine to see what you've done—" Brown bent over in a fit of coughing. He put his hand on the wall to steady himself then slumped into the snow, his musket clattering down beside him. Pitt looked around in alarm and took a step towards Brown then stopped, staring. John saw it too. Brown's head had rolled to the side exposing a red rash on his neck.

Pitt took two steps back. "You two pick him up and take him to the infirmary." He pointed at Louis and Mathieu, but neither one moved.

Pitt cocked his musket and aimed it at Mathieu. "Pick him up or I'll drop you where you stand, you heathen savage."

Mathieu stared at Pitt, and for a moment John thought that he would attack him in spite of the musket levelled at his chest. John bent down to take hold of Brown and his hand touched the handle of his bayonet. Brown's skin was pasty, and he was glassy-eyed with fever.

"Pick him up," Pitt screamed. John rolled Brown over onto his back and slid the bayonet out of its scabbard and pushed it into the snow beneath him.

Pitt's attention was focused on Mathieu, and Louis touched his arm and spoke to him in Mi'kmaq. Mathieu looked at Louis then took Brown's arm. Louis took his feet and Pitt called out to the guards at the cell. "Lock this one up," he said and pointed to John.

John sat by the fire and ate some of his bread. The brothers returned half an hour later, and Louis sat by him.

"We took the guard to the hospital. He'll die, and I won't be able to take revenge for his insults." John was astonished that revenge was the thing uppermost in Louis's mind.

"Did others have the fever?"

Louis nodded. "The hospital was full of sick and dying. There was no room for the English dog, so we left him on the steps."

The food didn't come until two hours past midday. It was brought by guards John hadn't seen before. The prisoners were grumbling about the delay as de La Tour dished out the fish stew. When they finished, de La Tour tried to engage the guards in conversation, but they wouldn't be drawn out. They took the cooking pot and bread basket and left. De La Tour looked at John and shook his head.

It was still dark when John awoke the next morning, but dawn was not far away. He went to the latrine bucket to relieve himself and stood stretching his back. Then he went to the fire, stepping carefully in the half light. The brothers lay side by side by the fire, and something about Mathieu made him stop. He lay on his back motionless with one arm thrown across his chest, and in the firelight John saw a sheen of sweat on his face. He crouched down and touched his forehead. Mathieu was burning with fever, and a shudder ran through him at John's touch, but he didn't wake.

Louis was a few feet away, curled up into a ball on the floor. John shook him gently, and he moaned and rolled over. His head fell to the side, and

John felt his blood run cold. A ring of red dots ran around Louis's neck and spread up one side of his face.

John sat on his heels in shock. "Smallpox," he whispered.

There was a gasp from across the cell. One of the soldiers was staring at him. His eyes went wide, and he cried out. "Smallpox. The Indians have smallpox. We are all going to die."

In a moment the other prisoners were on their feet, shouting in panic. One started to bang on the door with his fists, shouting in fear. "Smallpox. The Indians have the plague. Let us out of here." Others joined him, pounding on the door and screaming to be let out.

John piled wood onto the fire and prodded it till it threw enough light to see. Mathieu was burning with fever, and he was shivering at the same time. It was the same as John had experienced, but Mathieu was worse. John soaked a cloth in the water bucket and wiped his face. He moaned but didn't wake. Louis was sleeping. His breathing was ragged. His fever was less severe, and he showed no sign of the chills that wracked Mathieu.

De La Tour called out, "Do they have the smallpox?"

"I think so," John said.

One of the soldiers shouted, "You'll catch it. Stay back." John looked at him, and there was terror in his eyes.

"I had smallpox on the ship. They say you don't get it twice."

"I wouldn't take the chance."

"Someone must see to them," John said.

One of the soldiers, called Ogden, was pounding on the door with a stick. He stopped and looked across the cell. "The Indians brought this on us."

He hefted the stick in his hand, terror and fury in his eyes. John got to his feet and looked about for something to defend himself with, but the bar lifted and the door swung open. Four soldiers with bayonets fixed pushed the prisoners back, but they didn't enter the cell. The sergeant forced his way into the cell, and the prisoners surrounded him like a pack of dogs shouting and screaming to be let out.

"Quiet," the sergeant shouted, and they fell silent. "What's to do here?"

The prisoners all started to talk at once.

"Quiet. You." He pointed at Ogden. "What's this about?"

"The Indians have smallpox," Ogden said. "You must let us out or we'll all die."

The sergeant looked at the brothers, then around the cell. "There's smallpox in the town and in the barracks. Until it's over no one will leave the cell except to empty the slop buckets."

Ogden started forward, hefting the firewood in his hand. "You have to let us out. The Indians will make us sick."

The sergeant stepped back. "Troopers."

The soldiers pushed Ogden back with their bayonets and pulled the door shut, and the locking bar rang like a bell as it dropped into place.

The prisoners looked at each other in silent confusion, and Ogden turned on John. "It's their fault. They brought this on us."

Ogden was working himself up waving the stick around threateningly. John put himself between Mathieu and Ogden.

Then de La Tour stepped forward. "They didn't bring the sickness here. There was smallpox in the town during the siege. No one knows how it spreads, but it's best not to get close to someone who's sick."

Ogden stepped back alarmed, and the others took their lead from him and moved to the other side of the fire.

John breathed a sigh of relief and turned his attention back to the brothers. Louis's eyes were open but unfocused, and John knelt beside him.

"Louis, can you hear me?" he said. He wiped the sweat off his face and after a moment Louis seemed to recognize him.

"I have the sickness." His voice was weak, and his throat sounded raw. "What of Mathieu?" He rolled his head to the side and looked at Mathieu.

"You both have the sickness we call smallpox. You must rest and try to drink as much as you can."

"I will die," he said, his voice a whisper.

"I survived. I was sick on the ship and I got better."

"It's the white man's sickness. My people cannot survive it." His voice faded, and he slipped into unconsciousness.

John tried to make Mathieu and Louis comfortable. He folded Mathieu's tunic under his head as a pillow, and tried to get him to drink, but he was delirious. John covered him with a blanket, but he was burning with fever and threw it off. John didn't understand why but knew that in spite of the fever, he had to keep him warm, and he put it back each time he threw it off. Sweat poured off Louis, but he was in a deep sleep and lay perfectly still.

He awoke once in the afternoon, and John helped him drink, but he slipped back into unconsciousness again.

John tended to the brothers throughout the day, but there wasn't much more he could do. The fever had to run its course, and they would live or die.

CHAPTER EIGHTEEN

WHEN THE GUARDS BROUGHT THE food the next day, they levelled their muskets at the prisoners.

"Back," one man called. They pushed the prisoners back with their bayonets. Pitt was with them. Three other soldiers carried the food in and de La Tour took charge of divvying out the stew as normal.

"Form a line." De La Tour lifted the lid off the pot, and the smell of fish stew got the prisoners to their feet.

John brought Mathieu's and Louis's bowls as well as his own, and de La Tour ladled stew into them.

Pitt nudged de La Tour with his bayonet. "No food for the savages."

De La Tour faced him. "They are entitled to their ration."

John was down on one knee beside the pot. Pitt kicked at him, and he leapt back, trying not to spill the stew.

John backed away and put the bowls down beside Mathieu.

"I said no food for the savages," Pitt said.

"They're sick. They must eat, or they will die."

"Then they'll die." Pitt's face was red with anger. "Danny Brown died two days ago of the smallpox they brought to Louisburg."

"Smallpox isn't an Indian disease. They didn't bring it to Louisburg." John knew his temper was getting the better of him, and he forced himself to hold his tongue.

De La Tour spoke quietly. "We're all afraid of the smallpox."

Without warning Pitt kicked Mathieu in the ribs. "This savage killed Danny Brown," he screamed.

John heard Mathieu's ribs crack, and he launched himself at Pitt. "No," he cried.

Pitt drove the stock of his musket into his John's stomach, and he staggered back and fell to his knees winded.

"Animal, animal, animal." Pitt kicked Mathieu's inert body, driving his boots into his ribs and face. Mathieu was thrown onto his side, and Pitt kicked his kidneys again and again, stepping back to put more power into each kick. John lurched to his feet, but two of the guards pulled Pitt away. Pitt struggled wildly.

"Get your hands off me." One of the men grasped him by the lapels and shouted into his face. "That's enough, Harry."

As they dragged Pitt out the door, Louis called out in Mi'kmaq. John didn't understand the words, but the strength of his hatred was chilling. Then he struggled up onto his elbow to where he could see Mathieu.

"Does he live?"

"He lives, but he is badly hurt." Louis's eyes rolled up in his head and he fell back to the floor.

Mathieu's face was a bloody mess. His skin was clammy, and he was shivering violently. John washed the blood from his face, wrapped him in a blanket, and put his tunic under his head as a pillow. He ran his hands along his rib cage. He couldn't tell if anything was broken, but when he saw blood on his lips, his heart sank.

Louis slept through the day. He alternated between sweating and shivering. John managed to get him to drink some water, and made him as comfortable as he could. There was little change in the brothers' condition by nightfall, and John kept the fire burning high to keep them warm and to give him light to see. He wrapped his plaid around his shoulders and leaned against the wall by the fire for a while then curled up on the floor and tried to sleep.

John awoke as the first glimmer of daylight was coming through the cell window. He sat up aching from the hard floor and looked around. Louis had thrown his blanket off and, despite the cold, was soaked in sweat, but his breathing was even, and he was sleeping quietly. Mathieu was facing away from him. John stepped over Louis and as soon as he saw Mathieu's face, he knew he was dead. His eyes were staring blankly across the cell. His skin was grey and shiny, and a trickle of blood had run from his mouth and formed a pool on the floor.

John slumped down beside him and groaned.

Justinien de La Tour was watching him from the other side of the cell. "He's dead?"

John nodded numbly.

"I'm sorry," de La Tour said. "We must bury him quickly. It's dangerous to let the body lie."

John nodded and when he turned around, Louis was watching him.

"Mathieu is dead," he said.

"He was my brother," Louis said then he fell back onto the floor and closed his eyes.

De La Tour threw wood onto the fire and poked it into life.

"Another two are dead." He pointed across the cell. Two soldiers were wrapped in blankets beneath the window. "The dead spread the smallpox quicker than the sick," he said. "They must be buried straight away."

One of the soldiers climbed to the window and started calling out. "Guards, guards, there are dead men here. You must come. Guards, guards."

The other prisoners rushed the door and started to pound on it, calling to be let out. A few minutes later the door swung open, and four guards entered with fixed bayonets. The sergeant was behind them.

"Silence," he bellowed. "How many dead?"

"Three."

"Four." Ogden pointed to a body lying by the slop bucket. It was another British soldier. He was curled up on the floor like a child, his eyes staring into space, and his body was still as only the dead can lie.

Ogden rushed the door.

"Let me out. This cell is a death sentence."

"Hold," the sergeant barked, and the guards drove Ogden back against the wall with their bayonets. "No one leaves the cell." The prisoners were shouting with fear and inching forward. The sergeant stepped towards them and bellowed, "Quiet!" He glared at the prisoners, and as he turned his head John saw a flash of red at his collar, and there was a sheen of sweat on his face.

The sergeant pulled at his collar.

"The colonel has given orders that the dead are to be buried immediately and their belongings are to be burned." He pointed at John and the two Frenchmen. "You three will form one burial detail." He jabbed his finger at Ogden and two other soldiers. "You three will form the second detail."

Ogden shouted in the sergeant's face. "I won't touch a diseased body."

One of the troopers drove his musket into Ogden's gut.

"You'll do as I say, or I'll have you tied hand and foot to your pox-ridden friend." Ogden struggled to his feet, and there was madness in his eyes.

The sergeant turned for the door. "Bring the bodies."

John wrapped Mathieu in the blanket and looked at de La Tour. "Help me."

John and de La Tour each took an arm and Le Blanc took Mathieu's feet. Mathieu's body was heavy, and they struggled to lift him onto the cart. The soldiers threw the other bodies unceremoniously on top of him. The sergeant led them to a church in the south end of the town. A trench had been dug in the graveyard by the outer wall, and it was already half-full. Three men were working at the far end, and when they saw them approaching they dropped their tools and ran.

The sergeant pointed. "Put them in."

They laid Mathieu's body in the trench, and as he climbed out, one of the guards handed John a shovel.

"How many have died?" John asked.

"I don't know, but there are more buried outside the wall. Now get on with it."

De La Tour put his hand on his arm. We should say some words for him."

"I don't know what to say. Mathieu is Mi'kmaq, and I don't know their customs."

"There's no time for this." The sergeant prodded John with his musket. As he threw the first shovel of dirt over Mathieu's body, he was overcome with sadness. Louis and Mathieu had befriended him. He had only begun to get to know Mathieu, and now he was dead.

When they reached the barracks, the sergeant stopped.

"Leave the cart outside."

Ogden confronted him. "I'm not going back to the cell. They're all as good as dead."

The sergeant sneered at him. "You can walk back, Ogden, or we'll drag you."

"I'm a British soldier like you, not a criminal like the Frenchmen and the savages."

"You're a thief caught red-handed stealing from your comrades, and you will stay in prison until you pay back what you stole. The Frenchmen have committed no crime except to be captured when the town fell."

Ogden turned and ran crashing into one of the other guards. He threw a punch, but the guard drove his shoulder into Ogden's chest, sending him staggering back. The second guard slammed the butt of his musket into Ogden's ribs, and the fight went out of him.

"You robbed my brother that I buried two days past. You can expect no help from me."

He hit him again, and the sergeant called out, "That's enough now."

The sergeant looked at John and the Frenchmen. "Get him back to the cell."

They pulled Ogden to his feet, but he shook them off.

"Get off me," he cried, and he stumbled away towards the courtyard.

When John got back to the cell, Louis was still asleep, but his skin was cool and his breathing regular. John put the blanket over him and settled another under his head as a pillow. There was nothing more he could do, so he sat by the fire and tried to rest.

* * *

Louis slept through the day. Even the commotion when the food came didn't wake him. As night fell he was still asleep, and John began to feel uneasy. He watched him closely and kept the fire high until he couldn't stay awake any longer.

When John awoke at first light, Louis was looking at him. His face was pale and drawn, but his eyes were clear.

"Louis, you're awake." John moved to his side.

"Did you bury my brother?" His voice was weak, and he spoke each word slowly.

"I buried him with my own hands."

"It is good, for you were his friend." He closed his eyes, and John thought he had fallen asleep, but a moment later he opened them. "I will live for I must avenge my brother." Then he slipped back into sleep.

Louis awoke when the food came, but he was too weak to sit up, and John fed him stew, and he drank some water.

"I think the fever is broken."

Louis nodded, then lay down and was asleep in seconds. John was confident that Louis would live, but his face would carry the marks of the disease for the rest of his life.

The next morning when John awoke Louis was sitting next to him by the fire.

John sat up. "How are you?"

"The fever has passed."

"I'm sorry about Mathieu," John said. "I did what I could for him . . ."

"Mathieu was my brother. He is dead, and I will avenge him," Louis said.

Louis was changed, whether by his brother's death or by the fever, John couldn't tell. Before Louis had found humour in everything. Now he was stone-faced, as if all emotion had been drained out of him. John thought it would be long before he would see Louis laugh again.

On the second morning John told Louis how he had buried Mathieu and Louis nodded.

"I will sing the death songs for my brother, and, in time, my family will mourn for him." Louis retreated into himself. He sat by the fire or paced the cell, singing to himself quietly.

* * *

The next morning another soldier was found dead, which left nine prisoners in the cell. The soldiers sat in a group by the fire and spoke little. John was confident that he and Louis wouldn't get sick again, but the soldiers watched them fearfully. John began to believe that if they stayed in the prison they would die. The death of a prisoner meant nothing to the British. Smallpox was rampant in the town now, and there was no telling what they would do as the death count grew.

When the burial detail returned, the sergeant pointed at John and Louis. "You two on latrine duty." John looked at Louis and shrugged.

"You know what to do, so get on with it," the sergeant said. The latrine hadn't been cleaned since their last visit. The stench was overpowering, and the guard stayed outside. John was scrubbing furiously. Louis looked at him curiously, and he picked up the bucket.

"Keep making noise."

John stepped outside and knocked the bucket against the wall as if trying to dislodge something. The guards paid no attention to him, and he searched the snow around the entrance, but couldn't find the bayonet. There wasn't much time, so he picked a spot where he thought the musket had fallen, and bent down to scrub the bucket out with snow. His fingers brushed against the blade. He turned his back on the guards and scooped the bayonet into the bucket then hurried back to the latrine.

Louis looked up as he entered, and John held up the bayonet.

"This is good, my friend." He nodded approval.

"Keep an eye on the guards and make noise as if we're both working." John pulled his boots off and waded into the pool, and Louis looked on in surprise.

"What're you doing?"

"Just make sure the guard doesn't see me."

John felt his way forward; the water was knee-deep at the grating and he rolled his breeches above his knees. He slid his hand down one of the bars and confirmed his earlier examination: a bar ran across the bottom of the grating six inches above the floor. He waded to the centre. There were two rows of floor stones under the grating, and the floor dipped in the centre, increasing the depth below the bar.

John slid his hand through the grating, reaching as far as he could. The stone floor ended just beyond the grating. He slid the bayonet into the gap between the stones. It had a slim triangular blade, and he pushed it down easily into the gap between the stones. It was as he had thought. The water had softened the mortar until it was like mud.

Louis hissed and John looked around in alarm, Louis was waving him back. He jammed the bayonet into the gap between two of the stones and waded out of the pond.

"Hurry," Louis called. He stepped outside and busied himself cleaning the mops and buckets in the snow. John pulled his boots on and rolled his breeches down then hurried to help Louis.

As John came out of the latrine, the guards were coming towards them, but they were in no hurry, and John helped Louis put the mops and buckets away. The guards stopped halfway to the toilet and motioned for them to follow.

John knew one of the guards called Grant.

"Has the smallpox run its course?"

Grant frowned. "There've been more deaths, and I doubt it's finished yet."

"How many have died?"

Grant seemed lost in thought for a moment.

"Our regiment doctor died two days ago. Yesterday a doctor from the town came. He said they buried eighty in the last week. More die every day."

"How many soldiers are sick?"

"Half the garrison's sick. Eight died this week past." John wanted to ask more, but Grant seemed disturbed by his questions, and he let it go.

John sat close to the fire, pulled off his boots and rubbed his legs to get the blood flowing. Louis sat by him.

"The guard said many are dead in the town and half the garrison is sick, and I haven't seen the sergeant for days. Guarding prisoners is a growing problem for the British."

"I think you're right. When enough soldiers have died, the British will find a reason to kill us."

John pulled his socks and boots on.

"The mortar between the stones is soft. If we can remove two or three stones, we can slide under the grating, and we know the grating at the outer end is broken."

"We'll die if we stay here," Louis said.

"The Frenchmen told me the coldest months of the winter are yet to come. Can we survive in the wilderness?"

Louis took a stick and poked at the fire. "The Mi'kmaq know the ways of the forest, and we can travel in winter."

"How far is it to your village?"

"It is many days' journey. The British will hunt us, but they cannot travel far from their towns. We must stay ahead of them till they give up the chase."

"How will we survive the cold?"

Louis would only say that his people knew the forest. John couldn't draw him out any further, and he turned his mind to escaping from the prison.

The next day Grant and two guards John hadn't seen before took them to latrine duty. As soon as they stepped inside Louis picked up a bucket.

"I will clean. Work on the stones," he said. John pulled off his boots and his breeches and rolled his sleeves up. He waded to the grating and plunged his hand into the water. He had a moment of panic when the bayonet wouldn't come free, but he worked it back and forth, and it came away.

The mortar between the stones was like mud, and John dug it out easily. He worked his way around one stone and started on a second. He was shivering violently, and his hand was becoming numb, but he persevered. Louis hissed and John looked up. He was standing back from the entrance, and he held his hand up to wait. Then he ran into the latrine.

"Guard coming. Get out of the water."

John thrust the bayonet between two stones and splashed his way out of the pool and started pulling his breeches on. Louis shook his head.

"Not enough time." He filled a bucket from the pool and threw the water onto the floor so it splashed out through the door. There was a cry of alarm, and Louis stepped up to the entrance. "We're almost done."

The guard called something out. John didn't hear what he said, but Louis signalled it was safe.

The latrine had been washed down and swept clean. Louis had worked hard, and the guards would suspect nothing.

"How does it go?" Louis said.

"I dug the mortar out around two of the stones. We only need to remove one more, but the stones are frozen in place."

"I will try tomorrow."

"We need a stronger tool to loosen them. The bayonet will break."

Another soldier died in the night. The other men called the guards, and a short time later Grant and two men opened the cell door.

"Bring him," Grant said. The soldiers didn't move. John knew they were afraid to touch the body. He nudged Louis and got to his feet.

"We'll do it. He can't harm us now." He saw the look in Louis's eyes, but he didn't protest. The dead man was a regular soldier who had been jailed for breaking the nose of a tavern owner. He had been a big man, but his body was wasted by the disease, and John and Louis lifted him easily onto the cart.

When they crossed the ditch instead of going into the town, Grant turned left in front of the barracks and led them to a patch of ground against the town wall where a trench had been dug. The trench was a hundred feet long and half-full; the freshly turned earth stood in stark contrast to the white landscape.

Grant stopped at the ditch.

"Here." John and Louis lifted the body down into the ditch.

"Why're we burying him here? This isn't a cemetery. It's not hallowed ground."

"The cemetery's full. No more talk. Now get on with it."

"Will you say some words?"

"He's dead. There's nothing to say. Hurry up, so we can get back to a warm fire."

The soil was frozen, and they had to break it up with the shovels. They had barely covered the body when Grant called out.

"That's enough. He'll have company soon enough." They threw the shovels onto the cart and made their way back.

When they entered the courtyard, Grant called out, "Get the latrine cleaned and be quick about it. It's too damn cold out here." They dragged the cart down to the corner of the courtyard where it was stored, and Grant stood in the passageway watching.

"Let's get it done," John called to Louis. He handed a shovel to Louis, took the other one and hurried along to the latrine.

Inside the latrine, John held up the shovel and laughed.

"They didn't notice." He undressed and waded into the pool; he gasped at the cold, and by the time he reached the grating, he was shivering. He pulled the bayonet from between the stones and slid the shovel into the gap and pulled back. At first nothing happened, but slowly the stone began to move, and he kept the pressure on. Finally the stone broke free with only a ripple on the surface of the pool as it sank into deeper water.

John looked back. Louis had already cleaned most of the latrine and was washing the floor.

"Go on," Louis said. John slid the shovel behind the next stone and leaned back. The stone moved immediately. He pulled hard, and it fell over onto its side. He tried to slide it off the ledge, but it jammed and he couldn't move it.

The more he tried to break it free, the harder it seemed to hold. John gasped in frustration. His hands were almost numb, and he knew that he didn't have much time. He slid the shovel underneath the stone and pressed down, trying to lift it. The stone moved, and he slid the shovel farther in, inching it forward until it broke free and slid into deep water.

John looked behind him. Louis jogged down to the edge of the pool.

"It's enough. The guards will become suspicious."

"I only need to remove two stones, and it's done. See what the guards are doing."

John went to work on the next stone with the bayonet. The mortar came away easily, but his hand was frozen, and he was having difficulty gripping the bayonet. He dug the mortar out around one stone but couldn't hold the bayonet tight enough to reach the back of the stone. He slid the shovel into the gap and leaned back. The stone started to move. John worked the shovel back and forth until it rolled onto its side, and then he lifted it and pushed it under the grating.

John was losing the feeling in his hand. He jammed the bayonet between two stones and waded out of the pool and pulled his breeches and boots on, shivering violently. Louis was making a show of scrubbing the floor around the door.

"You're white with cold," Louis said.

"With any luck the guards will think I have the fever again."

The guards paid no attention to him. John thought they looked as miserable as he felt. He sat by the fire and let the heat seep into his body. He closed his eyes and had begun to relax when he smelt fish stew. When he opened his eyes Ogden was staring at him. He looked away quickly, and John's attention was taken up by the food. Later in the day he caught Ogden watching him again. Ogden looked away again, but it left John with an uneasy feeling.

* * *

The next day the guards didn't call them to clean the latrine until late in the afternoon. John saw that Grant was disturbed about something. He wouldn't respond to questions, but John heard the other guards talking about deaths in the barracks. The guards stayed by the cell door as usual, and Grant went back to the guardhouse. John stripped and waded into the pond. He had his hand on the bayonet when Louis cursed.

"The guard's coming. Get out of the water." John splashed out of the pool, dropped the bayonet, and hopped around on one leg, trying to pull his breeches on.

"Slow him."

"Faster, he's almost here."

John pulled his boots on then grabbed the bayonet and slid it into his boot. He was fastening his breeches when the guard arrived.

"Back to the cell."

"We're not done."

"We're wanted elsewhere, and there's no one to watch you." They stacked the tools in the corner and went back to the cell.

John grabbed the bars and pulled himself up to the window, but the guards had disappeared into the guardhouse, leaving a single sentry at the doorway. As he slid down, the bayonet jabbed his leg and he landed clumsily.

"What's happening?" de La Tour said in French.

"I don't know, but the guards seem agitated about something."

As John made his way to the fire he felt Ogden's eyes on him, and he slid down beside Louis and stared back. Ogden looked away, but John was shocked by the malice in his eyes.

De La Tour and Le Blanc shared out the food as normal, but the guards were impatient. De La Tour spoke to one of them, but John couldn't hear what he said, and they left again quickly. The soldiers went back to the fire. There was little talking. Many were sick, and they looked at each other with graveyard eyes, wondering who would live to see the morning.

As it started to get dark, de La Tour threw some logs onto the fire and kicked them into place. Then he came and sat between John and Louis. He was quiet for a moment, casting his eyes around the cell.

"Whatever it is you're planning, I suggest you do not delay," he said in French.

"What do you mean?" John said.

"Your clothes were wet when you come back from the latrine, and you were blue with cold. Others have noticed. Be wary of Ogden. He holds a grudge against you."

John exchanged a glance with Louis.

"What should we do?"

"The young guard told me a ship has come into the harbour. There's talk a new military commander is on board and additional troops to bolster the garrison. That means more guards."

De La Tour started to get up.

"It's late in the year. No captain will want to be trapped here for the winter, so Pierre and I could be sent back to France in a few days."

De La Tour moved away, and John spoke under his breath.

"You heard what Justinien said?"

"It must be tonight."

"Are you sure that you can find the way to your village in winter?"

Louis bristled. "I am Mi'kmaq, and this is our land," Louis said, dismissing the question as if speaking to a child.

John lay down and pulled his plaid around him, too keyed up to sleep. He listened as the guard made his rounds, counting his footsteps, gauging the time between passes. The cell became quiet and only the snores of the prisoners broke the silence.

The hours passed slowly, and when the fire had burned down, John sat up slowly. Louis, who was watching him, nodded, got to his feet, and moved to the window silently. John waited till Louis reached the window then slid the bayonet around to the side of his boot where he could reach it easily.

John stood and moved slowly, keeping out of the firelight, and made his way to the door. Louis was silhouetted by the glow from the fire, but he was so still John almost doubted his eyes until he grasped the window bars and pulled himself up.

The fire snapped, sending a shower of sparks across the floor. The sound seemed unnaturally loud, and John glanced around nervously. None of the prisoners moved and gradually his heartbeat slowed again. He looked at the window and Louis nodded.

John inserted the bayonet into the gap between the doors and slid it up until it touched the locking bar. A simple locking bar was all that the British thought necessary. The British thought the wilderness around them was a more effective deterrent to escape than locked doors. Louis appeared beside him, and they both grasped the bayonet and lifted. The blade made a scraping sound against the bar, and they froze. John glanced around anxiously, and forced himself to wait, listening to the snores of the prisoners until he was satisfied no one had heard them.

John nodded to Louis, but caught a movement out of the corner of his eye. He turned and a jolt of panic ran through him as Ogden stepped towards them. The firelight bathed his face in red as if it was covered in blood.

"I have you now." He made a gurgling sound as he spoke, and John saw a trickle of dark liquid slide out of his mouth.

Ogden hawked and spat a gob of phlegm into the darkness, and John could see him gathering himself to shout. He measured the distance and started to move, but he knew he couldn't reach him in time.

Ogden lifted his chin.

"Guar—" The word was cut off and Ogden staggered back clutching at his throat. A cawing sound came out of his mouth, and his eyes bulged in their sockets. He came up against the fireplace and John saw the black band around his neck and recognized de La Tour behind him.

De La Tour's belt was around Ogden's throat and he had his knee in the small of his back, strangling him. Ogden had the fever, or de La Tour wouldn't have been able to hold him. Even in his weakened condition he fought for his life. John watched in morbid fascination as de La Tour put all his strength into choking the life out of Ogden.

Finally Ogden's hands fell from his throat and he sagged to the floor, and de La Tour went down with him, pulling on the belt till he was sure he was dead. Finally de La Tour stood up. He was swaying on his feet, and his face was soaked in sweat.

"Help me carry him to his sleeping place," he whispered.

John put his hand on de La Tour's shoulder, and he and Louis picked Ogden up. They moved one step at a time fearful of waking the prisoners, and laid Ogden in the corner. John curled his arms and legs up like the others who had died of the fever.

De La Tour covered him with his blanket and moved to the far corner of the cell, motioning John and Louis after him.

De La Tour whispered in French. "The guards will think Ogden died of fever, and they'll be afraid to touch him. You must escape tonight, my friends. The chance may not come again." De La Tour shook their hands in turn then slipped away into the darkness.

CHAPTER NINETEEN

JOHN SLID THE BAYONET BETWEEN the cell doors, and he and Louis lifted, grunting with the effort; the blade scraped against the iron as it came free, but the door swung open. Louis grabbed the bar with his right hand and slid through, John followed him and lowered the bar back into place. Instinctively they crouched down and searched the courtyard, but the guard was nowhere to be seen. He was likely warming his backside by the guardroom fire.

John touched Louis on the shoulder, and they hurried to the latrine. John went to the pool and started to pull off one of his boots, and Louis hissed a warning.

"Guard coming." John pulled his boot back on, and when he looked up, Louis was gone. He crept to the entrance and looked outside. The light from the half-moon cast the courtyard into gloomy twilight.

John saw the guard on the far side of the courtyard. He had walked to the cell door and was on his way back to the guardhouse. His hat was pulled down over his eyes, but John could see the glow from his pipe. Then he caught sight of a figure behind him. It was only a silhouette, but he knew it was Louis. There was a glint of steel in his hand, and John's gut twisted in a knot.

The guard's feet crunched on the snow, and John heard him cough. Louis didn't make a sound as he moved, and John watched helplessly as he stalked the guard. Louis stepped onto the path and covered the last ten feet in three strides. The man started to turn, but Louis locked his arm around his neck, and John heard him grunt as Louis drove the bayonet into his back. The guard collapsed to his knees, and Louis pulled back and drove the bayonet into his back again and again. He sank to the ground, and Louis kept stabbing him. Finally Louis got to his feet and stood for a moment looking down at the body; then he turned and looked at John.

John was up and running and across the courtyard in seconds. He thought Louis had taken leave of his senses, but there was no time for recriminations.

"Take his feet," he hissed at Louis. He took the guard's arms, and they half carried half dragged him to the latrine. John ran back across the courtyard and picked up the guard's musket and slung it over his shoulder. Louis grabbed his hat and scooped snow up with his hands and covered the blood as best he could.

John could hardly contain his anger. If they were caught, they would both be hanged. He hurried back to the latrine and inside he put his face close to Louis.

"Are you insane?" He could barely keep himself from shouting. "Why did you kill him? He was no threat."

"Mathieu is avenged, and his spirit is at peace." Louis spoke in a whisper, but his voice was charged with emotion.

John turned the body over. It was Pitt.

"You've endangered us foolishly."

"It was my duty to avenge my brother's death."

John struggled to control his temper.

"There's no time for this. If they catch us, they'll hang us."

"Death will come this day or another. It's better to die than to live without honour." Louis spoke with such sincerity it took the heat out of John's anger, and he forced himself to concentrate.

"We must move quickly. Watch the courtyard."

John stripped and stuffed his clothes into his hunting bag and waded into the pool. He didn't relish the idea of immersing his body in the stinking water, but they had no other choice. He tied his bag to the iron grill and went to work on the last floor stone. It was a tight fit, and he could barely get the bayonet into the gap, but he persevered and managed to work the mortar out of the three sides. He slid the shovel into the gap and leaned back on the handle, but the stone wouldn't budge.

John was shivering violently, and his hands and feet were numb, but he couldn't stop.

"Louis, help me," he called, and Louis started to undress. "Is it clear?"

"No guards." Louis waded into the pool, and as soon as they put their weight on the shovel it popped out from between the stones, and they staggered back.

John pushed the shovel back into the gap.

"I'll stand on it," Louis said. He put his back against the grating and stood on the blade, and John pulled back on the handle, but the stone didn't move. John put his foot against the grill and pushed back with all his weight.

"Push, Louis." John was beginning to despair when he felt the stone shift. Louis felt it and increased the pressure grunting with the effort and the stone came free, sending John staggering backwards. John pushed the stone under the grill into deep water and measured the gap between the grating and the floor.

"I think it's enough." Louis put his hand in up to his armpit.

"We can pass through, but we must go now," he said.

As they waded out of the pool John looked at Pitt's body.

"We'll need his clothes." Pitt lay facedown, one arm thrown out to the side. The body was already stiff and difficult to turn over. John took his ammunition belt and boots, but the buttons on his greatcoat were frozen, and he had to cut them off with the bayonet. They tried to remove the coat, but Pitt's arms were frozen stiff.

"Wait," John said. He picked up the musket, opened the lock and blew out the powder. Then he drove the stock into Pitt's elbow. The iron cap on the stock made a dull crunching sound as it struck the arm, and the joint came loose.

John pounded all his joints, and by the time he was done, Pitt's body flopped around like a rag doll.

"It's enough." Louis pulled off the coat, and they stripped his outer clothes, tied them into a bundle, and hung them on the grating with the ammunition pouch. John took Pitt's arm.

"We need to hide the body. If they find it, the hunt will be up."

"The rats can eat his flesh," Louis said, and they dragged the body into the pool.

John felt his way along the floor with his hand, looking for sharp edges, then measured the distance between the grating and the floor again. He was soaked with stinking water and shivering violently, but he dreaded the idea of being trapped under the grating. He looked at Louis.

"I'll pull the body through," he said. John grasped the grating and steeled himself, took a breath and plunged below the surface. The cold was stunning, and he almost surfaced again. He turned face up, slid his head and shoulders under the grating and pulled himself through. His shins scraped on the bar, but he didn't notice the pain, and he broke the surface, gasping from cold and panic.

Louis had Pitt's body at the bars.

"Turn him face up," John said. Louis rolled the body over and pushed it under, John put his hand under the grating, grabbed a handful of his hair and pulled. The upper torso slid through, but his lower body became stuck. John pulled Pitt's arm, but he was snagged on something solid.

John started to speak, but Louis held his hand up.

"Wait." Louis waded out of the pool and went to the door, disappearing into the shadows. John slid his hand along the body until he found the problem. Pitt's underwear had snagged on the bottom of the grill. It was in a knot, and his hands were too numb to loosen it.

John heard Louis suck his breath in.

"Guards coming."

"How many?"

"Two." Louis pulled Pitt's legs, and John pushed, but his leggings were caught fast, and they were making it worse.

"Give me the bayonet." Louis handed the bayonet through the bars. John found where Pitt's woolen shirt and leggings had caught on the grating in a tangled knot.

John sawed at the wool, but the bayonet was clumsy in his frozen hand, and he had difficulty bringing pressure to bear on the material.

"Quickly," Louis hissed.

"I know." John took a breath and dropped below the surface. A wave of panic overwhelmed him, but he forced himself to go on. He felt his way along the body till he found the snag, and when he slid the bayonet into the knot, the wool parted easily.

John came to the surface gasping, and Louis pushed the body down, John pulled it under the grill and shoved it farther into the tunnel. Louis slid under the grill and surfaced beside him, and they untied the bundles of clothing and the musket from the grill.

"I'll take them," Louis said. He waded into the tunnel, pushing Pitt's body ahead of him. John held the musket and ammunition pouch above his head in his right hand and dragged the shovel beneath the surface with his left.

John was soon chest deep in water. The bottom of the tunnel was uneven, and he had to feel his way, stepping over stones and other debris. He sank ankle deep with each step, and the mud sucked at his feet, making progress painfully slow.

It was completely dark, but John could hear Louis ahead of him. He thought the tunnel was about two hundred feet long, but he had no sense of how far he'd come. He kept moving forward then something jabbed him in the chest, and he stopped gasping.

"It's ice." Louis spoke in a whisper, but it sounded eerily loud in the tunnel.

"How thick is it? Will it—?"

"Quiet."

John's arm was aching from holding the musket above his head. He rested it on top of his head and sighed in relief. A light flared in the latrine, casting shadows around the walls. Then two guards stepped up to the pool and started to urinate into the water. Their faces were in shadow, but their voices echoed along the tunnel.

"The lazy bastard's not here."

"He's probably hiding somewhere with a bottle of rum." John recognized Grant's voice.

"He'll lose the skin off his back if the lieutenant catches him."

"That's on his head. He's been warned often enough. It's cold and I'm for the barrack room's fire." Grant picked up the lantern and disappeared from view.

John felt a surge of relief as the voices faded, but now that the danger was gone, the cold brought him back to reality.

"We have to get out of the water." John placed the musket and the shovel on the ice and pushed them back from the edge. He put his hands on top of the ice.

"Help me, Louis." John cringed as his voice echoed off the walls.

"Wait."

John could hear Louis moving about, and he wanted out of the water badly. "What are you doing?"

"Pitt." There was a surging sound close by, and he realized that Louis was pushing Pitt's body under the ice.

A moment later Louis whispered, "The ice is thicker in the middle. Move this way." John felt his way along the edge of the ice until he met Louis coming towards him.

"Give me your foot." John legs were stiff, and it was difficult to bend his knee. Louis cupped his foot in his hands and heaved upwards, and John came out of the water and threw himself onto the ice. He spread his arms and legs praying that the ice wouldn't break.

The ice felt colder than the water, and John lay still for a few seconds, trying to fathom how that could be until he realized that Louis was calling to him.

"Louis, where are you?"

"Here." John crawled back to the edge of the ice and his hand came in contact with Louis's arm.

"Give me your hands." They gripped forearms. Louis's skin felt clammy, and his arms were bony and emaciated, but John winced at the strength of his grip.

John slid back trying to find some grip on the surface.

"Pull." John couldn't help himself sliding forward, but he felt Louis come out of the water and the weight came off his arms.

"I'm clear."

John retrieved the musket and ammunition pouch. He slid his hunting bag over his shoulder, and made his way along the tunnel dragging the shovel behind him. Louis followed with the bundles of clothes. John could see the entrance to the tunnel and the grating silhouetted in the moonlight, and he left the musket and ammunition belt and slid forward with the shovel. Without warning the ice gave way beneath him; he cried out in alarm, but the water was only a foot deep.

John pushed on the grating, and it moved easily. He leaned against the grating, put his feet against the wall, and pushed. Louis added his weight; the metal made a grinding sound against the stone, but it moved enough for Louis to slip through.

* * *

Louis disappeared into the darkness carrying the musket and their bundles of clothing, and as John waited for him to return, the cold gripped him like a vise. Louis seemed to be gone for a long time but he finally returned. He pulled the grating back, and John squeezed through. Louis snorted with the effort. John thought he sounded like an old horse blowing at the top of a hill, and he laughed to himself.

Still thinking about Louis as an old horse, John followed him onto the bank. He felt better on solid ground. The snow was not as cold as the water, and he almost began to feel warm. He watched as Louis used Pitt's greatcoat to rub himself dry and pull his clothes on. He thought his antics were comical as he hopped around on one leg.

Louis was rubbing his limbs and shivering, but John felt a warm glow spreading through him. He thought it was odd. Louis had grown up in this country and should be accustomed to the cold. Finally Louis looked at John.

John smiled at him. "You look—"

Louis struck him on the face with his open hand, and he staggered back in shock. Louis hit him again. Anger flashed through him, and he leapt at Louis, who was too quick, and struck him again, lighting up the side of his face in pain. Blood welled around his tongue, and he swallowed involuntarily. The metallic taste burned his throat, but it cut through the malaise that gripped his mind, and he felt as if he was in deep water, struggling to reach the surface.

Suddenly John was shivering so violently he could hardly speak. He clenched his fists.

"Cold, so cold." Louis took John's tunic and rubbed his arms and chest. The cloth chafed his skin and started a prickling sensation in his chest that grew to a burning pain, and he wanted Louis to stop but knew that if he did, he would die.

Louis took him by the shoulders. "Keep quiet."

John realized that he had been moaning out loud and clamped his jaws together. Louis wrestled his tunic over his head and pushed his arms into the sleeves.

"You must help yourself now." Louis guided his feet into his breeches, and John pulled them on, but his hands were stiff, and he couldn't fasten his belt himself. Louis helped him with his socks and boots; he pulled the guard's greatcoat on his back and put his hunting bag over his shoulder.

"Can you walk?" John's body was on fire. He wanted to lie down and sleep, but he nodded his head.

Louis slung the musket and ammunition pouch over his shoulder.

"Come." He set off. John followed, staggering like a drunk, but he forced himself to keep moving. Gradually the cramps eased, but the creeping lethargy pulled at him, and he fought it with every step.

They made their way along the town wall; the stones were coated in ice and sparkled in the moonlight, and John knew it meant the temperature was dropping. He lost track of how long they walked, but then he saw the gatehouse ahead of them, and they crouched in the snow to watch. The gate was closed and there were no lights or other signs of life. They listened for a while. The only sound John could hear was the waves breaking on the beach, and for some reason he found it comforting.

Louis moved forward again, and as they neared the gate he abandoned any attempt at concealment and walked openly. John felt a moment of panic, but he realized Louis was right. If they encountered a guard now, they would have to brazen their way through. No one challenged them as they passed the gate, and at the water's edge they looked back. The gatehouse was quiet, but John sensed something menacing about it and wanted to be far away.

Louis went north along the beach for a mile then turned inland.

"Where are we going?"

"This was our camp. There are things we will need." Louis passed between two large mounds in the snow, and John realized these were the remains of the dwellings the Indians called teepees. The support poles stuck out of the snow like the blackened bones of a monstrous animal. At the end of the camp, Louis stopped at a half-collapsed teepee and started to dig the snow away with his hands.

There was a sound like paper tearing, and Louis stepped back, pulling a flap of material away from the teepee; then he stooped and disappeared into the blackness. John followed, pulling the flap closed behind him. It was completely dark inside, and the air was damp and cloying as if it had been trapped in here for months. John heard Louis moving around as if searching for something, and after a few minutes a stream of sparks from flint and steel lit up the inside of the teepee.

The sparks flashed like tiny lightning bolts in the darkness, casting Louis's face in an eerie light as if the bones were shining through his skin. As John watched, a tiny flame appeared, and Louis blew it into life. He held a candle to the flame till it lit and set it on the ground. The inside of the teepee was coated with ice crystals that magnified the candlelight a hundredfold as if they were in a crystal cave, and John looked around him in wonder.

John was brought back to reality as Louis dragged two bundles of fur into the centre of the teepee and cut the bindings.

"These are our winter furs, Mathieu's and mine. We will need them to survive." Louis pushed one of the bundles to John.

"Open it. There isn't much time." The fur was stiff as a board, and it crackled like breaking ice as he straightened it. There were several garments: a tunic with a cowl attached, made from the fur of an animal he couldn't identify, and leggings made of lighter fur and a pair of fur boots. The boots were pale in colour, and the fur was long and fine grained.

Louis was walking on the furs to soften them, the ice crackling under his feet, and John found it oddly cheering. He did the same then worked the fur with his hands until it became flexible. Louis stripped off his leggings and pulled the furs on. He kept his deerskin tunic on and pulled the heavy garment over it.

"These are my furs." He pointed to the bundle at John's feet. "I will wear Mathieu's. Wear your shirt beneath the tunic, but your breeches will be too hot, and you will sweat."

It seemed impossible to John that he could sweat in this cold, but reluctantly he pulled off his boots and breeches, and put on the fur leggings. He tried to pull one of his boots on but it was difficult to bend the leggings, and he sat down to get better leverage.

"You must wear the mukluks."

"My hunting boots suit me well enough."

"Your feet will freeze. Your toes will blacken, and I will have to cut them off with the bayonet, and even then you will likely die."

Louis's voice was matter of fact, and John understood he was simply telling him the facts. He nodded and started to pull one of the boots onto his foot.

"No socks. They'll freeze your sweat." John grimaced but didn't argue. When he slid his feet into the boots, it was like submersing them in ice water.

John put his boots and his breeches in his hunting bag with his plaid. He pulled the fur tunic over his head. It was stiff, and he had a moment of panic when it became stuck, and he couldn't move his arms. Then he felt Louis pull it down over his shoulders.

John felt like he was encased in armour. The furs were so stiff that he could hardly bend to pick up his hunting bag. The cowl completely encased his head. He could only see a small area in front of him and had to turn his whole body to see to the side.

"Put your belt around your waist. You'll need it later." Louis had cinched the tunic around his middle with a belt of some sort, so he took the belt from his hunting bag and fastened it around his waist.

Louis handed him the last two pieces from his bundle. "For your hands."

They were gloves, but the strangest gloves he had ever seen. They were made of the same light-coloured fur as his boots and sewn tightly at the seams. They reached to his elbow and only had one finger section for his thumbs. John didn't waste time asking questions. He worked the fur until it was soft then thrust his hands into them. The gloves felt bulky but not uncomfortable.

Louis opened a deerskin bag and handed John a strip of leather.

"It's dried meat and berries. Break a piece off and chew it. You will need the strength." The mention of food made John remember he was hungry. He broke a piece of the meat off and put it in his mouth. It tasted like a dry stick and froze his tongue.

"Hold it in your mouth until it melts," Louis said. "It will freeze your gut if you swallow it now." John didn't want to offend, Louis, but he decided he would spit it out at the first opportunity.

Louis put the flint and steel in his bag and the dried moss he had used as tinder and slid a small axe into his belt. The handle was fifteen inches long, and the head looked too small to be useful for chopping wood. John assumed it was a weapon, but he couldn't see how it would be very effective.

John knew that the hunt would be up at first light, and he was anxious to get away.

"We must go."

"Wait." Louis took two wooden frames from where they hung on the side of the teepee and threw them at John's feet.

"What's this?" The frames were about two and a half feet long, oval shaped and tapered to a long tail at one end. The frame was made of wood with a lattice of skin strips stretched across it to form a net.

Louis placed John's foot in the centre of the latticework, and made it fast with leather bindings.

"What foolishness is this?" He thought Louis had taken leave of his senses.

"They're snowshoes. Without them you'll sink to your waist." Louis placed the other shoe next to John's right foot.

"Stand on it." John thought it was insane, but he let Louis fasten the frame to his foot.

John felt foolish standing in the teepee with these things on his feet. Only the front part was fastened to his foot, and when he moved the back dragged on the ground.

"I won't be able to walk in these things."

"You'll learn." Louis fastened another pair of snowshoes to his feet, working with the skill that came from years of practice. John was thinking about this when his mouth filled with a sweet taste that made his eyes water. The dried meat had melted in his mouth, and he was astonished at the flavour. He chewed and swallowed the meat then broke off another piece and popped it into his mouth.

Louis blew out the candle and dropped it into his bag. "We go."

John crawled out of the teepee and struggled to his feet. He fastened the ammunition belt around his waist, slung the musket and hunting bag over his shoulder.

"Louis, I can't walk in these things."

"Keep your body upright and take short steps. You'll learn," he said and set off towards the beach.

CHAPTER TWENTY

JOHN FELL TWICE BEFORE THEY reached the shoreline, and Louis waited above the beach.

"We must stay above the waterline to keep your mukluks dry."

"I can't walk in these contraptions. I will hold us both back."

"Do as I do." Louis moved away at a steady pace, but despite his best efforts, John fell behind. The snowshoes spread his weight, and he understood that without them, he would sink into the snow, but dragging them through the snow was exhausting. He increased his pace for a hundred feet, but he couldn't keep it up, and he fell back again.

John watched Louis moving away from him, his furs blending into the landscape like a forest creature. Then he realized what he was doing.

"Hopping from foot to foot." The sound of his voice startled him, and he looked around nervously. Louis took little hopping steps, lifting each shoe clear of the snow as he stepped. He tried to copy the motion and immediately grasped why the shoes were only fixed at the front. It made it easier to lift the shoe out of the snow. The tailpiece dragged in the snow but didn't slow him down, and he started to close the gap on Louis.

They followed the curve of the bay. To their left the forest had been cut down for firewood, and the land rolled away in snowy waves into the distance.

Beneath the snow, the stumps and debris would be impassable. They had to find a way around this barrier, and he hoped Louis knew where he was going.

A mile from the village Louis waited for John on the banks of a stream running into the sea. The trees hadn't been cut on the other bank, and the forest was a deeper black against the sky.

"Come." Louis turned inland. Broken branches and debris snagged John's snowshoes, and he had to feel his way forward. The sound of running water faded, and John realized the stream was frozen. He found Louis waiting for him farther up the bank.

"The trail to the south is there." Louis pointed to the far bank. "The ice will be thin. I will wait on the far side." Louis slid down the bank and disappeared into the darkness.

John waited a few minutes and then slid down onto the ice. His snowshoes floated on the snow, but he was still nervous of breaking through and took long strides to spread his weight.

Halfway across John realized that he wasn't cold anymore. In fact his feet were warm, and his fur tunic and leggings had softened and moved easily. He was so surprised that he stopped to relish the feeling, but there was a cracking sound behind him, and he rushed forward in panic. A dozen strides took him across, and he pulled himself up the bank.

Louis was waiting.

"We go," Louis said and set off along the bank to the north. The forest was dense, and John found it difficult to manoeuvre his snowshoes between the trees. After half a mile they broke out into open ground, and in the moonlight John saw they were on a narrow trail. Louis stood waiting.

"Here we turn to the south." Louis gave him more dried meat. "Eat. You'll need your strength."

"We go," Louis said.

The trail narrowed till it was a few feet across, and the snow became deeper. John began to feel more comfortable on his snowshoes, but months on board ship and in the prison had taken their toll on him. By the end of an hour he was breathing hard, and his hip joints were aching. He felt as if his thighs were on fire, but he followed on doggedly.

They stopped twice to rest and eat. They exchanged few words. Both understood they were running for their lives, and they had to save their strength for the march. John lost track of time, and the night became a journey through pain and fatigue.

At one point John realized that he could see the outline of the trees against the sky. He looked back and saw the first glimmer of daylight.

"Louis, day is coming." Louis waited for him to catch up.

"It'll be easier to travel." In spite of his exhaustion John's spirits lifted.

"The British will hunt us now," Louis said. "We must keep moving."

John's fatigue returned, but he pushed on, and the terrain began to change. The trees became smaller and took on a desiccated shrunken look, and the forest gave way to patches of open ground. John thought that in summer this whole area would be an impassable swamp. There was no longer a trail, and they moved from clearing to clearing wherever the going was easiest. The pace was quicker, but John felt vulnerable in the open.

John's stomach was growling, he was light-headed with fatigue, and he was glad when they stopped at the edge of a large clearing. It was about two miles across with a depression in the centre.

"We must cross quickly."

"Could we go around?" John said.

"We will lose too much ground."

"The British may not come this far."

"We have killed one of their people. They are well fed and will travel fast. We must cross."

"Let's not waste time, then," John said.

Downhill was easy at first, but the snow was deeper in the open, and John was not looking forward to climbing the other side. Louis led them to the left, avoiding the lowest part of the depression. They covered more ground, but there would be less uphill on the far side.

John was tired beyond anything he had ever known. Louis moved easily on his snowshoes and showed no signs of fatigue, and John wondered how long he could keep up with him. They had passed the centre of the clearing and started up the far side when Louis stopped and looked back. John looked at him, but Louis gestured for him to wait, and he held his breath and listened. There was no wind, and the cold made the silence deeper. It filled John with a sense of the immensity of this land. A tiny sound sent a shock through him. It was a hound howling on the scent, and without a word they started up the slope.

It was a long way to the treeline, and John felt panic rise in him. Judging distance in this black and white landscape was difficult, and he forced his panic down and concentrated on climbing the slope. He kept his head down and pushed as hard as he could. When he finally looked up, they were less than a hundred yards from the treeline, and he increased his pace again.

The ground levelled out, and Louis turned left towards a gap in the trees. John was gasping for breath, and he thought his legs would collapse under him, but he steeled himself for the final effort.

The snow had built a drift across the entrance to the trail, and even with their snowshoes, they sank to their thighs. John held the musket at shoulder level and forced his way forward. As he struggled through the drift, the silence was shattered by a musket shot. Then four more discharges close together. John threw himself down. His snowshoes tangled his feet, and he crawled around the snowdrift on hands and knees.

The musket shots echoed across the landscape, and John realized that whoever fired was a long way off. Louis had crawled to the side of the drift, and John moved over beside him. John searched the clearing. At first he saw nothing then he picked up movement at the edge of the trees. Six or eight men were moving into the open.

John looked at Louis. "Why did they fire? They're well out of range."

"They want us to know they're here, so we run ourselves to exhaustion."

"How many do you see?"

"Six or more. Soldiers and civilians. The men from the town will have the dogs."

They backed away from the snowdrift till they were under the cover of the trees.

"How did they catch us so quickly?" John said. "We didn't stop all night."

"We are weak from prison and the white man's sickness, but they have come far and will be near their limit."

"I don't know how much farther I can run."

"We must stay ahead of them until dark. They won't travel far from the town when it's so cold. The men will tire, but it's the dogs that are the danger."

At that moment the sound of dogs barking carried across the clearing.

"They've loosed the dogs." Louis strode away along the trail, and John had to stretch himself to keep up. He knew he was near exhaustion, but the need to survive drove him on. After half a mile they crossed a small clearing. The snow was deep, and he struggled into the trees on the other side where Louis was waiting. John looked back expecting to see a pack of savage dogs rushing at them, but the clearing was empty.

Louis pushed on for another hundred feet and stopped.

"This is a good place." The trail was only six feet across, and Louis bent a willow down on each side of the trail and tied them together with the strap from the food bag, leaving the bag hanging in the middle of the trail.

"Come." John ducked under the branches and followed Louis.

"What's the bag for?" Louis called over his shoulder.

"We must kill the dogs. The British can't hunt us without them."

* * *

Louis went two hundred feet along the trail, then forced his way into the trees, and started to work his way back towards the food bag. In the trees the snow wasn't as deep, and it only took a few minutes to reach the food bag. They crouched down where they had clear sight of the trail.

"Can you shoot one of the dogs from here?" Louis asked.

"Yes, I can hit one easily."

"There are three, I think. If you can bring one down, I'll kill the others."

John took off his gloves. He took one of the powder flasks from his bag, put a little on his fingertip and tasted it. It was dry and bitter, and he was confident it would fire. He poured powder into the flash pan and closed it firmly. He went down on one knee and brought the musket to his shoulder, checking he had a clear line of sight. Then he brought it down to the ready position and pulled the hammer to half cock.

"I'd like to draw the ball and recharge, but we don't have time."

Louis cocked his head and then dropped his voice to a whisper.

"They come." Louis undid his snowshoes and moved closer to the trail. John moved a few feet to his left and rested the musket on a fallen tree trunk, sighted along the barrel, and waited. He glanced at Louis, but his head was down listening. He was so still, he seemed to blend into the forest. It was a skill John didn't possess, and he wondered if Louis could teach it to him.

John's nerves were jolted by the sound of the dogs panting as they came along the trail. He could hear their paws crunching through the snow, but it was difficult to tell how close they were. He wiped his hand across his eyes and sighted along the barrel of the musket.

A moment later two dogs came into view, both large short-haired, bony animals of indiscriminate breed; one was black and the other a dull brown colour. They leapt at the food bag and bore it to the ground, and the tree sprung free, whipping back across the trail as the bag was torn loose. Both dogs had hold of the bag and were pulling it in different directions. The seconds ticked by, and even in the cold John's palms begin to sweat. The bag wouldn't hold their attention for long, and he had to bring one of them down before he lost the chance.

The opportunity came unexpectedly. One of the dogs managed to work its head inside the bag and stood still holding the bag down with its paw. The other dog tried to force its head inside, too, and for a moment both animals stood side by side. He pulled the hammer back to full cock. The metallic click seemed to echo around the forest, and he cursed silently for not fully cocking the weapon before. The nearest dog lifted its head and looked directly at him. John placed the front sight on its shoulder and pulled the trigger. The musket roared, and the dogs disappeared in a cloud of smoke. The recoil knocked John off balance, and he struggled to his feet as the smoke cleared.

The black dog lay still on the snow, its shoulder reduced to bloody pulp. The brown dog was howling pitifully, its hind legs shattered. John realized the ball must have struck the first dog, killing it, then gone all the way through and crippled the second one. Louis forced his way onto the trail and raised his axe. The wounded dog tried to drag itself away with its front legs, but Louis brought the axe down at its head. The dog twisted away, and the blade glanced off its head knocking it onto its side.

Louis stepped closer, and as he raised his arm to deliver the killing blow, a third dog came hurtling along the trail. It was larger and more powerful than the other two. It had a shaggy grey coat and a yellow cast to its eyes. A warning cry rose to John's lips, but it was too late. A deep growl came from the dog's chest, and it leapt at Louis. Louis spun ready to defend himself, and the hound seized his right arm in its jaws. Louis cried out in pain, and the axe fell from his hand. He was bowled over and landed on his side with the hound on top of him.

John tried to force his way through to the trail, but his snowshoes became tangled in the underbrush. He dropped the musket and tore at the leather thongs, breaking a fingernail as he freed himself. He grabbed the musket and lunged forward sinking knee-deep in the snow. Louis was on his knees. The hound had its jaws locked on his forearm and was jerking backwards violently, pulling him off balance. Louis punched the dog's muzzle again and again, but it didn't have any effect. The dog's jowls were covered in blood, and the snow beneath them was red.

John yanked the bayonet from its scabbard and knocked it against the stock to clear the snow out of the mount. The dog turned its yellow eyes on him as he slid the bayonet onto the end of the musket. John broke out of the trees and charged. The hound backed away, pulling Louis around in a circle. His face was set in pain as the dog worried his arm, pulling at it savagely.

The hound was almost broadside to him, and John moved behind it. It tried to turn away, but Louis held it. John drove the bayonet into the animal's side behind the ribs. The blade sank in without resistance. The dog let go of Louis's arm, howling in pain, and twisted its body almost in half trying to reach the bayonet. Its jaws dripped with bloody drool, and its yellow eyes were mad with pain and fury as it snapped at its side, and John braced himself as it thrashed back and forth.

John drove the bayonet in to the hilt, twisting it back and forth trying to find the heart or lungs. The hound snarled and twisted trying to reach him, dripping bloody foam from its mouth as it snapped at him in frustration. John felt the dog weaken. He pulled the bayonet half out and drove it in again at a different angle. The dog dropped to its knees, but it still tried to reach him with its jaws. He pulled the bayonet out and stabbed into its neck. The animal fixed him with its yellow eyes, and he held its gaze till the life went out of it.

John pulled the bayonet out and went to Louis. He was sitting in the snow, holding his arm against his chest. His face was white with shock, but his eyes were clear.

"How bad is it?" Louis didn't answer. John laid the musket down.

"Let me see." Blood was oozing from between Louis's fingers.

"Let me see the wound."

Louis pulled his sleeve back, gritting his teeth as it slid along his forearm. John blanched when he saw the wound. On either side of the arm between the elbow and the wrist were ten or twelve punctures oozing blood.

"Can you move your fingers?" Louis closed his fist and opened it slowly. John was relieved his hand still worked, but Louis winced with pain.

John pulled his fur tunic over his head and took off his linen shirt. The cold was fierce, and he pulled the tunic on again quickly. He tore the sleeve from the shirt and ripped it into two long strips.

"We need to clean and bind the wound." He took Louis's arm in his hand. Louis looked back along the trail.

"The British will not be far behind."

"I have to stop the bleeding, or you won't get far. This will hurt." He took a handful of snow and washed the blood off the wounds. Louis locked his jaws together but made no sound.

John washed the blood away, but it welled up again, and he bound one of the strips of cloth around the arm and tied it fast. The cloth started to turn red, and John wrapped the other strip around the wound and the bleeding seemed to stop.

John pulled Louis's sleeve down and got to his feet.

"Can you travel?" He took Louis's arm and helped him to his feet.

"I can walk."

"Wait." John ran into the forest and retrieved their snowshoes.

"Step on the shoes." John fastened Louis's shoes and then his own. The dogs had torn the food bag open, scattering its contents on the snow. He gathered up what food he could and stuffed it back in the bag and slung it over his shoulder.

John removed the bayonet, wiped the blood off on the hound's fur, and slid it into the scabbard.

"I must reload before we leave." Louis looked along the trail and nodded. John measured the powder, poured it into the barrel, and tamped it; then he wrapped a ball in one of the leather wads, pushed it into the barrel, and rammed it home. Finally he primed the pan and slung the musket over his shoulder.

"We must go," John said. "You lead." Louis nodded and strode away along the trail.

* * *

They set the best pace they could that would not exhaust them quickly. The trail ran in a straight line for almost a mile, and John kept looking back, fearful he would see the soldiers behind them. Finally the trail dropped into a depression, and he breathed a sigh of relief. The dip was only a few hundred yards across, and as they climbed the far side, he was surprised he was so close behind Louis.

Louis held his arm against his chest, and he swayed on his feet. At the top John called out, "Louis, stop."

"We must keep going; the soldiers may follow."

"This will only take a moment." John transferred the food to his hunting bag and used the bayonet to cut a hole in the side of the food bag.

"Put your arm in this." Louis slid his arm into the bag and John lifted the strap over his head and adjusted it till it took the weight of his arm.

"It is good," Louis said.

John could see Louis's pride was hurt at accepting help, but he was wise enough to know their survival depended on their ability to travel. Now that the immediate danger was over, John felt exhaustion begin to creep up on him. Each step was an effort, and his body ached with fatigue. He knew if the British caught them, they would hang them, and a fierce determination, born more of hatred for the British than fear of death, drove him on.

As they went on, the ground rose steadily, the trees became larger and there was more open ground. Late in the afternoon they entered a clearing on the side of a hill. The snow was deep, and it was heavy going. John felt exposed in the open, and as he searched ahead for danger he realized that the light was fading.

When they reached the trees, John looked back, but there was nothing moving.

"The British won't follow. They won't stay in the forest after dark," Louis said. They stood for a while, watching and listening, then moved on. John knew they were both exhausted. They were coming to the crest of a hill, and he started to look for shelter. The hill was crowned by half a dozen large pines. It looked promising, and he quickened his pace.

John caught up to Louis. He was about to suggest they seek shelter in the trees when he noticed the fur on Louis's tunic was almost black and glistening with moisture.

"Louis, stop." He touched Louis on the shoulder, and he stopped.

"Your wound is bleeding. We have to rebind it." Louis looked at his arm and nodded, but he didn't show any signs of concern, and John eyed him carefully.

"We'll rest in the trees. Can you make it to the top?"

Louis nodded.

They started uphill again, and John watched Louis carefully. Six huge pines stood close together on the crown of the hill surrounded by a circle of open ground. The pines were twice the height of the surrounding forest and their branches spread out to form a wide canopy that almost touched the ground. It was starting to get dark as they approached this island of trees. John began to imagine he saw shapes moving in the darkness, and his skin tingled with fright. He knew he was exhausted, and that his eyes were playing tricks on him, but it was an unsettling feeling.

As they crossed the open ground, Louis staggered. John put his hand on his shoulder to steady him, and was shocked when he saw blood dripping from Louis's wrist.

"Louis, stop. Your arm is bleeding," John said. Louis looked down in surprise as a fat drop of blood fell into the snow and spread out in a red stain. John looked behind them, and his eyes went wide in alarm as he saw a trail of bright red running back across the open ground into the forest.

Louis was looking at his arm glassy-eyed, and he didn't seem to comprehend what was happening.

"Come, Louis, we must—" The words froze on John's lips as a sound rose from the forest behind him that raised the hackles on the back of his neck. It was a high-pitched keening wail, a baleful sound like a lost soul crying in the night. John's fatigue fell away, and the blood pulsed in his head.

The sound came again, off to their right and closer. John spun around, searching the darkness for danger.

"We must go quickly." Louis hurried towards the trees.

"What is it? What is that thing?" Louis didn't answer, grunting with the effort as he pushed himself forward. Weakened though he was, Louis reached the pine trees ahead of John. Another wailing sound came from their left and changed to a low growl.

John had never heard such sounds but they touched some primitive part of him. His mind screamed with fright, and it took all his willpower not to panic. Night seemed to close in around them, and from the darkness, the sound came again, a long, high-pitched wail that made John's scalp tightened painfully. They were surrounded.

"What are these creatures?" John cried. Louis swayed on his feet, a sheen of sweat on his face.

"Wolves. They are wolves," he said. His eyes rolled up in his head, and he fell back into the snow.

CHAPTER TWENTY-ONE

IN THE LAST WEEK OF October, Scott was called to Major Coxe's office. When he entered the office, Coxe got up from his desk and stood with his back to the fire, obviously in a foul mood.

"Captain Scott, some time ago I instructed you to stop the bullying by the men under your command. Now my adjutant tells me two men were taken to the infirmary in recent days, both of them badly beaten."

Scott felt the colour rise in his face. He started to speak, but Coxe silenced him.

"I told you I wouldn't tolerate this behaviour. You have failed in your duty, Captain." Scott tried to interrupt, but Coxe wouldn't listen. "If your men are bored with garrison duty, then we shall give them the opportunity to see action sooner than later."

Coxe clasped his hands behind him. "You are posted to Annapolis Royal to reinforce the garrison against attack from the French and from the local native population. You will report to Major Paul Phelps who commands the garrison."

Scott's anger boiled over. "I'm being sent to this backwater as a result of a dispute between common soldiers. That's ridiculous, Major."

Coxe exploded. "I will decide what is and what is not ridiculous, Captain. You will obey my orders, and there will be no further discussion on the matter."

Scott was furious, but he bit his tongue. He didn't believe he was being sent to Annapolis Royal because of a few bloody noses, but there was little he could do about it.

After a moment Coxe went on. "You will sail on the brig *Spartan*, leaving Boston in the last week of November. Lieutenant Paine has been assigned to your unit. He will make the arrangements. That will be all, Captain. You are dismissed."

Scott left the room. Outside, Coxe's adjutant was studying the papers on his desk and didn't look up as Scott walked down the hall. Scott sent Lieutenant Paine to fetch Sergeant Crammer, but Crammer couldn't be found. Some of the troopers had been granted permission to visit Boston, and given Crammer's appetite for drink and debauchery, Scott knew he wouldn't be seen for days. No matter, he would deal with him in due course.

* * *

The following day Scott visited Mrs. Lockhart in the afternoon. As they took tea, Scott was preoccupied with his meeting with Major Coxe. Sending him to a backwater fort because his sergeant couldn't keep his fists to himself was absurd. He suspected Coxe had received his orders from London.

Mrs. Lockhart put her hand on his arm. "You seem withdrawn, Captain. Is something amiss?"

Scott clasped his hands together in front of him. "I am to be posted to Annapolis Royal as reinforcement for the garrison against attack from the local savages, it seems."

Mrs. Lockhart blanched. "Annapolis Royal? This cannot be. Who has ordered this? When did it happen?"

"Major Coxe delivered his orders to me in person yesterday."

"Major Coxe? I know him passing well, but this isn't his decision, I think."

"Major Coxe has a poor opinion of me, but I suspect there's more to it than that."

"What do you mean?"

Scott leaned forward. "You know why I was sent to Boston. I've made no secret of it. I believe Coxe's orders came from London."

"Are you certain? Most people in London don't even know that Annapolis Royal exists, far less what's transpired there."

"You are correct, but one backwater will do as well as another, I think."

"Coxe is sending you to Annapolis Royal to punish you for transgressions that took place a world away. It won't do. I won't have it."

Mrs. Lockhart got to her feet and paced to the fireplace. "I'll speak with Governor Shirley tomorrow and ask him to intervene."

Scott felt a cold shiver go through him, and he raised his hands to stop her.

"You cannot interfere. It's a military matter." Her eyes opened wide in surprise.

"Major Coxe doesn't have the authority to order you to some far-flung outpost on orders from the other side of the ocean, no matter how highly placed their origin."

Scott felt the colour rise in his neck.

"Elisabeth, you cannot involve yourself in this. I'm a soldier and must follow orders even though I find them distasteful. It's not fitting that you influence such things on my behalf."

"You cannot be serious, Captain. You must put such foolish ideas aside."

Scott got to his feet. "Foolishness has nothing to do with it. You cannot involve yourself in this. I forbid it."

Mrs. Lockhart's hands were shaking with tension. "Forbid it, Captain? Let me remind you that you are a guest in my house, and you have no right to forbid me anything."

"Then perhaps I'd best take my leave."

"Perhaps so."

Scott walked to the door. He was hot with anger and humiliation, but his gut twisted into a knot. Before he realized it, he had closed the door behind him and hadn't even bid her farewell. Mary hurried down the hallway with his greatcoat.

"Thank you, Mary."

"Good night, sir," Mary said as the door closed silently behind him.

Scott strode along the street, his heels tapping out a rhythm on the pavement. Night was coming and the square was almost dark. At the corner he looked back. Light was spilling from Mrs. Lockhart's house, and he thought he saw a shadow in the window, but it was too far to be sure. He walked back to his room with his mind in turmoil and turned and tossed for half the night before he found sleep.

Scott spent the following day discussing transport arrangements with Lieutenant Paine. He had little idea what to expect at Annapolis Royal, and he wanted to be sure they brought adequate supplies, particularly powder and shot. The lieutenant could hardly contain his excitement at the prospect of seeing action for the first time, and threw himself into the preparations with boundless enthusiasm. Scott wondered if his passion would be as ardent when he had seen the real thing. It was difficult to predict how a man would behave under fire until he was put to the test.

On the Friday morning Scott received a note from Major Coxe, advising him that the schedule for departure had been moved up. Over the next ten days Scott worked hard to ensure everything was in readiness. He needed to make sure they had enough supplies to last them through the winter.

Mrs. Lockhart was never far from Scott's mind. Several times he determined that he should speak with her, but the preparations for departure kept him busy. Two days before he was to board the *Spartan*, he sent her a note advising her of his departure date and suggesting that they meet, but he received no reply.

On Wednesday, November 11, Scott boarded the *Spartan*. He introduced himself to the captain, Thomas Blackwell, while Lieutenant Paine billeted the men. A hundred troopers were assigned to the garrison at Annapolis Royal, and sixty Iroquois warriors had been sent to act as scouts. They were lean, muscular men. Their bodies and hair were dyed in bright colours, and they dressed in animal skins and wrapped blankets around their shoulders against the cold. Scott knew little about these men. They were known as excellent scouts and good fighters, but they had a reputation for being bloodthirsty and cruel.

The ship weighed anchor the same afternoon, heading to the northeast, and Scott stood on deck watching Boston disappear over the horizon. Pain throbbed behind his eyes, and he felt as if the sky was pressing down on him, dulling his thoughts. He hadn't heard from Mrs. Lockhart, and he was distressed by this. It was an unfamiliar sensation, and he didn't understand what it meant.

Scott replayed the last words they had spoken to each other in his mind. He knew that her sentiments had been sincere, and in her mind she would be acting in his best interests. But he couldn't accept that she should use her influence to keep him in Boston. He would be the laughing stock of the regiment. He knew he had not behaved well. The feeling turned to acid in his stomach, and he went below to seek the solace of his bunk.

* * *

The voyage to Annapolis Royal was to take six days, but the weather turned stormy. A squall out of the northwest brought them to a standstill, and they spent three days holding position. When the weather abated, they returned to their northeast heading, but it was a rough passage. Scott's sea legs stood him in good stead, but Lieutenant Paine and many of the troopers were prostrated with seasickness. The Iroquois seemed inured to discomfort. They sat on deck, wrapped in their blankets, untouched by the motion of the ship or the cold.

Annapolis Royal was on the east side of the Bay of Fundy. It lay on an inlet that ran parallel to the bay. The inlet was separated from the ocean by a narrow strip of land and ran twenty miles or more to the north. The only entrance was through a narrow passage at the southern end of the channel, called "the cut." Blackwell pointed it out to Scott on the chart and emphasized it could only be navigated at slack water or running with the tide.

At first light on November 17 they were beating back and forth across the entrance to the cut when Scott came on deck. There was snow on the ground, turning the landscape to black and white. As the tide began to run, Captain Blackwell positioned the *Spartan* in the middle of the channel. The cut was less than a quarter of a mile across, and the volume of water that was forced through the gap had to be seen to be believed. Once the tide took hold of the ship, it was impossible to turn back and an error in judgment by the helmsman would dash them on the rocks.

Captain Blackwell kept the *Spartan* in mid-channel until they were well through the gap; then he put the helm over and the tide pushed them up the inlet, and Blackwell kept enough sail on to maintain steerageway. The high and low watermarks were over thirty feet apart. Scott had never seen such a tidal drop and remarked on it to Blackwell.

"It's the highest known tidal drop on the Eastern Seaboard, Captain Scott, perhaps in the world, and when the spring tides run, it can be half as high again."

Shortly after midday Scott saw a column of smoke to the north, and he went up to the bridge and watched Annapolis Royal take shape. The fort stood on a point of land on the eastern side of the inlet. It was constructed of earthen dykes built in a star configuration that created overlapping fields of fire. Cannons were embedded in the dykes, and Scott could see smoke rising from buildings behind the walls.

Columns of smoke were also rising from the forest along the inlet to the north, and Scott saw the outline of buildings along the shoreline and back amongst the trees. Blackwell told Scott these were the homes of the French settlers, who had been in this part of the country for generations. To the south of the fort a strip of flat land ran along the inlet for a mile. Blackwell told him this was drained marshland used to grow food for the fort and to send to Boston.

There was a flurry of activity on deck as the anchor splashed into the water. The tide was still pushing up the inlet, and the *Spartan* spun on the anchor as the crew dropped the sails. Even as she settled at anchor the crew were removing the hatch covers and preparing to offload the cargo.

Two boats left the dock below the fort. As the first one came alongside, two seamen dropped a ladder over the side. The first man to step on deck wore a lieutenant's uniform. He was in his twenties, shorter than Scott, and his skin was pale as if he'd suffered from a long illness. He was followed by a heavyset sergeant in his forties and a regular trooper. The lieutenant went to the bridge and saluted Captain Blackwell.

The lieutenant spoke with Blackwell for a moment, and Scott saw surprise in the lieutenant's face when Blackwell pointed him out. The lieutenant saluted smartly and followed Blackwell below. A few minutes later the lieutenant came back on deck carrying a package of dispatches and saluted Scott.

"I'm Lieutenant Millard, Captain. We had not anticipated reinforcements arriving until the spring."

"We're here now, Lieutenant. Please make arrangements to billet the men." The troops had gathered along the ship's rail to examine the fort.

"Yes, sir. If you'll follow me, I will escort you to Major Phelps's office."

Scott followed Millard to the ladder.

"Sergeant Hale, see that Captain Scott's belongings are brought ashore and taken to the officers' quarters."

"Yes, Lieutenant." The sergeant saluted, examining Scott closely. Scott waved Lieutenant Paine over.

"See that the men are billeted and report to me when they're settled."

"Yes, Captain," Paine said.

The cutter landed them at a wooden dock at the north end of the fort. On the flat ground above the beach stood four long narrow buildings that Scott took to be warehouses. To the left, houses spread along the shore, smoke rising from their chimneys.

Lieutenant Millard took a path between the warehouses and turned right onto a wooden bridge that crossed the ditch.

The gate stood open, and Scott stopped to examine the fort. He counted twelve buildings. They were constructed of stone with high-peaked roofs, chimneys spaced around the outer walls, and narrow glazed windows. There were four barracks blocks and a large L-shaped building that he guessed was the officers' quarters. There were also workshops and storehouses and a powder magazine built into the west dyke.

The fort was bustling with activity. Carts were coming and going through the gate; men were repairing the dykes in several places; and a blacksmith's forge was working against the north wall.

"How many men are garrisoned here, Lieutenant?"

"With the reinforcements, I believe it will be over four hundred, sir."

"This fort isn't large enough for that many men. Where are they billeted?"

"It becomes more difficult every day. We've had to billet some troops with the locals in the town."

Scott waved Millard on and he led him to the officers' quarters on the east side of the parade ground. As he stepped into the foyer Scott was struck by a wave of heat, and Millard closed the door quickly. The foyer was small with a staircase leading up on one side and a hallway running to the back of the building.

"Please wait here, Captain. I will inform Major Phelps that you're here." Millard knocked on a door on the right and entered. Scott removed his coat and a few minutes later Millard stepped out into the hall.

"Major Phelps will see you, Captain Scott."

Scott stepped into a large office with a high ceiling and windows looking onto the parade ground. It was furnished in plain military style, a desk and chair by the window, a table in the centre of the room, and a bookcase against one wall. A fireplace in the end wall of the building had a good fire burning, and the only concession to comfort were two leather-upholstered chairs by the hearth.

Major Phelps sat at the desk, and as Scott entered, he came forward to shake hands. Scott guessed Phelps was forty-five years old. He was the same height as Scott, slender and fit-looking. He had a long face and brown eyes. He was clean shaven, and wore his hair tied behind his head. He was dressed in a dark blue uniform over a white shirt and regulation black riding boots.

The major studied Scott as he shook his hand.

"Welcome, Captain Scott. I requested reinforcements after the French assault but, to be frank, I didn't anticipate their arrival before spring."

"Major Coxe didn't advise me as to why we were deployed at this time, Major."

"No matter. How many men have you brought, Captain?"

"A hundred soldiers and sixty Iroquois scouts."

Phelps nodded.

"Captain Gorham didn't travel with you on the *Spartan*?"

"No, Major. I hadn't heard he would be on board."

Phelps was lost in thought for a moment.

"What do you know of the situation at Annapolis Royal, Captain?"

"Major Coxe briefed me with regard to the French incursion in the summer and suggested that further French aggression was to be expected."

The major nodded. "The French can't attack us in winter. The cold is intense and the terrain impassable. Our patrols have found no indication of French troops in the area, and I now believe an attack in the spring is less likely."

"If that's the case, why were we sent to reinforce the garrison so late in the year?"

"Our political masters in Boston were shocked by the French attack in the summer, and alarmed that so large a body of men could reach Annapolis Royal undetected, so they're taking no chances."

Phelps went on. "My more immediate concern is with the local native population. In the first week of October the fort came under attack by a force of Mi'kmaq. Four men were killed and a dozen injured, some seriously. They attacked at night, and by daylight they had vanished. Shortly after the attack, the first snow fell, preventing us from pursuing them."

"How many natives were involved?"

"No more than a hundred, I would guess."

Scott frowned. "A regrettable loss of life, but such small numbers wouldn't present a real danger to the fort."

"That's true, Captain. However, the attack has had an effect on moral. Also the Mi'kmaq are allies of the French; it would set a dangerous precedent if they are seen to get away with it."

"I see." Scott began to realize that the situation was more complicated than he had thought.

The major drummed his fingers on the desk.

"The natives can be elusive. Captain Gorham is experienced in this type of action and was to lead an expedition against the Mi'kmaq in the spring. The Iroquois were to form the bulk of his 'Rangers,' as he calls his company."

"As I have said, Major, I was not told anything with regard to Captain Gorham."

"I'll speak with Captain Blackwell. Perhaps he can shed some light on the matter. For the present Lieutenant Millard will show you to your quarters. We will speak again when you're settled." They shook hands again.

Lieutenant Millard was waiting in the hall.

"Captain, the officers' quarters are at the other end of the building." Scott nodded and followed Millard along the corridor to the back of the building and up a set of stairs to the second floor. Millard opened a door at the top of the stairs.

"This is the only vacant room, Captain. I hope it's satisfactory."

The room contained a bed, a table and two chairs, a small desk, and a dresser. There was a fire burning in the grate, and the room was warm. The window looked out onto the parade ground and beyond that to the inlet. It was not Mrs. Broadhurst's house, but Scott had stayed in worse places.

"It'll do. Have my belongings brought up."

"Yes, Captain. A woman from the village will bring you fresh bedding, and I will arrange for more firewood. We keep the fires going in all the rooms, even if they're not occupied to keep the building warm."

Millard stepped into the corridor.

"If you'll follow me, Captain." Back on the ground floor they entered a large room spanning the full width of the building and facing onto the parade ground. A fireplace was set into the east wall with wooden benches and chairs arranged around it. A dining table and chairs took up the other side of the room.

Millard pointed to a door on the north side of the room.

"The kitchen is there. A French woman from the village cooks for the officers. The food is plain but plentiful." Scott nodded.

"Please seek out Lieutenant Paine and see that the men are billeted and find a place for Paine."

"Yes, Captain."

At dinner Scott met the rest of the officers. There were four captains and eleven lieutenants, including Millard and Paine. The officers welcomed Scott politely but remained reserved, and he wondered what rumours were circulating about him. Dinner was meat and vegetables. It was hot and a welcome change from the ship's fare. Scott retired soon after dinner and fell into his bed, and his last thoughts before sleep took him were of Elisabeth Lockhart.

* * *

Scott had Lieutenant Millard take him and Lieutenant Paine on a tour of the area. There were few horses kept at the fort, so they spent the best part of a day walking. The village stretched along the inlet for more than a mile. The land around the fort was heavily forested and dotted with small holdings. There were farms along the river to the north of the village, but after a few miles, they gave way to wilderness.

The following day Major Phelps sent for Scott, and they sat across from each other at his desk.

"I've had the opportunity to read the dispatches from Boston, and it appears Captain Gorham has been stricken with fever, hence the reason he wasn't on board the *Spartan*."

"What type of fever?"

"The dispatch isn't specific. I immediately thought of smallpox, but there hasn't been an outbreak in Boston for years."

"I heard nothing of an outbreak of fever before I left Boston."

The major nodded.

"In any case I am assigning you responsibility for leading the expedition against the natives in the spring." Scott was taken aback.

"I have no experience dealing with natives, Major. It would make more sense to have an officer with knowledge of the Iroquois lead the expedition."

"I've reviewed your career, Captain. You have considerable experience in the field, and I believe you are the best officer in the garrison to lead this expedition."

Scott was perplexed. It was irregular for a newly appointed officer to be assigned this type of command. Major Phelps got to his feet and went to the table.

"If you would, Captain." Phelps unfolded a map similar to the one Major Coxe had shown him and placed his finger on it.

"Here is Annapolis Royal." He slid his finger north along the coast. "This is the village of Shubenacadie, the home of the natives who attacked us. The French priest who lives in the village is known to have instigated the attack and also took part in it. His name is Father Jean-Louis Laporte. Your mission will be to retaliate against the village, and the capture of the priest Laporte will be a priority."

Scott placed his index finger on the map, measuring the distance between Annapolis Royal and Shubenacadie, then placed it on the scale.

"Thirty miles?"

"The scale is not accurate. It's likely closer to sixty miles to the village."

"What is the terrain like?"

"The land is forested and hilly. The best approach is along this river valley. It's some distance inland but that may improve your chances of approaching the village undetected."

Scott stepped back from the table.

"When do you want me to leave, Major?"

"As soon as the snow is gone and it's possible to travel. Early May, or if we're lucky, a month earlier."

"There's time to prepare, then."

"The Iroquois will be your best asset. They know the forest, and they are fierce fighters. Get to know them and their ways."

"They have a reputation for savagery, or so I'm told."

"Savagery has its uses, Captain, as I'm sure you're aware."

"May I take the map to study it?"

"Yes, but I'll require it to be returned to me in due course."

Scott rolled up the map.

"Lieutenant Millard will see to it that you have everything you need. He will also accompany you on the patrol." Scott raised an eyebrow.

"Millard has yet to see action, and it's past time he did."

"If that is all, Major."

"Thank you, Captain."

Scott turned at the door. "Major, this is an important mission. May I ask why you don't lead it yourself?"

Phelps's neck coloured. "I'm an engineer. Combat is not my forte. That will be all, Captain."

The following day Scott met with Paine and Millard in the officers' mess and gave them their orders. Both were excited at the prospect of action but were frustrated that it would be months before the mission would commence. Scott tasked them with making preparations. Lieutenant Paine was to create a list of supplies they would need and a training schedule to prepare the men. The Iroquois were ready to take part.

As Scott got up from the table Lieutenant Paine spoke.

"If I may, Captain, as I understand it, the purpose of the mission is twofold. We are to capture the priest Laporte. We are also to retaliate against the village for the attack on the fort. I'm afraid I don't understand what kind of retaliation we are to bring against the Mi'kmaq."

"We're to bring them death, Lieutenant." Both men shared a look.

"Military action isn't the parade ground. If you don't have the stomach for it, perhaps you should consider a career in the civil service."

Scott instructed both men to report to him the following week; then he donned his greatcoat and took the path along the river. He was troubled by the turn of events and wanted to be on his own, to think. There was something not quite right about the meeting with Phelps and his assignment to this mission. Completing the mission was of little concern. He had conducted many such actions. There was more to this than he knew, but there was nothing he could do about it for the present.

Scott's thoughts turned to Elisabeth Lockhart. She had been on his mind almost constantly since he'd left Boston. He was troubled by their parting and perplexed that she hadn't responded to his note. He wanted to unsay the harsh words that had passed between them, and his inability to do so nearly drove him to distraction. Such feelings were alien to him, and he struggled to understand them and to cope with the sense of foreboding that gnawed at his insides.

Scott walked for hours, and by the time he returned to the fort he was hungry and tired but no closer to resolving his feelings for Elisabeth Lockhart. There was nothing he could do to remedy the situation. The winter would be long, and he knew his discontent would only grow in this far-flung place.

CHAPTER TWENTY-TWO

JOHN DROPPED TO HIS KNEES beside Louis. He was unconscious and mumbling to himself in Mi'kmaq.

John pulled off his glove and touched Louis's forehead. He was burning with fever. A wolf howled behind him and another joined it on the other side of the clearing, making a fearful duet. John spun around, expecting to see dark shapes rushing at him, but saw only shadows in the forest, and somehow that was more frightening.

The pine tree behind him was tall, and the branches spread out, forming a broad canopy that almost reached the ground. There was almost no snow around the base of the tree. John pushed his way through, breaking off branches to open a passageway. He stood the musket against the tree, dropped his hunting bag, and removed his snowshoes.

John dragged Louis under the canopy, brushed a patch of ground clear of sticks and laid him on his back with the food bag under his head. He pushed up Louis's sleeve and frowned. His arm was swollen to twice normal size and inflamed. Grey pus and blood were oozing from the bite marks. A wolf howled, closer by and another joined it off to the left. John whirled around, but there was nothing there. He feared they had picked up the smell of Louis's blood, and he pulled the sleeve down.

The wolves howled again, first one then two others together. They were all around him, and John sensed they were gathering their courage. He used a dead branch to clear a patch of ground and used Louis's axe to hack dead branches from the tree until he had a large pile. Then he gathered twigs and pine cones as kindling.

John took the flint, steel and dry moss from his hunting bag. He set the moss on a stone and went to work with the flint and steel. The flint wouldn't spark; the edges were too smooth.

John let out a cry of frustration and one of the wolves howled in response as if it could sense his fear. The sound came from his right, and he turned wide-eyed with fright but couldn't see anything. A low growl put his nerves on edge, and he turned again, expecting to see some dark horror closing on him, but there was only the forest and the shadows.

John set the flint on the stone and struck it with the axe, shattering it into a dozen pieces. He picked up the largest piece and struck it against the steel and a spray of sparks flew immediately. He grunted in relief and struck again and again, throwing a steady stream of sparks onto the moss, but it didn't light, and he feared it had become damp during the chase.

Something made John stop. He looked around, and his blood froze in his veins. At the edge of the forest something was watching him. The hair stood up on the back of his neck, and his scalp tightened. The shadows were moving as if the darkness was shaping itself into a solid form. He couldn't see it, but its eyes flashed in the darkness as if lit from within.

John fought down a wave of panic, and struck the flint against the steel, furiously throwing off sparks onto the moss.

"Light for pity's sake, light." He struck the flint harder until his arm ached. Then he saw a red spark, and a tiny feather of smoke rose from the moss. He blew gently on it, and to his relief, it burst into flames. He held the candle over the flame, and the wick burned with a bright yellow flame. A wave of elation washed over him, and he set the candle down on the stone.

The wolf was twenty-five feet from him. John was astonished at its size. It stood waist high at the shoulder. Its legs seemed too long for its body. Its head was long and narrow, and its lip was curled back, exposing long fangs and a row of yellow teeth. It was covered in coarse hair, black on its legs and belly, fading to grey at the shoulder.

The wolf stared at John. Both the pupil and the white of its eyes were blue. He had never seen anything like them, and they were terrifying. The wolf focused on him with savage purpose. It lifted one paw and placed it delicately in front of it then froze. Fear rippled down John's spine as he felt the animal will him not to move. A burning pain shot his left hand. He cried out and pulled his hand away from the candle and fell backwards. The wolf snarled savagely and gathered itself to charge, but when it saw the candle it stopped and stepped to the side and John edged back till he came up against the tree.

John took the musket and set it across his knees, never taking his eyes off the wolf. It stood perfectly still, its eyes boring into his, and slowly it began to inch forward. John pulled the hammer back, it clicked to half cock, and the wolf lifted its head, sniffing the air. John raised the musket to his shoulder and pulled the hammer to full lock. The mechanical sound was unnaturally loud in the quiet of the forest, and the wolf dropped its head and moved to the right in front of him.

The wolf stopped, still standing side on to him. John placed the front sight in the middle of its shoulder and began to take up the pressure on the trigger. He was startled when he heard Louis speak.

"Wound him only." John glanced at Louis. He had raised himself on his good elbow. His voice was weak, and his chest rattled with fluid, but his eyes were clear, and John nodded.

John had only looked away for a second, but the wolf was farther to the right and closer. It was suspicious but he sensed it wouldn't hesitate much longer. John placed the front sight in the middle of the animal's body and squeezed the trigger. The musket's discharge shattered the silence. The recoil drove his shoulder back against the tree, and the wolf disappeared in a cloud of smoke. The wolf howled in pain and alarm and the other wolves set up a chorus of barking and howling. A wolf growled behind him and crashed away through the bushes, and John spun around alarmed at how close it had come without him hearing it.

The clearing was empty, but the sounds that came from the forest chilled his blood. The pack had turned on the wounded animal and were tearing it apart. Its squeals of pain and terror were harrowing, and John gasped in horror at the savagery of this land.

John forced himself to ignore the sounds. He had to work quickly before the wolves returned. He built a pile of twigs and pine cones and held the candle against them until they caught fire. Then he fed branches and twigs onto the flames till he had a good going fire. He blew out the candle and placed it in his hunting bag. He broke more branches off the tree and gathered deadfall until he had enough fuel to last the night.

John reloaded the musket and leaned it against the tree. The sounds of the wolf's torment had ceased, but he could still hear the wolves squabbling over the carcass. A wave of relief washed over him as he looked at the fire burning strongly. He took a long breath, and his heart began to slow.

John put his hand on Louis's brow. It was hot, and he was trembling and mumbling in delirium. John wiped his face and neck with snow and tried to get him to swallow some, but he coughed it up, and he stopped, afraid he would choke. He moved Louis closer to the fire and sat against the tree to gather his thoughts.

John fed wood onto the fire. He searched the forest for any sign of the wolves, but all he could see were shadows cast by the fire. He placed the musket across his knees and waited. He was tired and hungry and when the heat started to creep into his bones, he got to his feet and stood with his back to the fire, watching.

Later he sat against the tree to rest, and in spite of his best efforts, he nodded off for a few moments. He came awake with a start, looking around in alarm, and threw more wood on the fire. Once he thought that he saw a wolf's eyes flash in the firelight, and he leapt to his feet, but it was gone. Later in the night he heard the sound of an animal breathing close by and whirled around, musket at the ready, but there was nothing but darkness, and he couldn't tell if he'd imagined it. He kept watch as long as he could, but fatigue crept up on him like a thief in the night and, against every instinct, he let his eyes close.

* * *

John came awake. Some instinct had pulled him up from the depths of sleep, and he looked around anxiously. The fire had burned down to embers, and the first light was in the sky. A wolf was standing at the edge of the forest, watching him. It was perfectly still, but as their eyes met, it charged. John rolled to his feet cradling the musket in the crook of his arm. He was stiff from sitting in the one position all night, but fear flushed all stiffness out of him. He pushed the canopy aside and stepped into the open where he could get a clear shot.

The wolf was coming across the clearing in six-foot bounds, and the pack started howling in the trees. John forced himself to ignore them and concentrated on the wolf. He only had one shot, and for a fleeting moment he regretted not fixing the bayonet. He pulled the hammer to full cock and threw the musket up to his shoulder. The wolf came on silently, moving with unbelievable speed, and he focused his entire being on it. He followed it as it landed, gathering its hind legs under it for the next leap. It would be on him in seconds.

The world slowed for John, and as the wolf rose up out of the snow he placed the sight in the middle of its chest and squeezed the trigger. The musket roared and John saw the wolf thrown backwards before it disappeared in a cloud of smoke.

John stood breathing hard; his hands were shaking but his vision was crystal clear. The wolves were quiet and the cold air flowed into his lungs like sweet wine washing relief through him. A wolf snarled behind him and he spun around. He could see nothing, but he sensed something watching him.

John pushed back under the canopy and set the musket against the tree. He threw wood on the fire, feeding it until it was roaring. As if in response, the wolves set up a chorus of growls and strange little barking sounds. John ignored them and reloaded the musket. He sat beside Louis, whose breathing was ragged, face wet with perspiration. He cried out in his native tongue at whatever demons haunted his dreams. John wiped his face with snow and tried to make him comfortable.

John stared into the forest. He couldn't see the wolves, but knew they were there. The sound of a twig snapping, snow falling in the underbrush and low growls revealed their presence. He picked up the musket and stepped out into the clearing, and the wolves immediately became agitated, growling and snarling furiously.

The way they had torn one of their own apart the night before, John knew they were ravenous. The scent of the dead wolf would drive them mad. He knew that he had to give them the carcass, or they would come for it. Once they found their courage, they would press their attack on himself and Louis.

John stepped back under the canopy and set the musket down. He felt light-headed and put his hand against the tree to steady himself. The moment passed, but he let out a cry of frustration and threw more wood on the fire then grabbed the axe and went out into the clearing. The wolves greeted him with a chorus of growls and whines of frustration, and he forced his way through the snow to the dead wolf. He was astonished at its size. Head to tail it was almost as long as he was tall. It looked starved, but he thought it still weighed more than he did. The musket ball had struck the left side of its chest and had come out of its back leaving a massive exit wound.

John stamped the snow flat and pulled the animal's rear legs together, stretching the carcass out. He brought the axe down on the wolf's spine and the blade cracked as it struck bone. The wolves became frantic, and he glanced around nervously. He knew that they were close, but they didn't show themselves. John returned to the task. He hacked at the wolf's backbone forcing the axe between the vertebrae to separate the spine then cut ahead of the back legs. The wolf's hide was tough, and the axe was dull, but he persevered.

The smell of blood sent the wolves into a frenzy. John ignored them and chopped at the carcass until the rear haunches came away from the body. He straightened up and looked around. The wolves were becoming more agitated every moment. He sensed they were reluctant to break cover in daylight, but he didn't believe it would hold them for long.

John slid the axe into his belt, grasped the wolf's front paws and started to drag the carcass towards the trees. Even without its hind quarters the wolf was heavy, and it took all his strength. He could hear the wolves moving in the underbrush and once he caught a glimpse of a dark form deeper in the forest. He stopped twenty feet from the treeline. Some instinct told him to keep his eyes on the trees, and he backed away from the carcass. He was halfway to the fire when a wolf broke from trees and bounded towards the carcass. It was smaller than the animal he'd killed, and he guessed it was a female. Three others broke into the clearing; a fourth lingered at the treeline.

The wolves pounced on the carcass tearing at it ferociously. The largest wolf started to drag it towards the trees, and the other two pulled back. The larger wolf snapped at their muzzles in fury; they let go and it dragged the carcass back into the forest.

John dragged the wolf's haunches across the clearing and wrestled them under the canopy. Some instinct made him turn around. The female wolf was inside the canopy, creeping towards him on her belly. She snarled and launched herself at him, and John threw himself back over the carcass. She snapped at him but wasn't able to resist the smell of blood and started to drag the haunches out into the clearing.

John leapt to his feet. The musket was out of reach and he grabbed up a burning branch from the fire and lunged at the wolf. He landed with one foot on the carcass, and thrust the burning branch into the wolf's face. It let out a whine of pain and backed up, pawing at its muzzle and shaking its head. John stepped into the clearing. The wolf turned, snarling in pain and anger, and he thrust the burning branch into its face again. It let out a yelp and bounded away then turned again, but John charged at it, waving the burning branch in front of him and screaming at the top of his lungs. With a growl of fear or frustration, the wolf fled.

John stood breathing hard. He could hear the wolves tearing the carcass apart. It made his blood run cold, but he shook it off and went back to the comfort of the fire.

John kept the fire crackling. He looked up concerned that the tree would catch fire, but he'd already broken off all the dead branches, and the green ones wouldn't burn. He chopped the hind quarters in two, separating the legs and set about skinning one haunch. The axe was too blunt to be of much use, so he used the bayonet to punch holes along the leg. Then he slid the blade under the skin and made one long cut.

John peeled the hide off one leg. There was a layer of white fat between the skin and the flesh, and he cut through it and took the meat off in long strips. He peeled the bark off a branch, cut holes in two strips of meat and threaded them onto the branch. He held them over the flames, and the fat melted spattering in the flames as the meat began to roast. His stomach growled and he could barely contain himself, but he kept turning the stick to make sure the meat was cooked properly.

Finally John slid a strip of meat off the stick and bit into it. It was tough and gamey, but if it had been a prize cut of beef, it couldn't have tasted better to him. The fat ran down his chin, and he swallowed almost choking in his eagerness until he had eaten the whole strip. He sat against the tree and ate the second strip without stopping then licked his fingers clean.

John sat and let his stomach settle. He looked at Louis. He was burning with fever and moaning in his sleep. John crouched beside him and pulled his sleeve up. Louis cried out in his delirium. His arm was swollen and festering.

George Douglas

Soon his blood would become poisoned, and he would die. He had to get the poison out of him.

* * *

John searched around in the snow for the shards of shattered flint and selected a piece with a razor-sharp edge. He examined the bite marks on Louis's arm closely. There were two sets on the upper arm and one close to his wrist. He started at the elbow. He held Louis's arm against his chest and cut across the centre of the bite mark, and Louis cried out and thrashed in his sleep. John held him fast and cut again. He made incisions across all the bite wounds, cutting down until they bled and squeezed until the pus came out. He gagged at the smell, but kept working until all the wounds bled clean. He washed Louis's arm with snow and bound it up again. John tried to push snow into Louis's mouth. He choked and spat it out, but he managed to get him to swallow a little. Then he moved him closer to the fire and tried to make him comfortable.

John butchered the rest of the wolf's hind quarters, skinning the other leg and cutting the meat into strips. He built a framework of branches over the fire and roasted the meat. He took the food bag from under Louis's head and replaced it with his hunting bag. The meat filled the food bag, and there was enough to feed them both for several days.

With a full belly John's spirits rose. He sharpened the axe on a stone and gathered more fuel for the fire. He worked his way around the tree hacking off dead branches and stacked them around the base of the tree forming a rudimentary wall. It wouldn't stop the wolves, but it would make it more difficult for them to creep up on him.

There were five other pines in the grove, and John stripped the dead wood from two of them till he had enough fuel for several days. He knew he wouldn't use it all, but the work stopped him thinking about what he would do if Louis died.

By the time he had finished cutting wood, it was close to the middle of the day. John unbound Louis's arm and repeated the process of squeezing the wounds until they bled. Louis thrashed around, and he had to hold him down, but there was less pus, and it didn't smell as bad. He took that as a good sign, bound the wounds up and tried to get Louis to swallow more snow.

254

There was no sound from the wolves, John took the musket and walked around the trees but saw no sign of them. He found no tracks other than where he had killed the wolf earlier; he couldn't see them, but he sensed they were there in the shadows, watching and waiting.

John fed the fire, tended Louis's wounds, and slept off and on as the day wore on. The previous days had been exhausting, and he needed the rest. Better to sleep now than in the night when the wolves would become bolder.

John awoke as it was getting dark to find Louis awake.

"Louis, how are you?" Louis tried to speak, but he was wracked by a fit of coughing.

"Wait." John gathered a handful of snow and squeezed it into a ball.

"Put it in your mouth, and let it melt." He slid it between Louis's lips and tears welled in his eyes as he chewed the snow. John fed him more until he nodded it was enough.

"Don't try to speak. I'll get you some meat." He held a strip of meat over the flames to soften it and chopped it into pieces with the axe.

John helped Louis onto his side and fed him. He was weak but he ate half a strip before he became too exhausted.

"What of the wolves?" Louis said

"They're out there, but they're not so sure of themselves now." John looked at the darkening forest, and when he turned back, Louis was asleep. His skin was cooler, and John hoped the fever had broken.

John stoked the fire till the flames crackled. He was delighted Louis had been able to eat and drink, and he was sure he would recover. A wave of relief swept over him, and his spirits began to rise. He knew he couldn't survive without Louis, but they were also friends, and it would be good to have him back.

John's thoughts were interrupted by the howl of a wolf on the other side of the clearing. They were still out there waiting, and his temper flared at the relentlessness of these creatures.

"We will see who's hunting who," John said under his breath. He dug a fist-sized stone out of the ground and wrapped it in the hide with the scraps of fat and bone and tied it fast. John pulled the hammer to half cock and leaned the musket against the tree again.

John took the bundle of hide and bone and stepped into the clearing. Immediately there was a low growl behind him. He ignored it, and threw the bundle across the clearing. It landed silently, disappearing into the snow halfway to the treeline.

John marked the spot and drew a line to where he stood. Then he sat against the tree with the musket on his knees and pulled the hammer to full lock. He could hear the wolves yipping with excitement and building their courage. John kept his eyes on the edge of the trees. It was almost dark when he picked out a shadow creeping into the clearing.

John kept his eyes on the wolf and tried not to blink. It crept closer to where the hide had fallen and stopped sniffing the air. It was nervous, but it couldn't resist the smell of blood. The wolf hesitated for a moment longer; then another dark shape rushed past it and pounced on the hide. The wolf let out a snarl of rage and sprang forward.

John kept his eyes on the wolves and brought the musket to his shoulder. All he could see were shadows as they fought over the hide. He didn't have much time. If one got the upper hand, it would bound away into the darkness in seconds. He centred the front sight on the dark mass, picking the spot by instinct rather than sight and pulled the trigger.

The musket roared, and five feet of flame erupted from the end of the barrel. John's night vision was ruined, and he cocked his head to listen. The night was still. Only the crackling of the fire disturbed the silence. He waited and finally, deep in the forest, he heard it, the sound of a wolf squealing in pain and terror.

John reloaded the musket and sat with his back to the fire watching the forest. He slept in fits and starts, but he heard no more from the wolves, and finally he slept soundly.

CHAPTER TWENTY-THREE

JOHN AWOKE TO FIND LOUIS watching him, and he moved to his side. He squeezed some snow into a ball, and Louis was able to put it in his mouth himself. He chewed the snow and swallowed it, nodding his thanks.

"Is there food?" His voice was raw.

"I'll get you some." John roasted a strip of meat and chopped it into chunks that Louis could swallow.

Louis ate slowly, but he finished the whole strip. John roasted another, and he ate it as well and swallowed more snow.

John sat beside him.

"Let me take a look at your arm." He slid Louis's sleeve up and undid the bandage.

"The pain is less," Louis said. The swelling had gone down, and the wounds had closed up. John replaced the bandage and slid his sleeve down.

"It looks like . . ." John started to speak but Louis was asleep.

John busied himself around the camp all day gathering and stacking firewood, and he was surprised when he saw that darkness was falling.

John watched the forest. He felt he had turned the tables on the wolves, and he felt more confident. He had shot three wolves and reduced the odds against them. He should be pleased, but the animal's howls of terror as they

257

were torn apart stuck in his mind. The wolves' ruthlessness knew no bounds, and he wondered how he would survive in this savage place.

When John awoke Louis was on his side, trying to pull himself into a sitting position. John squeezed some snow for him.

"How do you feel?"

Louis chewed the snow and swallowed. "We must travel this day." His voice was still raw, but he sounded stronger.

"Can you sit up?"

"Give me your arm."

John helped Louis to sit against the tree; then he roasted more meat and sat beside him as they ate.

"What of the wolves?"

John finished chewing. "I shot three. I think there are three left, but they may be gone."

"They won't leave while there's food. They will follow."

Louis rolled to his knees, and John put his hand on his arm and lifted him.

"Are you strong enough?" Louis leaned against the tree unsteadily. John took his arm, and they walked around the fire. Louis was shaky on his feet, but by the third circuit he was walking on his own.

Louis sat down again.

"How much meat is there?"

"Enough for two days, perhaps three." John put two more strips on the fire.

"Maybe you should rest another day."

"Each day the weather will become colder. It's better to go south."

John wasn't convinced Louis could travel, but he said nothing. When they had eaten, John checked that the powder in the musket was dry then strapped on the ammunition belt and his hunting bag. Louis carried the food bag and slid the axe into his belt. They tied on their snowshoes and stood ready to depart.

"What about the fire?"

"Let it burn. It'll confuse the wolves."

"I haven't seen the wolves for some time. I think they've gone."

"We'll see," Louis said. John threw more wood on the fire. He was glad to be moving south, but the camp had been a safe haven and part of him was reluctant to leave it.

* * *

That night they camped under a fallen tree and ate roasted wolf meat.

"What's the journey to your village like?"

"My village is far to the south. It will take many days, perhaps the passage of a moon to reach it. This place is what the British call an island." He made a sweeping motion with his arm. "We must cross the gap to the mainland. Beyond that it is still far to my village."

John rolled onto his elbow. "Apart from Louisburg did the British take other towns from the French?"

"The French have settlements to the south along the seacoast, but I don't think the British have attacked them."

John tried to bring the map de La Tour had drawn on the floor of the cell to mind.

"What are your relations with the French?"

"Once we traded with the French, furs for tools and weapons. In my father's time the French took our women as wives, and lived amongst us. Now the fur is gone, and the French trade with the people of the north where the cold makes the fur grow thick. "

John rested his head on his hunting bag.

"Tell me of your people, Louis. Where do they come from? What is their history?"

"We are the people of the dawn," Louis said. "We have been on this land since before memory." He swept his hand across the forest. "We are of this land and will always be of this land."

John gazed at the stars on their endless journey across the sky. He wondered where his journey would take him and he realized that he didn't fear what lay ahead. His eyes were still filled with stars when sleep took him.

Before they set off the next morning he cut a notch in a stick and put it in his hunting bag.

* * *

On the day John cut the thirtieth notch, Louis said they would reach his home the following day.

When they set off next morning the forest was close around them, and John couldn't see far ahead. By the end of the morning they were climbing the side of a shallow valley, and as they approached the summit John called out excitedly, "Smoke! There's smoke on the horizon." He caught up to Louis at the top. A thin column of smoke rose in the distance, leaving a dark smudge against the blue sky.

"That must be your village. How far it is?"

"We will reach it before dark," Louis said.

John couldn't wait to meet Louis's people and to sleep with a roof over his head. They didn't stop at midday, and John chewed on dried meat to keep his strength up. In late afternoon they climbed a long hill, and to the south he could see clear sky. As they came to the summit, he smelt wood smoke and broke into a run.

He stopped on the edge of the hill, staring wide-eyed. Below him lay a broad valley running east to west across their path. The valley was thickly treed, and a river cut a path down the centre. Smoke was rising from the forest along its banks.

"What is this place?" John said.

"The valley is called Shubenacadie, as is the river. It is my home."

John had been eager to reach civilization, and now that it was close, he felt unsure of himself.

"How will your people receive me?"

"You are my friend, and they will make you welcome." Louis had shown little emotion since Mathieu had died, but as he looked down into the valley, his eyes were wet.

"Let's go down, then, and see my new home," John said.

CHAPTER TWENTY-FOUR

"YOU MUST STAND WITH US and fight the British." Father Jean-Louis's eyes bored into John.

John stood up abruptly. "It's late, Father, and I must take my leave."

The priest sank back on the chair, struggling to bring himself under control. He placed his palms together in front of him and drew a slow breath. When he looked up, John saw something that might have been regret in his eyes.

Father Jean-Louis was fifty years old. His body was lean and hard from years spent in the wilderness. His face was lined from the sun, and his eyes were dark, almost black. He wore the black robe of a priest, and a crucifix hung around his neck.

John picked up his tunic. "Thank you for your hospitality, Father, and for the food."

Father Jean-Louis nodded. "Wait." He took a leather bag from a shelf above the desk and held it out to John.

"You carry the Brown Bess musket. The balls will fit the barrel, I think." The bag contained thirty or forty lead balls and a flask of powder.

John smiled. "Thank you, Father. This is a gift, indeed."

"Use them well, my young friend. Ammunition is worth more than gold in this land."

"I will, Father. Thank you again."

Father Jean-Louis stood by John as he tied his snowshoes and made the sign of the cross. "Go with God, my young friend, but come and see me again. We have much to discuss."

John jogged across the clearing. At the trail to the river, he looked back. Father Jean-Louis raised his arm and waved.

John stopped at the river to gather his thoughts. He was hungry to learn all he could about this country. The priest possessed vast knowledge of the land and its people. He was fanatical about his religion and his hatred of the British, and he tried to force John to attend his church and to submit to his authority. John had visited him once shortly after he arrived in the village but had avoided him since.

The winter had passed quickly, and John had regained his health and strength. Louis's mother and two brothers had died of smallpox the previous year, but his father, Joseph, had welcomed him to the village and treated him like a son, and Louis's sister Françoise was teaching him to speak Mi'kmaq.

That night John asked Louis about the priest.

"He came to live amongst us when I was a boy. He brought Frenchmen from Port Royal to build his cabin and the building he calls a church."

"Your people have made him welcome, then?"

"The French know our ways. They have been our allies for generations."

A few days later John decided to visit the priest again. He hoped to learn more about the conflict between the British and the French. He also hoped Father Jean-Louis could help him find his way in this land.

Father Jean-Louis boiled water for tea, and they talked about the coming spring. The priest seemed eager to put John at ease, and showed none of the fanaticism that had made him uncomfortable on his previous visits. The priest's journal was open on the desk.

"What's the date, Father?" Father Jean-Louis looked up from his kettle.

"It's April seventh." John was astonished. It was a month later than he had calculated, and suddenly he was filled with the need to plan for the future.

"What can you tell me about this land, Father? There is so much that I don't know."

Father Jean-Louis poured the tea and took the cups to the table.

"Let me show you what I can." John sipped the tea, savouring the heat as it warmed his insides. Father Jean-Louis lifted a trap door and climbed down to the cellar. A moment later he emerged carrying a leather sleeve. He slid a map out and spread it on the table. It covered the east coast of the British and French colonies, but to the west it was blank. The map was finely drawn by an expert hand, and John was delighted with it.

Father Jean-Louis ran his finger along the map.

"This is the St. Lawrence River, here are Quebec, and Mont-Royal. These towns are the heart of French Canada." He moved to the south.

"This is Boston. It was from here that the attack on Louisburg was launched."

Father Jean-Louis pointed to a bay to the north.

"This is Hudson's Bay. This area is rich in fur." He put his hand on John's shoulder. "I see the light of adventure in your eyes, my young friend, but making a fortune in the fur trade is not as simple as you might think."

"What do you mean, Father?"

"There's tremendous wealth in the fur trade, and those involved will do almost anything to protect their interests."

"The land is vast, Father. There must be fur for the taking."

"It's difficult work, and the natives are highly skilled in the art. If you go into their lands to trap, they'll kill you."

"How do you become a trader, then?"

"That's not so simple."

The priest ran his finger over Hudson's Bay. "The exclusive rights to trade fur in Hudson's Bay were granted to a group of British companies over a hundred years ago in the form of a royal charter. The natives in this area send their furs to the British through Albany and Boston."

John nodded. "What of the French?"

Father Jean-Louis pointed to the north of Hudson's Bay. "The natives from the north and eastern parts of Hudson's Bay trade their fur with the French."

"What then of the British monopoly?"

"The French deny the British have the right to such a charter. It's been a source of discord and often violence between them for many years. But as you say, the land is vast, and it's impossible to enforce such a monopoly."

"Where are we on the map, Father?"

The priest placed his finger on a point on the eastern coast of the Bay of Fundy. "Shubenacadie is here and this is Port Royal." He slid his finger southwest to a long inlet off the bay.

"Is that the place the Mi'kmaq attacked?"

The priest's mouth tightened. "The British have much to answer for in this land." He strode to the fire and set more water to boil.

John sat on the bench by the fire. Father Jean-Louis's hands were shaking as he spooned tea into the kettle.

"Why did the Mi'kmaq attack the British? Why would the villagers provoke them?"

Father Jean-Louis pulled a chair to the fire and sat opposite John.

"Last fall, Gabriel—you will know him from the village—went to Port Royal to trade. One of the merchants gave him blankets. It was old inventory he said, a gift from the fort, and Gabriel shared them with the villagers."

Father Jean-Louis leaned forward.

"A few days later, some of the villagers became ill. It was smallpox, I have seen it before. There were British blankets in every teepee where there was sickness."

"How many became sick?"

"Before the smallpox over three hundred souls lived in the village. There are less than half that now."

Father Jean-Louis sat very still.

"Was there smallpox in the fort?" John said.

The priest's voice became brittle. "There was no sickness at the fort. They knew the blankets were riddled with the smallpox."

"I don't understand, Father," John said. "I thought that smallpox was carried by noxious vapours in the air."

Father Jean-Louis shook his head. "We don't know how it spreads, but it's a rule of our order that the clothes of a brother who has smallpox must be burned."

"If it's true, it's an evil deed even for the British."

"It's been done before by the British and others."

Father Jean-Louis looked away. Clearly this was a subject he didn't want to discuss.

"And the villagers attacked the fort in revenge?" John said.

Father Jean-Louis nodded. "More than forty warriors took part, I went with them."

"When did this take place?"

"We arrived as the first snow fell. After dark we crept through the town to the eastern dyke." The priest stopped speaking.

"Father?"

The priest shook his head. "We waited until the change of the guard, when there were many soldiers on the dyke, and fired on them. They were taken by surprise and fell into a panic firing randomly into the darkness. Later we heard that more than twenty soldiers were struck down."

Father Jean-Louis fell silent, and after a few moments he went on.

"In the darkest part of the night we withdrew."

John sensed the priest was struggling with some personal conflict.

"Did you fight, Father?" The priest covered his face with his hands, and after a moment he looked up.

"I shot one soldier, and I fired on several others." The man I shot died, and I don't know if I struck any others." John nodded, encouraging him to go on.

"I lashed out in anger at the evil that was done to this village. I believe that my God will know this and understand." There were tears in the priest's eyes, and for a moment John glimpsed something of the man behind the robes and the fanatic's voice.

The priest went on.

"The snow fell steadily the next day and the temperature dropped. The British don't venture far from the fort in such weather."

John sipped his tea, but it tasted bitter, and he set it down.

"I know little of this land, but I know the British, and they won't let such an assault go unpunished. They will seek revenge."

"Let them come. God will strengthen our hand, and we will throw them back."

John visited Father Jean-Louis several times in the following weeks. The priest shared his knowledge freely, but he continued to pressure John to conform to his doctrine and beliefs. John refused to let the priest control him, and their meetings ended in angry words. On his last visit Father Jean-Louis was more conciliatory, they parted on good terms, and he gave John a journal and pen and ink as a parting gift.

John wrote in the journal every day. He recorded the date, what he had done, and his thoughts and feelings. He found great solace in this. The act of writing his thoughts helped him to come to terms with his situation and to accept that he might never see his homeland and family again. The journal was a valuable gift, and John was grateful for it, but he remained wary of the priest and kept his distance.

At the beginning of May, John wrote of his astonishment as spring seemed to arrive overnight. The snow melted, leaving the landscape bright and clean. Buds appeared on the trees, and wild flowers carpeted the landscape with colour.

John's spirits rose with the season. He put away his furs, and he and Louis sat outside the teepee to eat their evening meal for the first time.

"Tomorrow will be a good day to hunt." Louis nodded. "The snow is gone, and the ground is dry."

They had hunted throughout the winter, ranging farther afield each time as game became scarce. John had become adept at travelling on snowshoes, but he looked forward to hunting on solid ground.

"We will leave before sunrise." John nodded. Louis still grieved the loss of his family, but John sensed that the shadow was lifting, and he hoped to see again the light-hearted man who had become his friend in Louisburg.

John awoke before dawn to find Louis already on the move. He had slept in his breeches and socks, and he slid his shirt and buckskin tunic on and pulled on his hunting boots. He took his hunting bag and musket and ducked under the entrance to the teepee.

Louis was looking to the east. The first light was in the sky. He was dressed in a buckskin tunic and leggings, and he had moccasins on his feet. He carried his bow, a knife, and a tomahawk on his belt, and he had a blanket slung over his shoulder.

"It will be a good day to travel," he said. John slung his hunting bag and plaid over his shoulders and slid the tomahawk Louis had given him into his belt and took up the musket.

"Let's go." He was eager to be on the move and looking forward to the feel of solid ground under his feet again.

A veil of mist covered the river. It flowed over the banks and around their feet like a soft cloud. The trees rose from the mist like dark sentinels guarding the riverbank. The sun came up over the edge of the valley and burned away the mist, turning the surface of the river to silver, and John squinted against the glare. The buds were sprouting, the valley was bursting with life, and he felt his spirits rise at the prospect of the hunt.

A mile from the village they came to the first ford. John set his musket down and pulled his boots and socks off. He rolled his breeches up and stuffed the boots into his hunting bag. Louis was already wading into the river. The water was ice cold. John gasped as it splashed over his feet and ankles, and he was thankful that it only came as high as his knees.

On the north bank Louis led off to the northeast. The trail was wide, and the ground dried quickly as they moved away from the river. They fell into an easy loping run that they kept up all morning, and John revelled in the feeling of freedom. The smells of the forest were like wine to his senses, and after the black and white of winter, the colours of spring were a feast to his eyes.

At midday they stopped to eat pemmican and drink. There was little need to talk, and they saved their breath to run. John knew the game moved inland in the spring, and they didn't expect to find good hunting till they were out of the valley. In the late afternoon they reached a range of small hills and decided to make camp. They lit a fire and built a shelter, a process they had refined on their journey from Louisburg.

Louis heated water on the fire. John had become accustomed to the bitter tea the Mi'kmaq made. On the journey from Louisburg he had learned to his astonishment that it was proof against scurvy. He hadn't believed it at first, but since he had started drinking the tea, his gums had healed and the rash on his skin had vanished. He was incredulous that the British hadn't learned this, and he wondered what other knowledge the Mi'kmaq possessed.

John wrapped himself in his plaid. It had been a good day, but his muscles ached, and he was ready to sleep. Louis poured tea into a bowl for John and for himself. John blew on the steaming liquid and took small sips, savouring its warmth. Louis lifted his chin.

"We shall see game tomorrow, I think."

"What've you seen?"

"A buck and four does on the trail before we made camp."

John was constantly astonished by Louis's abilities as a tracker. He could recognize the smallest sign an animal left and knew what it meant. He had taught John the basic things to look for, but Louis's skills had been honed by a lifetime in the forest, and he would never match them.

"I will watch," Louis said. Standing watch had become a habit on the trail from Louisburg and even in Louis's own country they continued the practice.

"Wake me when you're ready to sleep," John said. He rolled himself in his plaid and was asleep in minutes.

CHAPTER TWENTY-FIVE

IN THE FIRST WEEK OF May, Scott met with Lieutenants Paine and Millard and instructed them to prepare to depart two days hence. Scott impressed on them the need for discretion. The local people would hear about the patrol, but the less time they had to warn the priest or the natives, the better. Preparations were to be treated as a practice drill until the day they were to depart.

Lieutenant Paine was excited at the prospect of seeing action for the first time. Scott cautioned him to contain his enthusiasm lest he let something slip. Millard was more subdued and had few illusions about what to expect. Scott took Millard aside and instructed him to stay close to Lieutenant Paine on the patrol. The last thing he wanted was an amateur under his feet.

The following day Major Phelps sent for Scott. He handed him a two-page document and instructed him to read it in his presence. The document instructed Scott to lead a patrol to Shubenacadie and to conduct a raid on the village in retribution for the attack on the fort the previous October. It also instructed him to capture the priest Father Jean-Louis Laporte and bring him to Annapolis Royal to face charges of treason.

Major Phelps faced Scott.

"Do you understand your orders, Captain?"

"Yes, Major. However, there's no reference to the degree of retribution to be exacted from the villagers."

"That will be at your discretion, Captain. Bear in mind that twelve British soldiers were killed during the attack on the fort."

The orders gave Scott carte blanche to act as he saw fit. They also severed Major Phelps from responsibility for the action. Scott turned to leave, and Phelps spoke again.

"Captain Scott, I expect this mission to be a completed expeditiously and with vigour, do we understand each other?" Phelps's voice had taken on a petulant tone, and his eyes glittered with malice.

"We understand each other, Major." Scott walked out, leaving the door open behind him.

Scott was seething with anger. Phelps was distancing himself from responsibility for the raid; he knew that if anything went wrong he would make Scott a scapegoat and would use his past record against him. Scott didn't doubt his ability to lead the patrol but the major's behaviour soured his stomach.

Scott sent word to Millard and Paine to bring a map of the area to the officer's mess.

"Lieutenant Millard, you're familiar with this area?" Scott pointed to the Shubenacadie village.

"I've been as far as this river thirty miles north of the village." He pointed to an unnamed river. "I was part of a patrol led by Captain Grove."

Scott ran his finger along a valley to the east of the fort. "What's the terrain like in this area? Are there usable trails?"

"There is no direct route, but there's a network of trails crisscrossing the valley that we used to reach the river."

"Could you find your way to here?" Scott pointed to where a river branched off the valley to the west.

"I believe so. The trails change all the time, but it shouldn't be difficult if we use the Iroquois to scout for us."

Scott nodded. "Will the ground be dry enough for us to travel?"

"It's difficult to say, Captain. The snow is almost gone on the coast, but it may still be deep in the interior. It's not normal practice for patrols to enter the interior before the end of May."

Scott snapped at Millard. "I'm not interested in normal practice, Lieutenant. Will the ground be hard enough to travel or not?"

Lieutenant Millard straightened up. "I believe it will be, Captain." He stepped back, pale-faced.

"We will leave the day after tomorrow; we will take eighty regular troopers and the sixty Iroquois scouts." He looked at Millard. "You will command forty men, two groups of twenty each with a sergeant."

Scott turned to Paine. "Lieutenant, you will have similar responsibilities, but your group will accompany me. The Iroquois scouts will be under my command."

Lieutenant Paine nodded but was clearly unhappy to be under Scott's direct command.

Scott put the map in its carrying case. "There will be no talk of this with the men. I want them paraded before first light with weapons and rations for ten days in the field."

He turned to Millard. "Lieutenant, you will bring the leader of the Iroquois scouts here tomorrow night. See to it that rations are made available to the scouts before we depart."

"Yes, Captain."

"Very good," Scott said. "Dismissed."

* * *

Two days later the patrol left Annapolis Royal at first light. Scott had wanted to be on the march before the village was awake, but Major Phelps had insisted on addressing the men. The delay only increased Scott's resentment of the major.

Scott sent the Iroquois ahead. He'd met with their chief the night before and laid out the plan to him. The chief was called Swatana; he was about thirty-five years of age, lean and tough-looking. He spoke good English and grasped what Scott had planned immediately. Scott felt confident he would perform his part as required.

Scott pushed hard, stopping only once in mid-morning to rest then driving on again. Lieutenant Paine was ten years younger than Scott, but he struggled to keep up. At the midday break he was sweating heavily and sat with his head in his hands. Scott only allowed half an hour to eat, and then he had the men back on the trail.

They followed the patchwork of trails through the forest, and by the end of the first day they were deep into the valley. They camped off the trail, and Scott set up a picket line for the night. The troops were weary, and there was little talk as they made camp, and Lieutenant Paine was asleep as soon as he had finished eating.

The next day Scott kept the pressure on. There was some grumbling from the ranks, but Sergeant Crammer's fists soon put an end to it. They stopped to eat at midday and the troops were subdued, saving their strength for the march. That night Scott ordered no campfires to be lit. They were still some distance from the village, but he didn't want anything to alert the villagers of their presence. The next morning they were on the move at first light, and in less than an hour they reached the river Scott had seen on the map.

Scott called Swatana and the lieutenants together and spread the map on the ground. Scott motioned to Swatana.

"You'll scout the approach to the village. Send word to me of any difficulties we may encounter."

Swatana nodded.

Scott turned to Millard. "We will proceed along the south bank of the river to here." He put his finger on a point two miles from the village. "Lieutenant Millard, you will take forty men and approach the village from the south. Lieutenant Paine and I will approach along the riverbank. When you hear our musket fire, you will attack. Is that clear?"

"Understood, Captain."

Scott gave the Iroquois a fifteen-minute start and sent for Sergeant Crammer.

"Captain Scott, sir," Crammer said.

Scott pointed out the village on the map. "The French priest Laporte has a church somewhere in the village. I want you to take ten men, find the church, and bring the priest to me."

"Yes, Captain."

"Alive and uninjured, Sergeant, is that clear?"

"Yes, Captain."

They moved along the riverbank in single file for half a mile; then the trail opened up, and they moved two abreast. Scott ordered the troops to maintain silence. Anyone talking or making a sound that could give them away would be flogged.

They moved west for two hours. The river was forty feet across and swollen with melted snow. Just before midday the line came to a halt, and Scott went forward to find Swatana and Lieutenant Millard waiting for him. Millard pointed.

"The village is a mile to the west, Captain."

"Take your men to the south as we discussed. I will give you ten minutes start; then we move forward. Now go."

Millard motioned his sergeant to follow and hurried away.

Scott ordered the men into the forest out of sight. They'd been lucky so far, and he didn't want to lose the advantage of surprise by encountering a villager on the trail. He waited ten minutes by his watch and signalled the advance.

Over the next mile the trail broadened out, and the land became flat. Scott saw smoke rising from the trees ahead, and he caught the tang of saltwater in the air. He was preparing to send a scout to find Swatana when the silence was broken by the report of a musket. A volley of fire followed, and the Iroquois war cry rang through the forest.

Scott broke into a run. "Forward at the double."

Lieutenant Paine was at Scott's heel, Sergeant Crammer close behind. They came on teepees and cabins scattered along the riverbank, and could see fighting amongst the trees.

Scott signalled to Lieutenant Paine. "See to it, Lieutenant."

Paine broke off, calling for his sergeant, and Scott kept heading for the centre of the village.

Scott emerged into a large cleared area. Teepees stood in a semicircle at the edge of the forest, forming a rude amphitheatre. A pitched battle was going on in the clearing between the Iroquois and the villagers. The villagers outnumbered the Iroquois and were holding them off.

Scott ordered the men to form a line and open fire. The first volley caused bloody mayhem. After the second volley, resistance collapsed, and the villagers broke for the forest, pursued by the Iroquois whooping with delight.

"After them," Scott called. "Don't let them get away." The troopers charged after the retreating villagers, firing their muskets on the run.

There was a volley of musket fire from the trees to the south. The villagers were trapped between Millard's and Paine's troops and cut to pieces in the crossfire.

Scott called out to Crammer. "Sergeant, find me the priest."

"Yes, Captain." Crammer ran off, his platoon trailing along behind him.

Scott strode to the south side of the clearing. Some of the villagers were still fighting, but there were less than a hundred on their feet, and more fell with every volley. Scott spotted Lieutenant Paine on the edge of the forest and waved him over.

"Call them off, Lieutenant. I want some alive to answer questions."

"Yes, Captain."

"Platoon to fall back," Paine shouted, trying to make himself heard above the musket fire. His sergeant worked his way around the edge of the fray, ordering the troops to cease fire.

The troopers stepped back, but the Iroquois kept on attacking.

"Break that up, Lieutenant," Scott called.

Lieutenant Paine had twenty men force the Iroquois back with their bayonets. Lieutenant Millard emerged from the woods and added his men to the task. Swatana and Millard came face-to-face, both of them shouting. After a tense moment Swatana spat on the ground and waved his warriors back, and the troops surrounded the villagers with a ring of bayonets.

Scott called Millard and Paine to him.

"Disarm them and bring them to the clearing." Scott walked to the centre of the village and waited while the villagers were forced to sit on the ground. Scott saw Sergeant Crammer wading across the river, and he went to meet him.

Crammer stopped on the beach and saluted. "The church is there and the priest's cabin." He pointed to the forest on the other side of the river. "But the priest is nowhere to be found."

Scott slammed his fist into his hand, and Crammer rushed on. "We searched the other dwellings, but there's no one there."

Scott held up his hand. "The villagers will know where he is. Pick one and make him talk, Sergeant."

Crammer licked his lips in anticipation. "Yes, Captain."

Smoke was rising from the forest on the other side of the river, and Scott lifted his chin in question.

"We burned the church and the priest's cabin."

"Find me the priest, Sergeant."

"Yes, Captain." Crammer ran off along the riverbank, his men on his heels.

Scott went back to the clearing and waved the two lieutenants to him. "Report."

Lieutenant Millard spoke first. "We have the entire village, Captain. There are sixty-eight prisoners, over a hundred dead, and we are still counting."

"Did any escape?"

"Some escaped. We don't know how many."

Scott looked at Lieutenant Paine.

"We cleared the riverbank and swept the village to the east of the clearing. Most of the villagers were killed, and we captured ten more."

"Has the priest been seen?"

Both men shook their heads.

"Keep a firm hand on the men. There's more to be done."

Both men exchanged an uncomfortable glance.

Crammer dragged three men to the edge of the forest, and the villagers watched silently as he placed a noose around the neck of each man and threw it over the branch of a tree. None of the men spoke English or was willing to admit they could. Swatana spoke to one of them, but he shook his head, and Swatana struck him in the face with his fist. The man was over sixty years old, and as he staggered back, Swatana hit him again and screamed in his face, but he remained silent.

Crammer separated them and looked at Scott. Scott nodded and Crammer called, "Haul away."

The old man let out a strangled cry as he was lifted off the ground. A moan went up from the villagers, and a female voice wailed in despair.

Lieutenant Paine ran over to Scott. "Captain, I must protest."

"Be quiet, Lieutenant Paine."

"Captain . . ."

Scott glared at him. "I said be quiet, Lieutenant. Return to your post, or I'll have you court-martialled for disobeying orders under fire."

Paine went white and walked away, averting his eyes from the clearing.

The villager's body hung limply from the tree, and Crammer and Swatana were now questioning another prisoner. Crammer held him by the hair while the Iroquois smashed his fist into his face. The man didn't cry out, and Crammer looked at Scott and shook his head.

Scott nodded and Crammer called out, "Have done with it now."

The troopers walked back with the ropes, lifting the two villagers off the ground. There was a communal sigh from the villagers, and two men got to their feet, but the troopers clubbed them to the ground.

Crammer came jogging up to Scott. "They're stubborn, Captain. I don't think they'll talk."

Scott didn't reply. Anger had been eating away at him since he'd left Boston, and months of enforced idleness and the conflict with Major Phelps had added to his frustration. The priest's escape turned to acid in his stomach, and he swept his arm around the village.

"I want nothing left here, Sergeant. Is that clear?"

Crammer nodded. "And the villagers?"

"You know what to do."

"Yes, Captain." Crammer backed away and called to his men to form up on him.

Scott sent for the trooper carrying his gear and retrieved his writing case. He sat on a tree stump and wrote a notice advising any who read it of the consequences of conspiring against the sovereign power of the British Empire. He signed and dated the document then dusted the ink and packed up his writing case while it dried.

Lieutenant Paine came back across the clearing and stopped in front of Scott. "Captain Scott, what is Sergeant Crammer preparing to do?"

"Sergeant Crammer is obeying orders as should you."

Paine drew himself up to his full height. "Captain Scott, I cannot countenance this . . ."

"This is war, Lieutenant. If you don't have the stomach for it, then you have no business in the army."

"Captain, I must tell you it's my duty to report this action to our superiors."

"You can report it to the devil himself for all I care, Lieutenant, but you will obey my orders."

"I will—"

"Enough, Lieutenant, you're dismissed."

Paine strode away pale-faced and shaking.

Scott waved Millard to him. "Burn the village and ready the men to march. I want to be gone within the hour."

"Yes, Captain. Will that be all?" Millard's face was pale.

"Send Sergeant Crammer to me."

Crammer came at the run. "Send a man to post this on the church." He handed the paper to Crammer. "Is everything ready?"

"Yes, Captain. On your order."

"Then finish it." Scott started along the riverbank, and a volley of musket fire rang out behind him, then another and another, until it rolled across the forest like distant thunder.

CHAPTER TWENTY-SIX

ON THE SECOND DAY, JOHN and Louis selected a spot on the bank of a creek as a base to hunt the area, and spent the reminder of the day constructing a shelter and setting up camp. The next morning they were ready to move before first light. Louis had an arrow knocked on his bow, and John carried the musket at the ready.

They moved up the bank of the creek in single file. There were many tracks along the creek, and John searched the foliage expecting a deer to break from cover at any moment.

"The wind is behind us. They have our scent," Louis said.

"Can we track them?"

"They will run many leagues. Better to seek other game."

John un-cocked the musket and slung it over his shoulder.

Louis found a trail going upstream and swung into a run. John ran five strides behind, matching his pace. John was not entirely disappointed. It felt good to be moving—he wanted to see more of the country, and if they killed an animal, it would mean the end of the hunt.

They followed the creek all morning, and when they stopped to eat at midday John said, "Have we chased all the deer out of the country?" Louis shook his head.

"There is game in the forest, but in the spring they range farther afield." As John started to get to his feet, Louis gripped his arm and put his finger to his lips. John was startled to see a buck and three does on the other side of the creek, heads cocked listening.

John began to reach for the musket, but Louis shook his head, and he sat still. The buck took two steps towards the creek and stopped sniffing the air. Then he moved forward slowly and the does followed.

As the buck came to the water Louis slid his bow across his knees and knocked an arrow moving infinitely slowly, keeping his eyes on the buck. The buck stopped at the water and sniffed, turning his head from side to side. He lowered his head to drink, and the does trotted down to the water. Louis came up on one knee and drew the bow in one smooth motion. John saw the buck's ears go up. In the same instant Louis loosed the arrow. The buck broke to the right bounding away, and the arrow struck him behind the shoulder.

John leapt to his feet and ran to the creek. Louis was already halfway across, and John cocked the musket and stood ready. The buck ran halfway across the beach then collapsed, its legs still trying to run. Louis was on it in three strides, and struck the buck behind the ear with his tomahawk, killing it instantly.

John un-cocked the musket and rested the butt on the ground.

"It was a good shot, Louis, but how did you know which way he would turn?"

Louis looked at John as if speaking to a child. "A buck will always turn downstream."

John couldn't help but smile at Louis's expression. He pulled off his boots and waded into the creek. "I'll bring our gear across," he said.

The water came to his knees. It was ice cold, and he sucked in his breath in shock. In the middle of the creek he looked downstream to the south. The sky was deep blue with a hint of cloud on the horizon. He hoped that the clouds would pass. Carrying the buck back to the village in the rain would be a miserable task.

John hauled their baggage across the creek and set it on the bank while he dried his feet and pulled his boots on.

"You must teach me to shoot a bow like that."

"I've tried, but you must practice every day."

John had tried the bow, but he knew it would take years to master. Louis had hunted with it since childhood, and he would never attain his skill.

John tied a rope to the deer's back legs, and threw it over the branch of a tree. The animal was heavy, and it took both of them to haul it off the ground. Then they set to work.

They had done this many times and each knew his task. Louis slit the animal's belly open, and the entrails spilled out onto the ground. Then he cut out the heart and lungs. John went to a cluster of small trees and cut a carrying pole and hacked the branches off.

In fifteen minutes Louis had gutted and cleaned the buck, and its internal organs lay in a bloody heap at his feet. The easy part was done. Now they had to carry the carcass back to the village. John wasn't looking forward to it, and he glanced at the sky hoping that the rain would stay away.

He could only see a narrow patch of sky. It was deep blue, but a vague sense of unease crept into his mind. On impulse he pulled off his boots and socks and waded to the middle of the creek. The sky above was bright blue, but the clouds to the south had thickened into a dark line on the horizon. He stared at the sky, oblivious to the ice cold water washing over his legs, and his mouth went dry as he realized what he was looking at.

Louis called out from the bank. "What do you see?"

"Smoke. I see smoke."

Louis dropped his knife and waded into the creek. "The village is to the south." Louis shook his head. "It's too far for a cooking fire. It takes much smoke to be seen from this distance."

"What could cause it?" John spoke half to himself.

"It's an ill omen. We must return to the village."

They splashed ashore, and John pulled his socks and boots on and began to pack up his gear. "What of the buck?"

"Leave it." Louis dropped the buck and stuffed the rope into his pack.

"We must travel fast." John slid his hunting bag and musket across his shoulder.

Louis led; they waded across the creek and took the game trail through the forest. John followed ten paces behind, and they fell into a run. The trail twisted back and forth through the trees, but it was wider than the trail along the creek, and they moved faster. They ran through the morning, not stopping to eat at midday, and reached their previous camp in the middle of the afternoon, half the time it had taken the day before.

They pushed on without stopping. When they came to a clearing, John searched for smoke, but the sky was clear. He knew there were many things that could have caused the smoke, but he couldn't shake the feeling of dread in his gut. Late in the afternoon they stopped to eat some pemmican then pushed on again. They ran until nightfall, slowing to a walk and picking their way along the trail as it got dark.

As they crossed a clearing John said to Louis, "We should stop for the night."

"It's not yet dark. We can go on."

"It will do no good to break an ankle in the dark." John saw a flash of frustration in Louis's eyes; then he nodded.

"We'll make camp," Louis said.

They lit a fire at the edge of the clearing but didn't bother to construct a shelter. John's feet and legs throbbed, and his shoulder ached from the musket. He bit into his pemmican hungrily. Louis sat staring into the darkness.

"We'll start at first light," John said.

After a moment Louis said, "It's better to rest now. We will travel faster tomorrow."

There was tension in Louis's voice, and John sensed he feared what they would find at the village, but he knew Louis would not thank him for speaking about it.

"I will watch first," Louis said.

John wrapped himself in his plaid and fell into a dreamless sleep. He was awakened by Louis shaking him.

"Light is coming," Louis said. John got to his feet and stretched. There was a hint of dawn in the east. Louis hadn't wakened him to stand watch, but there was no point in bringing it up.

John threw wood onto the fire and kicked it into life as he chewed his pemmican and warmed himself. He would need his strength today, and he forced down as much as he could stomach.

Louis came and squatted by the fire. "We must reach the village today."

John knew Louis was telling him they wouldn't stop till they reached the village. Louis's features were calm, but John sensed the tension in him.

They were on the move as soon as it was light enough to see, picking their way along the trail. John was stiff from the hard ground, but he walked it out of his muscles in the first mile. They gradually increased their pace to a run they could both keep up all day. The discipline John had learned hunting in the mountains around Glen Nevis stood him in good stead, but his strength and endurance were now beyond anything he had possessed in Scotland.

Before midday they entered the Shubenacadie valley. When they reached the river John drank greedily then pulled off his boots and socks and waded across. Even in his urgency to reach the village he remembered the importance of keeping his gear dry.

As they followed the trail along the river John searched the sky. There was little sign of smoke, but as they neared the village he smelt burned wood on the wind. Louis smelt it too, and he ran flat out for the village.

As they approached the village, John saw birds circling in the sky. Crows and ravens were roosting in the trees in the hundreds, and their screeching put his nerves on edge. When they came to the river, Louis cried out in alarm and stopped. The village had been destroyed. The teepees and cabins were burned to blackened husks, smoke was spiralling up from piles of ashes, and the smell of charred wood and burnt meat assaulted John's senses.

They splashed across the river, and as they came into the centre of the village John saw the bodies. Sixty or seventy villagers lay dead in the clearing. The men were in a circle around the women and children. They had been butchered like cattle. Some had been shot and many had been bayoneted. They had terrible wounds to their heads as if their skulls had been torn open. Their faces were red, and black blood had pooled in their eyes, making them look like tormented souls.

Louis fell to his knees. He turned his face to the sky and cried out in anger and despair; in anguish, he tore at the earth with his fingers. John stood frozen in horror at the carnage around them.

Louis struggled to his feet and stood staring. John put his hand on his shoulder.

"The British have done this," Louis said.

"Could it have been some other enemy?"

"Only the British have this many muskets, and they have brought their hunting dogs. He pointed to one of the bodies. These are Iroquois arrows."

"What have they done to their faces? What horror is this?"

"They've taken their scalps," Louis said. "The British pay silver for each Mi'kmaq scalp brought to them."

Without warning Louis leapt away across the clearing. John followed, with the weight of the musket he couldn't catch him, but he knew where he was going. Joseph's teepee was a charred ruin. The skin covering had been burned away, leaving the blackened twisted poles standing. Joseph lay on his back in front of the teepee. The right side of his chest had been torn away by a musket ball, and his body was covered in bayonet wounds. The crows had feasted on his face, tearing his cheek open and leaving blackened gashes where his eyes had been.

Françoise was a few feet away. She was naked, and her legs were splayed apart. Her belly had been cut open and her entrails had spilled out covering her sex in a grim parody of modesty. Her eyes stared blankly at the sky, oblivious now to the torment that had been visited on her.

Louis stood clasping and unclasping his hand convulsively. A wave of anger swept over John at the heartless cruelty of it all. He put his hand on Louis's shoulder. "We must bury them."

Louis looked at John. "We will bury them; then we hunt the men who did this." There was a tic working on the side of his face, and his eyes were cold.

John knew this might cost him his life, but he didn't hesitate. We hunt them and kill them if we can," he said.

John searched through the wreckage for the digging tools the villagers used to harvest clams. When he returned, Louis had wrapped his father and sister in buckskin bed rolls.

"Our burial ground is north along the river."

John used two teepee poles to make a crude stretcher. They carried Joseph to the burial ground a mile upstream from the river then returned for Françoise. They dug one grave and laid Joseph and his daughter side by side, and covered them gently with the rich black soil of the valley. Louis stood for a long time, singing softly in Mi'kmaq, and John waited while he took his last leave of his family.

Finally Louis turned away. "One day we will conduct the funeral rites to help them to pass on."

"What of the other villagers?"

"There's not time to bury them if we are to catch the British before they reach the fort."

284

"Let's go now."

As they ran alongside the river John went over what must have happened in his mind. The British must have attacked the village the morning after they left. That gave them a day or a day-and-a-half start. Louis had said the fort was a three days' march, and a large group would move slowly. If they pushed hard they could catch them. He didn't know what they would do when they caught the British, but he put the thought from his mind for now.

As they passed the trail to the priest's cabin John called halt.

"We must find out what happened to the priest." John didn't wait for Louis to reply, but he fell in behind him. He was halfway to the cabin when the smell of charred wood reached him. John stopped at the edge of the clearing. The priest's cabin was a smoking ruin. The walls were blackened, and the roof had fallen in, leaving the stone chimney standing. The church's roof and two walls had collapsed leaving the gable ends standing, and the remains of the door creaked on its hinges.

Louis came up beside John. "The priest is dead or he has fled."

"There's nothing here." John shifted the musket to his left shoulder, and as he started to turn away, the breeze swung the door closed, revealing a white square in the centre.

"Stop, Louis." His voice was loud and Louis looked at him sharply.

John ran to the church. A square of white paper had been nailed to the door and a message written in well-formed English script covered the paper. John stepped closer to read it.

May 8, 1747

The action against the Mi'kmaq village in the place known as Shubenacadie was conducted in retribution for the lawless and unprovoked attack carried out by the people of this village on the British colony of Annapolis Royal during the month of November 1746 where twelve British subjects were murdered.

The French priest Jean-Louis Laporte, resident at Shubenacadie, is known to have instigated and participated in the attack on Annapolis Royal. He is known to have killed two British soldiers by his own hand. Father Jean-Louis Laporte is hereby named traitor and murderer. Any man who will deliver

285

said Jean-Louis Laporte to Annapolis Royal or to authorities at other British settlements will be eligible for a reward of not less than one hundred pounds sterling.

Captain Frederick Arthur Scott

Annapolis Royal

John read the paper twice. The name at the bottom of the page burned itself on his mind like a hot iron, and he stumbled into Louis. John read it again, and as he read "Captain Frederick Arthur Scott," his head swam with nausea and the cry of rage that came out of him left him panting for breath.

John became aware that Louis was shaking him. "What does it mean? What do the words say?"

John forced himself to focus. "It's written by the man who killed my uncle." Rage clouded his vision again, but Louis's grip on his shoulder brought him back to reality.

Louis looked closely at the notice. "Say the words for me."

John removed the note from the door carefully and read it aloud, speaking each word slowly as much for his own benefit as for Louis's. His mind went back to the day his uncle Murdoch had been killed, and Captain Scott had been arrested. The major in charge of the dragoons had spoken of a lieutenant who had been the son of a rich Englishman. It had to be the man John had killed in his uncle's cottage. Somehow they had held Scott responsible for his death. John didn't understand how this had all come about, but his instinct told him it was the same man.

John held the paper tightly.

"We must find them." His mind seethed with anger and confusion, and he had to force himself to think clearly.

"It's the same soldier who killed my family?" Louis said.

"I don't know how that can be possible. How he can be here? But there can't be two captains with this name in the British Army."

"You're here. Why shouldn't he be?" Louis pointed to the paper. "Have they killed the priest?"

"He lives, or they wouldn't have named him wanted." John looked at the sun. He folded the paper and put it in his hunting bag. "They're more than a day ahead of us." He started across the clearing when a thought struck him.

"Wait."

John ran to the cabin and stepped inside testing the floor with the stock of the musket.

"The day is wasting. We must follow the British," Louis said.

"We need powder and shot. The priest has a cellar under the floor. Help me." The floor was covered with charred wood. John used a broken plank to scrap the debris away from the trapdoor. Louis slid the blade of his axe under the trap door, and they heaved it open.

John climbed down into the cellar, stooping under the low ceiling. It was dark inside, but the contents looked undamaged by the fire. The barrels and wooden cases stacked around the walls were intact. Six ammunition boxes were stacked against the south wall, and John brought one to the steps where he could examine it.

"Six powder flasks in each," he said, and handed it up to Louis. "One will be all we can carry."

John started to climb up the ladder then stopped.

"Wait." The map case lay on top of one of the barrels beside a wooden box that contained a compass. He handed the map and the compass to Louis and on impulse lifted the lid of the barrel. It contained pemmican. He took six packages and handed them up to Louis. A naval cutlass in its leather scabbard stood against the barrel and he took that, too.

John closed the trap door, and divided up the food and ammunition between them. John removed the map from its case and folded it in a square and put it in his hunting bag with the compass.

Louis looked skeptical. "It's more weight to carry."

"It will help us find our way in the wilderness."

Louis shrugged.

John hung the cutlass across his back and arranged it so he could reach the hilt with his right hand and shouldered the musket and other gear.

Louis stood ready beside him. "Now we seek our revenge."

The ravens rose screeching into the air as they entered the village, and when they had passed, they dropped back down to continue their grizzly feast. They took the trail to the south, and the quiet of the forest fell about them like a shroud.

CHAPTER TWENTY-SEVEN

SCOTT'S NOTE BURNED IN JOHN'S mind. Sorrow, anger and guilt from that last day at Fort William welled up in him. Captain Frederick Arthur Scott. Could two men carry that name in the British Army? John repeated the question over and over. He would know soon enough.

They pushed hard. They both had reason to catch the British before they reached Annapolis Royal. The foliage became denser as they went south, limiting their view of the trail ahead. John kept his eyes sharp. The British were at least a day ahead of them, but he still expected to come on them at every turn in the trail. In the middle of the morning Louis stopped and put his finger to his lips and sniffed the air. John smelt it too—wood smoke—and he eased the musket to half cock.

The trail opened into a clearing, and John stepped left to open up his line of sight. Smoke was rising from the remains of fires scattered around the clearing. John moved around the left side of the clearing, Louis went to the right. The British had broken the lower branches from the trees to feed their fires.

Louis was examining the ground where the trail led off to the south. "They are a day ahead."

John lifted an eyebrow. "We've made up a lot of ground."

"They are moving slowly; perhaps they have wounded. The fire is less than a day old."

John nodded and they picked up the chase.

The British trail was easy to follow, and they ran side by side. As the day went on, John's instincts told him they were closing the gap quickly, and he increased the pace. When darkness fell, they camped by the side of the trail and didn't light a fire. John slept fitfully, his dreams haunted by images of his uncle's death, and he was awake before first light. Louis stood ready, and as soon as there was enough light, they shouldered their gear and moved off.

They started slowly, easing the stiffness out of their muscles, and as the light grew, they increased the pace. A winter of good food and exercise had brought John's strength back, and he pushed hard, driven by anger and the desire to come face-to-face with Scott. At midday they stopped to eat, and he forced down as much pemmican as he could and drank till his stomach ached; then they ran on.

Some miles farther on, the trail descended into a hollow. It was heavily treed with dense foliage on either side of the trail. A creek ran through the hollow. It was twenty feet wide where the trail crossed, and narrowed again downstream. They stopped to listen. John heard nothing but water splashing over the stones and birds singing in the bushes.

Louis spoke in a whisper. "This creek joins the river that runs close to the British fort."

"How far to the fort?"

"We're close."

The creek bank had been churned up by the soldiers' boots. It was obvious that the main body had crossed the creek, and a small group had gone downstream. John started to speak, but Louis held his finger to his lips. He followed the tracks downstream and a moment later he came hurrying back.

"We must go quickly."

"What's wrong?"

Louis pointed downstream but didn't reply. He waded into the creek, and John pulled the hammer to half cock and followed. The water was only ankle deep. He glanced over his shoulder as he stepped onto the bank and hurried to catch up with Louis. John had learned to trust Louis's instinct for danger, and he resisted the urge to ask him what had alarmed him.

As John came up beside Louis, there was a shout behind them, and he looked back. A British soldier had come out of the trees on the other side of the creek. His red coat stood out against the green of the forest. He called over his shoulder and ran for the creek, and a moment later two other soldiers stepped out onto the bank of the creek.

There was a bend in the trail ahead, and John ran hard. The redcoats carried muskets, and they needed to get to cover quickly. John realized they wouldn't make it and skidded to a halt.

"Louis," John called. He cocked the musket and brought it up to his shoulder as he turned. The first soldier was almost across creek, and the other two were still in the middle. They made a solid mass of red. John placed the front sight in the middle of the leading man's stomach and pulled the trigger.

The soldier saw danger and threw himself to the side as John fired. The musket roared and John was unsighted by the powder burn, and he turned and ran, not waiting to see if his shot had struck home. Birds burst from the underbrush, flapping away in alarm as the crash of the musket echoed through the forest.

John ran hard, expecting to feel a musket ball slam into his back every second. Louis squatted at the turn in the trail, and John dropped down beside him. He lifted his chin towards the creek. Two redcoats were struggling back across the creek. One was bent over clutching his stomach; the second man was supporting him and the third soldier was nowhere to be seen.

Louis nodded. "It was a good shot."

"They'll hang us if they catch us."

"The British don't need a reason to kill."

John got to his feet and leapt away. Louis waited, watching the redcoats for a moment, then followed. As Louis came up beside John he called a halt.

"This trail leads to the river then turns along the bank on this side. We can cut the corner through the trees."

John grasped what Louis was saying. "The British will have heard the shot and will be coming along the trail. We can go around them." Louis nodded.

"Move now."

Louis pushed into the trees. The underbrush was dense at first, but it opened up after the first twenty feet. John looked at the sun. They were heading roughly southeast. They were safer off the trail, but John was frustrated at their pace. He estimated they had gone a mile when he heard the sound of the river ahead. As they moved closer, it became a roar.

The underbrush was dense, and John lost sight of Louis as he struggled through to the trail on riverbank. The river was swollen with melted snow and roared past, blocking out all other sounds. As John looked around, searching for Louis, he caught a blur of colour to his left and spun toward it. Two redcoats were coming around a turn in the trail. They were only thirty feet from him. One of them cried out in surprise, and both men froze.

Louis burst from the forest behind the soldiers and rushed at them screaming his war cry. Both men looked around in alarm, but Louis crashed into them. He locked his arms around the nearest soldier, and the momentum tumbled them down the riverbank.

The second soldier staggered backwards to keep his balance, struggling to get his musket off his shoulder, and John charged at him. The soldier brought his musket across in front of him, and John heard the hammer click, but John was on him before he could bring it to bear. John drove the stock of his musket at the soldier's face. The redcoat brought his weapon up to protect himself but John's musket slammed the barrel into his face.

The soldier staggered back, blood pouring down his face. His finger caught on the trigger and his musket discharged with a tremendous roar. He cried out in pain as the recoil tore the weapon from his hands. The barrel was close to John's face, and he stumbled back stunned by the blast.

The redcoat let out a bellow of rage and charged at John. John gasped his musket by the barrel like a club, but the redcoat would be on him before he could swing it. He dropped the musket and launched himself at the redcoat. The soldier tried to lock his arm around John's neck, but John blocked his arm, and head-butted him in the face. The soldier grunted and fell backwards. John butted him again. It was a solid blow, and he felt his nose collapse under the impact. The man staggered back, screaming in pain, and covered his face with his hands.

John turned, searching for the musket, but the redcoat roared in anger and rushed at him. He slammed into John, and his weight carried them both off their feet. John twisted and broke his fall with his arms, but his left elbow landed on a stone, numbing his arm.

John rolled to his knees holding his arm. The redcoat was down on one knee. One eye was swollen shut and his nose and mouth were a bloody mess. He wiped the blood from his eye with his right hand, and the gesture stirred something in John's memory. He reached around to his left side, and a flash of dark metal against his red coat told John he was trying to free a pistol from his belt.

The redcoat looked up at him, and John felt a shock of recognition. It was the man who had almost killed him in Glen Nevis and who had hunted him across the mountains. His taunts echoed in John's head and a cry of rage came out of him. He pulled the priest's cutlass from its scabbard and launched himself at the redcoat. The pistol was tangled in the soldier's coat, but he managed to pull it free as he staggered to his feet. He held it in both hands, pulled the hammers back, and turned his right arm sweeping around towards John.

John hurled himself across the gap, reaching for the pistol with his left hand and throwing the cutlass back. The soldier brought the pistol to bear, but he didn't fire. John realized his right eye was filled with blood, and he was trying to focus on him with his left. It was a momentary delay, but it was enough. John pushed the soldier's wrist to the side; one pistol barrel discharged with a crack and acrid smoke stung John's eyes.

John grasped the soldier's wrist, pulled him off balance and drove the cutlass in under his arm. The point struck below the armpit. It sliced through his coat and ran six inches into his side. The soldier's eyes went wide. He coughed and blood erupted from his mouth. John stepped back, the cutlass made a sucking sound as it came free, and blood spurted from the wound. The soldier dropped the pistol and put his hand over his side, trying to stop the bleeding, and sank to his knees.

John looked down at him. Blood was pulsing from between his fingers, and he knew it was a killing blow. The redcoat looked up at him. His right eye was filled with blood, but hate and contempt blazed from the other.

"You killed my uncle, Englishman, but you have not killed me," John screamed at him.

"You." Shock and bewilderment twisted the soldier's face as recognition dawned on him.

A cry of hate came out of John, and he swung the cutlass striking down at the redcoat. He raised his left hand to protect himself. The blade severed his fingers and struck below his right ear biting into his neck. The stroke carried through, and the blade came free, spraying blood into the air. The soldier fell onto his side, blood pumping from his severed arteries.

John took a step back panting, and a cry came out of him that was part elation and part anguish. He felt no guilt, as when he'd killed the young lieutenant in Scotland. He felt no remorse for killing this man, and his death brought only a grim sense of completion.

There was a sound behind him, and John whirled around to see Louis scrambling up from the riverbank. He carried a British musket and an ammunition pouch slung over his shoulder.

"It's done. We must go." John saw the body of the redcoat half-submerged in the river.

John picked up the pistol. It had two barrels side by side. It was a plain weapon, but the workmanship was good. One barrel had discharged during the fight, and he un-cocked the second one. Voices called out from upstream. They both turned, and after a moment they came again.

"We must go," Louis said.

"Wait." John opened the redcoat's ammunition pouch. It contained lead balls for the pistol, leather patches and a powder flask. There was also an iron mold to cast lead balls. He put the pouch and the pistol in his hunting bag and leapt to his feet.

As they ran along the trail, John's mind was reeling. The soldier he'd killed had hunted him in Scotland. He didn't understand how he could be here, but he was. If he was here, then the Captain Scott that signed the notice on the church door had to be the same man that had killed his uncle. He was elated and furious at the same time, and he knew in his heart that there would be a reckoning with Scott.

The trail turned away from the river into the forest, and the sound of the water gradually diminished until all John could hear was their footfalls on the trail. There were soldiers ahead of them and behind them. John knew they could blunder into a patrol at any moment, but they had no choice, and he ran on. The trail turned west then east again. John heard the sound of the river begin to grow again and they slowed their pace, creeping along the side of the trail.

The trail came back to the river at a ford. The river was over a hundred feet across, and narrowed again above and below the ford. They pushed into the undergrowth and crept up to the ford on their bellies. The riverbank had been churned up by dozens of footprints, and John searched the other bank for any sign of the redcoats.

"Do you know this place?"

Louis nodded. "The trail on the far bank leads to the fort." He pointed downstream.

John started to speak, but the sound of voices calling out on the other side of the river made them both freeze.

"Come." Louis broke cover and ran, taking a trail at the water's edge.

Downstream of the ford, the river narrowed, and the current increased turning the river into a boiling maelstrom that was impossible to cross. The trail skirted a small hill and brought them back to the river at a smaller ford that would only be passable in summer when the river was low. Now it was a boiling torrent of standing waves and whirlpools—anyone trying to cross would be dashed to pieces.

There was a clear strip of beach downstream from the ford. Then the trail led off into the forest. They crept forward to where they could see across the river. As John crawled up beside Louis he saw three soldiers coming down to the other bank. Each carried a musket and a heavy pack and they were struggling on the slope.

Louis put his mouth to John's ear. "Wait to see what they do."

The redcoats dropped their packs, stacked their muskets against a tree, and took their water bottles down to the river. John could see their faces clearly, but the sound of the river drowned out their voices. Farther up the bank, movement drew John's eye. Another man was coming out of the forest. He was dressed in an officer's greatcoat over a blue officer's uniform, and he wore a sabre strapped to his waist.

There was something familiar about the way this man walked. He called out to the soldiers. John couldn't make out the words, but the tenor of his voice carried across the river. He'd heard that arrogant tone before in Glen Nevis and again on the shores of Loch Linne.

Something turned over in John's mind, and he leapt to his feet.

"Scott."

Louis made a grab for him, but he burst out into the open and charged down the beach. The men on the other side of the river looked around in alarm, and John ran along the beach until he was opposite them. He cocked the musket then realized he hadn't reloaded it, and threw it down.

He stepped to the water's edge and called out. "I see you, Scott. You killed my uncle, and I will have your life for it." John glared across the river in impotent rage.

Captain Scott walked down to the river and looked at John. Two soldiers came and stood beside him. Scott stared at John, confused as to why this madman had emerged from the forest to scream at him. One of the soldiers said something to him. Scott dismissed him with an irritated gesture, but a moment later his eyes widened as recognition dawned on him, and John saw his lips move.

"You!"

John shook his fist and called out. "You know me now, Scott. I'll have your life."

He tore the pistol from his hunting bag and cocked it. He'd never fired a pistol, but he'd seen it done. He turned to the side and raised his arm adopting the classical stance.

As John brought the pistol to bear, Scott grabbed the soldier beside him and pulled him in front of him. John squeezed the trigger and the pistol discharged with a loud crack. His arm was thrown up by the recoil, and he lost sight of Scott in a cloud of burning gunpowder. A musket discharged behind him, and John ducked instinctively and spun around. Louis was standing behind him, smoke coming from the barrel of his musket and he motioned to him.

"Come." On the other bank one of the redcoats was slumped on the ground, one soldier stooped down beside him, and Scott and the other man ran for the trees.

Louis grabbed John's arm and dragged him to his feet. "We must move."

John realized that Scott and the redcoat were running for their muskets. He picked up his musket and reached for his ammunition pouch. A musket shot rang out, and they both ducked, and Louis grasped John by the shoulders.

"There will be another time. We have to go."

John looked across the river. Scott and the redcoat were running back, each carrying a musket.

"This way." Louis ran downstream. John followed; his feet sank deep into the gravel, and his limbs felt heavy as if he were running in a dream. The ground in front of him exploded, throwing dirt and gravel into his face. An instant later he heard the report of the musket, and he dodged to the right, shaking his head to clear his vision. The beach ended abruptly. The bush grew right down to the water, forming a solid barrier in front of them, and the only break was where the trail began.

They would be easy targets on the trail, and Louis ran straight into the forest. John was two paces behind. The branches whipped at his face and tangled his legs, but he drove on until the foliage swallowed him up. A musket ball tore through the brush to his right, followed by the crack of the discharge. John ducked involuntarily and kept going. He pushed forward for a hundred feet then turned and made his way back to the trail and crouched down to reload his musket.

A moment later Louis came out of the bush and squatted beside him. "The man in the long coat killed your family?"

John waited till his breathing slowed. "He hung my uncle while I was forced to watch. I don't understand how he can be here, but it's him. There is no mistake."

"Then he killed my family also. One day we will kill him, but you must hold your anger for that day."

John nodded, but he was too overwhelmed to speak.

Louis started back along the trail. John finished loading the musket and followed. Twenty yards from the beach Louis set his musket on the ground. John laid his beside it, and they crept back to where they could see across the river.

Scott was pacing back and forth on the beach. One soldier sat with his back against a tree. There was blood on his shirt, and a soldier was winding a bandage around his shoulders.

"You wounded one, Louis. It was a good shot at that range."

"A good shot would have killed him."

As John watched Scott. He felt his anger rise again. He forced it down, but it soured his stomach.

"Where is the other man?" Louis pointed to the riverbank. The soldier came out of the trees followed by a group of natives.

John counted eight. They were big lean-boned men, and their skin was burned brown by the wind and sun. Some of them wore their hair in an elaborate headdress, others in a long plait down their back. They were dressed in deerskin breeches and tunics. A few wore only a loincloth made of the same stuff.

Each man carried a bow and an axe in their belt, two carried muskets, and each had a sleeping roll slung over their shoulders. It was too far to see their faces, but John sensed something ruthless about them. Scott met them at the riverbank and engaged one of them.

"Who are they?"

"They are Iroquois. They are the hunting dogs of the British." There was contempt in Louis's voice, and he stared fixedly across the river.

Scott was speaking animatedly and pointed across the river. The man John took to be the leader of the Iroquois looked in their direction for a long moment. Then the Iroquois dropped their sleeping rolls and leapt away. Scott set off after them. The two redcoats fell in behind, helping their wounded comrade, and in moments the riverbank was deserted.

They made their way back to the trail and Louis grimaced. "He has sent the Iroquois to hunt us."

"They will have to go back to the ford to cross the river."

"They carry only their weapons, and they are fresh to the chase. We must go quickly."

CHAPTER TWENTY-EIGHT

THEY RAN HARD, BUT THEIR muskets and gear slowed them, and John knew it was only a matter of time before the Iroquois caught them. The trail had turned west. John couldn't hear the river anymore, and he called out to Louis.

"Do you know this trail? Where does it lead?"

"The trail leads to a point of land to the west of the British fort. The sea is to the west, and the river runs between us and the fort."

"We'll be trapped on the point. Can we go around to the north and slip past the soldiers?"

"The sea is close. The soldiers will cut off escape in that direction."

John heard a sound and turned to listen, but it was too faint to identify. "What is it?"

Louis shook his head. "I don't know."

In his gut John knew the pursuit was closing. A mile farther and he felt himself begin to tire. They'd run for days, and he wondered how long he could keep going. Louis showed no sign of fatigue, and John gritted his teeth and pushed any thoughts of weariness aside.

The trees gradually became sparser and they finally broke out into a large clearing, planted with grain and corn. A farmhouse and a barn stood on the other side of the clearing, and two men standing by the barn looked at them in surprise.

"There." Louis pointed to where the trail began on the south side of the clearing. They passed six farms in the next two miles, and John knew they were nearing some type of settlement.

The forest began to open up, and the breeze carried the smell of salt water. John breathed it in, and felt his spirits rise. It didn't make any sense, but he was grateful for it anyway.

A half mile later they broke out of the trees, and John saw a body of water on their left, which had to be the sea inlet. A town spread along the east bank of the inlet. John could see wooden houses and barns amongst the trees, and a church at the edge of the water surrounded by a graveyard.

To the south a fort stood on a point of land extending into the inlet. It was built of earthen dykes lying at sharp angles. Cannons were placed as the points of the star where they could defend any section of the wall. This must be Port Royal, what the British called Annapolis Royal. To the south the inlet broadened out, stretching away into the distance. John was surprised to see a ship anchored in the inlet. It carried three masts and must have been a hundred and fifty feet long. He thought it must have recently arrived, as he could see men securing the sails and rigging.

John felt vulnerable in plain sight of the town, and he looked around nervously. He exchanged a look with Louis, and by mutual assent they increased their pace. Their pursuers were not far behind, and they had to find a way to get off this peninsula.

They ran along the bank of the inlet, and John could see the fort clearly across the water. They had only gone a few hundred yards when he heard a shout behind them. He looked back and was alarmed to see the Iroquois half a mile behind them. John couldn't believe they had been able to catch them so quickly.

John looked around desperately. A quarter of a mile ahead he saw a cluster of buildings on the edge of the inlet that looked like fishermen's shacks. Behind the buildings the ground dropped to the shore; the ship was riding at anchor off the beach. If all else failed they could swim across the inlet.

"There," John called, and they ran flat out. A musket shot cracked behind them, and John looked back. There was powder smoke on the breeze, and one of the Iroquois let out a war whoop when he saw him turn. John pointed to the buildings. The fishing shacks stood close to the inlet, and they left the trail without breaking pace.

As they approached the shore, the ship filled John's field of vision. There was frantic activity on board, and he could hear men calling out from the rigging down to the deck. The ground fell away in front of them, and they went straight over the embankment and slid down to the beach. A fishing boat similar to the ones John had seen in Louisburg was drawn up on the beach. John was on his feet in a moment and reached the fishing boat in four strides. It was twenty feet long and carried two masts. It was gaff rigged and the mizzenmast was eight feet taller than the foremast. A birch bark canoe lay next to it on the beach.

John dropped his musket and hunting bag into the boat and put his shoulder under the bow.

"Lift," he called. Louis put his shoulder against the other side and they heaved but the boat didn't move. John ran along the side splashing into the water.

"Rock her free." He pushed down on the starboard side, and Louis lifted the port gunnels. They alternated lifting and pushing down, but the boat wouldn't budge. John came round to the port side, and they lifted together grunting with the effort. John felt the hull move a little. They redoubled their efforts, and it broke free and they began to ease the boat into the water.

John knew the Iroquois were close.

"We can't launch it before the Iroquois are on us," John called. Louis slid his axe from his belt, and John drew the cutlass and they ran up the beach. As they reached the bottom of the slope a voice called out behind them.

"Get down, lads. Get down."

It was a quarterdeck voice that carried clearly across the inlet. John turned to see a row of seamen standing along the side of the ship each with a musket in his hand.

"Down." John picked a man out standing by the foremast shrouds making a downward motion with his arm.

John heard a cry above them and looked up to see six Iroquois warriors at the top of the embankment. They looked like wolves that had scented blood. The leader let out a war cry, and leapt down the slope. John threw himself at Louis, knocking him to the ground as musket fire crashed out across the inlet, and the air was filled with whirring musket balls.

When John looked up, he saw that the volley had caught the Iroquois in a tight group and chopped them to pieces. Four lay still, their bodies torn to pieces by the one-ounce lead balls. One warrior stood holding his hands over his stomach staring wide-eyed at the blood spurting from between his fingers. Then his eyes rolled up, and he pitched forward onto his face. The men on the ship cheered and called out in delight at the carnage they had wrought.

John leapt to his feet and ran to the fishing boat.

"More will come." They put their shoulders under the bow and heaved. The boat moved six inches. One more heave and it slid down the beach. They splashed into the water. John grabbed the foremast shrouds and rolled over the gunnels into the boat.

"Wait," Louis called. He slid the canoe into the water, boarded the fishing boat and tied it to the stern.

John set one of the oars in its slot in the gunnels and pulled, and the boat turned in its own length. He slid the oar aboard and hauled up the mizzen sail. The breeze filled the sail and the boat started to heel. He put the tiller over, and the bow came around heading away from the shore.

"The canoe will slow us."

"We may need it later," Louis said.

"Take the tiller."

Louis took the helm, and John went forward and hauled up the foresail. He started to unfurl the jib, but the boat lost way and started to drift towards the ship. Louis was struggling to bring it around.

John rushed to the stern. "Let me have her." He put the tiller over to starboard. "Use the starboard oar. Pull hard." Louis grabbed an oar and used it like a paddle sweeping around the stern.

The boat came around to port, the sails filled and John steered her across the stern of the ship.

Louis set the oar down and sat beside John. "I haven't done this thing with the cloths."

"I'll teach you, but first we must escape." John brought the bow hard to port to bring them under the ship's stern, giving it as wide a berth as possible.

The ship loomed above them, a massive black presence swinging on her anchor, seemingly weightless in the breeze. They came within thirty feet of the stern, and the seamen gathered along the rail, calling out greetings. The man who had called out to them forced his way to the rail. He was squat and broad shouldered with a shock of black hair, and John guessed he was the bosun.

"What's your name, lad? Where are you from?"

John pointed to the head of the inlet. "We're from Shubenacadie to the north."

"Why were the savages hunting you?"

"They attacked us in the woods, and we ran for our lives."

The bosun frowned and looked to the shore.

"Are you French? Do you have family here?" John realized that his Scottish accent was out of place, and the bosun was suspicious. He kept pace with them along stern rail.

"Come aboard, you'll be safe here." They rounded the stern, and John put the boat on a course across the inlet.

"We best be on our way. You have our thanks." The bosun called for them to come aboard, but John pretended not to hear, and he stood watching them as they moved away.

John knew the soldiers could come out of the woods at any minute, and they needed to get away while they had the chance.

"Take the tiller," he said. "Hold her steady for the fort." He hurried to the bow. The jib lines were tangled. He swore as he struggled to free them, but finally he hauled the jib aloft, and the boat surged forward.

By the time John took the tiller again they were across the inlet almost opposite the fort. The fort had extensive earthworks, and men were repairing them in several areas. He could see smoke rising from buildings inside the walls, and there was a great deal of coming and going through the main gate. Redcoats patrolled the top of the dykes, but they paid no attention to the fishing boat.

John put the tiller over and brought the boat on the other tack heading away from the fort. The wind was coming up the inlet, and they would have to tack back and forth against it. It was a tedious process, but the fishing boat sailed well, and he held her as close to the wind as he could.

John looked back. Challenger Boston was painted on the bow of the ship, and the bosun stood to one side watching.

John handed the tiller to Louis and went forward. He was sure there would be a larger jib, and sure enough it was stashed under the bow cover.

"Put the helm up." He motioned to Louis to put the tiller to starboard, and the boat turned into the wind and came to a stop. He hauled the jib aloft quickly, came back to the stern and brought the boat on the wind again. It surged forward under the larger jib.

As they bore away across the inlet, both of them looked back. A boat put out from the ship pulling for the west side of the inlet, and Louis touched his arm.

"There." He pointed to where the bodies of the Iroquois lay. It was over a mile, but there was no mistaking the red jackets of the soldiers.

John turned his attention back to sailing the fishing boat.

"We should dump the canoe. It is weight we don't need."

"The Iroquois are good trackers. It will be hard to elude them. When it's dark we should sink the fishing boat and take the canoe. We can carry it ashore and hide it in the forest."

John inclined his head. Louis made sense, but he would be reluctant to abandon the fishing boat.

"How far to where the inlet joins the sea?"

"We will reach it by dark if the wind holds, but when the tide is running it's not possible to pass through to the sea."

"We'll take our chances." As he spoke small currents and swirls began to appear on the surface of the water. "The tide turns."

"We'll take advantage of it while we can." Louis looked back up the inlet. "We must be through to the sea before the tide turns again, or we'll be trapped."

The wind freshened, and John began to wonder how they would fare on the ocean. His uncle, Murdoch, had taught him to sail on the sea lochs, but he'd never sailed on the open sea. He hoped he'd be up to it, but first they had to get through the passage, and he drove the fishing boat until the gunnels were almost awash.

As they continued south the inlet broadened to two miles across. Low hills ran along the eastern shore, and the peninsula that separated them from the sea was flat and heavily treed. Broad mudflats had been exposed by the tide and flocks of sea birds were feeding at the water's edge. John tracked the passage of the sun. The ship had long since disappeared below the horizon, and he estimated there was less than three hours of daylight left.

Louis tapped his shoulder "There." He pointed to the western side of the inlet.

John searched the shoreline for long minutes; then he saw it, a flash of white. "A sail."

John watched the white speck move across the inlet, tacking into the wind as they were. "Could be another fishing boat," he said, "but knew it wasn't true.

"It comes quickly," Louis said.

John looked down the inlet, searching both shores. "Can we put ashore and escape into the woods?"

"There's not time to sink the boat. They will see where we go ashore, and the Iroquois will run us down. The tide will turn before nightfall. If we can get through the gap to the bay, we can lose them in the dark."

John looked back and the sail already seemed larger. "You said the bay? I thought the ocean was on the other side of the peninsula."

"It's an inlet from the ocean, but it's many miles across. The western shore is below the horizon. The British call it the Bay of Fundy."

"How long to the gap?"

Louis swept his hand across the sky.

"It'll be a close-run thing. The tide has already begun to slacken."

John looked behind them, and his heart sank. The ship was hull up on the horizon, carrying all sail. He knew they couldn't outrun a vessel of that size for long, and he concentrated on getting as much speed out of the fishing boat as he could.

CHAPTER TWENTY-NINE

THE IROQUOIS COVERED THE GROUND like hounds on the scent. Scott hadn't been able to keep up with them, and Sergeant Crammer and his troopers were some distance behind him. Scott heard the crash of musket fire. He wanted the boy alive, and he cried out in frustration.

As Scott emerged from the forest he saw a ship anchored in the inlet, likely a merchant vessel out of Boston, he thought. He had run himself out and was down to a trot when a shout brought him to a halt, and Swatana stepped out of the forest. Scott motioned to him and kept moving. Swatana and two of his warriors ran across the open ground, and he came to a halt.

"What's happened? Where is the boy?"

Swatana scowled and pointed to the ship. "The British fired on us. Four of my warriors are dead, and another will not live to see another dawn."

"That's insane. Why would the British fire on you? Where's the boy?"

"The white man and the Mi'kmaq are on the ship."

Crammer and the troopers came out of the trees, and Scott held up his hand for Swatana to wait.

"Sergeant, the ship fired on the Iroquois. Hail them and make our presence known," Scott said.

"Yes, Captain." Crammer took off his jacket.

"The boy's on the ship. I want him alive, Sergeant."

"Yes, Captain."

Crammer trotted away holding his red jacket aloft.

"On, me lads," Crammer called and the troopers fell in behind him.

Scott set off towards the ship and motioned the Iroquois to follow. When he came up to Crammer, he was engaged in a shouted conversation with the ship, and demanding that they send a boat.

A short while later Scott saw a longboat leave from the ship and pull for the shore.

"Sergeant Crammer you and four troopers will accompany me on board to apprehend the boy."

"Yes. Captain."

The Iroquois lay on the embankment, only two were moving. Scott motioned to Crammer. "What of the scouts?"

"One will live, the other will be dead in an hour."

"See that we're not delayed burying him."

Scott came down the embankment as the boat touched the beach. There were four seamen at the oars, and the fifth at the tiller saluted Scott.

"Bosun's Mate Hopkins. Mr. Larkin, first officer of the *Challenger*, requests that you come aboard." Scott took a seat beside Hopkins, and Crammer and the troopers pushed off and climbed aboard.

"Get on with it, man," Scott said.

There was no talk as they rowed to the ship. They made fast to the starboard side, and Scott climbed the rope ladder to the deck. As Scott stepped onto the deck a man stepped forward and offered his hand.

"I am James Larkin, first officer of the *Challenger*." Larkin was in his forties, a slow talker with a shock of dark hair and a weather-beaten face. Scott shook his hand and looked around the deck.

"Where's the boy?"

"I am sorry. I didn't catch your name, Captain, and what boy are you referring to?"

"The boy my scouts were chasing when you fired on them." The colour rose in Larkin's face.

"We couldn't know the natives were your scouts."

"Where's the boy?" Scott barked. "He is a murderer, and I want him."

Larkin looked towards the stern. "He's not on board."

"Where's the boy? Do not test my patience," Scott shouted.

The colour rose in Larkin's neck, and he pointed to the stern. "They took a fishing boat down the inlet."

Scott climbed to the bridge and looked over the stern. A fishing boat was tacking across the inlet, already over a mile away.

Scott returned to the main deck. "Weigh anchor and overhaul the fishing boat. The boy mustn't escape."

Larkin hunched his shoulders. "We'll do no such thing, Captain. We're not yours to command."

Scott shouted at him. "You allowed a murderer to escape justice, killing half a dozen of our scouts in the process. You will do as I say, sir." Spittle flew from Scott's mouth and Larkin flinched.

Scott called out, "Troopers."

Crammer barked an order and the troopers surrounded them. Scott never took his eyes off Larkin. "You will follow my orders, Mr. Larkin."

Larkin's jaw set. "Bosun's mate," he barked. Eight sailors rushed forward, muskets at the ready.

Hopkins jabbed his musket into Crammer's back. "Give me an excuse, Sergeant, and I'll blast your backbone out through your belly." His voice was soft, but the tone left no doubt he'd pull the trigger.

Scott looked from Larkin to the seamen. His frustration was boiling over, but there was nothing he could do for now.

"Sergeant Crammer, stand down." The sailors fell back, but kept their weapons trained on Crammer and the troopers. Scott held Larkin's eye.

"Who's the captain of this ship?"

"Captain Harwood commands the Challenger. He's ashore meeting with Major Phelps."

"We shall speak again, Mr. Larkin."

Before Larkin could say more, Scott strode to the ladder.

"Sergeant Crammer." Scott swung onto the ladder and climbed down to the longboat. Crammer and the troopers followed, rocking the boat wildly as they boarded.

"Take me ashore." The sailors exchanged glances but didn't move.

"Take me ashore." Scott barked, and the man nearest to Scott leaned forward and put his knuckle to his forehead.

"Begging your pardon, Captain, but the bosun must . . ." He was interrupted by Larkin's voice from the deck.

"Hold below."

Scott looked up to see Larkin swing onto the ladder and climb nimbly down to the longboat, followed by the bosun.

Scott climbed onto the jetty and strode towards the fort with Crammer and the troopers trailing behind him. Larkin and Hopkins followed some distance behind. Scott went straight to Major Phelps's office knocked and entered. A man Scott took to be Captain Harwood was standing with his back to the fire. He was in his mid-sixties, short with a belly hanging over his belt. He had a head of dark hair threaded with grey and a face lined by years at sea.

Major Phelps stood next to him. He blinked in surprise when he saw Scott then scowled.

"Captain Scott, what do you mean by bursting into my office like this? Why was I not informed of your return?"

"I'm only just returned, Major, and have come to request that—"

Phelps interrupted him. "We heard musket fire a short time ago. What has happened?"

'The musket fire was from the *Challenger*. The crew fired on and killed six of the Iroquois scouts under my command."

Captain Harwood took a step forward. "What's that you say? The *Challenger* fired on you?" There was a rap on the door and Larkin and the bosun stepped into the room.

"Mr. Larkin, what's happened? Is what this man says true?"

Larkin shook his head.

"We sighted two men running along the inlet, one white, the other native. There were eight or ten savages close on their heels, and we provided covering fire to enable them to escape."

Scott exploded.

"They were our scouts, Captain. They were pursuing a man who murdered the heir of one of the most important families in England." Scott turned to Captain Harwood, his anger rising. "Your first officer allowed the man to escape in a fishing boat and refused my request to pursue him."

Larkin's face was red, and his voice rasped with anger.

"I heard no request," he barked. "You attempted to force me to your will, and I'll not have it."

"You brought arms to bear on a British officer, sir. That is a capital offense."

Phelps stepped between them.

"Be quiet both of you. I won't tolerate such behaviour." Phelps walked to the fireplace and turned.

"Captain Scott, what's the status of your mission?"

"The mission has been completed, Major. The village at Shubenacadie has been destroyed. Major, it's vital that we pursue this man before he disappears into the wilderness." Scott clenched his fists in frustration.

"Captain Scott, you will contain yourself and answer my questions." The major's voice rose in pitch, and his face became pale with anger. "What of the natives at the village, Captain?"

"The majority were killed during the action."

"As I understand it, there were several hundred villagers?"

"That's correct, Major, and most of them died during the raid."

Phelps's eyes narrowed. "You killed them all? Are telling me you wiped out the entire village?" Scott could barely contain his temper.

"Your orders were to exact retribution for the attack on this fort. I have carried out my order to the letter."

Phelps stared into space, and the room went quiet. Harwood and Larkin watched, tight-lipped, and finally Phelps looked at Scott again.

"Who is this man you were pursuing?"

"The man I am pursuing killed Lieutenant Sackville, the son of Lord Sackville, the Duke of Devon, in Scotland a year ago. As the duke is personal advisor to the prime minister, I believe it would be in your best interest to ensure this murderer is brought to justice."

"I'll decide what's in my best interest, Captain. How can you be sure it's the same man? How could he be here in Acadia?"

"I don't know how he came to be here, but it's the same man. He called me by name and fired on me."

Phelps frowned.

"Where is he now?"

"He escaped down the inlet in a fishing boat. We must pursue him immediately."

Phelps looked at Larkin. "Is this true, Mr. Larkin?"

Scott burst out angrily. "Do you doubt my word, Major?"

"Captain Scott, you will be silent." Phelps's voice was harsh.

Larkin glanced at Harwood and he nodded. "What the captain says is true. The man and the native took the boat and sailed down the inlet."

Phelps and Harwood shared a look, and Phelps turned to Scott and Larkin. "Gentlemen, will you excuse us."

Scott started to speak, but the major pre-empted him.

"Captain Scott, you will wait outside."

Scott bit his tongue and left the room before he lost complete control of his temper. He paced in the hallway. He had little regard for Major Phelps, but for now he needed his cooperation. He was astonished that the boy was here in Annapolis Royal, and the humiliation he had endured at the hands of Lord Sackville welled up in him again. No matter—he wouldn't let the boy escape a second time.

Finally the door opened and Phelps motioned for them to enter.

"If this man is who you say he is, Captain Scott, then he should be brought to justice." He held up his hand. "Captain Harwood has agreed to pursue the fishing boat."

"We're wasting time. We must leave immediately . . ." Phelps's cut him off, and his face took on a pinched look.

"You will hear me out, Captain. You will take a complement of men on board the *Challenger*. Captain Harwood will run down the fishing boat, and you will bring this man back to Annapolis Royal."

Scott nodded not trusting himself to speak further lest it delay their departure.

"Carry on, Captain Harwood," Phelps said. Scott started to leave, but Phelps motioned for him to stay. When the others had left Phelps spoke again.

"Captain Scott, let me be clear, I will not tolerate a repeat of the incident that took place on the *Challenger*."

Scott bit his tongue, anxious to get after the boy. "If you have no further instructions for me, Major, I'll take my leave."

Phelps glared at him. "You're dismissed, Captain."

When Scott stepped on board the *Challenger*, there was frenzied activity on deck. The sailors were high in the rigging, shaking out the sails, and the windlass was creaking as it took up the strain. Harwood was on the bridge talking to Larkin. Both watched Scott as he crossed the deck.

Scott climbed to the bridge and stood with his back to the stern rail. He felt the anchor break free, and the ship pirouetted neatly and came on the wind. In spite of his anger Scott was impressed by how efficiently they got underway. There were clouds over the Bay of Fundy to the west, but the sky to the south was clear. The wind was in the south, and they started tacking down the inlet.

Scott had brought ten troopers and a dozen Iroquois. Harwood had objected to so many armed men on board, but Scott had ignored him. The troopers stood along the rail looking at Annapolis Royal. None seemed happy to be relinquishing the comforts of the fort to chase a fugitive. The Iroquois sat at the bow watching the sailors work the ship. The death of their warriors had created a blood feud, and Scott watched them lest they try to take revenge on the crew.

Scott searched the horizon, but there was no sign of the fishing boat.

"Captain, how long do you estimate before we overtake the fishing boat?"

Harwood looked at Scott. "They are at least two hours ahead of us, and an empty fishing boat will make good time. He looked off towards the stern. We are making six knots, perhaps seven. If the wind holds, we will come up with them in three hours, four at the most."

"It'll be dark by then. Can you make more speed?"

"We're carrying all sail, Captain. This is our best speed." Hardwood's tone made it clear he had nothing more to say.

Scott paced the bridge, willing the ship to greater speed. He was determined that the boy wouldn't escape him. It was late in the afternoon when he heard a cry of sail ho from the masthead, and Larkin called out.

"Where away?" Scott looked up at the crow's nest. The sailor called out again, his words were carried away on the wind, but he pointed to the south. Larkin waved and the man came sliding down the rigging. He was only a boy of fourteen or fifteen years of age.

"It's a small boat, Mr. Larkin, two masts hull down."

"How far?"

"Five miles, sir, maybe more."

Larkin looked at the rigging. "Good, lad. Back aloft with you. Don't lose sight of it."

"Aye, Mr. Larkin."

Scott stepped up to Larkin. "How long until we come up with them?"

Captain Harwood came on deck, and Larkin turned to him. "The fishing boat is hull down five miles ahead."

"Very well, Mr. Larkin, carry on."

"How long until we come up with them?" Harwood looked up at the sails.

"An hour, perhaps two, depending on how well they handle the boat."

"You must make more speed, Captain. We must catch them before dark." Harwood's face darkened. He started to speak but thought better of it and turned his back on Scott.

It was an hour before Scott picked out the sail against the background haze. A moment later a shout went up from the deck, and the troopers gathered at the bow to watch. Scott watched the boat for a while; then he went to where Harwood stood by the wheel. "We are gaining on it quickly."

"The tide's turning. We make better speed against it than they can."

"Can you bring us alongside?"

"Aye, if they don't reach the gap before us."

Scott looked at Harwood sharply. "What do you mean?"

"The tide's turning, Captain. In an hour it will be in flood. We can't transit the channel against it." Scott strode to the rail. He remembered the surge of water in the gap from the outward journey, and he returned to the wheel.

"We mustn't lose this fugitive, Captain. We must make more speed."

"That will depend on the wind and the tide," Harwood interrupted him before he could say more. "We are making our maximum speed, Captain Scott, there's no more to say." Larkin looked at Harwood, a question in his eyes, and Harwood shook his head.

Scott didn't know what had passed between them, but a seed of doubt was planted in his mind. He kept his temper under control. Provoking Harwood further wouldn't help, and he didn't want to chance losing the boy. When he looked again, the fishing boat was in plain sight two miles ahead, but as he watched, the motion of the ship began to change. The bow was throwing off spray as it took each wave. The tide was running against them now, and their forward motion was slowing.

Scott watched the fishing boat cut across their bow from port to starboard. The gap was less than a mile ahead, and he realized what they were trying to do. Now he understood what the look between Larkin and Harwood meant, and he strode to the wheel and faced Harwood.

"We must catch them before they reach the gap."

"It'll be a close-run thing, Captain."

"Why are we bearing away from the fishing boat?" His voice became strident, and he felt his temper rise. "We must come about and pursue it directly." The *Challenger* was on the starboard tack with the wind coming over her starboard rail. The fishing boat was on the opposite tack.

"I'll decide how to handle my ship. That will be all, Captain Scott."

Scott was furious. The *Challenger* was a mile behind the fishing boat, but the two vessels seemed to be moving farther apart now. He heard Larkin give the order to come about. He knew changing tack with the wind behind them, jibing they called it, was a dangerous manoeuvre, and they could be dismasted. As the ship came around, the sails slammed over hard and the rigging groaned under the strain. Harwood looked up sharply, but the *Challenger* surged forward again.

Scott saw what Harwood was doing: the *Challenger* was now lined up for a run across the inlet that would take them through the gap. He breathed a sigh of relief and went to the port rail. The fishing boat was a mile away, and it was making little headway against the tide. The *Challenger* was closing the distance between them quickly, and half an hour later they were within a quarter of a mile of the boat and Scott could see the two men clearly.

Scott turned to Harwood. "Can you capture the boat, Captain?"

Harwood pointed to the forward deck where two groups of sailors were readying grappling irons. The fishing boat would come up on the port side, and Scott moved to the rail and waved Sergeant Cramer over.

"Have four troopers ready to drop into the fishing boat and take the fugitives prisoner."

"Aye, Captain. I'll do it myself."

"I want the boy alive, Sergeant. Do you understand?" Crammer nodded and went down to the main deck.

The fishing boat changed course several times, and Harwood matched each turn and continued to gain on it. They were less than a quarter of a mile from the inlet. Scott didn't know how close they could come, but Harwood showed no sign of concern. The fishing boat turned hard to port with the wind across her stern. The sails slammed over to the starboard side, and the boat heeled until the rail seemed to go under. Harwood cursed and called to the helmsman to let her fall off. The ship came around to port, but Harwood shouted at the helmsman to bring her up to starboard again.

The fishing boat had turned around and was heading back up the inlet and would pass along their port side.

Scott strode to Harwood. "You must come about, Captain."

"We can't come about with the wind behind us. We'll be dismasted."

"These men must not escape." Scott was shouting, furious with Harwood's faint-hearted behaviour.

Scott was startled by the crack of a musket from the main deck. He rushed across the bridge, and as he slid down the stairs to the main deck a volley of musket fire rattled from the bow.

"Hold your fire, damn you." He saw Crammer tear a musket from one of the troopers. He reversed the weapon and drove the stock into the back of the man next to him sending him to his knees. Crammer swung the musket like a club striking another trooper on the side of the head and knocking him senseless.

"Sergeant Crammer, these men will be flogged when we return to Annapolis Royal. You will see to it."

Scott saw the fishing boat moving past their port side. Then it turned again onto the starboard tack across their stern. He ran to the bridge rail. The boat was now three hundred yards behind them, and he realized that their course would take them into the inlet with the wind on their beam.

Harwood called out to the helmsman. "Starboard your helm."

The ship came around to starboard and the wind came on her beam, lining the bow up with the centre of the gap, but the ship almost came to a stop as it met the incoming tide and the four-foot swell it drove ahead of it.

Scott kept his eye on the fishing boat. It was being thrown around wildly by the tide, the bows almost disappearing between each swell, but they were still making forward progress. The ship shuddered as if it had struck a reef and a burst of spray broke over the bow and flew across the deck. Another shudder shook the ship, and the bows were thrown to port. The helmsman corrected it, but Scott saw Larkin look at Harwood questioningly.

As the ship struck the next wave, it felt as if they had hit a solid wall. The sails backed and then snapped tight again. They slid to port and the helmsman struggled to bring her back on course again.

Harwood called out, "Hard to starboard. Bring the ship onto the port tack." The seamen ran to work the yards, and Scott felt the ship begin to turn, and he put his hand on Harwood's shoulder.

"What're you doing, Captain? They have almost reached the gap."

"The tide is against us, Captain Scott. We can't make the gap." Harwood pointed to the cliffs along the bottom of the inlet. "We'll be driven onto the rocks."

"You cannot let these men get away, Captain."

"I will not endanger my ship any further, Captain Scott. Step aside."

Scott stepped back and called out, "Sergeant Crammer."

Harwood looked at him sharply as Crammer came across the deck with six troopers behind him. Crammer stopped beside Scott, and the troopers took up positions on either side of him. The ship was already bearing away, and Scott realized that even if he forced the issue, they could not come about in time to make the gap.

Harwood stared at Scott stone-faced. "Captain . . ."

Scott pre-empted him. "Stand down, Sergeant Crammer."

"A wise decision, Captain Scott," Harwood said.

Harwood stepped up to the helm. "Mr. Larkin, launch a boat and send two men with a telescope to climb that cliff." He pointed to the headland at the northern end of the gap. "I want to know which way the fishing boat is heading. Then bring us to anchor on the east side of the inlet."

"Aye, Captain."

Harwood turned away, but Scott spoke up. "How long till the tide turns, Captain?"

"Six hours, Captain, but it will still be dark. We will make the passage in morning."

"There will be a half-moon tonight, light enough to make the transit."

Harwood turned to Scott. "We will not chance the gap in the dark."

"This man must not escape."

Harwood held Scott's eye. "The spring tides are running and will carry the fishing boat across the bay. We will follow at first light, Captain, and not before."

CHAPTER THIRTY

JOHN WATCHED AS THE CHALLENGER slowed, the sails backed and filled, and she came to a halt. The tidal surge pushed the bow around, and she started to drift towards the rocks at the south side of the inlet. There was surge of activity on deck; John saw the seamen haul the sails around, and she came onto the port tack and bore away across the inlet.

John breathed a sigh of relief and turned his attention back to sailing the fishing boat. They were in the teeth of the tidal surge, and each time the bow took a wave, he was afraid they would be swamped. John gave the helm to Louis and went to the foremast. The boat began to pitch violently, and he held on to the mast as another wave broke over them. He took a reef in the foresail and reefed the mainsail down to half its size and returned to the stern.

Louis looked at him uncertainly, but John put the tiller over and brought them onto the starboard tack. Under reduced sail the boat became more stable. John brought her up two points closer to the wind, and they cut away from the cliffs into the gap.

John looked back. The *Challenger* was halfway across the inlet. As he watched she came up into the wind. He guessed she would heave-to or anchor. Either way they wouldn't be able to transit the gap until the tide turned.

With the wind on the starboard quarter they rounded the headland and the tidal surge eased, and the fishing boat rode the swells easily. John put her on a course to the north away from the shore. He still thought the canoe was of little use, but it rode the swells easily and didn't slow them down. Behind them, the inlet was already out of sight.

"Your skill with the boat is good," Louis said.

John shook his head. "I know a little, but I think good fortune was on our side today."

"It may be so, but we came through the gap, and they did not."

John looked back again.

"When the tide turns, they'll follow. By then we must be far away. Will you make the journey to Quebec with me? Perhaps we can trade for furs and become wealthy?"

Louis stopped bailing and looked at John. "My people are no more, and I have no home. It will be a good journey to make, and we will kill more English and their Iroquois dogs," he said.

John looked at the darkening sky. "Do you know the trail to Quebec?"

"My father travelled there, and he told me of the journey. It is many days to the west, and we must pass close to the land of the Iroquois." Louis pointed to the northwest. "There, a river empties into the bay. It is the start of the journey to the place the French call Quebec."

John looked back at the peninsula to get his bearings, and brought the bow around to the northwest. The wind was in the starboard quarter, and the fishing boat took the swells in its stride. Behind them darkness was falling, but he knew the British would come at first light.

The tide was pushing them up the bay, and John compensated, keeping the boat heading to the northwest. As darkness fell he put another reef in the mizzen. He'd never sailed at night, and he didn't want to chance swamping the boat in the dark. Later the sky cleared. He was able to find the North Star and held their course as best he could.

John showed Louis how to keep them on course, and they took turns resting. John lay down by the mizzenmast and put his hunting bag under his head and closed his eyes. Later he awoke, surprised that he had slept at all, and sat beside Louis at the helm. A half-moon rode high in the sky, casting the ocean in an eerie light. He was thinking that the moonlight made the swells look like monsters bearing down on them when he realized that something had changed.

"The tide has turned."

"You slept for a quarter of the moon. The night is half gone," Louis said.

"You should sleep." He took the tiller and Louis went forward, disappearing into the gloom, and a few minutes later John heard him snoring softly.

The night clouded over, hiding the stars, and the moon faded, leaving the ocean in darkness. The wind turned cold and John wrapped his plaid around his shoulders. It was two hours before John saw the first light in the eastern sky. It grew slowly, revealing a grey day with low clouds scudding across the sky. John brought the boat up a point. The change in motion wakened Louis; he sat up and looked at the ocean.

"It's getting light. I hope we'll see land soon." Louis came back to the stern seat.

John put the tiller over, bringing the boat into the wind, and they lost all forward motion.

"Take the tiller. We can carry more sail in daylight." John went forward.

When he had hoisted the foremast mainsail, Louis called out, "Drink." He pointed to the water keg under forward bench.

John had drunk nothing since the previous day and his throat was raw. There was a metal cup fastened to the keg by a chain. He held it under the bunghole and dribbled water into it. The water was brackish, but he gulped it down. Then he drank another cupful more slowly.

John kept the boat stable while Louis drank; then he brought them on the wind, heeling hard to port. Louis sat by the starboard rail and handed John a piece of dried meat.

"You'll need your strength." The sweet taste of the berries made John's eyes water, and he ate the pemmican with relish.

The wind held, and John kept on to the northwest, searching the horizon for the first sign of land. After an hour he began to think they had underestimated how far it was across the bay. Louis was standing by the mizzenmast, searching the ocean.

"There." He pointed to the west, but it was some time before John picked out a darker line on the horizon.

"I see it."

John kept as much sail on the boat as he could, but for a time it seemed they weren't getting any closer. There was nothing on the horizon in any direction, but he knew the British wouldn't have given up the chase. The ship could outrun the fishing boat in the open sea, and he was anxious to reach the land.

As the boat plowed on, the line on the horizon faded to grey; then John realized what he was looking at.

"Fog. There's fog along the coast."

"There is much fog in this season," Louis said. "We must be careful, but the British will not enter it with their ship."

"Let's hope so," John said. "The captain of the *Challenger* knows his business too well for my liking."

They held their course for another hour, but the land didn't seem closer, and John couldn't tell where the sea ended and the sky began. The fog began to thin. Then as if a curtain had been pulled back, it parted to reveal the coast. They were a quarter of a mile off a muddy beach exposed by the tide. Low cliffs rose abruptly from the beach, topped with dark green fir and pine trees that John found startling after the grey of the sea.

Louis went to the bow and studied the coastline.

"We're too far to the north." He pointed south.

"How far is the river?"

"I can't tell. The shore is rocky to the north of the river, to the south the forest runs down to the shore. This is what my father has told me."

The fog still lay a mile offshore, hanging like a grey curtain across the sky, separating them from the ocean. The wind dropped and John brought the fishing boat around to the south, and they tacked back and forth between the fog bank and the shore for another hour. The wind came in flurries, and the fog bank churned in the breeze, closing in around them then receding again. There was something menacing about the fog. It enveloped them in a world of silence, and John and Louis spoke in whispers as if the fog would carry their voices to their enemies.

Ahead, the shoreline curved to the east, and John put the helm over to give them room to manoeuvre. As they rounded the headland the wind picked up, and he felt the tide begin to run.

"This is the mouth of the river," Louis said.

"Are you sure?"

"It can be no other."

Above them, a high-pitched screech pierced the air, and John turned, searching for danger. On the headland to the north an eagle launched itself into the air and glided gracefully downward. It cried out again as it swooped over the water. It was a haunting sound, and John felt the hackles rise on the back of his neck. The eagle floated across the surface, effortlessly took a fish and winged its way into the sky.

John was startled out of his reverie as the fishing boat lurched, as if the eagle had signalled a change, and the tide surged under them pushing them into the mouth of the river. John could see currents swirling on the surface, and as they entered the estuary a swell began to build. The boat heeled over, and the bow threw spray back at them as they took each wave.

"I've never seen a tide like this," John said.

"The sea is there." Louis pointed to the southeast. "The tide comes straight in from the ocean and runs into the river."

John looked at Louis then over his shoulder.

"The ship," John cried out. The wind was blowing the fog to the north, slowly revealing the British ship a mile offshore. She was holding her position against the tide, and John realized they must have been cruising back and forth at the mouth of the river waiting for them.

A longboat was tied to her starboard side and as he watched, a dozen men stepped aboard and it pulled straight for them. John put the helm over and drove the boat into the estuary; with the wind behind them and the tide surging, they might be able to outdistance the longboat.

John brought the bow up a point, trying to con every bit of speed he could out of her, but Louis gripped his shoulder and pointed to the north shore.

"There." John sucked his breath in. Another longboat was pulled up on the beach at the mouth of the river. Even as they watched, men were pushing it into the water. The seamen handled the oars, and John saw Iroquois amongst them. The boat was heavily laden, but it was moving across the river to where it would intersect their path half a mile ahead.

John searched the shore looking for a place to land.

"We have to beach the boat and take to the woods."

"The longboat will be on us first." Louis pointed behind them. The oars were dipping rhythmically as the longboat drove towards them.

John started to put the helm over.

"Wait," Louis called, "we'll take the canoe." He took the rope and started to pull the canoe in.

"The longboats are faster. They will be on us before we reach the shore." Louis pointed out to sea.

"It's the season you call spring. The tide will turn the river into a torrent."

"We can't outrun the British on the ocean. We must chance the river in the canoe."

John looked across the estuary. The longboat was coming on quickly. The second longboat was being thrown around by the tide, but they were still making headway and would soon block their path.

Louis gripped John's arm.

"We must take the canoe."

"We'll be overwhelmed in the canoe. It's madness."

"The tide grows stronger now. You must trust me in this," Louis said.

John heaved a sigh. "All right. We take the canoe."

John brought the boat into the wind. Their motion through the water stopped, but the tide still carried them forward at astonishing speed. The canoe looked old, but it was heavily made, and John hoped it wouldn't be torn apart by the sea. Louis held the bow and John piled the muskets and their baggage into it. A wave struck the port side, and John had to grab the gunnels to steady himself.

John struggled to his feet. He looked around. The longboat was less than five hundred yards behind them now. He pointed but Louis pre-empted him.

"Bring it around." The canoe was on the port side where the waves were coming in, and they manhandled it to the starboard side.

"I'll hold her," Louis said. John lowered himself into the bow of the canoe and held fast to the sides and Louis slid into the stern. There were three paddles wedged under one of the seats, John freed two and handed one to Louis.

John glanced at Louis, and they pushed away from the fishing boat. He felt vulnerable in this tiny vessel, and he hoped Louis knew what he was doing.

"Back," Louis called. John dug his paddle in driving astern. "Back. We must clear the boat." The fishing boat was being thrown around wildly and could crush the canoe if it struck them.

They back paddled till they were thirty feet astern of the fishing boat, and Louis brought the bow around towards the entrance to the estuary. They rose to the crest of a wave and John looked around; the fishing boat was a hundred feet away drifting to the north. The second longboat was half a mile ahead holding position in the centre of the river. He looked behind them and cried out in alarm. The longboat from the ship was less than three hundred yards away.

John could see the faces of the Iroquois. He looked at Louis and motioned to the longboat.

"They're almost on us."

"Wait. We must wait for the tide," Louis said. John glanced at the longboat again. The oars were rising and falling rhythmically, driving them forward.

"Louis we have to go now." John was perplexed that Louis didn't seem to understand the danger.

John turned and dug his paddle in, and the canoe swung sideways to the tide and rolled perilously, but Louis brought it around again quickly. John turned and looked at him.

"What are you doing, Louis? The British are closing fast!"

"I see them, but we must wait for the tide to rise."

"The British will hang us if they catch us."

"Wait," Louis called. John threw his hands up in frustration.

"There," Louis called. He pointed past the longboat.

John looked out to sea. The *Challenger was* cruising on the starboard tack, but there was nothing else to see.

"There. Get ready," Louis called. John watched as a single wave lifted the ship and threw it thirty degrees to port, shredding her topsails and tearing two spars loose. The wave moved across the inlet growing in height and strength as it came on.

John swore under his breath.

"What is it?"

"It's the season of the great tides. The surge will carry us up the river. We must stay ahead of the wave, or it will drive us under." John turned around and looked around the estuary. The tide had carried the canoe into the mouth of the river. The longboat behind them was pulling hard trying to stay ahead of the wave, and the second boat was moving towards them oblivious to the danger.

The canoe was thrown around wildly, but Louis steered it expertly keeping it stern on to the tide. As the mouth of the river narrowed, the wave increased in height and gained speed. It was a terrifying sight as it bore down on them.

"Wait," Louis called, "until it's almost on us."

John could see the masts of the British ship beyond the wave. The topsails were in tatters, and she was clawing her way out of the estuary.

The wave was two hundred feet behind them, and John steeled himself as he watched it rush towards them, six feet high and spanning the width of the river.

Louis sat perfectly still, watching the wave; then he called out.

"Now. Paddle now." John dug his paddle in, putting all his strength into it. Louis fell in time with him, and the canoe surged forward. Louis steered for the centre of the river angling across the front of the wave. John looked back, and his stomach lurched. The wave was less than a hundred feet behind them and coming fast. It was smooth in the centre of the river, but at the edges it curved forward and crashed onto the riverbanks destroying everything in its path.

John paddled with all his strength, drawing great gulps of air.

"Harder, drive harder," Louis shouted. John could hardly hear him over the roar of the water. The wave was fifty feet away rushing at them like a wall of moving stone.

John felt the stern lift, and Louis shouted, "Keep paddling. Don't stop."

John held his breath as the canoe rode up the front of the wave. He braced himself for it to break over them, but the canoe held position below the crest of the wave. John glanced behind him. Louis was digging his paddle in to hold them in position.

"I'll call the strokes. Follow my lead." The wave carried them forward at breakneck speed, and in spite of the danger John let out a whoop of elation.

John saw the longboat from the ship to their right. It was staying ahead of the wave, but making heavy going of it. It suddenly turned across the face of the wave and almost broached, but the helmsman brought the stern around and averted disaster. He was astounded to see the second longboat two hundred feet ahead of them. The helmsman's face was set with concentration as he steered the longboat towards them. Four Iroquois sat in the bow with their weapons ready.

The canoe started to slide to the right across the wave and John heard Louis call out.

"Paddle left." John swapped his paddle to the other side and dug it in countering the roll of the canoe. They steadied below the crest, and John felt a surge of admiration for Louis's skill at handling the canoe.

John heard a popping sound from his right, and he turned in time to see a cloud of powder smoke blow away across the estuary. One of the sailors set a musket down and took up his oar again. John thought it was an act of frustration rather than a serious attempt to hit them. The helmsman was shouting orders and waving his right arm. The sailors on the port side stopped rowing, and the boat spun around and surged across the front of the wave straight for them.

John watched the longboat, trying to judge if it would reach them before the wave struck it.

"Be ready to change direction," Louis called. John nodded but kept his eyes on the longboat. The helmsman knew his business. His eyes moved between the canoe and the oncoming wave, and he shouted orders to the oarsmen as he made adjustments to their heading.

When the longboat was a hundred feet from them, two seamen in the bow raised their muskets and fired. The water exploded in front of the canoe and a moment later John heard the reports of the muskets. John saw the helmsman bark an order, and he put the tiller over and started to bring the longboat bow on to the oncoming wave.

John felt Louis shift his weight; then he called out, "Right!"

John dug his paddle in, driving the bow to port, and Louis brought the canoe around almost broadside to the wave. John's stomach lurched as the canoe almost tipped over, but it righted again, and they slid across the face of the wave away from the longboat.

"Left," Louis called. John dug his paddle in. He felt the canoe slow down, and they held position below the crest of the wave again.

John looked to his right. The seamen were pulling desperately, as the longboat rose up the face of the wave until it was almost standing on end. The seamen held fast with one hand and grasped their oar with the other; an Iroquois warrior tumbled over the side and clung to the boat half in the water. The weight started to drag the boat around. John thought it would broach, but one of the seamen struck the warrior on the head with a belaying pin, and he disappeared beneath the surface.

The helmsman put the tiller over, and the boat righted, but as it crested the wave it came half out of the water, and four seamen were thrown into the ocean, limbs flailing. The longboat hung in the air for a long moment then crashed down on top of them driving them under. John caught a final glimpse of the longboat wallowing in the trough half filled with water, with the crew bailing for their lives.

The river narrowed ahead, and the cliffs on both sides compressed the tidal surge increasing its height. John watched in awe as the incredible volume of water pouring down the river collided with the tidal surge, to form a huge standing wave. He could barely believe what he was seeing, but the tide had brought the river to a halt and was forcing it to flow upstream. Fear tingled in his gut as the canoe was carried towards this maelstrom like a leaf on the wind.

The second longboat was a hundred yards to their right. It was being thrown around by the tidal surge, and the seamen were fighting to keep it from broaching. John looked back. Louis's face was set in concentration.

"We must keep to the left side of the river," Louis called. John nodded. He changed his paddle to the right side, and Louis brought them to within a hundred feet of the cliffs. John searched the rocks for a place to land, but the cliffs towered above them smooth and shining with moisture.

The river made a turn to the left, and as they were carried around John saw it turned to the right again four hundred yards ahead. The river narrowed as they approached the bend and the wave began to break up near the centre of the river. The top curled over and collapsed into a churning maelstrom that was driven ahead of the wave.

John glanced at the longboat. The crew was pulling furiously trying to stay ahead of the wave, steering for the north shore. John had to admit grudging admiration for the helmsman, and in the same moment he realized that the fishing boat wouldn't have survived this.

"Closer, we need to be closer to the left side."

"What lies beyond?" He looked back, but Louis shook his head. The longboat was close to the north side of the river now, and John could see the helmsman shouting orders and stabbing the air with his hand.

At they came into the bend Louis brought the canoe under the shadow of the cliffs. An outcrop of rock blocked John's view ahead, and the sound of the river grew to a deafening roar. Louis steered the canoe around the outcrop, and John's stomach lurched. Ahead of them the river narrowed to half its width and fell into a hole, forming a huge whirlpool.

Louis struck the side of the canoe, and John looked back. He leaned forward and shouted, "Hold back." The roar of the water drowned his voice, but John read his lips and dug his paddle in. The tidal surge lifted the canoe,

328

and as they fought to hold it below the crest John stared at the whirlpool in fascination and horror. It was forty feet across and dominated the north side of the river, turning like a great wheel and spiralling down in the centre as if it were pulling the river down into some vast cavern below the earth.

The canoe lurched, and John came back to his senses. The stern broke through the crest of the wave. Louis leaned forward paddling furiously, but the canoe began to tip backwards. John threw himself over the bow and dug his paddle in deep, and they slid onto the front of the wave again.

A four-foot standing wave lay directly in their path. There was no way to avoid it without broaching, and John looked at Louis.

"Stay high on the wave," Louis called. As they bore down on the wave, they worked their paddles back and forward to maintain position. Just before they struck the wave, John thrust his paddle under his seat and grasped the sides of the canoe. John hung on grimly as the water battered him like a giant fist.

As the canoe crested the wave, John called out in surprise. The longboat was close to the north side of the river, the tidal surge was carrying it towards the whirlpool, and the seamen were pulling desperately for the north bank. The longboat was moving across the face of the tidal surge aiming for a shelf of rock at the bottom of the cliff. It was polished smooth by the water. It was an almost impossible landing, but it was their only chance. John couldn't help but admire their courage, and a tiny part of him willed them to make it to shore.

As he watched the longboat claw its way across the river, John knew they wouldn't make it. The tidal surge struck them side on and the longboat was thrown into the air and turned over tumbling the sailors into the mouth of the whirlpool. John saw one of the Iroquois surface on the edge of the whirlpool, but he was sucked under immediately. The longboat struck the water stern first and seemed to balance for a moment; then it fell bow first into the whirlpool and was pulled under.

John felt the canoe falling, and he dragged his eyes away from the whirlpool. The canoe slewed to the left almost broaching, but Louis pulled the stern around. John leaned out to the right and pulled the bow back in line and looked back at Louis.

"Make for the centre of the river." John only heard half of what he shouted, but he understood.

The tide carried them around the turn, and John stared spellbound as the tidal surge swallowed the whirlpool like a great beast devouring its prey, leaving a churning torrent in its wake. He tore his eyes away. The surge was driving them towards the cliffs on the south side of the river. Louis banged on the side of the canoe, and he looked around.

"Back paddle."

John dug in leaning back as he paddled. The canoe broke through the crest of the wave, and his stomach lurched as they dropped into the trough. The wave rushed on towards the cliffs, and they paddled for the middle of the river. The wave broke against the cliffs exploding forty feet into the air with a clap like thunder, but the tidal surge carried them around the turn.

The cliffs fell away, the river began to broaden out, and the tidal surge collapsed to three feet in height. John was astonished they had survived, and he cried out in relief.

"Keep paddling," Louis said. "The tide will carry us far up the river." John looked back, and he was astonished to see Louis grinning from ear to ear. It was the first time he had smiled since Mathieu's death, and he found himself laughing out loud.

"Paddle."

"Aye." The canoe was half filled with water, and John looked at Louis. "Can you hold her?"

Louis didn't reply, and John bailed with his hands until he couldn't scoop up any more water. There were still two inches in the bottom, but the canoe rode higher in the water.

The river continued to broaden, and as the wave pushed them upstream John began to relax. They passed between two islands, and a bay opened up on their left. The river turned south, then northwest, and broadened till it was almost like a lake, nearly half a mile wide.

The lake ran to the west, but John saw another arm to the north.

"Do you know of this lake?"

"My father has told me that many rivers feed it."

"Did your father describe the journey to Quebec?"

"He said he and his brothers kept moving west and north until they came to the great river."

The north arm of the river was larger, but John had no way of knowing where it led. He looked at the watery sun peeking through the clouds and took a bearing on the west arm.

"We'll follow your father's guidance."

"It's the only wisdom we have to guide us," Louis said.

The tidal bore carried them twenty miles to a fork branching to the west before it finally lost its strength.

"Do we take the west arm again?" John said.

"It is as my father has told. The river has many branches, but we must keep to the west." The fork was narrow, but the current was stronger and John took that as a sign it was a main branch of the river.

The sun was well past its height as they moved into the west fork. The tidal bore had lost its power, and they settled into a steady rhythm with the paddles. There were several hours of daylight left when they spotted a creek on the south bank. The trees grew down to the water's edge and cast it into shadow.

"This is as good place to make camp," Louis said. The creek was narrow and only a few feet deep. They landed at a clearing on the north bank. John stepped ashore and dragged the canoe out of the water, and they unloaded their gear and turned the canoe over to drain.

John couldn't remember when they had last eaten, and he was exhausted. He sat with his back against the canoe and ate some dried meat; it was soggy from being immersed in salt water, but when the taste of the berry juice hit his tongue his eyes watered at the sweetness.

Louis slumped down beside him and John handed him some pemmican. Louis was grey with fatigue, and his eyes were bloodshot. He took a bite of pemmican and rested his head against the canoe.

"I can't go any farther," John said.

"We survived, but the Iroquois have a blood feud with us now, and they'll follow if they can. We must move at first light."

John unpacked their gear, spreading it out on the canoe to dry, and lay down with his hunting bag as a pillow. Images of the day flashed through his mind: the *Challenger* emerging from the fog like a ghost ship, the tidal surge, and the terrifying power of the cataract. The last image he saw before sleep claimed him was of the longboat and its crew being pulled down into darkness.

CHAPTER THIRTY-ONE

SCOTT PACED THE BRIDGE OF the *Challenger* restlessly. The boy had escaped. Six troopers had been drowned and they had lost eight Iroquois. He cared little about the troops and less about the savages, but losing the chance to hang the boy soured his stomach. He didn't know if the boy had survived. He didn't think anyone could have survived that maelstrom, but it brought him no comfort.

It was mid-morning, but the day remained overcast, and the *Challenger* was plowing its way across the Bay of Fundy. The wind was steady from the south, and Harwood had told him that if it held, they would reach the inlet in time for the evening tide. Harwood had made it clear that he wanted Scott and his men off his ship at the earliest opportunity.

In the end they didn't make the tide and the *Challenger* had to beat back and forth off the inlet all night. Scott stayed on deck until the rain drove him below around midnight. He dozed in a chair until first light then went back to pacing the bridge. When the tide turned Harwood conned the ship through the gap and by early afternoon they dropped anchor off Annapolis Royal. Scott went ashore as soon as the boat was lowered.

* * *

Scott went directly to Major Phelps's quarters and requested a meeting. Phelps kept him waiting for half an hour, and when he was admitted the major was standing by the fire in the same position Scott had seen him last.

"Well, Captain, have you captured the murderer?"

"No, Major, the fishing boat made it through the inlet. We pursued them across the Bay of Fundy, and they escaped into a river. We sent boats to capture them, but they were overwhelmed by a tidal surge."

"Yes, the tidal bore can be fearful in the spring."

Phelps pursed his lips. "And the fugitive?"

"The boy was likely drowned in the river, but I don't know that for certain. We lost six troopers and a number of the Iroquois scouts."

Phelps shook his head and looked down at the floor for a moment.

"The loss of a few troopers isn't important. They can be replaced, as can the Iroquois, but it's a pity you couldn't capture the fugitive. It would have been a feather in your cap and would have added impetus to your career."

Scott knew the major cared little for his career. What he really meant was it would've enhanced his reputation. To capture the man who had killed the Duke of Devon's heir would have played well with his superiors.

Phelps warmed his hands at the fire.

"You will provide me with a full report on the action against the village at Shubenacadie and the pursuit of this fugitive by the end of the week. That will be all, Captain."

Scott turned to leave but Phelps stopped him. "A letter for you was included in the mail package brought by the *Challenger*. It's on the table."

The quality of the paper set the letter apart from the other correspondence on the desk, and Scott's heart missed a beat when he recognized the handwriting. He thrust the letter inside his tunic, saluted Phelps, and pulled the door closed behind him. He went to his quarters and set the letter on the table by the window. He removed his jacket, took a paper knife, broke the seal, and smoothed the letter out on the table. His pulse quickened at the sight of that elegant hand, and he sat down to read it.

Captain Scott,

I am writing to you on the evening the Challenger sailed for Annapolis Royal. I must tell you that your note informing me you were to leave for Annapolis Royal did not reach me until the day you were to sail. I do not fully understand how this could have happened but I assure you that I will uncover the cause of this error and take steps to ensure it does not occur again.

Captain, I am distressed that we should have parted under such painful circumstances and that I did not have the opportunity to speak with you or at the very least to correspond with you before you departed. I admit that the things I said when we last met were said in anger and frustration. I was wrong to suggest that I should attempt to influence your posting to Annapolis Royal. It would compromise your independence and offend your pride and self-esteem. Please accept that my suggesting such a course of action was motivated by the sense of dread that overwhelmed me when I thought that we should be apart.

I hope that this correspondence finds you in good health and in strong spirits. Please be assured that my affections for you remain the same. I hope that when you return to Boston we may resume our friendship as if this disharmony had not arisen to cast a shadow over our lives. I pray that you will write and share your thoughts and, I hope, your feelings.

I remain your true friend and companion.

Elisabeth Lockhart.

Scott got to his feet and walked to the fire and back. He read the letter again, and a weight lifted from his chest. The sense of dread that had gnawed at him since he'd left Boston melted away as he sat down and started to read again.

PART THREE:
BELONGING

CHAPTER THIRTY-TWO

JOHN WAS AWAKENED BY LOUIS shaking him.

"Day is coming. We must go."

"We didn't set a watch."

"We have far to travel. It was good to rest," Louis said.

John got to his feet, aching from the hard ground. Louis inspected the canoe, and John went through their gear to see what could be salvaged. The muskets were undamaged, and he cleaned them and sharpened the flints. The powder they'd taken from the priest's cabin was still dry, and he loaded both weapons. There was enough dried meat for one day.

John spread the map out on top of the canoe. Water had soaked one corner of the cloth, staining it dark brown, but otherwise it was undamaged. He traced the west shore of the Bay of Fundy with his finger. There were two rivers marked on the map, neither one named. The most northerly river had tiny waves drawn at its mouth, and its course was close enough that it had to be the river they were on.

Louis squatted beside him, and John traced the river with his finger.

"Here's the Bay of Fundy, and this is the river we're on." Louis tapped the map with his finger. "It stops."

"It's not complete."

"Then we travel south and then west."

They loaded the canoe and slid it into the water. They drifted to the mouth of the creek and held position searching for any sign of danger. Mist clung to the river. A watery sun broke through the clouds stirring it into motion, and a heron took to the air, trailing ribbons of white from its wingtips as it skimmed the water. John was spellbound by the beauty of this place, and in spite of its savagery he felt drawn to it.

Louis nudged the canoe forward, and the spell was broken.

"I see no sign of pursuit," John said.

"The hatred of the Iroquois is strong. They will follow if they can."

John put his paddle in the water and fell in time with Louis.

"We have meat for one day. Tomorrow we must hunt. The powder survived, and it's dry enough to use."

"Better to use the bow and make no sound," Louis said.

The current was slow, and as they went upstream the river widened and became more of a lake than a river. It ran north and west as far as they could see. Both banks were heavily treed, and John saw no sign of habitation. By the time they had been paddling for an hour his arms and back were on fire. He wouldn't allow himself to show any sign of distress, but he was relieved when Louis turned the canoe into a cove at midday.

They ate pemmican and drank from the river.

"How far is it to Quebec?"

"I don't know. My father told only that it was far." Louis was watching the river intently. "We should go," he said.

* * *

Late in the afternoon they came to where a smaller river joined the main branch from the northwest, and Louis turned the canoe in.

"We hold to the northwest," John said. He tried to hold an image of the priest's map in his head. Gradually the river turned to the west and narrowed, and they had to work harder as the current increased.

They paddled until dark, and John spotted a side channel on the left bank.

"We should camp away from the river." Louis didn't answer, but he steered them in. The channel turned back on itself, hiding them from the river.

"There." Louis pointed to a clearing on the west bank.

They pulled the canoe out of the water, and John started to set up camp.

"I will hunt," Louis said.

"Be quick." John said. He'd paddled all day and was hungry.

Setting up camp was second nature now. John lit a fire and gathered fuel for the night. He turned the canoe over and inspected the muskets, blowing out the pans and replenishing them with fresh powder.

John sat close to the fire to keep the mosquitoes off and watched the river. The setting sun turned the inlet to red then gold, and as he listened to the sounds of the night, a sense of quiet seeped into him, and he sat perfectly still until he heard Louis's footsteps returning.

Louis carried four squirrels. He set his bow on the ground and started to gut the animals. John looked askance.

"They are good to eat," Louis said.

"I've never eaten a squirrel. It doesn't seem right somehow."

"They were all I could find, and we must eat."

Louis skewered the squirrels and set them on the fire to roast. John was dubious, but the smell of the roasting meat was appealing. Louis passed him one of the carcasses, and he bit into it tentatively. To his surprise the meat was sweet and juicy, and he ate hungrily. Louis was watching him from the corner of his eye.

"It is good?"

John nodded. "I'm surprised."

Louis threw the bones on the fire and passed another squirrel to John. He ate slowly. The edge was off his hunger, and he wanted to savour the taste. The night had cleared, but he couldn't find a constellation he recognized.

"We should watch tonight." Louis took the first watch. John was tired. His arms and shoulders ached from paddling, and his lower back was numb. He rolled into his plaid and was asleep in moments.

The next morning John went to the river and splashed water on his face to shake off his fatigue; then he helped Louis launch the canoe. They held steady at the mouth of the inlet and searched for danger. John was awed that such a huge mass of water could make no sound as it moved past.

* * *

The fifth night after they made camp, Louis brought down a deer with his bow, and they ate their fill for the first time in days. With a full belly John slept soundly. When he awoke, Louis was prodding the fire to life. The aroma of roasting venison filled his head, and he got to his feet and stretched. He was becoming accustomed to paddling, and felt the strength growing in his arms and shoulders. Louis handed him a strip of venison, and he bit into it with relish.

The sky was overcast and threatening rain, and John looked at the river. "The river runs more north than west now. How did your father describe the land?"

"My father and his brothers travelled much of the way to the great river on foot"

"How will we know when to leave the river?"

"We will know when it's time," Louis said.

John found it frustrating when Louis spoke like this. He needed to plan the journey even if it was in a rudimentary way, but Louis was content to see where each day led. He unpacked the map and studied it, trying to find some landmark he could identify.

The question of when to leave the river came to a head sooner than John had anticipated. In the first part of the morning they started to see signs of habitation. They passed a fishing camp on the west bank that had been used recently. A trail ran north from the camp along the west bank of the river, and another came down to the river from the west.

Louis turned the canoe in towards the trail. John started to speak; then he caught the smell of wood smoke on the wind. They hid the canoe under an overhang on the bank and crept to where they could watch the trail.

The trail looked well used.

"There must be a village close by. Could it be Iroquois?" John said.

"The Iroquois lands are to the south and the west," Louis said, "but I don't know the people in this country."

"Do we have reason to fear them?"

"There is no reason, but we are two, and there will be many in the village."

John was curious about the village, but something made him uneasy. The forest seemed too quiet, and there was nothing moving on the trail. He whispered, "We should take the trail to the west." Louis nodded.

"Let's go."

"We must hide the canoe," Louis said.

They pulled the canoe into a creek downriver. They had to drag it over the sandbar at the mouth and walk it upstream.

"There," John said. Louis nodded, and they dragged the canoe into the underbrush.

"It won't be seen till the leaves fall," Louis said.

They made a long loop and came back to the trail well to the west of the river. They waited until darkness began to fall then set off. The trail was broad, and they ran side by side until it became too dark to travel. That night, they slept away from the trail and took turns standing watch.

They were on the move at first light. John's legs ached at first, but after half an hour he was running easily beside Louis. The river valley was heavily forested, and they scouted the trail carefully, wary of encountering the occupants of the village, and by the end of the morning they had climbed the west side of the valley.

They concealed themselves below the crest of the hill and waited for an hour, watching the trail for signs of pursuit.

"No one knows we're here."

"It is better so," Louis said.

As they crested the hill John looked back. Smoke rose from the trees where the village must lie, but otherwise the valley looked deserted. To the west the land rolled away into the distance, and his spirits rose at the prospect of the journey.

CHAPTER THIRTY-THREE

BY JOHN'S RECKONING THREE WEEKS had passed since they'd left the river. They had held to the west and south guided by the sun and the priest's compass. The forest was endless, and John had given up trying to estimate how far they had come, how many lakes they had skirted, or creeks they had forded. They followed game trails where they could and found their way through the forest when they had to. That morning they had come on the first trail they'd seen in days and were following it west. Hardship and endless miles of travel had hardened John's body, and he ran at a pace he could keep up for hours. Louis was fifty feet ahead running effortlessly.

That night they camped away from the trail, and John roasted venison on a small fire.

"The trail is well used. There must be a village close by."

"We have come far to the west," Louis said. "We must be close to the land of the Iroquois."

"Word of our fight with the British couldn't have travelled ahead of us."

"That is true, but we must go carefully. The Iroquois guard their lands jealously, and they won't welcome our presence."

John stoked the fire, and it threw off a shower of sparks.

"What did your father tell you of the great river?"

"My father said they journeyed for many days. He said that they had passed through the lands of the Iroquois but didn't encounter them."

John watched the sparks rising into the darkness.

"We shall see where the trail leads tomorrow, Louis." John smiled to himself. These could be Louis's words. Louis's sense of time and distance ran counter to his, and he wondered if he was starting to become like him.

John lay on his back and looked at the stars moving across the sky until he slept, and later when it was his turn to watch, he sat with his back to the fire looking out. An owl hooted in the distance, but he was accustomed to the sounds of the forest and sensed no danger. He understood this land now, and felt drawn to it with all its savagery and beauty; as night turned slowly to day, he wondered what it held in store for him.

They ate their venison and broke camp.

"We should wait until it's light."

John nodded. "Better we see the Iroquois before they see us." John blew the powder out of the musket pans and replenished it with fresh powder, and they started off.

The trail was wide enough for them to travel side by side, and they scouted each turn and stopped often to listen. By midday John thought they had covered ten miles.

In the middle of the afternoon, as they came around a turn, Louis crouched at the edge of the trail. John squatted beside him. Ahead the trail ran half a mile straight to a lake.

"There." Louis pointed. Through the trees John could see a structure close to the lakeshore.

"There's no smoke."

"No, but we will go carefully."

They stepped into the forest and swung in a wide loop down to the lake. They crept within two hundred feet of the structure, and John saw it was the remains of a longhouse. They kept the building between them and the lake as they approached.

"It's abandoned."

"There are others." Louis pointed to lakeshore. "This was a village many years ago."

"Why would they leave?" Louis shrugged.

"I don't think they have gone far."

Louis walked around the longhouse and sat looking at the lake. John crouched close by, cradling the musket on his lap.

"Longhouses become used up. The Iroquois dig pits to store their food. It's good for many summers." He spread his fingers. "Then the insects infect the pits, and they move to a new place."

John could see the shape of the village. There was a cleared area a few hundred feet back from the lake, ringed by the remains of longhouses. The lake was a mile across and ran southeast to northwest as far as he could see.

"The Iroquois will be close?"

"They would move a day's journey, perhaps two, but no farther."

John searched the other shore for smoke or signs of life, but could see nothing moving. He was about to get to his feet when a movement caught his eye on the lake.

John put his hand on Louis's arm.

"It's a canoe. More than one, I think." Louis rolled onto his stomach and crawled to the side of the longhouse; John followed, holding his musket across his elbows. Three canoes moving along the edge of the lake each held four warriors. They looked the same as the men who had hunted them at Port Royal. They made clean smooth paddle strokes that drove the canoe forward with deceptive ease. He thought they would be hard men to fight.

They watched until the canoes passed to the northwest.

"We'll need a canoe to cross the lake," John said.

"We must follow." Louis led off across the clearing, and they took a trail that followed the shoreline. It was overgrown, and petered out after a mile, forcing them into the trees, and they lost sight of the Iroquois.

Louis moved away from the lakeshore where there was less underbrush and they could move faster.

"We must keep pace with them," he said. "Their canoes were empty. Their camp will not be far."

They kept moving parallel to the lake for a mile or more then carefully moved back towards the water.

John spoke in a whisper. "Where did they go?"

Louis shook his head and sniffed the air. "Smoke." He pointed west to where a point of land ran out into the lake. Now John smelt wood smoke and he nodded.

They worked their way across the base of the point to where it formed a bay on the northwest side. Then they swung back into the forest and approached from the north. Spring was becoming summer, and the underbrush was thick along the lakeshore. It gave them cover, and they crawled on their bellies till they could see the Iroquois camp.

There were six lean-to structures scattered along the point, and four canoes lay belly-up on the beach. A dozen Iroquois sat around a fire cooking meat and fish. Their voices and laughter carried to John and Louis in their hiding place.

Louis put his lips to John's ear. "It's a hunting camp. They have set meat in the sun to dry."

Racks had been set up on the rocks at the end of the point, exposed to the sun and wind.

"They have much meat. I think they won't stay long here," Louis said and signalled that they should leave.

As they backed away, something caught John's attention behind the camp, and he put his hand on Louis's arm.

"There." He pointed to the shape of a canoe in the bushes back from the lake. Louis nodded, and they crept away. Two hundred yards back they got to their feet. John pointed to rising ground to the east and they climbed to where they had a view to the west. The lake was more than a mile across. A breeze rippled the surface, but they couldn't see any movement on the water.

Below them, John could see smoke rising from the Iroquois camp.

"There's no village."

"This is a hunting camp. Their village will be a day's travel."

"Is this the lake of the Iroquois that your father described?"

"It may be, but I can't tell for sure."

They camped two miles from the lake and didn't light a fire. John spread the map on the ground and examined it, but this part of the country was blank.

"The lake runs to the northwest. There may be a river that will carry us to the St. Lawrence."

"It may be, but we must cross the lake or go around."

The next morning they made their way back to the hill, and Louis pointed to the camp.

"There's no fire."

"They've gone."

"We shall see."

They crept back to the lakeshore to find the camp deserted. The meat racks were empty, and the canoes were gone. A feather of smoke rose from the fire, and they watched for a long time before they approached. John carried his musket at the ready, but the shelters were empty. If it wasn't for the smoking campfire, it would have been difficult to tell when the camp had been used last.

John went to the canoe they'd seen the day before. It was fifteen feet long and two and a half feet wide at the middle. The bow and stern were elegantly curved, but it was old and dried out. Louis turned it over and found a hole at the stern big enough to put his fist through.

"Here." Louis pointed to where one of the seams had opened, but the frame looked solid, and there was no other obvious damage.

John looked at Louis.

"Can you patch the holes?"

"Gather resin. I'll make the repairs." John dropped his gear and took only his axe.

In the winter Louis had shown John which trees produced the best resin, and he trotted along the beach to a stand of pine trees. He chopped a square of bark from a tree and started to scrape resin onto it with the axe, and in half an hour he had filled the bark with resin.

When John returned to the camp, Louis had propped the canoe upright with stones and fashioned new bindings for the seam. John squeezed the seam together and Louis pulled the bindings tight and made them fast.

"Will it hold?" John said.

"The seam will hold, but the bark is old and will absorb water."

Louis examined the resin, squeezing it between his fingers. "It's good. Make a fire. I'll repair the other damage."

John added kindling to the ashes of the Iroquois fire and blew on the embers until the flames took hold. He filled the iron cooking pot with resin and set it on the flames. He didn't like melting the resin in their cooking pot, but it was the only metal pot they had.

John took the square of bark to Louis.

"Will this work for the patch?" Louis turned it over.

"Thicker would be better, but it'll do." He set the bark on a log and fashioned a patch to cover the hole in the canoe. He made holes for the binding with his knife and threaded strips of buckskin through the holes and used a stick to twist each one tight before he tied it off.

The resin melted into a clear liquid that filled the air with the scent of pine. John added more resin and stirred it till it melted and carried it to the canoe.

Louis tilted the canoe until the patch was on the top.

"Pour slowly." John dribbled the resin along one side of the patch and Louis used his knife to trap it until it solidified. They worked their way around the patch adding layers until the resin formed a smooth seal.

"Now the inside," Louis said. They used all of the resin John had prepared, and he made another trip to gather more. The repairs took several hours, and when it was done John was pleased with the result.

They floated the canoe in the lake, and after ten minutes with no leaks Louis deemed it a success. Louis knocked down one of the shelters and used the wood to fashion two paddles. They were rough and heavy, but they would do the job.

It was late in the afternoon by the time they were finished, and John was hungry. He poked the fire into life and roasted some meat. Louis sat by him, and John motioned to the fire.

"The Iroquois may see the smoke."

"It's possible, but there will be other hunting parties on the lake." They ate in silence for a while; then Louis lifted his chin.

"We should cross tonight."

John nodded. "The sky is clear, and there will be a quarter moon."

They left at dusk on a northeast heading, and almost immediately John's knees were wet and he found an inch of water in the bottom of the canoe.

"We're taking on water."

"The bark is old and the water softens it."

"Give me the cooking pot, and I'll bail." John started to bail, and Louis turned the canoe, making directly for the opposite shore.

By the time they reached the west side of the lake John was bailing constantly just to keep them afloat. They came ashore in a small inlet, and John dragged the canoe up the beach. Louis handed him their gear and stepped ashore.

"What do we do with the canoe?"

"Hide it in the forest."

They half dragged and half carried the canoe into the trees, and John cursed as he stumbled and tripped in the underbrush.

"This will have to do." In the dark, there was no way to tell how well the canoe was concealed, but they'd have to take the chance. They went back to the lake, and Louis took a stick and brushed away the drag marks on the beach.

They moved away from the lake; it was almost completely dark in the forest. The ground started to rise, and they forced their way uphill for a couple of hundred yards until John felt the ground level out. The underbrush was thick around them, and John inched his way forward until he felt the ground begin to fall away.

"I think this is a good place to sleep," he said.

"Yes," Louis said, "but no fire, and we stand watch."

John took the first watch, and later when Louis woke him the light was growing in the east. He got to his feet and stretched. Louis handed him some pemmican, and they squatted down to eat.

"We should travel northwest. The St. Lawrence lies in that direction."

"We must go carefully," Louis said. "We're still in the land of the Iroquois."

John examined his musket. It had lain in the bottom of the canoe, and the powder was wet. He was pleased to see that the priest's powder flask was still sealed, and he drew the balls and reloaded both muskets.

As they started to descend, Louis held his hand up. John could see a trail running around the base of the hill, then back to the lakeshore. He couldn't see more than a hundred feet in either direction. Louis raised his eyebrows in question.

"We'll travel faster on the trail, but it's well used, and we must be cautious."

"It's early in the day. Perhaps we can use the trail for a few hours."

Louis headed north, and John followed ten paces behind him. They stopped at each turn and checked the trail ahead, and John kept watch to the rear. It was slow-going, and John found it frustrating, but the consequences of running into an Iroquois hunting party were not appealing, so he persevered.

They travelled for several hours and saw no sign of habitation. Everything was green and lush and the only sounds they heard were the songbirds in the bush. A breeze sprang up off the lake, carrying the scent of pine and a sweet plant John couldn't identify. John's spirits started to rise, but then he saw Louis duck and come running back along the trail.

John pushed into the underbrush till he was well back from the trail, and Louis dropped down beside him and mouthed, "Iroquois."

They crawled to where they had a partial view of the trail. John lay still, and as the moments passed it became so quiet he thought he could hear his own heart beating. Then he heard voices, muted by the trees but coming closer. He looked away. Louis always said he shouldn't look directly at an enemy as he may feel your eyes on him. He didn't really believe it, but he watched out of the corner of his eye anyway.

John only caught a glimpse of the Iroquois as they crossed a gap in the trees but there was no mistaking their dress and the distinctive way they wore their hair. They carried sleeping rolls, food bags and were armed with bows and axes, and a few carried muskets. Fifteen warriors passed in single file. In a moment they were gone, and the forest was silent again.

They lay still, watching, but there was no further movement. John leaned close to Louis.

"Will they guard their rear?"

"This is their home ground. None will trail."

"That was close. We must be on our guard."

"It's not safe to use the trail. There will be other parties."

They moved west into the forest, stopping now and then to listen, then moving on. They climbed a ridge a mile from the lake. From the top John could see the lake running to the northwest.

"The ridge will be easier going."

"And there will be fewer mosquitoes to eat your soft flesh." John looked at Louis, surprised. His face was expressionless, but there was laughter in his eyes.

The ridge was treed with pine and spruce. The trees were widely spaced apart, and they made good progress till they stopped at midday to eat. They hadn't come across any water on the ridge, and John looked at the lake longingly.

John unpacked the map and spread it on the ground searching for a landmark that he could identify.

"The great river is to the west. The cloth won't help us to find it."

"It may not, but when we reach it, I'll be able to draw the route we followed."

Louis looked at the map again. "The box with the needle, how is it used?" J

John took the compass from its box and set it on the map and aligned the map to the north on the compass.

Louis examined the map and turned the compass, watching the needle track to the north. "I don't see its value, but I will think on it."

John was about to say something, but he thought better of it, and packed the map and compass away.

Louis curled his legs under him. "The priest said that we could trade fur with the French?"

John nodded. "He said that the French don't like outsiders, and we must find some way to gain their trust."

"Where will we find fur to trade?"

"You said you can trap beaver. Perhaps you could teach me."

"I can trap beaver and other animals, but the people of the north will kill us if we trap on their land. It's better to trade for fur and sell to the French."

"Then we must have trade goods."

"Where will we get such goods?"

"I don't know," John said," but we must find a way."

They had followed the ridge for an hour when John saw smoke through a gap in the trees and hissed at Louis. Louis turned and John lifted his head motioning to the sky, and Louis trotted back.

"There must be a village to the west."

"We must go carefully."

They followed the ridge for the rest of the day. The ridge gradually descended and the foliage became thicker again. As it started to get dark, Louis pointed to a knoll a few hundred yards ahead.

"We should camp." The knoll was heavily treed and the undergrowth was dense.

John selected a pine tree with branches growing low around the base. He started to push his way into the canopy.

"Wait," Louis said. He moved back along the ridge and dropped to his stomach. John almost cried out when he saw Louis lying next to a pool of water.

John threw himself down and scooped handfuls of water into his mouth. It tasted of leaves and moss, but he drank and drank again until his belly was swollen.

"How did you know it was here?"

"Sometimes you can smell water if you really need to drink."

They sat with their backs against the base of the pine. "I'll take first watch." Louis nodded.

The next morning, John was awakened by Louis holding his hand over his mouth. He gripped his wrist, and Louis held his finger to his lips and tilted his head. John nodded and moved around beside him. There were voices along the ridge to the north: five or six men calling out and laughing. John couldn't understand what they were saying, but there was a taunting tone in their voices that that he found troubling.

Louis leaned close. "Iroquois."

"Can you understand them?"

"I don't know their language."

John started to rise, but Louis put his hand on his shoulder. "They are many. We should let them pass."

John shook his head. "I must see. I'll be careful."

John checked that his musket wasn't cocked and gathered up his gear, ready to move. Louis knelt beside John.

"It's better to let the Iroquois go on their way."

"I have to see." Louis shook his head in exasperation and motioned for John to lead.

John crept along the ridge. Louis followed to one side, and they'd only gone a short distance when John saw a trail ahead. It cut through the top of the ridge, forming a hollow thirty feet across. The undergrowth grew waist-high on both sides of the trail, carpeting the depression in green.

John saw four Iroquois standing on the trail, and he was shocked to see a girl in their midst. The Iroquois were spinning her around. One of the warriors drove the heel of his hand into her back. The girl cried out in pain as she was thrown against the other warriors, and they jeered and laughed at her cries.

Louis touched John's arm and mouthed, "We must leave." John shook his head and pointed down into the hollow. He started to crawl forward. Louis gripped his arm and motioned for them to leave, but John gently pulled his arm free and shook his head.

John passed the musket to Louis and took the pistol from his hunting bag. He hadn't examined it since they'd crossed the lake, and he hoped the powder was still dry. He swore that he would take better care of his arms in future.

John slid down the side of the hollow, taking care not to disturb the foliage or make any sound that would betray his presence. He inched his way forward to where he could see the clearing.

There was a tiny sound behind him, and John looked back. Louis was behind him, pulling himself along on his elbows, dragging his musket with him. He motioned again for them to leave, and John couldn't help but smile that Louis had been able to come so close before he heard him.

John got up on one knee and pushed a branch aside to clear his view. The Iroquois were young men. They wore buckskin clothes and moccasins, and dressed their hair with some type of gum that made it stand out from their heads. Sleeping mats, weapons, and other gear were scattered around the clearing.

The Iroquois jostled the girl back and forth, but John couldn't see her. He could hear her calling out in Iroquois, anger and distress in her voice. Then one of the warriors dragged her clear of the group. John almost cried out when he saw that she was European. She was no more than sixteen years of age. A shock of black hair hid her face, but he caught a flash of blue eyes. Her limbs were long and slender, and the skin on her arms was burned brown by the sun. She wore a buckskin dress that fell to below her knees and moccasins on her feet.

John felt Louis touch his arm, and he leaned close.

"She's a captive, likely taken when she was a child." Louis inclined his head for John to come away, but the girl screamed, and John turned back to the clearing. The Iroquois had his left arm around her neck, and his right hand was inside her dress pulling at her breast. John started to get to his feet, but Louis gripped his arm.

"We must help her."

"There are too many. They will kill us, and she will still be a captive."

The warrior held her and two others pulled up her dress. She was naked beneath the dress; her skin was pale where the sun hadn't touched it and somehow it made her seem more vulnerable. She lashed out at the warriors who were pawing at her, but her struggles only amused them, and they laughed at her distress.

One of the warriors lifted the girl's legs, and they bore her to the ground. Two of them held her legs and another pinned her shoulders to the ground.

The warrior who had held her by the neck seemed to be their leader. He undid his leggings and fell on top of her.

John's mind went back to a similar scene in the farmhouse in Glen Nevis and white anger flashed through him. He started to get to his feet, but Louis grabbed him, pinning his arms to his sides, and hissed in his ear.

"There are too many. I will fight with you but it will be our death." There was no fear in Louis's eyes. He was simply stating the facts. They couldn't win. John nodded and Louis relaxed his hold on him.

The girl screamed and fought but she was no match for the warriors. The leader of the Iroquois whooped and laughed and when he was finished, another warrior took his turn. John knew Louis was right. There were four Iroquois, and there could be others close by, but his anger and frustration all but consumed him as he watched them rape the girl. Louis was watching him carefully.

The second warrior got to his feet and another took his place, but as he came over her the girl reared up and struck him in the face. He roared with anger and slammed his fist into the girl's face, and she fell back to the ground. The other warriors laughed and cheered as he started bucking away at her. John felt Louis's hand on his shoulder, and he cast his eyes down and shook his head. He knew they had to do whatever it took to survive, but he was maddened by this, and he felt as if something was tearing loose inside him.

A bark of laughter brought John's attention back to the clearing. The Iroquois stood over the girl fastening his leggings. The girl was lying on her back rolling her head, half-conscious. The leader motioned to the fourth man, but he shook his head and walked away much to the amusement of his companions.

The Iroquois slung their sleeping rolls onto their backs and moved off in single file, taking the trail on the north side of the clearing. The last warrior called to the girl. She didn't respond, and he followed the others down the trail. After a moment the girl rolled to her knees, her dress still pulled up around her neck. Her body was startlingly white. Her back was straight, and her hips and legs were slender and shapely. John was captivated by her, and at the same time he was ashamed to be a silent witness to her distress.

The girl dug her hand into the earth and pulled up a handful of soil. She put her hand between her legs and rubbed it into her groin. She made a keening sound like an animal in terror that built to a cry of rage. She stood up and threw the dirt across the clearing and screamed, cursing the Iroquois. It was a cry so filled with humiliation and grief that John looked away. It took a moment for him to realize that she had called out in French and that he understood her. He had leapt to his feet, shaking Louis off and forced his way into the clearing before he knew what he was doing.

CHAPTER THIRTY-FOUR

"Mademoiselle," John said.

The girl turned and the alarm in her eyes changed to surprise. She pulled her dress down and looked down the trail. She was almost as tall as John. Long dark hair hung down her back, streaked with mud and leaves. She brushed it over her shoulder revealing an oval face and intense blue eyes. She had a wide mouth, small even teeth and blood was oozing from her lip and running down her chin.

The girl stared at him wide-eyed.

"Who are you?"

"I am John Wallace. Come, we must get away before the Iroquois return." He held out his hand to her.

"The Iroquois will kill you." Her voice had a lilting quality as if she was singing a nursery rhyme as she spoke, but her words carried no emotion.

"You're French. I can't leave you here."

John saw something flash in her eyes, and he turned to see an Iroquois warrior running silently across the clearing. He wore only buckskin leggings and moccasins on his feet. He carried a tomahawk in his right hand, thrown back to strike. John launched himself at him. He threw up his left arm to block the tomahawk and slammed his shoulder into the warrior's chest and the breath went out of him with a whoosh. John grabbed his right wrist and swung him, sending him staggering across the clearing.

The Iroquois regained his balance quickly, let out a yell of rage and charged at John again. John reached over his shoulder and yanked the cutlass from its scabbard. His uncle had taught him the basic sword strokes, and his response was instinctive. The Iroquois swung the tomahawk at his head with all the power of his arm and shoulders. John parried the blow, deflecting it to the side.

The Iroquois recovered instantly and swung at his hip. John leapt back alarmed at his speed and swept the cutlass around in an arch. It struck the tomahawk below the head and deflected it to the right. The Iroquois was thrown off balance, his right foot slid out from under him, and John slashed the blade across his thigh, cutting down to the bone.

The warrior grunted in pain and lashed out backhanded. John slid to the left and brought the cutlass down in a high arc striking at the warrior's neck. He threw the tomahawk up in defense and the cutlass clipped the tomahawk and deflected, striking the warrior below the ear. John stepped back as the Iroquois collapsed, blood pumping from his neck.

"Behind," the girl called out.

A second Iroquois was almost on him. John recognized him as the leader. He was taller and heavier than John, but he moved lightly on his feet. He held a tomahawk in his right hand and struck down at John's head. It was too late to deflect the blow. John grasped the cutlass with both hands and threw it above his head to block the blow.

The warrior let out a blood-curdling scream as he struck; the cutlass caught the tomahawk two inches below the head shattering the shaft, and John was driven back, struggling to keep his balance. The warrior dropped the axe and lunged at John's throat, and John cut right to left in front of him. The Iroquois arched his body back and the blade left a red line across his chest, but he kept coming. John dug his heel in and prepared to lunge again, but the Iroquois went rigid. His eyes glazed over, and he dropped to his knees. Louis jerked his axe from the head of the Iroquois, who slid to the ground.

John started to speak, but over Louis's shoulder he saw the two remaining Iroquois standing at the entrance to the trail, a look of horror on their faces. One of them let out a cry of alarm, and they both fled down the hill.

John dropped the cutlass and ran to the trailhead. He pulled the pistol from his hunting bag and cocked the hammers. The warriors were thirty paces away, moving downhill, and he could only see their upper bodies above the scrub. He placed the front sight between the shoulders of the nearest warrior, dropped it to allow for the downhill shot, and pulled the trigger. Louis fired a heartbeat later and the roar of the musket overwhelmed the pistol discharge, and John fired the second barrel at the last warrior.

Louis launched himself down the trail. John scooped up the cutlass and went after him. The hill was steep and John slid his way to the bottom and broke into a run. Twenty paces from the bottom he found one of the Iroquois face down on the trail with a musket wound below his left shoulder. He was making a choking sound and there was blood on his lips. John knew it was a lung hit, and he would be dead in minutes.

Louis came trotting back along the trail. "He ran like a deer. I couldn't catch him."

"He'll bring others."

Louis nodded. He crouched and pulled the Iroquois's head back, cut into his neck with his knife, and watched the blood spurt onto the ground. He wiped the blade on the warrior's shoulder. John was shocked at such a cold-blooded act and he turned away lest it show on his face.

When John entered the clearing, the girl was tying up a sleeping roll, and she stood and faced him.

"What's your name?"

She lifted her chin. "My name is Chantal Marie Elisabeth Garnier."

"How long have you been a captive of the Iroquois?" Her steel blue eyes met his unwaveringly, and John realized that beneath the dirt and grime this girl was beautiful.

John started to speak, but Louis interrupted.

"Is the Iroquois village near?"

The girl looked at Louis. "Who's your companion?" Her voice was empty of emotion.

"His name is Louis Pictou. He is Mi'kmaq. The British and the Iroquois destroyed his village and killed his family, so he has reason to hate the Iroquois."

The girl nodded, but her eyes were wary.

"Are the other Iroquois dead?"

John shook his head. "One escaped."

"The village is an hour's travel to the north. There are other villages within half a day. The Iroquois will send word, and many will come."

John started to gather up his gear.

"We must go." Louis pointed towards the lake.

"We take the lakeside trail. We must travel fast if we are to elude the Iroquois." John turned to the girl.

"Can you travel?" She held up her hand to wait.

"The trail leads to the great river and to Quebec. The Iroquois will expect you to go that way."

"Do you know Quebec? We're making our way there."

"It's where I was born."

John waited, and she went on.

"The Iroquois will be relentless. It will be better to take a different trail."

"Which trail?"

"The men you killed had travelled to the north of the river the French call St. Lawrence, to the place the British call the Bay of Hudson." She lifted her chin to John, and he snapped at her.

"I'm Scottish. Don't confuse me with the British."

The girl's eyes flashed with anger, but she went on.

"The Iroquois trade for fur with the tribes in the frozen lands. The fur is rich and highly valued. Their canoes are hidden along the lakeshore. I will bring you to them."

"How far?"

"Half a day to the east. The Iroquois will hunt to the north. They won't look for you in their own lands. Better to take the canoes by night and follow the river at the north end of the lake. It joins the St. Lawrence. From there you can reach Quebec."

John looked at Louis.

"The girl speaks wisely. It will be difficult to evade the Iroquois on their own ground." John looked at the girl.

"We go east as you say."

They retrieved the muskets and their gear and John held up his hand.

"Wait," John said. He reloaded the pistol and both muskets, and readied their gear. The girl stood by, her bundle slung over her shoulder.

"We go quickly."

Louis took the lead. The trail was steep and wound back and forth across the hill for the first half mile. On level ground Louis increased the pace. They ran for half an hour, and John was pleased that the girl showed no signs of discomfort. Louis waved them to a stop three hundred feet from the lake and went forward to scout the shore. After a few minutes, he waved them on.

"There are many tracks. It will make it difficult for the Iroquois to track us." Louis looked at the girl. "How far to where the canoes are hidden?"

She pointed south along the lakeshore. "Half a day's walk. At this pace we will be there before dark."

"The canoe is sound and will carry us across the lake?"

"There are three canoes and many furs. You can trade them to the French in Quebec."

"First we must elude the Iroquois."

John nodded and Louis leapt away. John followed and the girl fell in behind him. The trail ran along the lakeshore, skirted the base of a hill, then came back to the water. John stayed a hundred feet behind Louis. Louis's ability to sense danger was superior to his, and he would react quicker.

It was two hours before they stopped where a creek entered the lake. When they came up to Louis, he was examining the ground, and the girl knelt to drink.

"Several groups have travelled this way in the past days."

"Can you tell how many?"

"It is difficult. There are many tracks." The girl nodded.

"It's one of the main trails. It leads to Iroquois villages to the south." Louis put his hand to his mouth for silence and motioned them off the trail.

John pushed into the underbrush. The girl followed. He knew Louis would ensure they left no sign of their presence. John circled a rise in the ground and crept up the slope to where he could see the trail.

The girl lay to his right, Louis to the left close enough to speak. The foliage was thick, and John could only see a small section of the trail. A few minutes later an Iroquois warrior came into view. He had a bundle slung over his shoulder and carried a musket in his right hand. John only saw him for a second then he passed out of sight.

More Iroquois passed in ones and twos. John counted twenty-two. There was a long gap; then another warrior passed, hurrying to catch up with the group. Louis put his mouth to John's ear. "Wait."

John nodded, and Louis slid back into the forest.

John looked at the girl. Her eyes were on the trail, but she sensed him looking and turned.

"They're not hunting us. Where do they come from?"

"I think they are from the villages to the south of the lake. I know their dress. They are hunting for furs to trade and slaves." John had not spoken French since Louisburg. The girl spoke with a heavy accent, and there was something in the way she spoke of the Iroquois that he didn't grasp. Louis hissed from the bottom of the slope, and they made their way back to the trail.

An hour later the girl signalled to stop. "The creek is half a mile ahead. The Iroquois often camp where it enters the lake."

"I'll scout the creek," Louis said, and slipped away.

John moved into the forest and sat against a pine tree. He took some pemmican from his bag, broke it in two and offered a piece to the girl. "Eat while you can."

The girl hesitated then took the meat and ate it slowly.

Since they'd left the clearing she had only spoken a few words. She sat on the ground with her legs tucked under her and gave off a sense of quiet intensity that didn't welcome intrusion.

Finally John spoke.

"How did you come to be a prisoner of the Iroquois?" The girl became still, minutes passed, and finally she looked at him.

"I was twelve years old when they took me. My father traded fur with the natives, and he would travel to their territories to trade. He said it was more profitable, but he really thought of himself as an explorer and trading fur was just an excuse to go into the wild lands. He drew maps and recorded everything he saw. When we were old enough he took my brother and me with him and my mother refused to be left behind."

She looked into the distance for a moment and then went on.

"Four seasons ago we travelled far to the north of the big river to trade for fur. We spent the summer travelling and trading with the natives in the region. They are kind-hearted people and were happy to trade with us. I made friends with the children in the villages we visited, and they taught me their language. We were returning to Quebec in the fall of the year when the Iroquois attacked us."

The girl stopped. Her eyes were wet, and she was struggling to control her emotions. John waited and she went on.

"The Iroquois killed my father." She stopped and seemed to steel herself. "They tortured him. I heard him screaming through a whole night and in the morning I knew he was dead. My mother died the same way after the Iroquois had used her." She rubbed her hands on her thighs as if brushing something off her skin. "They brought me back to the lake and sent my brother to another village."

"What became of your brother?"

"I didn't see him again."

John was feeling more comfortable speaking French. He started to ask another question, but the girl interrupted him.

"Why did you risk your life to help me? I mean nothing to you." She was looking at him intensely, searching his face.

"You're French. I saw what they did to you . . ." He stopped realizing what he was saying. The girl's eyes blazed, but he couldn't tell if it was from anger or hurt.

"I . . ."

"Do not speak to me of these things." Her voice was sharp as flint.

"As you wish." John looked away, stung by her tone.

John felt the heat rise in his neck. Silence grew between them, and he got to his feet to listen for Louis returning. He heard only the leaves rustling in the breeze and a songbird in the distance. He knew that he wouldn't hear Louis, and after a few minutes he looked at the girl.

She was sitting on the ground watching him. She possessed a kind of serenity that protected her and contained her emotions. John slid down till his eyes were level with hers. He was about to speak, but there was a sound to his left and Louis emerged from the forest.

Louis squatted beside John.

"There are many Iroquois. They make camp where the creek enters the lake. They will pass the night there."

"How many?" Louis spread the fingers of both hands, opening and closing them twice.

John looked at the girl. "Where are the canoes hidden?"

"In the creek some distance from the lake."

"Are there other villages near?"

She shook her head. "There's a village a mile to the east, but it has been abandoned for years. The Iroquois use the mouth of the creek as a travelling camp."

John looked at the sky.

"It will be dark soon. We could wait until they travel on tomorrow."

"The Iroquois will hunt the trail to the northwest. When they don't find us there, the warrior who escaped will lead them to the furs."

John looked at Louis. "Can we reach the upper creek without being seen?"

Louis nodded and looked at the girl.

"Show us where the canoes are hidden."

Louis led them west away from the lake in a circle that brought them to the creek less than a mile from the lake. The creek was only six feet across. The water was black in the shadow of the trees. John and Louis stopped to listen, and John was surprised when he saw the girl do the same.

John pitched his voice in a whisper.

"Which way?"

"There." The girl pointed downstream, and he motioned for her to lead. She led them along the creek bank, barely making a sound as she moved. A few hundred yards downstream, she picked her way through the underbrush to the bank of the creek and waved him up beside her. The creek was twice as wide now, but the trees hung low over the water, and the undergrowth was so dense it was difficult to see the other bank.

The girl pointed across the creek.

"There." John searched the bank but didn't see anything.

"I don't see it."

"They are there."

The girl pulled her dress above her knees and stepped into the creek and John's eyes were drawn to the water splashing on the back of her slender legs. Louis moved up beside him. He felt the colour rise in his face and looked away.

Louis lifted his chin. "Do you see?"

John shook his head. "I see only the undergrowth."

"There, upstream of the pine. There's a gap in the foliage."

John looked where Louis told him to, but saw only leaves and branches; then he gasped in astonishment. Through the gap he saw a flash of silver, and as if a veil had dropped from his eyes, he saw the shape of a canoe against the bank. It was camouflaged so cunningly that even at this distance it was difficult to make out. Once he knew what to look for, he found the other two canoes quickly.

John pulled off his boots and waded across the creek. There were three heavily built canoes, each fifteen feet long and four feet wide at the middle.

Each was loaded with square bales wrapped in deerskin and bound fast, but the canoes rode high in the water.

John didn't know how much furs traded for but, based on what the priest had told him, he judged that the contents of the canoes were worth a great deal. It was a windfall that could establish him in Quebec or fund his return to Scotland. The priest had told him the French would only trade with their own, but he would deal with that later. First they had to escape the Iroquois.

John looked at Louis. "They are strong canoes."

"Can we handle three?"

"We can take one each if the girl can paddle, but it will be slow."

"Better to take one and make good our escape."

"There's much fur. It will be worth a great deal to the British or the French."

John realized that he didn't see the girl, and he started to look around.

"There." John saw her emerging from the forest, and he felt uneasy that he hadn't noticed her absence.

"How many Iroquois live in the village where you were held?" John asked.

"Three hundred, I think."

Louis frowned. "Too many. We must escape tonight."

John nodded. "Somehow we must get past the Iroquois at the lake."

"I'll scout the camp," Louis said, and slipped away silently.

John examined the first canoe. The centre was packed tight with bales, leaving space for paddlers at the bow and stern. He stepped into the stern, the canoe moved under him and he put his hand on one the bales to steady himself. There were two paddles in the bottom. He took one and made a backward stroke and the canoe responded easily, pulling against its ropes. He set the paddle down and climbed onto the bank.

John looked at the creek, wondering how they could escape with all three canoes. The girl was sitting on the ground watching him. John sat opposite her.

"The priest from Louis's village told me that the French will not trade with outsiders. It may be better to hide the fur in the forest and make our escape in one canoe."

"My uncle is a merchant in Quebec. He and my father were partners. If you bring me to Quebec, he will trade with you." John felt a thrill run through him, and knew now that the furs could change their fortunes.

John brought his mind back to the present. "We came on a fishing camp on the east side of the lake. Are there others close by?"

"Not on this side of the lake. There's a village to the south, but it is abandoned." The girl sat with her legs tucked up under her and her back straight. There was something compelling about her, but he found the directness of her gaze disconcerting, and he looked away.

They sat in silence for a few moments; then John got to his feet and checked the priming on his musket and the pistol. As he slid the pistol into the bag he heard a sound behind him, and turned to see Louis emerge from the forest.

Louis squatted down. "The Iroquois are making camp for the night. They have two fires, but they've set no guards."

"They have nothing to fear in their own country."

"There are fewer warriors now." He held up his hand and spread his fingers to indicate the number. "This many are gone."

"Five less for us to be concerned about." Louis didn't reply, but he seemed uneasy.

The girl spoke just above a whisper. "We must reach the lake. By tomorrow others will hunt us."

"Tell me of the village to the south. How long has it been abandoned?"

"There were many longhouses, teepees, and some cabins. It was abandoned when I first saw it three summers ago."

John was lost in thought for a moment; then he turned to Louis. "Can we load the furs into two canoes? I don't think we can manage three."

Louis nodded. "We can paddle one canoe and tow the other. If we need to escape, we can abandon one."

John nodded, but he didn't like the thought of abandoning the furs. "Let's load the canoes."

They offloaded the furs from one canoe and split them between the two others. John was pleased that they still floated high in the water.

He made the empty canoe fast to the bank, but as he climbed out the girl said, "You must destroy the canoe. The Iroquois could use it to pursue us." John pushed his dirk into one of the seams and opened it up till he'd made a two foot gash. He pushed the canoe away from the bank watched as it sank. Only the raised bow and stern protruded from the water. Even if the Iroquois found the canoe, they couldn't repair it quickly enough to pursue them.

John looked at Louis and the girl. "Can we bring the canoes to the lake without being detected?"

"The creek is overgrown and has many turns, but at the lake there is no cover," Louis said. "We can't pass the camp without being seen."

"Then we have to draw them off."

John took one of the priest's powder flasks from his hunting bag.

"Bring the canoes as close to the lake as you dare; I'll set fire to the deserted village. When the Iroquois come to investigate, we can slip through to the lake." Louis nodded.

"We should walk the canoes downstream while there's still light."

They put the muskets and gear in the lead canoe and the girl put her sleeping roll in the second vessel. John pulled off his boots and stepped into the water. Luis took the bow of the lead canoe.

"I'll lead. Help the girl to hold back against the current." John moved back and took the gunnels opposite the girl.

Louis kept the canoes in the middle of the creek. The canoes floated high, but they were slow to turn, and John wondered at the wisdom of trying to escape in such clumsy vessels.

The creek widened and became deeper as they neared the lake. John stepped in a hole and sank up to his waist, and he held on to the canoe and tried not to make any sound. The water was cold, and he was shivering. He looked at the girl, but she was concentrating on keeping the canoe on course and showed no discomfort. After what felt like an hour, Louis stopped. He pointed ahead to where the creek widened out, and they brought the canoes to the bank and made them fast.

John retrieved his hunting bag and the musket and climbed onto the bank; Louis sat beside him as he pulled his boots on. John pointed east. "How close is the camp to the creek?"

"The camp is on this side where it enters the lake."

John looked at the sky. "We must wait until it's fully dark. When I set fire to the village, the Iroquois will go to investigate, and we can slip into the lake."

"I'll watch the camp," Louis said.

John checked his flint and steel; then they waited in silence. The girl stood a few feet away, but as darkness fell, she was so still she almost became a shadow in the forest. The creek made no sound as it slid past them. The only sound John could hear was the evening chorus of the songbirds.

John saw a glow in the direction of the Iroquois camp. The girl's eyes flashed and she turned her head. Her ears were better attuned to the forest than his, and a moment later Louis came out of the darkness and squatted beside him.

Louis pitched his voice low as if the shadows were listening. "The camp is quiet. They cook food and prepare for the night. Time to move." Louis led them away from the creek and in a few minutes they came to the lakeshore trail.

The Iroquois camp was a hundred yards away, where the creek entered the lake; the ground was open with only a few trees to provide cover. Three fires were spaced out along the lakeshore, and John saw the shapes of the Iroquois moving in the firelight.

He leaned close to Louis. "They're settling for the night."

"They won't leave the camp, I think."

They moved back to where the girl stood, and John handed Louis his musket. "I'll follow the trail to the village. When it's done, I'll return through the forest."

Louis nodded.

John turned to the girl. "Can you help Louis bring the canoes to the lake?"

She shook her head. "It will be difficult to find the village in the dark. I will come with you."

"It would be better if you helped Louis—"

She interrupted him. "I will go to the village with you." Clearly she was determined, and there was no time to argue.

John looked at Louis. "Can you manage the canoes alone?"

Louis nodded. "I'll bring them to the lake, swim out on the north side of the creek, and I'll find you," he said.

John kept to the trees until they were out of sight of the Iroquois camp then stepped onto the trail. He picked a large pine on the lakeshore and fixed its position in his mind. He wanted a landmark he could recognize so they wouldn't blunder into the Iroquois camp.

John set off slowly, alert for any danger. Moving helped ease the tension in his gut, and he gradually increased the pace. The girl kept up and her feet made no sound as she ran. Only her breathing gave away her presence.

They broke out of the trees onto a bay, and John followed the trail round to the right.

"Stop," the girl hissed, and John looked at her.

"There." She pointed behind them. John saw it immediately. The ruins of the village were spread out along the lakeshore. The trail was overgrown, and he'd run right past it.

There were thirty or forty dwellings in the village scattered between the lakeshore and the forest. The remains of six longhouses stood in a row in the centre of the village, sixty feet long and twenty wide. Most of the roofs had collapsed, and the walls sagged inwards. They had been constructed of spruce logs imbedded in the ground, with the outer walls and roof made of bark. John selected the building second from the end of the row. The roof had collapsed, forming an untidy pile at one end. The wood was dry as tinder, and he whispered to the girl, "Gather kindling to make several fires."

John chopped a section of the debris into kindling, set it against the wall by the entrance and stacked dry wood on top of it. Then he built another three fires along the wall. The girl came behind him, adding fuel to each fire.

When they finished, John nodded in satisfaction. "One more fire where the roof has fallen in."

"The wood's dry. It will burn," she said.

"I want to be sure."

John went to the other end of the building, hacked a section of the wall into pieces, and built a fire between the collapsed roof and the wall. He placed the powder horn on the pile and heaped bark and dry wood on top of it.

"It'll act as a fuse and give us time to get back to the creek."

John ran back to the entrance. The girl had set a mound of dry moss beside the first fire, and he thanked her silently and set to work with flint and steel, sending a shower of sparks onto the moss. The girl knelt beside him and blew onto the moss, but nothing happened, and his arm began to tire.

"Keep going," she said. John redoubled his efforts, and to his relief he saw a feather of smoke rise from the moss.

"Stop now." The girl blew on the moss, pulling the material apart with her fingers and a flame flared. She pushed the burning moss into the base of the fire. The dry bark caught, and in seconds it was snapping and crackling.

John leapt to his feet and stuffed the flint and steel back into his bag.

"Quickly light the other fires." He grabbed a piece of burning bark, ran to the far end of the building and lit the fire under the powder horn. By the time he came back to the entrance the girl had all the fires along the wall burning. He started to speak but the wall behind her exploded into flames, cutting off their escape.

John changed direction.

"This way," he shouted, and pointed to where a section of the side wall had collapsed, creating an opening at ground level. The girl dropped to the ground and wriggled through. John pushed his hunting bag through and squeezed himself into the opening. His shoulder jammed against one of the supporting logs, and he couldn't pass through. He tried to back out, but he was stuck. A wave of panic overwhelmed him, and he dragged himself back inside tearing the skin on his forearm in the process.

The heat inside the building was intense, and John knew he couldn't last long. He pushed his right arm and shoulder through first and dug his heels in trying to find purchase in the soft ground. His left shoulder jammed against the log and panic seized him again as he realized he couldn't move forward nor back.

The girl grasped his wrist and started to pull. He was astonished at her strength as her fingers dug into his flesh. He pushed, scrabbling to find purchase with his feet and twisted his body back and forth. The girl leaned back, gasping with the effort. He thought his shoulder would come out of its socket, but he moved forward a little. Then suddenly he was through and gasping for breath.

John got to his feet.

"Thank you."

"We must go quickly now." He followed her along the side of the building. When they reached the trail he looked back. The longhouse was burning fiercely. The fire had jumped to the next building, and the flames were already licking up the walls.

John was elated, but the fire was moving faster than he had anticipated.

"Go quickly. Run." The girl leapt away like a deer in flight, and John had to stretch himself to catch her. It was almost completely dark and they were running blind. He knew it was madness. If one of them twisted an ankle their plan would be in ruins. John felt as if he was running in a dark tunnel. The girl was a shadow ahead of him.

There was a cracking sound behind him, and John skidded to a stop. The whole village was ablaze. The fire had spread to the forest, and he saw a tree explode into flames with a hissing sound that seemed to draw the breath out of his lungs.

John took to his heels again, and the fire lit the sky ahead of them, painting the forest red and gold. John's shadow moved ahead of him, flitting through the trees and leading him on recklessly. As he came around a long turn in the trail, he saw the pine tree he had marked highlighted by the fire.

John stopped and stepped into the forest. He could see the Iroquois moving in the firelight and calling out in alarm. The girl appeared beside him.

"They don't come. I don't understand," he said. He could see the girl's eyes now.

"When the forest burns, it can move quickly, and they've learned to fear it."

"Stay close lest we become separated in the dark."

John kept to the trees moving parallel to the trail. The girl moved so quietly he had to look to make sure she was still there. He came to within two hundred feet from the camp. It was dangerous to come so close, but he needed to see what was happening. He stood in the shadows between two trees, where he could see the camp clearly. The girl was beside him. He could feel the heat of her in the narrow space. Despite the danger, he found her presence distracting, and forced his attention back to the Iroquois.

The camp was in turmoil, and the Iroquois were milling about by their campfires. Many warriors were waving their weapons around and shouting.

"What are they saying?"

"Some want to go to the fire, but their leader thinks they invite danger for no reason."

"What will they do?"

"I've seen this go on for hours, but in the end they will do nothing."

John waited, hoping that something would change. The creek was thirty feet from the nearest campfire, and he could see its reflection on the water. It would be impossible to slip past the camp without being seen, and on this side of the lake it was only a matter of time till they were trapped.

John leaned close to the girl. "We must go."

As they started to move back, an explosion crashed through the forest, and they looked back.

"The powder horn. I'd given up hope." The camp was in uproar. The Iroquois were screaming and waving their weapons in agitation. A group of six or eight warriors broke from the camp and rushed along the trail, whooping their war cry. The rest of the group grabbed their weapons and streamed out of camp in pursuit.

John looked at the girl. "Let's go."

He skirted the camp and turned upstream along the creek bank. Louis would know to bring the canoes down to the lake. The light from the camp-fires faded, and John felt his way forward. And as his eyes adjusted to the darkness, he made out a shape moving on the creek.

"Louis," John hissed, and a canoe materialized out of the darkness.

"The bank's too high. Go to the camp."

John turned downstream. The girl was already moving ahead of him. They came out onto open ground and stopped where the trail crossed the creek. The fire was raging through the forest faster than he thought possible. It was moving in their direction, and he feared it would drive the Iroquois back to the camp. John felt the girl touch his arm, and he turned. The canoe glided out of the darkness, Louis dipping his paddle silently. The second canoe was ten feet behind. John went to meet it, and Louis called out, "Beware."

CHAPTER THIRTY-FIVE

JOHN TURNED TO SEE TWO Iroquois warriors running across the camp, one thirty paces ahead of the other. The nearest warrior's face was cast half in shadow. The other half blazed red in the firelight. He let out a war whoop and threw back his right arm and John saw the tomahawk flash in the firelight.

John knew if he hesitated he was lost, he yanked the cutlass from its scabbard and he threw himself at the warrior. John grasped the hilt with both hands and dived at his chest.

The Iroquois cried out in surprise and threw himself to the side wind milling his arms to keep his balance. The cutlass struck his groin, and John felt it hit bone. The Iroquois screamed in pain and fell backwards, but John's weight carried him on, and he twisted the cutlass gouging along the bone. Blood splashed onto John's face, and he knew it was a mortal wound.

John fell hard, grunting from the impact. The second warrior howled with rage and leapt at him, swinging his tomahawk. It was a wild swing and once committed, he couldn't change direction. John threw himself to the side, and the axe slid past his shoulder burying itself in the gravel.

The Iroquois landed half on top of John. He tried to throw him off, but he was heavily built, and John was half winded from the fall. The Iroquois used his weight to drive John down and swung the tomahawk at his head. John grasped the cutlass with both hands and threw it up to block the blow. The blade bit into the wooden shaft and stuck fast. The Iroquois screamed in rage and threw himself back, almost tearing the cutlass from his hands. John saw a shadow move behind him; then Louis slid his knife into the Iroquois's neck.

John got to his feet.

"Quickly," he called and slid the cutlass into its scabbard as he ran for the canoe. He lifted the bow and heaved, and the girl added her weight. Louis climbed into the stern and the canoe slid into the creek.

"Get in." The girl climbed nimbly into the canoe and John pushed off and leapt aboard.

John back-paddled away from the bank then switched sides and pushed the bow downstream. Louis brought the stern around, and they fell into a familiar rhythm. John could feel the drag of the second canoe, and he dug the paddle in hard trying to gain every inch of purchase he could. He looked behind them and gasped, the fire was rushing along the lakeshore at frightening speed. Trees exploded in flames as it came on. The firelight turned the surface of the lake blood red, and created a fearful shadow play on the trees as if there were monsters moving in the forest.

The creek bent to the right as it entered the lake. A mud bank followed the curve on their left running out into the lake, and John pushed hard for the darkness of the open water.

Louis hissed, "There's danger. Be ready."

John searched the creek banks. He couldn't see anything, but he trusted Louis's instincts. He cocked both barrels of the pistol and placed it on a bale in front of him. The girl took a paddle and leaned over the left side adding her strength to their effort.

The current was pushing the canoes towards the north side of the creek. John feared they would be thrown up on the bank but Louis managed to bring them around.

John searched the treeline for danger. Thirty feet more and they would be clear. There was a cracking sound behind them, a huge pine tree crashed to the ground sending sparks exploding into the air, and in the firelight John saw a group of Iroquois running along the mud bank aiming to intercept them at the point.

"There." John stabbed his arm at bank. The leading warrior brandished his tomahawk and let out a war cry that was taken up by the others.

John gauged the distance.

"They'll be on us before we reach the point."

"Drive hard," Louis cried, "the mud will slow them." The girl was leaning over the gunnels, using her whole body to drive the canoe forward. The Iroquois were halfway along the mud bank. The flames bathed their bodies in red, and it flowed over their skin like blood oozing from open wounds. In the firelight they seemed like a legion of demons called up from hell to hunt them.

John was startled at the report of a musket behind him. One of the Iroquois cried out and fell face-first into the mud, and Louis threw the musket down and took up his paddle. The other warriors screamed in rage and redoubled their efforts to reach the canoe. John put all his strength into his paddle, and as they approached the end of the mud bank Louis brought the canoe round to clear the point.

"Push hard on the left." John switched sides and leaned into it.

The bow cleared the mud bank by ten feet, but Louis called out, "Behind."

Four warriors had almost reached the end of the mud bank. John grabbed the pistol, aimed at the centre of the group and fired the left barrel. The pistol cracked, his arm was thrown up by the recoil, and the warrior at the front of the group went down clutching his stomach. The others leapt over him screaming like mad men.

John levelled the pistol at another warrior and pulled the trigger. The ball struck him in the hip and spun him around, and he dropped without a sound.

John grabbed his paddle and dug it into the creek, and as the bow cleared the mud bank he looked back. The two remaining Iroquois warriors threw themselves into the creek, they sank chest deep but they reached the canoe. One warrior lunged out of the water at Louis, tomahawk in hand. John started to call out a warning, but Louis drove his paddle into his face then swung it like an axe driving him under.

Louis had leaned over the side of the canoe, and he had to drop his paddle and grasp the side of the canoe to pull himself back. The last Iroquois grasped Louis's wrist, pulling him off balance. He reared out of the water and struck Louis with his tomahawk below the shoulder. Louis cried out in pain. He wrenched his left hand free and grabbed the warrior's wrist as he tried to strike again.

John rolled over the fur bales and swung his paddle at the Iroquois's head. The warrior broke free of Louis's grip and threw his tomahawk up in defense. The paddle struck him on the shoulder and the tomahawk fell from his hand. John almost toppled into the creek. He dropped the paddle and tried to throw himself backwards.

The warrior grasped John's shirt and jerked him out of the canoe. He felt the Iroquois reaching for his throat, and he thrust his left hand up to protect his windpipe. The warrior was heavier than John, and his strength was fearful. He was crushing John's left hand and closing off his windpipe. Panic surged through him, and his chest started to heave as his lungs were starved for air. He began to feel light-headed, and he knew unconsciousness was just moments away.

John got his feet under him and thrust up with all his strength and threw the Iroquois against the side of the canoe. His grip loosened and John drew a gasping breath and reached for his dirk; then his eyes went wide. The girl leaned over the side of the canoe and wrapped her left arm around the Iroquois's head. He saw a knife in her right hand, and in the time it took him to register what was happening, she struck three times, cutting into the warrior's throat.

The Iroquois had grasped the girl's hair, trying to pull her out of the canoe, but she held his head against the gunnel. Blood was spurting onto her face, but she kept stabbing his throat. John pulled the dirk from its scabbard, but the Iroquois went limp. The girl released him, and he slipped beneath the surface. The girl wiped the blood from her eyes, and said, "It's done. We must go."

They had drifted towards the shore, and John pulled the canoe into the bank. Louis was slumped against the fur bales holding his arm against his body.

"How bad is it, Louis?"

"It's not a killing blow, but I can't paddle."

"Let me see."

John used the dirk to slit Louis's jerkin and turned him, trying to see the wound by the light from the fire, but all he could tell was that the wound was bleeding freely. He pulled Louis's jerkin over his head, took off his own shirt and put it over the wound.

"Lean back." He sat Louis against one of the bales, trapping the shirt in place.

John dragged the canoe around the end of the mud bank. He had the sense that the girl was trembling, but the forest fire cast her face into shadow, and he couldn't say if it was from fear or anger.

"Take the front paddle." She moved to the bow, and John pushed them out into the lake and climbed into the stern.

John paddled in time with the girl. The drag from the second canoe held them back, but they gradually built up forward motion. John steered straight out into the lake until he was sure they couldn't be seen, then turned north parallel to the shore.

When he looked back, John was stunned. The whole lakeshore was ablaze. The fire had jumped the creek and was moving north along the shore at an unbelievable pace. He was aghast at the havoc they had wreaked on the forest.

John could see Louis hunched over against the fur bale.

"How is it, Louis?"

"I will live, but I won't be able to paddle for some days."

John watched the fire running ahead of them consuming the forest like a ravening beast. It would be madness to try to land there, and he called to the girl.

"We must cross to the eastern shore." He was surprised how easily he slipped into French.

She spoke over her shoulder. "How is it with the Mi'kmaq?"

"He's struck in the shoulder. I think the wound is deep."

"We'll need him to paddle when we leave the lake."

"We must reach the shore before daylight," John said, and he turned the canoe towards the east.

The light was growing in the sky when John saw the outline of the eastern shore. He was near exhaustion. The fight with the Iroquois and paddling through the night had drained him. The fire raged along the western shore of the lake. The blaze was enormous and again he felt a pang of guilt at the damage they'd done to the forest. Black smoke and ash rose into the sky and blew across the lake. It burned his eyes and throat, but he was thankful that it would cover their escape.

John had stopped paddling and let the canoe drift to a stop. Louis had wrapped himself in a blanket and was asleep, and the girl watched him from the bow.

"That way to the northwest," she said. John brought the canoe around, and they fell to again. The eastern shore was heavily forested. John could see the girl searching for something, but he didn't question her. Finally she pointed ahead.

"There." She changed her paddle to the left side. "Turn here." John couldn't see anything but undergrowth; then he felt the motion of the canoe change, and he realized they'd entered a creek, and the current was slowing them.

As they came to shore the girl pushed the foliage aside. John ducked under the branches, and they slid into the creek. He pulled the second canoe alongside them, and the canopy fell back over the entrance. Louis had awakened and was looking around. "It is a good place."

John looked at the girl. "How do you know this place?"

"The Iroquois have hunting camps on this side of the lake. Once I ran away and hid here for a day and a night. The Iroquois don't know of it. We'll be safe here for a while."

John slid his paddle into the water, and it touched bottom.

"We should pull the canoes farther into the creek." He pulled his boots off and stepped into the water up to his knees. The girl slid in on the other side, and they pulled the canoes upstream until they bottomed out and John made them fast to the bank.

The girl took her sleeping roll and climbed onto the bank. "There's a good place to camp a little way farther."

John helped Louis climb onto the bank and gathered up their gear and weapons. The creek was heavily overgrown, but the girl led them to a clearing on the south bank.

John dropped the gear. "Let me see the wound."

Louis sat on the grass and uncovered his shoulder. The tomahawk had cut into the muscle below the shoulder blade. The wound was four inches long and oozing blood. John filled his water flask and soaked a piece of his shirt to wash the wound.

"We should sew it closed, but I don't have the instruments." He tore up his shirt and made a bandage.

The girl came and squatted beside him.

"Rub it into the wound first." She held a handful of crushed berries and leaves.

"What is it?"

"It will stop the wound from putrefying." The pasty substance looked unsavoury, and John was skeptical.

"It's good," Louis said. "The girl is right." Louis scooped the paste out of the girl's hand and rubbed it into his shoulder and bound it up.

John started to gather wood.

"There's so much smoke in the air. I don't think a fire will give us away." He knew they needed warmth and rest. They were exhausted, and Louis had lost a lot of blood.

John spread their gear out to dry in the sun then built the fire up and made leaf tea. He sipped his tea, and as the sun warmed him, the tension of the last day and night began to wear off. He pulled his boots off and lay down and stretched out, trying to relax. Sometime later, John sat up. He hadn't intended to fall asleep, but he felt refreshed. The sun was high in the sky, and he realized that he had slept for hours. Louis was snoring softly, and the girl was nowhere to be seen.

John got to his feet carefully, trying not to wake Louis, and pulled his buckskin tunic on. There was little firewood to be found around their camp, so he loaded the pistol, slid his tomahawk into his belt, and went looking for more fuel. The clearing was off the beaten track. There wasn't even a game trail along the creek, so he went into the forest and started upstream. A few hundred yards from the camp he came on a dozen trees that had been blown down in a tangled heap.

John was pleased. The deadfall was close to camp and would provide firewood for several days. He dragged the larger limbs out of the pile and cut them into manageable lengths with the tomahawk, working until he had enough fuel to last them through the night. He started to stack the branches into a pile when a sound behind him made him made him freeze. He dropped to the ground and turned in a circle searching for danger, but he saw nothing moving in the forest.

John couldn't identify the sound, but he was sure it had come from the direction of the creek. He took the pistol from his belt and crept towards the creek. Louis had taught him how to move quietly, and he placed his feet where they would make no sound, stopping every few minutes to listen. The sound of the creek gradually increased, and he guessed he was close to a waterfall.

John moved downstream where the underbrush grew close along the bank, got down on his stomach and crawled forward. He caught a flash of colour through the foliage. He lay still and listened, then inched forward till he was only a few feet from the creek.

The creek was no more than six feet across, but upstream it opened into a pool. On the other side of the pool, the creek ran over a rock face. It made a low rumbling noise as it tumbled into the water. This was the sound he had heard in the forest. John felt a little foolish, and he got to his feet and pushed through the underbrush to the side of the pool.

John was startled by a cry to his right and he turned, bringing the pistol up. The girl rose out of the pool. She was naked and water streamed off her body, pouring down her flanks and over her hips. Her breasts were tight with the cold, and tiny drops of water clung to them, shining like beads of light. The water reached the top of her thighs and the current lapped against the dark triangle at the base of her belly. The pistol dropped to John's side. He felt the colour rise in his face, but he couldn't tear his eyes away.

The girl pushed her hair back from her face, and her eyes were fierce.

"Have you have come to use me as the Iroquois? Are you no better than the savages, then?" John felt as if she'd struck him in the face.

"I didn't mean . . ."

She talked over him. "Do you have the courage to take me yourself, or will you have the Mi'kmaq hold me down?" Her anger was sharp as a blade, but it was the disappointment in her voice that made him ashamed.

She was like a creature of the forest, a wild thing that won't be tamed, and the fierceness of her spirit made him want her all the more. John felt the bank crumble under him, and he stumbled back.

"I'm sorry I did not mean . . ." The words froze in his throat, and he looked away, "I'm sorry," he said and stumbled into the forest.

John wandered aimlessly; he was ashamed and humiliated, and felt that he had failed the girl in some way. He felt foolish and gullible. He lost track of how long he walked, but finally he returned to the deadfall.

John hacked at the deadfall until he had accumulated a huge pile of firewood. It was more than they would need, but the work helped to relieve the tension in him. When he dragged the first load to the camp, Louis was sitting up by the fire. John made two more trips, and when he returned with the last load, the girl was roasting pemmican on the fire. As he sat by Louis, she looked at him, and he felt the colour rise in his neck, but her eyes were empty, and she turned back to the meat.

Louis was weak, and as soon as they'd eaten he wrapped himself in his sleeping roll and fell asleep. John sat across the fire from the girl. Twice he made to speak, but the words froze in his throat, and finally he wrapped his plaid around his shoulders.

"I'll take the watch," he said. He didn't look at her as he stepped away from the camp. He sat with his back to the fire and watched the forest, but the image of the girl naked and unafraid continued to intrude on his thoughts. Finally fatigue overcame him, and he stretched out on the ground and closed his eyes. He had meant the girl no harm, and now he felt that something had been lost.

CHAPTER THIRTY-SIX

THE LETTER FROM ELISABETH LOCKHART changed everything for Scott. It stirred emotions he didn't understand that caused him to feel at once elated and vulnerable. He started to compose a response to her, but he was incapable of putting pen to paper. He realized that he didn't know what it was he felt for Elisabeth Lockhart nor did he understand why her letter had such a profound effect on him. He thought of what had passed between them on the *Raven* and after, and in his heart he knew something had changed. He pulled on his coat and took the trail to the head of the inlet. The river was high with melted snow, and he sat on the bank and let the sound of the torrent wash the turmoil from his mind.

Scott made his way back to the fort and sat down at the table and wrote a letter to Mrs. Lockhart, sealed it and put it in his trunk for safekeeping. He went to bed, but sleep wouldn't come, and his mind ran on consumed by thoughts of Boston and Elisabeth Lockhart. The next day he added the letter to the package of documents the *Challenger* would carry to Boston.

* * *

In the following weeks Scott led patrols along the coast, never more than a day's march from the fort. It kept his mind occupied and the physical activity burned away the nervous energy that consumed him. Since the action at Shubenacadie he'd seen no sign of the native population. The French settlers had heard about the raid and kept their distance from the soldiers.

A month after the raid, the fort received reports of native activity to the east, and Scott was dispatched to investigate. He took Sergeant Crammer, twenty troopers and four Iroquois scouts. Scott drove them hard across the long valley to the east, but they found no sign of natives in the area.

It was late when they returned to the fort, and Scott was astonished to see a merchant ship anchored in the inlet. When Scott arrived at the officers' quarters, Lieutenant Paine was eating dinner in the common room, and he came to his feet when Scott entered.

"Captain Scott, Major Phelps has asked that you report to his office first thing in the morning."

"Very well, Lieutenant. What ship is anchored in the inlet, and from which port does she hail?"

"She is the *Eagle* out of Boston, Captain Benjamin Jeffry commanding."

"Very well, Lieutenant. Carry on." Scott went to his room to wash, and he retired immediately after dinner.

The next morning Scott reported to Major Phelps, but it was half an hour before the orderly showed him into his office. The major was sitting at the table, and he got to his feet and walked over to the fire.

"Come in, Captain Scott."

"You asked me to attend you this morning, Major?"

Phelps clasped his hands behind his back.

"I will come right to the point, Captain. Our masters in Boston are organizing a campaign along the border with the French territories, and troops are being recalled all along the Eastern Seaboard to support it." Phelps paused as if gathering his thoughts. "You and your men will return to Boston immediately to take part in the action. The *Eagle* presently lying at the anchor in the inlet will convey you."

A surge of excitement welled up in him, but Scott kept his features neutral.

"When does she sail, Major?"

"In two days' time. You will make arrangements to board your men no later than sunset tomorrow."

"If that is all, Major . . ." As Scott turned away Phelps spoke again.

"One more thing, Captain. The Iroquois scouts will accompany you."

"Yes, Major."

Two days later the Eagle sailed on the ebb tide, and Scott watched Annapolis Royal fall below the horizon. They reached the gap by mid-afternoon, but the tide was against them. Scott had been assigned a cabin, but he stayed on deck. The weather was warm, and he stood at the rail as Jeffry brought the ship to anchor.

Jeffry was in his fifties, slow moving and running to fat, but his mind was sharp. Scott had spoken with him when he came aboard, and he'd been polite but reserved. Scott didn't doubt Major Phelps had told him of his background, but such matters were of little importance to him. Shortly he would be in Boston, and that was all that mattered.

The evening was long, and there was light enough to steer as the ebb began to run, and Captain Jeffry conned the ship through the gap and put her on a southerly heading. The sky was clear, and Scott identified the constellation Ursa Major and used it to find the North Star. There was something comforting about letting the stars guide him and he stayed on the bridge until the need to sleep drove him to his bunk.

Six days later the Eagle clawed its way into Boston Harbor against an easterly wind. Jeffry tacked the ship back and forth across the harbour until they were within reach of the pilot boats. Each boat had ten rowers known as Hobblers. The Eagle required four boats to tow her into harbour.

It was late afternoon when the Eagle made fast on the north side of the harbour, and Scott and his troops disembarked within the hour. Scott ordered Sergeant Crammer to march the men to the barracks. He told Swatana, the chief of the Iroquois, about the expedition to the French border and that he wanted him and his men to join him. Swatana said he was returning to his village, and that if Scott sent word when the expedition was to leave, he would join him.

A boy was waiting on the dock with a horse and trap for him, but it was almost dark by the time Scott arrived at the base. He instructed the boy to wait and went inside to find the orderly. It was the same man, but Scott couldn't remember his name.

"Good evening, Captain Scott. Your old room is ready for you."

"Have my chest and other boxes unloaded from the gig, and also advise the cook that I would like dinner as soon as possible."

"Dinner has already been served for the evening, Captain, but I am sure the cook can prepare something for you."

Scott went to the dining room while his belongings were taken upstairs. The cook sent cold cuts, bread, cheese and a bottle of red wine to the dining room for him. He hadn't eaten since morning. He was famished, and both the food and the wine were excellent. In his room he unpacked his writing case and wrote a note to Mrs. Broadhurst enquiring if his old rooms were still available then sought out the orderly.

"Have this delivered to Mrs. Broadhurst's rooming house first thing tomorrow."

"Begging your pardon Captain Scott. Major Coxe has requested that you attend him first thing in the morning."

"Very well."

Scott had been on his feet since before first light, but in spite of his fatigue and the effects of the wine, sleep didn't come quickly. He lay staring at the trees moving in the breeze. In his mind he ran over everything that had happened since he'd left Boston. Uppermost in his mind was Elisabeth Lockhart. He wanted to see her, but he was apprehensive. Her passion and her strength drew him to her, but somehow those same qualities disarmed him.

Scott reported to Major Coxe at nine o'clock the next morning. Coxe got up from his desk, motioned Scott forward and stood to shake his hand.

"Welcome back, Captain Scott." He waved him to a seat.

"Thank you, Major." Coxe dashed off a signature on a document and pushed it to the side.

"Well, Captain, how did you find Annapolis Royal?" He sat back and raised an eyebrow.

"It gave me the opportunity to experience the wilderness, Major, but I must admit it was not the most rewarding posting I've had."

Coxe picked up another document, glanced at it, and threw it down.

"This is Major Phelps's report on your deployment to Annapolis Royal. It's a perplexing report, Captain. It suggests that you provoked conflict on a British merchant ship." He tapped the report with his finger. "And if Major Phelps is correct, came close to taking the vessel by force of arms." Scott's gut tightened, but he didn't let his face betray his feelings.

The major cocked his head to one side.

"On the other hand, Captain, Major Phelps speaks highly of the expedition you led against the Mi'kmaq village at Shubenacadie. He considers the mission a success and anticipates no further conflict with the natives for the foreseeable future." Scott was surprised, and he inclined his head in acknowledgement.

Coxe placed his hands on the table.

"In truth, Captain, I don't know what to make of you, but Colonel Havilland's expedition will provide you with ample opportunity to demonstrate your capacity for ruthlessness. No doubt we shall have occasion to discuss your military career again at a later date." Scott kept silent and waited.

Coxe pursed his lips.

"As you are aware, Captain, we are at war with France. Over a year ago we captured the town of Louisburg. Since then there have been skirmishes but no major actions. Now we have been instructed to conduct a campaign along the border with the French. The purpose of the expedition is to demonstrate dominion of our territories."

Scott raised an eyebrow. "Is this to be the first step in a larger incursion?"

Coxe shook his head. "There's no plan to annex French territories. With the war in Europe our forces are stretched too thin. My personal feeling is that an invasion is inevitable, but it won't happen until the war in Europe has come to an end."

Coxe handed Scott a document. "These are your orders; in short, you and your troops will make your way to Albany, where you will place yourself under the command of Colonel Havilland. I believe the expeditionary force will be in excess of two hundred strong."

"When do we leave, Major? How long should I plan to be in the field?"

"You'll leave no later than the end of July. That gives you six weeks to prepare, and you should expect to be in the field until winter sets in."

Coxe got to his feet and extended his hand.

"Lieutenant Paine will see that you have everything you need. He will also take part in the campaign under your command. Report back to me a few days before you leave."

"Yes, Major." Scott saluted and left the office.

When Scott returned to the officers' quarters, the orderly presented him with two notes that had arrived shortly after he had left. The first was from Mrs. Broadhurst. He looked at the second note, and his pulse raced as he recognized Elisabeth Lockhart's hand even before he read the salutation. He slid both notes into the inside pocket of his tunic.

"That will be all. Thank you."

Scott went to his room and slid a paper knife under the seal of Mrs. Lockhart's note. It contained only four lines of script. She expressed her pleasure at Scott's return to Boston, enquired after his health and the journey from Annapolis Royal, and invited him to take tea with her on the following Wednesday, tomorrow, at two o'clock in the afternoon. The note was signed Elisabeth.

Scott paced to the door and back then read the note again. He was confounded by the effect she had on him, and he barked a laugh when he realized he was acting like a schoolboy. When he opened Mrs. Broadhurst's note, she expressed her pleasure in hearing from him again. The rooms he had occupied had been let in his absence, but she indicated she had another set of rooms that would suit him admirably and invited him to view them at his convenience.

Scott scribbled a note to Mrs. Broadhurst advising her that he would call tomorrow before midday. He didn't respond to Mrs. Lockhart. She would know he would come. He instructed the orderly to send the note to Mrs. Broadhurst to have his clothes laundered and pressed, and to have a bath prepared for him. He wanted to wash the smell of the ship off his skin and the melancholy from his mind before he saw Mrs. Lockhart.

Scott presented himself at Mrs. Broadhurst's shortly before noon the following day, and the maid showed him into the parlour. Mrs. Broadhurst came bustling into the room a few minutes later gushing with pleasure at seeing him again.

"First, let me show you the rooms I have for you, Captain; then we can have a cup of tea and catch up on everything that's happened since you left."

Mrs. Broadhurst led Scott upstairs and showed him into a suite of rooms at the back of the house that looked onto the river. They were larger than his previous accommodations and more comfortably furnished.

"What do you think, Captain?"

"They will do admirably, Mrs. Broadhurst. When can I take possession?"

"The rooms are available immediately." Scott couldn't help but smile.

"I will have my belongings sent over in the morning, and I will take up residence tomorrow evening if that's acceptable."

By the time they finished it was past midday, and Scott took his leave declining Mrs. Broadhurst's invitation to take tea with her. He walked to the library and asked for any maps or other geographical materials related to the French-British border region to be made available to him the following day. He took his midday meal at an inn close to the library and walked to Garden Court Street.

* * *

The maid curtsied as she opened the front door.

"Captain Scott, sir, Mrs. Lockhart is expecting you. She is in the upstairs parlour, sir." She led Scott upstairs and closed the door silently after him. Mrs. Lockhart was standing by the window, smiling. She was wearing a blue silk dress and a white blouse. The buttons of her blouse were undone revealing white skin, and her hair was loose and swept forward over her shoulder.

"It is good to see you, Captain Scott."

"Indeed, Mrs. Lockhart."

Mrs. Lockhart crossed the room and stopped. She put her hands on his chest and looked at his eyes.

"Captain, I regret the manner in which we parted. It is my wish that nothing should come between us." Scott breathed in the scent of her, and a rush of emotion welled up in him.

"That is also my wish, Mrs. Lockhart." He was astonished that he had uttered those words. He hadn't contemplated such a response. It wasn't his nature so speak so. The words had come unbidden to his lips, but the greater revelation for him was that they were true.

Mrs. Lockhart slid her arms around his neck and pressed herself against him.

"I have missed you, Captain." She put her hand on his face and pulled his mouth to hers. The taste of her made his head swim, and all that had happened since he'd seen her last ceased to exist, only his want for her remained, and he crushed her mouth to his.

After a moment they broke apart, and she led him to her bed. She unfastened her dress and let it fall to the floor and stepped out of it naked. Scott drank in the contours of her body and the whiteness of her skin, and she pulled back the bedspread and slid between the sheets.

"Come, Captain, we have long been apart. Do not make me wait any longer."

Later they took tea in the downstairs parlour. Mrs. Lockhart wore a green velvet dress and a white blouse, and she bound her hair up with a black ribbon. Scott left his jacket off and rolled up his sleeves. The maid brought a pie made from blueberries with cream to dress it. Scott ate the pie and called for more when it was finished.

Mrs. Lockhart wanted to hear about Scott's posting to Annapolis Royal, and he described the voyage, Annapolis Royal and its surroundings, Major Phelps and the military situation in the region. She was interested in his account of the tidal drop and the spring tides. She hadn't visited the area and professed an interest in seeing it for herself.

Scott described the expedition against the Mi'kmaq. He passed over the details of the raid, but she insisted on hearing everything.

"Captain, there's talk that many of the villagers were killed; is that true?" Scott hesitated, and she pressed him further. "Captain, it's not my intention to judge your actions, but I have placed my trust in you, and I wish there to be no secrets between us."

Scott was apprehensive speaking of these things with Mrs. Lockhart, but he couldn't deny her.

"As you wish. My orders were to conduct a putative raid against the Mi'kmaq in retribution for the attack against Annapolis Royal last year. I led the attack on the village. Many were killed, and the village was burned."

"How many were killed, Captain?"

Scott hesitated a second time, but there was no going back.

"I don't know the exact number, but I don't believe that many escaped."

"Women and children?"

"Yes."

Mrs. Lockhart went still.

"I understand that you were following orders, Captain, but I struggle to reconcile such actions with the man I have come to know and admire." She looked at him with that unblinking gaze as if she would see into his soul, and Scott looked back, hiding nothing.

"I'm the same man, Mrs. Lockhart. I don't pretend to be other." After a moment she smiled and took his hand. She seemed to accept what he said, but there was something sad in her eyes that he found disquieting.

Scott took her hand in both of his. "Now you know everything that's happened to me, tell me what you've been doing these last months."

She laughed. "My life is not nearly as exciting or dangerous as yours. The only challenges I face are the demands of my business enterprises."

"Let me be the judge of that."

She inclined her head.

"The war with France has driven commodity prices up, and we've been hard-pressed to keep up with demand. My people have been working round the clock for months to keep our warehouses full and our vessels loaded. In recent months I've also signed trading agreements with three locations in the Caribbean Sea. I am pleased to have established a foothold there as the region holds much promise for the future."

Scott knew little of mercantile affairs, but he was impressed with her grasp of the markets. She was fearless and capable of bold action when she deemed it worthwhile.

"What will you do when you have conquered the Caribbean?"

She laughed in that soft lilting tone that he found so appealing and put her hand on his arm. "I haven't conquered the Caribbean, Captain. I have simply launched a business enterprise."

It was Scott's turn to laugh.

"From what I have seen of your business acumen I expect it is only a matter of time until you establish dominion over the whole region."

Mrs. Lockhart smiled.

"To answer your question"—she tilted her head as she looked at him—"the sugar trade will prove rewarding in due course, but conducting one's affairs at such a distance is complicated, and I have extended myself as much as is wise for now. For the present I will turn my attention to markets closer to home."

"What do you have in mind?"

Mrs. Lockhart placed her elbows on the table. "I believe there are opportunities in the fur trade worth exploring."

"I have little knowledge of the trade, but as I understand it, the Hudson's Bay Company has the exclusive monopoly to trade for fur."

She laughed out loud. "Ah, yes, the honourable Hudson's Bay Company. They do indeed hold such a charter. However, there are merchants in Boston and other places . . . who have found ways to participate in the trade."

Scott frowned. "Does Hudson's Bay not have the support of the British government? Would they not take steps to control such activities?"

"That's true, Captain. They do have the support of the British government, and they do take steps to maintain their monopoly. However, the land is vast, and the north is an ungovernable wilderness. Issuing a charter is one thing; enforcing it is something entirely different."

Scott started to speak, but she pre-empted him.

"Things are changing, Captain. We're at war with France. A year ago the expeditionary force from Boston captured Louisburg. Tensions are high between the British and the French."

He saw what she was getting at. "You think Britain will invade the French territories?"

"Truly, I don't know, but where there's change, there's opportunity, and it's wise to be prepared."

Scott became thoughtful. "You may have something. I was recalled from Annapolis Royal to participate in a campaign along the border with the French territories."

Mrs. Lockhart's eyes opened in surprise. "You didn't tell me of this, Captain?"

Scott smiled. "Indeed, madam, we have had little time to talk until now."

She laughed and squeezed his arm. "Touché, Captain. Tell me then of this campaign."

"I know little enough, only what Major Coxe conveyed to me. I am to proceed to Albany where an expeditionary force is being assembled. It is commanded by a Colonel Havilland. The purpose of the campaign is to show the flag and demonstrate control of British territory."

Mrs. Lockhart sipped her tea and placed the cup delicately in the saucer.

"There's been talk of military action in recent months, but I hadn't heard it was to be on this scale."

"As I understand it, the intent is to demonstrate possession of our territories, and no doubt, make the French nervous. However, I don't believe we'll be invading with two hundred troops."

Mrs. Lockhart put her hand on Scott's arm. "When are you to leave?"

"We're to leave for Albany by the end of next month." She eased her grip on his arm, and her eyes sparkled.

"Well, at least we have some time, Captain. How long is this campaign to last?"

"Coxe said I'll be in the field until the first snowfall."

Mrs. Lockhart was lost in thought for a moment; then she took Scott's hands.

"I have a business engagement this evening that I must prepare for. Will you dine with me this coming Saturday, Captain?"

"With the greatest pleasure."

As she saw him to the door, she seemed preoccupied. Scott slipped his tunic on, and she placed her hands on his chest and kissed him on the mouth.

"I'll look forward to Saturday." His head was filled with her scent. He breathed it in, and she laughed out loud and pushed him away.

"Until Saturday, Captain."

Scott inclined his head. "Until Saturday, then."

As he turned to the door, she put her hand on his arm. "We must speak again of this campaign to the French territory. I believe it may contain the seeds of an opportunity."

CHAPTER THIRTY-SEVEN

THE NEXT MORNING SCOTT SENT word for Lieutenant Paine to meet him in the officer's quarters at midday. He instructed the lieutenant to conduct an inventory of the equipment they'd brought back from Annapolis Royal and to develop a list of the supplies they would need for a three-month campaign. He told Paine to report back to him when the task was completed.

When he had finished with the lieutenant, Scott went to the stables. He was pleased to find his horse, King, hadn't been reassigned. The stable master informed him that King was to have two shoes replaced that afternoon, and he gave instructions for him to be brought to the stables close to Mrs. Broadhurst's in the morning. He had six weeks before his departure for Albany, and he intended to use the time to further his knowledge of the French border region.

Scott spent the next few days working in the library, examining any maps and other materials that he could find related to the border region. He came across two maps that had been completed in the last ten years and one report that described the areas potential for homesteading and farming. There wasn't much useful information, but one thing was clear: as Mrs. Lockhart had said, the territory was vast and mostly unexplored.

* * *

On the Saturday evening, Scott joined Mrs. Lockhart for dinner at her house. She wore a black satin dress and a string of rubies. She radiated health and well-being and a subtle sensuality that Scott found more than compelling. The food and wine were excellent, and they floated through the evening, speaking of what was in their hearts and their minds. Scott felt at ease with this woman, as if he'd known her all his life, and he sensed she felt the same.

In the morning they bathed and took breakfast in the dining room. Mrs. Lockhart wore a simple grey dress and bound her hair behind her head. Scott's appetite was keen, and he did justice to everything that was placed before him. Mrs. Lockhart ate sparingly, but she enjoyed watching Scott indulge himself.

The maid cleared away the breakfast dishes and poured coffee. Mrs. Lockhart took a sip and set her cup down.

"Do you intend to spend your entire career in the military, Captain? Have you considered what you might do when you are done with the army?" Scott looked at her in surprise. There was a smile on her lips and a sparkle of mischief in her eyes.

"In truth I haven't thought on it a great deal. The army has been my life since I was a boy."

"Do you believe there will be opportunities for you in Boston for advancement within the military?"

Scott hesitated, and a he felt a pang of discomfort. Her capacity for directness could be disconcerting, and she had the ability to get to the heart of a matter.

"Do you mock me, Mrs. Lockhart?"

She became serious. "No, Captain. I do not mock you. I'm simply stating what I think must be obvious to you also. Society in Boston, military or other, follows traditional conventions. Your background will be an impediment to advancement, and your actions have offended influential elements of the establishment."

Scott felt his temper rise, and he burst out, "The devil with Boston and its establishment. I'll not behave like a fawning sycophant for the privilege of being acceptable to society."

"I'm not suggesting you should, Captain. I'm simply stating the obvious, unpleasant as it may be."

"What would you have me do, Mrs. Lockhart? Open a tavern in the town or grow turnips perhaps?"

"No, Captain. I was about to suggest that you go into business with me."

Scott was dumbfounded and fell silent, and she went on before he could gather his thoughts.

"As I said the other night, I believe there will be opportunities in the fur trade in the coming years. A venture in this area, if it's to succeed, must have a number of key ingredients. It will require careful planning, investment to launch the venture, and bold action to carry it to fruition."

Scott finally found his voice. "I've no taste to be a kept man."

The heat was rising in his face, but she forestalled him.

"Captain, I'm not suggesting that you be in my employ." She put her hands on the table and held his eyes. "I believe the campaign you are to take part in will present a unique opportunity. Much of the fur that comes out of Hudson's Bay passes through the region you'll be campaigning in. Ultimately the fur goes to Boston or Mont-Royal and Quebec."

"I know nothing of the fur trade or commerce for that matter."

Mrs. Lockhart held up her hand.

"Hear me out, Captain. The area is little known. The French and the Iroquois protect it jealously, and Hudson's Bay Company is even more secretive. Only the Hudson's Bay people and the French venture into the region."

"What's this to do with me?"

Mrs. Lockhart got up and retrieved a map from the dresser and spread it on the table. Scott was impressed by the cartography: it was beautifully executed, and the detail was superior to what he'd seen in the library.

Mrs. Lockhart placed her finger on a point where two rivers met. "These are the St. Lawrence and Ottawa Rivers. The Iroquois have territories in this region."

She swept her finger over an area to the north and west of the rivers. "The Iroquois have traditionally acted as middle men trading with the people in the north for fur, then trading it to the British in Boston."

In spite of himself Scott was intrigued. He got to his feet and leaned over the map. "What are you proposing?"

She leaned her elbows on the table next to him. "The Iroquois have been losing ground for years. They will kill to protect the trade, but Hudson's Bay has eroded their position. The Bay men are greedy. They want the trade to themselves, but there are others who avoid both the Iroquois and the Hudson's Bay."

She tapped the Ottawa River with a slender finger. "There are a few merchants from Boston and other parts of Massachusetts who have traded with the natives coming down from the Hudson's Bay. The French have been trading with them for generations."

"How do they avoid conflict with the Iroquois and the Hudson's Bay Company?"

"I have little knowledge of how the trade is conducted. They don't maintain trading posts in the wilderness, so they must have some other way of coming in contact with the natives. This much I do know. The trade through Mont-Royal and Quebec equals or exceeds that of Boston."

Scott sank into his chair and took a sip of coffee. "I'm still not clear what it is you are suggesting."

Mrs. Lockhart sat opposite him. "I'm suggesting that if we can find a way to establish trading relations with the natives in the far north, and bring fur out without interference from Hudson's Bay or the Iroquois, I believe there's a fortune to be made."

"If the Hudson's Bay Company found out, they could make things difficult for you in Boston."

"Then we'll deal with the French through Mont-Royal."

Scott laughed out loud. "You continue to surprise me. We're at war with France. Wouldn't that be treason?"

She smiled and her eyes twinkled.

"War is just another business opportunity, Captain, and this war won't last forever."

Mrs. Lockhart pulled her chair closer.

"The campaign along the border will present an opportunity to explore the region. The force is large enough that you won't be easily challenged. Indeed most will avoid you, native and French alike." Mrs. Lockhart tapped the Ottawa River then ran her finger over the north. "This entire region is largely unknown. If you can find a route to this area, the more remote and little known the better, then we will have our opportunity"

"Where no one has traded previously."

"Precisely."

Mrs. Lockhart rested her hands on the table. "What I am proposing is this: use the campaign as the launching point to find a route to the north and a way to trade with the natives. We'll make detailed plans over the winter, and in the spring you'll lead the first expedition."

She held up her hand. "Hear me out before you say anything. We will form a new company for the purposes of trading for fur. You and I will be equal partners. I will provide the finance to launch the expedition with the understanding that I'm to be repaid from the first year's profits. Thereafter we share equally."

Scott searched her face. She returned his gaze unblinking, and finally he sat back. "In truth I don't know what to think, far less how to respond."

"Then don't respond for the present." She laughed and put her hand on his arm. "This is not a decision that you make every day."

Scott took his leave before midday, and as Mrs. Lockhart walked with him to the door, she became serious.

"I've presented you with a dilemma, Captain, but I want you to know that I am sincere in this."

Scott's mind was reeling. "I don't doubt your sincerity, but I must think on what you have said."

"Then know this, Captain: we have a bond between us that I will nurture and strengthen if I can, whatever you decide."

She put her arms around his neck, and he pulled him to her. He breathed in the scent of her, and a surge of such confusing emotions welled up in him that he crushed her to him until she gasped.

After a moment Scott released her. She slid her arms under his tunic and locked them around his chest. Finally she stood back and smiled.

"Until Wednesday, Captain."

"Until Wednesday."

The door closed behind him, and he set off with a head crowded with conflicting thoughts and feelings. He needed to walk to clear his mind.

* * *

In the weeks that followed, Scott and Mrs. Lockhart spoke often of her proposal. Scott was hesitant, and she didn't press him. The army had been his life since he had been a boy, but he knew she had the right of it. Major

Coxe tolerated him because he had no other choice at the moment, but that could change in a day, and he could find himself without a command.

His third week back in Boston, Major Coxe sent word for Scott to report to him the following Monday morning. When he entered Coxe's office he was writing at his desk and waved him to a chair while he finished. Coxe dusted the document he'd been working on and added it to a pile to his left.

Coxe looked at Scott.

"The timing for the French campaign has been moved up, Captain. Colonel Havilland has sent word from Albany of increased activity on the French side of the border."

"When am I to leave?"

Coxe slid a letter across the desk.

"You're to leave a week from Thursday. I take it you've have made all necessary preparations?"

"Yes, Major. We have fifty-five troopers ready to march, and I'll send word for the Iroquois scouts to join us on route. Arms, ammunition, and supplies have all been assembled and transport wagons secured."

Scott opened the letter and read the orders, but when he read the final sentence the heat rose in his face.

"It states that at the conclusion of the campaign I'm to return to my post at Annapolis Royal. It was my understanding that my home post was to be Boston."

"Your orders state that you are posted to Annapolis Royal. You have been recalled to take part in the French campaign. When the campaign is over, you'll return to your home posting."

Scott threw the letter down.

"I protest in the strongest terms. I completed my assigned task in Annapolis Royal, and there's no further need for me there." The blood drained from Coxe's face, and he slammed the palm of his hand on the desk.

"You, sir, will not raise your voice to me. You were sent to Massachusetts in disgrace, guilty of gross incompetence and dereliction of duty. You should consider yourself fortunate to have a post of any kind in the British Army."

Scott stood, sending the chair sliding backwards.

"I completed the mission you knew Major Phelps wasn't capable of. It seems when there's bloody work to be done I'm competent enough. No doubt there will be more of the same on the new campaign."

Coxe struggled to his feet. His face was red and spittle flew from his lips as he roared at Scott.

"I'll not tolerate such behaviour, Captain." He jabbed at Scott with his finger. You'll follow your orders, or I'll have you court-martialled."

Scott put his hands on the desk and leaned towards Coxe.

"I'll play my part in the French campaign, Major, a part that the likes of you don't have the stomach for, and when I'm finished we'll speak of this again."

He scooped up the letter and turned for the door. Coxe came to the end of the desk and stamped his foot.

"You'll not turn your back on me, sir. I am your commanding officer."

Scott slammed the door behind him. The adjutant froze halfway to his feet then averted his eyes and sat down.

Scott stormed out of the building and strode to the stable. He kicked King into a canter and took the river path to Mrs. Broadhurst's house, and walked into the town to let his temper cool. Mrs. Lockhart was right about his future with the army. He didn't understand why he hadn't seen it before, but now he knew where he stood. He went to the library. He asked to see any maps they had of the French border and sat down to make his plans.

Mrs. Lockhart sent a note to Scott that a matter of some urgency had come up, and she wouldn't be able to take tea with him on Wednesday, but she looked forward to meeting him for dinner on Saturday. Scott was disappointed. He'd been eagerly anticipating their meeting, and in a moment of insight he realized that he was becoming dependent on her. Part of him rejected the notion, and he felt resentful of it, but presently his anger dissipated, and he found himself looking forward to seeing her.

On the Saturday it rained and Scott delayed leaving for Mrs. Lockhart's until it had eased. As he came up the steps the maid opened the door.

"Let me take your coat, sir. Mrs. Lockhart is waiting for you in the parlour."

"Thank you." She took his coat and opened the parlour door for him. Mrs. Lockhart was standing by the fireplace. Even though it was summer, the day was cold, and a fire burned in the grate. She wore a light blue dress that flattered her figure and a black scarf tied around her shoulders. She glowed with health. Her skin was white as porcelain and so transparent he could see the web of veins beneath.

She smiled as he entered.

"Captain Scott." She came to him, moving with her easy grace, put her arms around his neck and kissed him. Scott savoured the taste and the smell of her as if it were a drug he had to have. She pressed herself against him, and he squeezed her till she gasped and broke away.

"Careful, Captain. I'm more delicate than you might think." She laughed and led him to the sofa and settled next to him.

She took his hand and twined her fingers in his.

"I'm sorry we couldn't meet on Wednesday, but an issue arose that required my immediate attention that I'll tell you of presently."

Scott laughed to himself.

"I must tell you, madam, I was sorely disappointed. It's a circumstance to which I'm not accustomed."

She laughed and slapped his shoulder.

"You mean you're not accustomed to a woman making you wait, Captain?" Her eyes were full of mischief.

"No, madam. It's simply that I haven't previously felt so at a loss for the want of a woman's . . . your company."

The colour seemed to deepen in Mrs. Lockhart's eyes, and she put her hand on his face.

"It's the same for me, Captain. I want you to be part of my life now." She was interrupted by a knock, the door swung open, and the maid froze in embarrassment. Mrs. Lockhart laughed and slid along the sofa.

"Begging your pardon, ma'am, but cook says to tell you dinner's ready."

"Very well, Mary. We'll be along shortly."

"Yes, ma'am." The girl curtsied and fled pulling the door closed behind her.

The food was excellent as Scott had come to expect. They couldn't speak freely with the serving staff coming and going, and Scott reflected on the things he'd said to Mrs. Lockhart. The words had simply come out as if by their own volition. He was embarrassed to have uttered such an expression of . . . he struggled to put what he'd said into context. The only word that did it justice was belonging.

After dinner they retired to the parlour. The maid brought in a decanter of red wine and two glasses then retreated. Mrs. Lockhart added a log to the fire and jabbed at it with the poker. She slid the table closer to the sofa, poured wine for them and sank onto the sofa beside him.

"Now, Captain, tell me of the French campaign. Is all in a state of readiness? And I wonder if you've given further thought to the matter we've discussed over the past few weeks."

Scott took a deep breath.

"I've thought much on what you proposed. I will tell you my feelings on the matter, but first I must tell you of what has recently transpired."

"Oh?" She raised an eyebrow. "Go on, Captain."

Scott told her of his meeting with Major Coxe and his departure for Albany the following week. She was alarmed at this but held her peace until he finished. He kept nothing back, not attempting to understate the acrimonious tone of the meeting.

When he finished, Mrs. Lockhart nodded.

"This doesn't surprise me, Captain, as I've previously said Major Coxe and his colleagues will never accept you. That it has become blatant so quickly is not unexpected. "

Scott inclined his head.

"I had already decided to accept your proposal."

She started to speak, but Scott held up his hand. "Let me be clear, the conflict with Coxe had no bearing on my decision to join with you. It has merely moved things forward. Rest assured that I will embrace our partnership to the fullest extent of my commitment."

Mrs. Lockhart took Scott's hand. She looked down at her lap and her grip tightened; then she lifted her head and looked at him. He eyes were shining with delight, and she took his other hand and folded it in hers.

"Captain Scott, I have another proposal to make to you beyond what we have already discussed." Scott lifted an eyebrow, and she took a breath and went on. "It is my wish, Captain, that we marry and be man and wife."

Scott opened his mouth to speak, but she put her finger on his lips. She got to her feet, went to the fireplace and placed her left hand on her stomach.

"The reason I think we should marry, Frederick, is that I am carrying your child."

Scott came to his feet. This was the last thing he'd expected to hear. It was also the first time she'd called him by his given name.

"I thought that . . . I thought . . ." He stammered to a halt.

Mrs. Lockhart clasped her hands.

"One of the reasons my husband rejected me and was unfaithful was because I couldn't have children." A smile crossed her lips. "It seems that in the end, the fault was not mine; it was he who wasn't capable of fathering a child. I find a certain irony in that."

Scott found his voice again. "Are you certain? How can you be sure?"

"The matter that prevented me from meeting with you on Wednesday was the need to consult my physician. He has confirmed that I am recently with child, and that I am well and healthy."

Scott went to her and took her hands in his, and she went on. "It's no doubt a shock for you to hear this. I would have waited to tell you, but your imminent departure has made it imperative that I speak sooner."

Scott nodded and found himself laughing.

"You have the right of it. It's not what I had expected to hear this evening." In spite of the shock he found he was not displeased, and Mrs. Lockhart laughed with him.

"I understand that it is somewhat irregular for a woman to propose marriage. It's not done in polite society."

"It has been my experience that irregularities are of little consequence where you are concerned."

She put her hand on his arm. "I understand that it's a shock. You will need time to think on what I have said."

Scott's mind reeled, but he saw how the future could unfold, and he turned her towards him. "I don't need time to decide, Elisabeth. When I return from this campaign, we will marry."

She threw her arms around his neck and clung to him fiercely. After a moment she eased herself away from him.

"Come, we have little enough time together. Let us make the most of it."

CHAPTER THIRTY-EIGHT

WHEN JOHN AWOKE, THE LIGHT was growing in the eastern sky. When he entered the camp, Louis was wrapped in his sleeping roll, watching him from under hooded lids. There was no sign of the girl. John kicked the fire into life and warmed his hands.

"You move like a wounded bear in the forest. Do you remember nothing of what I taught you?"

"I didn't want you to put a musket ball in my backside, and I thought it better to let you know I was there."

Louis sat up stiffly. John almost helped him, but he knew Louis wouldn't thank him for it.

"Where's the girl?"

"She didn't sleep in the camp." He looked at John questioningly. "If she didn't share your bedroll, she must be in the forest."

John's eyes opened in shock. "I didn't lay hands on her."

"It's clear that you want this woman," Louis said. "I don't understand why you make a simple thing difficult? If you want this woman you should take her."

John massaged his temples. "It's not our way."

"Your people are hard to understand," Louis said. "The summers of your life pass swiftly. There's not time for such foolishness."

John took the iron pot and filled it from the creek, and as he returned, the girl came out of the forest with her sleeping roll over her shoulder. She dropped the bundle and started threading pemmican onto a stick to roast. John set the pot on the fire and dropped a handful of the leaves and pine cones into it.

John sat across the fire from her. "You didn't sleep in camp?"

She looked at him, her face impassive. "The forest is safer in hostile lands." She held his gaze for a moment, unflinching, then went back to tending the meat.

John wanted to speak about the day before, but he was at a loss for how to begin.

Instead, he turned to Louis. "How's the shoulder?"

"It's stiff."

"Let me see." He removed the bandage, soaked a piece of his shirt in the creek and washed his shoulder. The wound had closed; the skin was pale and dry and there was no sign of putrefaction. Louis wiped his fingers across the wound and sniffed them.

"It will heal."

John turned to the girl. "Do you have more herbs for the wound?"

She took a leather pouch from her bed roll and threw it to him. "Mix it with water to make a paste. Use only a little."

John mixed the paste on a piece of bark, applied it to Louis's shoulder, then bound the wound again. Louis nodded his thanks.

The girl handed John one of the skewers of meat.

"Your friend must eat. We'll need him to help with the canoes." John handed Louis a skewer of meat, and bit into his own.

When he had finished, John turned to the girl.

"How far is it to the river they call the St. Lawrence?"

"It's two, perhaps three, days to the head of the lake."

"How do we reach the big river?"

"There's a river that flows from the lake to the St. Lawrence.

John nodded. "We move as soon as it's dark?"

"The canoes are heavy, and will move slowly," Louis said. "Perhaps it's best to take one canoe and leave the furs."

"We can trade the furs for supplies for a whole year, I think."

"Perhaps it's so." John thought Louis was about to say more, but he fell silent. John got to his feet and took the pistol and the tomahawk.

"Rest while you can; I'll check the canoes are secure."

The canoes were undisturbed, but John was curious about the furs. The girl had said the furs were good quality. He was tempted to open one of the bales, but when he examined it, he didn't' think he wouldn't be able to seal it again properly, so he left it. He couldn't guess how much they would bring in trade, or if the French would even trade with them, but he understood they were the key to establishing himself in this land.

John walked downstream. The creek banks were heavily overgrown, and he was ten feet from the shore before he saw the water. John crept through the underbrush to where he could see across the lake and the shoreline in both directions. The fire was still raging on the west bank; it had burned the forest as far as he could see. The wind was driving it north, and the smoke blackened the sky for miles. John was aghast at the damage the fire had done, and he felt another pang of guilt at having caused such carnage.

John watched the lake for a long time till he was satisfied there was no danger. When he turned to leave he was startled to see the girl sitting ten feet from him. He was unnerved that she'd been able to come so close without his hearing her.

She lifted her chin to the lake. "The fire moves to the north. The Iroquois must move out of its path."

"Then they won't be waiting for us at the head of the lake."

"They won't be able to go around the fire, but they can still use their canoes. The Iroquois are strong, and they are cunning. We must be careful."

"The sooner we leave, the better I'll like it."

The girl was so still she seemed to blend into the foliage. Only her blue eyes stood out against the forest around her.

"Why did you follow me?"

"I came to see if there was danger."

"How did you get so close to me?"

She shrugged. "I was a slave of the Iroquois, and I learned their ways." She started to get to her feet.

"Wait."

She sank down again.

"Yesterday at the pool I . . ." He tried to say three things at once, but they became confused and he stumbled.

"I meant you no harm." He opened his hands. The colour rose in his face, and he fell silent.

The girl stared at him fiercely, searching his face. He returned her stare but as the moments went by his temper began to stir. He'd risked his life to rescue this girl. He hadn't harmed her, and he resented being judged like this. She looked at the water.

"The wind's changing." John looked across the lake. Great clouds of smoke were rolling towards them. When he turned back, the girl had vanished.

When John got back to the camp, the girl wasn't there, and Louis was asleep. That he didn't wake when John entered camp was an indication of how weak he was. He took the iron pot to the creek for water, and when he returned, Louis was awake. He made tea and sat while they passed the pot between them.

Later the girl stepped silently out of the forest and sat across the fire.

"Can you travel?"

"I can travel, but I can't paddle," Louis said.

She looked up at the sky. "We should leave as soon as it is dark. There's much ground to cover."

John was in the stern of the first canoe, the girl in the bow, and Louis in the middle. John had difficulty dissuading Louis from trying to paddle, but he convinced him it was better to save his strength in case they encountered the Iroquois. They turned north along the shore, towing the second canoe. It made turning more difficult, but they soon became accustomed to it.

By John's reckoning there should have been a quarter moon. The smoke from the fire obscured it. It gave them cover, but it made finding their way difficult.

John and the girl fell into a rhythm with the paddles. Soon it was almost totally dark, and the only way John could gauge the passing of time was by his growing fatigue. What seemed like hours later, the wind shifted, and the sky began to clear. He realized they'd strayed too close to the western shore, and turned northeast.

The wind held steady, and as they approached the northeast shore the quarter moon finally broke through. John's shoulders and back were aching, and his arms felt as if they were on fire. Dawn wasn't far away and he knew they should get off the lake.

He spoke quietly. "The night is almost past. We must find a place to hide the canoes."

The girl stopped paddling. "There's a river where we can hide. I think it is close."

"How can you tell where we are?"

"The far shore turns to the east. You can see the fire on the shoreline. The river is close, but I don't know how far."

"We'll follow the shoreline till we find the river or another place to camp."

John kept them heading east until he could see the outline of the forest; then he turned northwest again. They edged closer to the shore, searching for a place to hide the canoes, but the land along the lakeshore was bare, and John began to despair of finding a place to hole up for the day.

Ahead of them a point of land jutted out into the lake. They would be exposed rounding it. He turned to the girl, but she spoke first.

"I think the river is on the other side of the point. We must hurry. Daylight is coming."

"Are you sure?"

The girl nodded. "It's there."

John didn't have a better suggestion except unloading the canoes and dragging them into the forest, so he pushed on.

As they approached the end of the point the wind came up almost bringing them to a stop. John dug in hard, and Louis took up a paddle and added what effort he could. The river was a little way past the north side of the point. The trees grew down to the water on that side and John breathed a sigh of relief as they slid into the river and under the shadow of the forest.

They hid the canoes on the north bank of the river and made camp farther into the forest. As soon as he had eaten John rolled himself in his plaid and fell into an exhausted sleep. He awoke late in the afternoon to the smell of roasting meat. Louis was sitting by the fire, and the girl was packing up her sleeping roll. John checked the canoes then sat by the fire to eat as they waited for darkness.

The wind was behind them for the first part of the night, and they made good progress. The fire was still burning along the west bank of the lake. Ahead, John could see where the shore curved to the east, and he guessed they were nearing the head of the lake. The girl had said the river left the lake on the east side, and he steered in that direction.

The night clouded over, and John navigated by intuition. At one point he felt the canoe pull to starboard. He corrected it and then he realized that it must be the river pulling them, and he let it come around. The current was sluggish and gradually the light from the fire faded as they slid into the river.

There was enough light from the quarter moon for John to see. The river was three or four hundred feet across, wider than he had expected. Dawn wasn't far away, and he guided them into a creek on the eastern bank. The mouth of the creek was fifteen feet across, and the whole area was densely forested. After a hundred feet they struck a gravel bar. John and the girl dragged the canoes over the bar, but the water quickly shallowed and they tied them to the bank.

They made camp in a clearing some distance from the creek but didn't make a fire. John slept until midday. Louis was asleep, but as he got to his feet, he sat up.

"Where's the girl?"

"She sleeps in the forest. She's wary of the Iroquois and of us."

John looked at him questioningly.

"The Iroquois treat their women harshly, and she doesn't want to be a slave again." John wasn't sure what Louis was saying, but the girl walked out of the forest, and he said no more.

They sat in a circle as they ate.

"I want to scout the river while there's still light," John said.

"My wound is much improved. I will go with you."

"Good." John looked at the girl, but she shook her head.

John took the pistol and the musket and followed the creek down to the river. The river was four hundred feet across. The banks were heavily treed, but there was little undergrowth to give them cover. They stayed back from the water and went downstream for three miles but found no sign of habitation.

It was early evening when they returned, and after they broke camp John asked the girl to sit with him.

"Do you know what it's like downstream?"

"I haven't travelled this river. I heard the Iroquois say that a canoe can pass, but that's all I know."

"How long will it take to reach the St. Lawrence?"

"The Iroquois don't count numbers as we do, but I think it is takes two days, perhaps three."

"We shall find out soon enough," John said.

They made good time the first night. The river was wide, and there were no sandbars to navigate. They pushed on steadily, and at one point John realized that the river had widened, and he couldn't see the banks. The current had also diminished, and he turned west till they found the riverbank again. Dawn wasn't far away, and they hid the canoe in an inlet and waited for daylight.

The river had emptied into a lake running north to south as far as he could see. For the next two days they travelled north and entered a smaller river flowing to the northwest. Wildlife was abundant. They saw deer and moose, and John caught sight of a bear for the first time. He was astonished at how black its pelt was and how fast it moved when they disturbed it.

On the fifth night the sky was clear and the quarter moon was bright enough to see the riverbanks. The river separated into several channels, the land along the banks became flatter, and they encountered more gravel bars and backchannels. Late in the night John saw an expanse of water ahead. He knew it was the St. Lawrence River, and he stopped paddling.

"It's the great river," Louis said, "but we must still take care."

John looked at the girl. "Your instincts were true. You've brought us to the St. Lawrence."

She nodded. He could only see her shadow, but recognized tension in her.

The current carried them towards the south bank. John steered them back to midstream, and they paddled to the mouth of the river. The moon was gone, leaving them in darkness, but John could sense a huge body of water ahead of them. He turned into the north bank and called to the girl.

"We must hide the canoes until daylight." She didn't answer, but she changed her paddle to the left side and brought the bow around. The mouth of the river spread into a delta with many channels and inlets and they stumbled blindly into a side channel that had enough cover to hide them.

They spread their sleeping rolls on the riverbank. John didn't think there was any danger, but he didn't want to be far from the canoes. It was hours till daylight, but he couldn't sleep, and he lay back and looked at the sky while he waited for the dawn.

At first light they moved the canoes to a larger channel where there was better cover and set off along the bank. John led, keeping under cover of the trees and after a mile they found themselves on the banks of the St. Lawrence River.

John was astonished at the size of the river. It was a mile across. To the north it looked more like a lake than a river, and the banks on both sides were heavily treed as far as he could see. John sat down and looked at the girl.

"It's magnificent."

"I learned in school that it's one of the great rivers of the world." For a moment he sensed sadness in her, but she went on.

"We should wait till dark to travel. To the north is Trois-Rivières. It would be better if the townspeople didn't see the furs."

"You're right," John said. "We'll wait till dark."

They stayed on the riverbank through the morning, sleeping and watching the river. Even though it was a major trade route, they saw nothing moving on the water. At midday they returned to the canoes and made a fire to cook.

Later, as John walked along the bank of the channel, the seed of an idea started to grow in his mind. The channel ran at ninety degrees to the river, and narrowed and ended after a quarter of a mile. The head of the inlet was overgrown with reeds and would suit his purposes well.

John went back to camp and motioned to Louis and the girl.

"I think we should hide one of the canoes here. We don't know what will happen when we reach Quebec, and I don't think it's wise to risk the furs all at once."

Louis nodded.

"We don't know if we can trust the French."

John glanced at the girl, but she didn't react.

The girl turned to John and once again he found her unblinking gaze disconcerting.

"There are men on the river who would steal the furs. I heard my father say there are men in Quebec who will kill for the silver that the fur brings."

"We'll hide one canoe here and come back for it when we're ready. We'll count the bales so each will know what their share will be."

The girl looked at John sharply. "I want nothing from the Iroquois. I'll have no part of their fur or the silver it brings."

John was nonplussed. "I've little knowledge of the fur trade, but I believe the furs are worth a great deal. You led us to them and helped to bring them here. You should share in the reward."

"I want nothing of them. They are yours to do with as you please." She got to her feet and walked into the forest.

John and Louis dragged the lead canoe into the channel. John was amazed at Louis's ability to arrange the foliage, so it appeared natural. When they were finished, he had to look closely to see where the canoe lay hidden.

They set out as soon as it was dark, paddling with the current, and with one canoe they made good time. John guessed they had been on the river for three hours when he saw lights on the west shore, and the girl spoke over her shoulder.

"I think this is Trois-Rivières."

The river narrowed as they approached Trois-Rivières, and John kept them close to the east bank. There were lights from fires or torches along the river for a mile and on the hills behind the town. The moon hadn't risen, and it was almost completely dark as they drifted past.

John called softly to the girl. "How many people live here? Do they farm or what's their business?"

She stopped paddling and looked back. "I was small when I came here, and I don't remember it well. There's a fort built of wood and houses along the shore. I remember other buildings, but I don't know what they were used for. My father brought us here to trade fur. That is all I know, but my father said to trust no one in the fur trade except family and people you know well, so I think it's best to pass by."

They drifted past the settlement. John brought them back to the middle of the river, and they kept moving till the light began to grow in the east. The river was vast, and there were many creeks and side channels that offered cover for the canoe. John picked a channel on the east bank, and they made camp. The riverbank was heavily treed, and they'd seen no sign of life since Trois-Rivières, so they felt safe lighting a fire to cook and to dry their clothes and gear.

John slept until midday and awoke hungry and thirsty. Neither Louis nor the girl were in camp. He took his water bottle to the river and found the girl sitting on the bank.

"You were not in camp when I awoke. Did you sleep in the forest?" He knelt and filled the bottle.

"I'm accustomed to the forest. It's been my home for many years."

John sat against a tree. "How far do you think it is to Quebec?"

"Come." She led him along the channel back to the St. Lawrence. She walked with a natural grace that John found captivating. She measured each step, placing her foot as if it were part of a dance, and she seemed to float over the ground. She made almost no sound as she moved, and she disturbed the leaves no more than a breeze in the forest.

John found her perplexing. He was drawn to her beauty and her courage, but she was like a wild thing. She'd killed the Iroquois in the canoe without remorse, and he knew she would kill again if she was threatened. Yet there was sadness in her and a kind of fatalism that kept her apart from the world.

When she reached the St. Lawrence, she turned upstream towards a patch of willows close to the bank. John kept to her right, where he had a view of the river and to maintain a respectful distance. He looked across the river but he couldn't see anything moving.

"There." She pointed to the far bank. The river was almost a mile across, but even at that distance he was sure he would be able to detect movement on the water.

"I don't see anything."

"On the other bank downstream from us."

John exclaimed in surprise and looked at the girl. "A wagon."

"I think it's the Chemin du Roy, the King's Road. It runs from Quebec south to Mont-Royal."

"A road. I hadn't expected to find a road in this wilderness."

"We're two days from Quebec, perhaps three. There will be travellers on the road and more people on the river now."

John nodded. "We will travel at night until we're close to Quebec then push through the last day to reach the town."

That night they saw lights in two places on the west bank of the river, and they kept moving until almost daylight before finding a place to lie up. Apart from the lights they had seen in the night, the country was empty. The river seemed endless, and John thought he'd never become accustomed to the vastness of this land.

They hid the canoe in a creek; John estimated the river was over a mile wide now. Low hills rose up on both banks, running away into the distance. He could see movement on the north bank, along the Chemin du Roy, and they began to see signs of habitation. They came on several abandoned dwellings, and there was smoke on the horizon to the north.

They slept through the afternoon and were on the river as soon as it was dark. The sky was clear and the first quarter of the new moon rose over the horizon. It bathed the river in a yellow glow like a golden path stretching out before them, and John wondered where it would lead and what fortune it would bring.

The river began to narrow again, and John could see the outline of the hills on the banks. There were lights on both banks now, and John saw the shape of farmhouses and barns along the shore, and the smell of wood smoke was in the air.

John called to the girl. "Do you recognize this place?"

She looked back. "I don't remember this place, but I think we'll reach Quebec today."

"We will push on through, then." She nodded, but there was sadness in her eyes, and she looked away.

As the light grew, John began to see farms along both banks. Each farm consisted of a narrow strip of land running back from the river, and he judged each to be a mile in length. These farms were clustered together ten or twenty in a row. As they went downstream they became closer until they formed a solid line on each side of the river.

John called to the girl.

"I've never seen anything like these farms, narrow strips of land and so close together."

"They're called seigneuries. They were originally laid out by a seigneur who was granted the land by the French crown. The Seigneur was required to build a mill and a church in each seigneury and to rent the plots to habitant families who came from France. These farms have been here since the first people came from France many years ago."

John steered closer to the shore to get a better view.

"Why are the farms laid out in long narrow strips? It doesn't make sense."

"It's to give the seigneuries access to the river. There were no roads when the settlers first came, and they used the river to travel and transport what they grew to market. All seigneuries are like this. There are more roads now, but I don't think this will change."

John's attention came back to the river. A few miles ahead the river narrowed, and hills rose steeply on each bank. On the right the land rose almost vertically, forming an escarpment above the river. The wind began to pick up, breaking the surface of the water into whitecaps and driving a swell upstream. It was late in the afternoon when they reached the narrows. The river was half a mile across at that point, but the force of the wind coming through the narrows almost brought them to a standstill. There were houses and buildings scattered along the banks and boats plying the river in both directions now.

As they fought their way through the narrowest part of the river, John called out to encourage Louis and the girl. He kept the canoe close to the bank, trying to find shelter from the wind. As soon as they were through the narrows the wind dropped.

John let out a shout of surprise as he caught his first sight of Quebec. The land along the west bank rose to form a bluff five hundred feet above the river. There was a stone citadel on the top that dominated the river. The town spread out along the bank of the river and up the hill to the bottom of the fort. A stone wall that enclosed the town ran two miles along the shore. Warehouses and workshops were situated along the shore, and farther back were houses and taverns built against the town walls.

Stone wharves had been constructed in several places, and boats of all shapes and sizes were made fast to them. Smaller boats were drawn up on the beach and men were carrying out repairs to them and stringing fishing nets to dry in the sun. Half a dozen sailing ships lay at anchor off the town, and men were busy offloading their cargos onto barges. John had been in the wilderness for so long it felt strange to watch people going about their daily business.

John steered the canoe away from the bank to get a better view of the town and to pick a spot to land. The first thing that struck him was the smell: wood smoke, roasting meat and baking bread, rotting fish and sewers all jumbled together. As they got closer he heard men laughing and shouting in French. It was an assault to his senses after the silence of the forest.

The people working on the beach took little notice of them, and the girl motioned for John to go farther along the shore and directed them to a jetty some distance past the citadel. The jetty was built of logs driven into the riverbed and ran twenty feet out from the beach. Half a dozen men were offloading barrels from a lighter tied to the jetty, and as they approached, the girl hailed them.

"Is this the dock of the merchant Jacques Garnier?" One of the men looked down at her. He was forty years old and heavyset with workman's hands. John guessed he was the foreman.

"This is the property of Monsieur Garnier, and he is indeed a merchant in Quebec."

"I am Chantal Garnier, his niece. Would you be kind enough to inform him that I have returned to Quebec?"

The man was taken aback.

"But Monsieur Garnier's brother and family were killed by the—" He stopped, realizing what he was about to say. He barked an order to one of the workers then came to the end of the pier and knelt to look at the girl. He studied her face for a moment then turned to the boy and called.

"Run to Monsieur Garnier's house and tell him that his niece is returned from the wilderness alive. Run now, boy, and don't stop for anything." The boy glanced at the girl then took to his heels, calling out for the men to get out of his way.

The man looked at John and Louis, and nodded.

"Bring the canoe to the beach on the far side of the pier." John back-paddled and brought them to the shore downstream of the pier. The big man dragged the bow up onto the beach, and they stepped out. John left the musket in the canoe, but thrust the pistol into his belt.

The man looked at the girl with a quizzical expression on his face.

"I am Pierre de Launay. I've worked for Monsieur Garnier for many years. Before that I worked for your father. If you are indeed his daughter, you may remember me." An expression of pleasure lit the girl's face. John was astonished at how it changed her, and he realized that he'd never seen her smile. It transformed her.

"I remember you, I think, but I was very young when the Iroquois took me." Pierre de Launay's face broke into a grin, but a shadow crossed it at the mention of the Iroquois.

"It's best not to talk of such things."

Pierre was about to say more, but there was a shout and a man came hurrying along the shore towards them. John examined him closely. He was in his late forties, about the same height as John, broad-shouldered and thick through the middle. He had a square jaw, a nose that had been broken more than once, and thinning black hair and a full beard.

He stopped a few feet from the girl, studying her. Nothing about this man resembled her, but then John realized they had the same eyes.

"You are Chantal. I would know you anywhere. How can you be here? How can you be alive?" He stepped forward and pulled her into a bear hug. She did not resist, but John saw her tense. He stepped back and held her at arm's length. He started to speak, but a piercing screech stopped him.

John looked around to see a large matronly woman hurrying towards them, making heavy going of the beach. She screeched again, a plaintive sound that grated on John's nerves. Monsieur Garnier's mouth tightened, and he stepped back as she came up and enveloped the girl in a smothering embrace. John guessed this was Garnier's wife.

Monsieur Garnier turned to John and Louis, looking at them with a mix of curiosity and suspicion.

"I am Jacques Garnier." He extended his hand, and John took it.

"I am John Wallace, and this is my friend Louis Pictou." Garnier shook hands with Louis.

"How is it that you are here with Chantal?"

"We were travelling from Louis's village in Shubenacadie to Quebec when we came on a party of Iroquois. She was their hostage. We freed her, and we came here to return your niece to her home and to escape the Iroquois."

Monsieur Garnier's eyes opened in surprise.

"You killed Iroquois warriors and escaped to tell. You are both brave and fortunate, I think."

"The Iroquois are fierce fighters. We were lucky to survive."

"You will be safe here. You have done us a great service in returning my niece to us."

Madame Garnier let out a howl of despair, and all eyes turned to her.

"They were killed in front of your eyes." Her face was red, her breathing was becoming laboured, and she made to clutch the girl to her breast again, but she stepped out of her reach. She turned to her husband and gasped.

"The Iroquois butchered her father and mother in front of her. What a horror for the child." She put her hands on the girl's shoulders and burst into tears.

Monsieur Garnier's face showed his irritation at his wife's outburst, and he looked at the girl kindly.

"I'm sorry, my child. The loss of your parents is a tragedy, but you've returned to us now, and we're grateful for that." She nodded and John was shocked to see tears in her eyes.

Madame Garnier put her arm around the girl.

"Come, my dear, we'll go home now." She set off up the beach holding the girl close, but she broke free and ran back to where John stood.

"Thank you, John Wallace, for what you've done for me. You risked your life to save me, and I'm grateful to you." She directed the same unflinching gaze at him, but it didn't make him feel uneasy as it had before. There was no reservation or doubt in her eyes, but John saw sadness there.

He nodded but no words came to his lips.

She turned to Louis. "Thank you, Louis Pictou, for what you've done for me. I'm grateful to you."

John was taken aback when Louis's face broke into a smile.

"Go well in your life now," Louis said.

She nodded then looked at John. "You may call me by my given name, John Wallace, if it pleases you."

"It pleases me well enough. I wish you good fortune, Chantal."

As she turned away, Madame Garnier enfolded her in her generous embrace uttering squeaks of delight and anguish.

John was relieved that Chantal was safe. She could put the years of captivity behind her now and embrace the future in the safety of her family. But as he watched her move away, her slender form dwarfed by her matronly aunt, a sense of unease crept over him as if there was something important that he should do or say that he couldn't bring to mind.

A crowd had gathered on the beach. As the story of Chantal's rescue spread, they favoured John and Louis with looks of admiration and nods of approval. John thought this boded well for them. He'd been apprehensive about the reception they would receive in Quebec. Now it seemed they were considered heroes.

Monsieur Garnier watched his wife and Chantal move away along the beach then turned to John. "What plans do you have now, young man?"

"We had no plans beyond reaching Quebec and returning Chantal to her family. We had hoped there would be opportunities for us in the fur trade, but we know little of the business." Monsieur Garnier was looking at the canoe and John caught the glint of avarice in his eyes. It was only there for a second, but it put him on his guard.

Monsieur Garnier lifted his chin. "You have many bales of pelts."

John turned and looked at the canoe to give himself time to think. "We took them from the Iroquois when we freed Chantal. I believe they're valuable, but I understand that it's not easy to trade fur in Quebec."

"That is so, young man. Outsiders are looked on with suspicion, particularly the British, but you have friends here now. I am one of the largest merchants in the town. I will trade with you for the fur if you wish, and I'll treat you fairly."

John looked at Monsieur Garnier and nodded. "You have my thanks, monsieur. We will trade with you, but I must tell you that I am Scottish and love the English no more than you do."

A bark of laughter burst from Garnier, and he slapped John on the back. "Well said, young man. I'll remember not to make that mistake again."

Garnier walked the length of the canoe and back. "I count thirty-six bales. Do you know where they were harvested?"

"I believe they are from a place called Hudson's Bay. That's far to the north, I am told." John saw surprise in Garnier's eyes, but he hid it quickly.

"They will be winter furs, then. That is very good, very good indeed." John felt a twinge of apprehension, but he tried not to let it show.

"I'll have my men bring the furs to my warehouse for safe keeping. You will be my guests tonight. With the addition of Chantal, my house will be overflowing, but we'll find a place for you even if it's in the kitchen. Tomorrow you can make your own arrangements."

"That'll suit us well enough. It'll will be strange to have a roof over my head again after so many nights in the forest."

Garnier directed them to his warehouse at the north end of the town, and as they paddled the canoe downstream, Monsieur Garnier and his men kept pace with them on the shore.

John spoke quietly. "What do you think of Monsieur Garnier's offer?"

"I think that it would not be wise to trust this man." Louis looked over his shoulder. "While you spoke with the girl he had eyes only for the furs."

"I think you're right, but we must accept his hospitality for now."

Louis didn't reply and Garnier hailed them from the beach.

The warehouse was close to the end of the town at the base of the hill. It was a long narrow stone building with two floors. There was a set of wooden doors in the centre of the building with a smaller access door next to it, and John was surprised at the variety of trading goods inside. The ground floor was stacked to the ceiling with barrels and wooden cases. John had seen similar barrels on the Orion, and he knew they would contain everything from iron nails to fat or grease. Garnier's men carried the fur bales upstairs. Garnier followed and led John and Louis to a desk by the window.

Garnier took a seat and motioned John and Louis to chairs on the other side. John pulled a chair around and Louis stood by the window, watching the men bring the last of the bales up from the canoe. The second floor was only half-full, but the goods were more expensive. John saw rolls of sail cloth stacked along one wall and smaller barrels that he guessed contained wine or brandy. The far end of the building was dedicated to fur. There was a long table set against the wall and shelves with materials for binding bales of fur. The rest seemed to be set aside for storage, but there weren't many bales of fur in the warehouse.

Monsieur Garnier looked at Louis, then John.

"You have thirty-six bales in total. What fur do they contain?"

"There's been no time to open them, monsieur. Chantal told us they contain beaver and lynx."

"How did the Iroquois acquire these furs? Did they trade for them or take them by force?"

"In truth I don't know, monsieur. We killed the Iroquois who were transporting them." Garnier blinked in surprise and looked at John curiously then pushed back his chair and got to his feet.

"Shall we examine these mystery goods, then?" He called to Pierre de Launay to bring one of the bales to the table at the far end of the warehouse. He slid his knife under the binding and looked at John. John nodded and the foreman cut the binding, removed each pelt, and laid it out on the table. Garnier examined the fur carefully, holding it up to the light and rubbing it between his palms.

"This is excellent quality beaver, good size, a mature animal," he said, half to himself. It took the foreman some time to unpack all the furs and lay them out on the table, and John counted fifty-four.

Garnier examined each fur and organized them into piles by size and quality. He worked methodically, rechecking several furs and moving them to different piles. John watched, carefully noting everything he did, but his knowledge was too limited to understand how he was assessing the quality and the value.

Finally Garnier seemed satisfied.

"These are good quality furs. I believe you are correct that they came from the north. The animals grow thicker fur to protect themselves from the cold. This quality of fur is only found in the extreme cold, likely in Hudson's Bay."

John resisted the urge to ask what the furs were worth. His father had taught him never to rush into making a bargain. His father was a cattle dealer, but the principles would apply as well to the fur trade, and he remained silent. Monsieur Garnier frowned and put his hand on John's shoulder.

"As I said earlier it would be difficult for an outsider to trade fur in Quebec. We owe you a great deal, and I am willing to make a bargain with you."

"I'm grateful, monsieur." John ran his fingers through one of the furs. "As you have said these are fine pelts, so a bargain will be to our mutual benefit."

Impatience flashed in Garnier's eyes.

"I'll make you an offer for all the fur you have. I have good quality muskets, powder and shot, lead to make musket balls, knives and all the tools that you'll need to survive in this country." John inclined his head.

"That's most kind, monsieur, but I haven't given much thought to the future. In all honesty I don't know if we'll need all of the items you have mentioned. Perhaps it would be better to consider a combination of trade goods and silver."

Garnier frowned.

"Silver doesn't normally change hands in this type of transaction. I must remind you, my young friend, that you're new to Quebec and are not familiar with how these affairs are conducted. It would be best to be guided by someone who has your best interests at heart."

"You are kind, monsieur, but it's been a long day. Perhaps we should rest now and conclude our dealings in the morning when we're both rested."

Garnier was tight-lipped. "Very well, we'll find a place for you to sleep."

Garnier left the foreman to secure the warehouse and led John and Louis along the road to the town. Garnier pointed out the citadel, several churches, the town hall, and other locations that he thought were important. John felt uncomfortable walking openly after so many months in the forest, but he was also delighted to see this bustling town with its sounds and smells.

Inside the town wall the houses were built of stone and stood closer together. The main street was cobbled and wide enough for two coaches to pass. It was lined with houses, bakeries, and other establishments on both sides. Garnier turned right at the third street. It was narrower but also cobbled, and John wondered if all the streets in the town were so well-made.

Monsieur Garnier's residence was actually a small compound. The house was an elegant stone building of three floors, and the main door was accessed by a short flight of steps. The window glass was expensive, and the doors and window frames had been recently painted. The house faced south and John guessed the upper floors had a view of the river.

The street ended at the town wall, and a stone wall ran from the house to the wall. Monsieur Garnier let them in through a door in the wall and locked it behind him. John found himself in a square courtyard formed by the house on the left and two flanking walls running to the town wall on the right.

Monsieur Garnier led them across the courtyard to a stone building. The main door was in the centre of the building, and there were glassed windows on either side set high above the ground. Garnier unlocked the door, and they stepped inside and John saw it was a small storehouse where Garnier kept his more expensive trade items. The walls were lined with shelves stacked with bolts of cloth, cooking utensils, crockery and one shelf was dedicated to navigation instruments.

Garnier turned to John.

"Please wait here. There's something I must attend to." And he hurried off. John looked at Louis and raised an eyebrow, and Louis shrugged. The room was a treasure house of trade items. John couldn't estimate its value, but clearly Garnier was a wealthy man.

John caught the glint of metal on the wall nearest the house: a row of muskets stood in a rack containing fifty weapons or more. Shelves at the end held powder flasks, boxes of flints, musket balls and tools to maintain and repair the weapons.

In the centre of the wall four muskets were mounted horizontally on pegs. John had never seen anything like them. The barrel was half as long again as the Brown Bess musket and the bore looked half the diameter. They were beautifully made. The stocks were made from a single piece of hardwood that enclosed the barrel and flowed smoothly into the stock and cheek piece, and the lock and trigger mechanism were finely finished in brass and steel.

John was so absorbed in examining the weapon that he didn't realize that Garnier was standing behind him.

"This is the Kentucky Long Rifle," he said. "It is one of the finest weapons ever made." He took the rifle on the lowest pegs down and pointed out the details to John.

"The barrel is forty inches in length and fires a forty-eight calibre ball." He went to the window, squinted down the barrel then held it so John could see. "See the spiral grooves inside the barrel. They impart spin to the ball as it flies, making it incredibly accurate. This is called rifling."

Garnier handed the rifle to John, who he brought it to his shoulder and sighted along the barrel. He inspected it from every angle, turning it over and examining the lock and trigger mechanisms and the hinged plate on the stock that covered a compartment to store ball patches and flints. This was the finest weapon he'd ever handled, and he knew he had to have it.

He looked up to find Monsieur Garnier looking pleased with himself.

"It's a fine rifle, is it not? There are not ten like it in Quebec."

"I've never seen anything like it. What range does it have?"

"A good marksman can strike a circle." He held his hands twelve inches apart. "At three hundred yards four times out of five. The same has been claimed at five hundred yards, but I haven't seen that myself." John ran his hands lovingly along the stock, testing the weight and balance.

Monsieur Garnier took down a second rifle and handed it to Louis.

"These rifles were made in Massachusetts by Swiss and German gunsmiths who brought their craft from their homelands. They're expensive and difficult to obtain. I had to pay a great deal to secure the four you see here." John realized he'd been foolish to show enthusiasm for the weapons, but there was nothing he could do about it now.

John handed the rifle back, and Garnier returned it to its place on the wall.

"We can discuss a price for one of these rifles tomorrow when we complete our negations," Garnier said. He'd lost his sense of urgency and now seemed content to wait until the next day to complete their transaction.

"Come, you must eat, and we'll find you a place to sleep."

Garnier led them directly into the kitchen. The smell of baking bread and cooking meat filled John's nostrils, and he remembered he hadn't eaten since early that morning. Three women were busy in the kitchen: a dark haired woman of forty was making pastry at a table, and two girls were tending to pots and pans suspended over the fireplace and the hob beside it.

Garnier spoke to the dark-haired woman.

"Madame Crevet, do you have a moment, please?"

"Yes, Monsieur Garnier." She wiped her hands on her apron as she crossed the kitchen.

"You will have heard that my niece Chantal has returned alive from the wilderness." She looked at John and Louis curiously. "We have these two young men to thank for rescuing her from the Iroquois and returning her to us." Her eyes went wide.

"I've heard nothing of any Iroquois, but we shall hear all in due course, no doubt."

Garnier introduced John and Louis to Madame Crevet, and she nodded to each in turn.

"They will be staying with us tonight. Can you provide them with supper and find them a place to sleep?"

"Supper you shall have." She addressed herself to John and Louis. "A place to sleep is more difficult. The house is full to bursting."

"We've slept under the stars for many months," John said, "and our needs are simple."

"You have an accent. Are you English?" A frown creased Garnier's face.

"Our young friend is from Scotland," Garnier said. "Be warned he may take it ill, if you name him British." Madame Crevet laughed.

"I shall see their needs are seen to, monsieur."

Garnier looked at John.

"I will leave you in Madame Crevet's capable hands. I have much to do this evening, and I will be engaged until after midday tomorrow. I suggest you take the opportunity to explore the town in the forenoon. Let us agree to meet here shortly after midday."

"That will suit us well enough." Garnier started to walk away then looked back.

"Word of Chantal's rescue will go through the town like wildfire and will come to the attention of the commander at the citadel." He pointed up. "It may be best to report to the commandant on Chantal's rescue."

"We will surely do so, monsieur."

Garnier nodded and disappeared up the stairs.

Madame Crevet motioned for John and Louis to follow her. "Come, let me show you where you can sleep." She led them to a door under the stairs that opened into a laundry room with wooden wash basins and a large bathing tub along the wall. She went to the far end and opened a door to a storage room with a window that looked out onto the courtyard.

"This is the best I can offer you." The room was filled with wine barrels and beer kegs, boxes of tea and spices.

John nodded.

"It'll do very well, madame. We're accustomed to rougher accommodations than this." Madame Crevet smiled.

"We're grateful to you and your companion for bringing Chantal back to us. I was here when her father owned the house, and I knew her as a child."

"Does she remember you?"

"I haven't seen her yet, but I hope she remembers me. She was a sweet child, strong-willed and clever."

John waited for her to go on, but she was lost in thought.

"What were her parents like?"

"They were brave, kind people. We all loved them. I was distraught when they were lost." Her eyes were wet, and she wiped them with her sleeve.

"Chantal's father built this house. He started the trading company from nothing, he was a man of tremendous energy and a respected merchant in Quebec. His brother, Monsieur Jacques, inherited the house and the business when he was killed." She frowned and averted her eyes.

John thought that there was more to tell than Madame Crevet had said.

"We're grateful for your hospitality, madame." She snapped out of her reverie and smiled.

"It's not much. Come to the kitchen presently. We shall give you supper, and perhaps we can talk more. I would like to hear how you came to rescue our little Chantal from the savages."

"We shall come presently, madame."

John and Louis spread their sleeping rolls on the floor, and John slid his pistol and tomahawk into his hunting bag. He blew the power out of the musket pan, set it against the wall and sat down on one of the crates. Louis sat opposite him.

"Tomorrow we must make a bargain for the furs."

428

"I know little of such things," Louis said. "I trust you to make the bargain."

"I'll do my best."

Louis was silent for a moment.

"I don't trust the man Garnier. He'll cheat us if he can."

"I don't trust him either, but we're guests in his house and strangers to Quebec. It would be wise not to offend him."

Louis nodded.

"It's good we brought only one canoe."

"I want nothing of his trade goods. I think we should bargain for two of the long rifles and silver." Louis nodded, and John got to his feet.

"Let's see what the cook has for us."

Madame Crevet sat them at the kitchen table and gave them a meal of chicken, pork, potatoes, and freshly baked bread with creamy butter and surprisingly good red wine. She kept bringing food until John held up his hands.

"I can eat no more, or I will burst, but I must tell you that was the best meal I've had in as long as I can remember." Madame Crevet smiled. "Now I think we must sleep."

"I shall expect to see you early in the morning for breakfast."

CHAPTER THIRTY-NINE

THE NEXT MORNING MADAME CREVET gave them a breakfast of eggs and fried bread washed down with coffee from an island in the Caribbean Sea that John had never heard of. When they had eaten their fill John asked Madame Crevet for the name of the commandant at the citadel.

"His name is Colonel Philippe Amyot, but he's at Mont-Royal. There have been clashes with the British in the last year, and they make plans."

"Perhaps we shouldn't waste our time, then."

Madame Crevet spoke quietly.

"The colonel is an arrogant man and wouldn't see you anyway. You should seek out Captain François Aubert. He's in charge of the citadel guard, and you will find him grateful for any information about the British or the Iroquois. Also, the town is alive with talk of how you rescued Chantal; it would do no harm to have the captain as a friend." She winked as she got up from the table.

John and Louis made their way up to the citadel and enquired at the main gate for Captain Aubert. The sergeant of the guard looked at them skeptically and demanded to know their business. When John told him the purpose of their visit, his attitude changed immediately, and he invited them into the guardhouse while he sent a trooper off to inform the captain.

A few minutes later the trooper came hurrying back, and led them inside. The citadel was massively constructed of stone blocks. Inside, the fortress was laid out in the same star formation he'd seen in Scotland but on a colossal scale. John couldn't imagine how the walls could be breached or how such a fort could be subdued.

The centre of the fort consisted of a parade ground surrounded by stone buildings on three sides. The trooper led them to a long building on the south side of the parade ground, and up to the second floor landing. He knocked on a door and held it open for them. They stepped into a square room with a window looking out to the river, and a fireplace in the wall beside the door. There was a heavy table and four chairs beside the fire and a bookshelf against the other wall.

Captain Aubert stepped forward to greet them. He was forty years of age, half a head shorter than John and twice as broad across the chest. He looked like the kind of soldier who was accustomed to life in the field. He had short dark hair, a grizzled beard, and deep laughter lines on his face.

"Welcome my friends." He shook hands with John and Louis and invited them to sit at the table.

Captain Aubert motioned to a man standing by the window.

"Come, François, and meet these young men." François was in his early thirties tall and strongly made. He had a long face with sharp featured and a wide mouth. He was clean shaven and wore his dark hair pulled back behind his head. John was struck by the oddest sensation that he'd met this man before. It couldn't be true, but there was something familiar about his eyes.

John shook hands with him.

"I am François de La Tour. I'm very pleased to meet you." He shook hands with Louis and took a chair by the fire. Captain Aubert dragged a chair around and sat opposite John.

"Tell me what I can do for you, my young friends, but first I would like to hear what you can tell us about the activities of the British and the Iroquois. I understand you have recently had dealings with them."

John related the events of the last few months starting with the massacre at Shubenacadie, their pursuit by British and subsequent escape. Captain Aubert interrupted to ask for more details on British weapons and manpower. When he described the fight with the Iroquois and Chantal's rescue, he sat quiet watching John. Then he sat back and shook his head.

"It is not often you hear such a story, particularly from ones so young."

The captain went to the door and shouted for his orderly to bring mulled wine.

"You're from Scotland. Your French is good, but I hear it in your accent. How is it that you find yourself here?" John told them a version of the raid in Glen Coe, his flight across the Highlands, and subsequent capture. When he described his uncle's death, he stopped as tears of anger and grief welled up in him.

John described the voyage on the Orion, his imprisonment below decks, and the damage done to the ship in the storm. He told them that the ship had put into Louisburg for repairs and how he was taken ashore to the prison. Then all of a sudden he realized what it was about François that was so familiar, and he looked at him.

"Are you Justinien de La Tour's brother?" François went very still and the blood drained from his face.

"What do you know of my brother?"

"I met him in the prison at Louisburg." François grasped John by the shoulders.

"When did you see him? Is he well? What's happened to him?"

John resisted the urge to break free, but Louis was watching François warily. John shook his head then looked at François.

"I saw him less than a year ago at the prison in Louisburg. He was well and in good spirits." François took a breath and released his hold on John.

"I'm sorry, but I've had no word of my brother for almost two years, and after the British took Louisburg there were stories of killings and worse."

"When I last saw him he'd been told he and the other French prisoner were to be sent to France. A ship had come into port during the last week we were in the prison, and I think they would have put him onboard." François face broke into a smile.

"That is the best news I have heard in a long time. I'm in your debt."

Captain Aubert prompted John.

"Tell us what you know of Louisburg, I would also like hear how you escaped." John told them how they had escaped from the prison and travelled south to Louis's village. Captain Aubert and François listened without interrupting. When he'd finished, Captain Aubert looked at Louis and John incredulously.

"You tunnelled out through the latrine? Then you travelled the length of the country in winter just the two of you? I've never heard the like."

They were interrupted by a knock at the door and the orderly entered with a jug of wine and four glasses. Captain Aubert filled a glass for each of them.

"What can we do for you, my young friends?"

John shrugged his shoulders.

"We seek nothing, Captain. Monsieur Garnier told us that you would want to know what we could tell of the British and the Iroquois."

"We're grateful for any information we can gather. The British have made three incursions into our territory in the last year. We don't know their purpose, but after Louisburg we must be prepared for all eventualities."

François looked at Louis, then John.

"What are your plans now?"

"We've agreed to trade the furs we took from the Iroquois with Monsieur Garnier. We thought that if the trade goes well we might seek more fur to trade." A frown crossed François's face, and he looked at Captain Aubert.

"How much fur did you take from the Iroquois?"

"We brought thirty-six bales to Quebec."

"Thirty-six bales is a no small amount. If it's good quality it would be worth a great deal."

John got the sense that François and Captain Aubert were uncomfortable discussing Monsieur Garnier.

"We know little of the value of fur. We would like to trade the fur for two Kentucky Long Rifles that Monsieur Garnier has in his possession and the remainder in silver."

"It's not my place to advise you, but I doubt that Monsieur Garnier will trade for silver. He will want to bargain for trade goods."

"That's the sense I have, but we're not known in Quebec, and it may be difficult to find someone willing to trade with us."

Captain Aubert broke in.

"It wouldn't be right to advise you against trading with Monsieur Garnier. That would be a grave offense, but Monsieur Garnier has a reputation in Quebec . . . let me simply advise you to look to your own interests."

"I'm wary as it is, but I don't think it would be wise to offend someone like Monsieur Garnier, so we must trade with him this time whatever the outcome."

Captain Aubert nodded.

"You must know that François is a merchant and also trades in fur."

"Of course. Justinien told me that you were partners." François inclined his head.

"My enterprise is modest in comparison to Monsieur Garnier's, but should you wish to pursue future endeavours in the fur trade I would be pleased to assist you if I can."

Captain Aubert got to his feet.

"I'm afraid there are some things that I must attend to." He shook hands with John and Louis. "It's been a pleasure to meet you both. I'm sure that we shall meet again, so until then, farewell."

"Thank you, Captain. The day is wearing on, and we must meet Monsieur Garnier, so we shall take our leave."

François fell in with them and as they passed through the main gate he shook hands with them both.

"My establishment is outside of the wall at the north end of the town. Anyone will direct you. I would be pleased if you would visit with me when you have the opportunity. I'd like to hear more of the time you spent with my brother."

"Thank you. We'll make sure to do so in the coming days." They parted outside the gate but François turned around.

"Wait." He stood close to John and spoke quietly. "If I were to trade for good quality beaver fur, I will calculate it in British coin to make it simpler for you. I would expect to pay two to three shillings for each pelt. I would sell it in France for the equivalent of five shillings per pelt. You can multiply it by however many pelts you have. Garnier may drive a harder bargain, but at least you will have an idea of where to begin."

John grinned from ear to ear. "Thank you, François."

When they arrived back at the house, Monsieur Garnier hadn't returned and Madame Crevet gave them bread and cheese and sat with them as they ate.

"You saw Captain Aubert. He is well?"

"Yes, we met Captain Aubert, and he is well. He was interested in what we could tell about the British and was very helpful." John wondered if Madame Crevet's interest in the captain was more than casual.

"What will you and your friend do now?"

"We'll trade our furs to Monsieur Garnier. Beyond that we've made no plans. Since we freed Chantal we have thought only of returning her to Quebec."

Madame Crevet smiled.

"I saw Chantal this morning. She remembers me from when she was a child." She kept smiling, but she wiped a tear from her face with her apron.

"How is she? Can we speak with her?"

A frown crossed her face, and she shook her head.

"I don't think that Madame Garnier will let her out of her sight, but you'll see her again in due course." John thought she wanted to say more, but they were interrupted when Monsieur Garnier entered the kitchen.

Garnier led them to the warehouse. He was in bad humour and spoke abruptly.

"I must attend to some things. It'll take a few minutes. You may examine the rifles again if you wish." He didn't wait for a reply and went to the far end of the building.

John took the four long rifles down and examined each one. He looked for cracks in the stock and worked the pan and trigger mechanisms. He held each up to the light, so he could see the grooves inside the barrel. It was a marvellous invention and he was curious to see how accurate they would be. He found a crack in the stock of one rifle but other than that there was nothing to choose between them.

John looked at Garnier, head down at his desk.

"What do you think?"

Louis kept his eyes on the rifle.

"I think the Frenchman will cheat us if he can, but I would trade all of the fur we have for one of these weapons" He shrugged his shoulders. "We took the fur from the Iroquois. It's like a gift."

"I feel the same, but we'll make the best bargain we can."

Garnier called out and motioned for them to join him, and they returned the rifles to their pegs and took the chairs at the desk.

"Let us conclude our business, shall we?"

"May I first ask how Chantal is?" A look of surprise flashed across Monsieur Garnier's face, but he recovered quickly.

"She is well. My wife is seeing to her needs." He hesitated. "When a white girl has been held captive by the savages, it's difficult for her to be accepted back into society."

"I don't understand." Garnier's eyes strayed to Louis again, and he shrugged.

"To be blunt, no man will have her after she has been the slave of the savages, Iroquois or other."

John felt the colour rise in his face.

"You're her uncle. How can you speak of her in such a way?"

Garnier was taken aback and his tone hardened.

"You're a stranger here, but I don't think this would be very different in a British town."

"It's as well that I'm not British, then." Garnier's face went blank.

"You should speak of this when you know Quebec better." It was obvious to John that Garnier cared little for his niece and that further talk wouldn't change that.

John composed himself. "Perhaps we should conclude our dealings."

Garnier's face betrayed the flicker of a smile.

"Very good. Here's what I propose. You've shown interest in the Kentucky Long Rifles. I suggest that we make a straight trade. Your furs for two of the rifles. I wouldn't normally make an offer for weapons of such quality, but I am indebted to you for the return of my niece."

John stared at Garnier.

"You're correct, monsieur. My friend and I are interested in the rifles. However, I believe your estimate of their value is higher than I would have thought." Garnier frowned, but John pressed on. "I believe you would pay two to three shillings in British coin for good quality beaver pelts. I don't know what the equivalent is in French livres."

Garnier interrupted John angrily.

"What do you know of the value of beaver pelts? What you're suggesting is preposterous." John held up his hand to forestall him.

"It's not difficult to find the value of any type of pelt in Quebec, monsieur."

"Remember you are outsiders here," Garnier barked. "I've made you a fair offer for your merchandise. I assure you that you won't find another merchant willing to trade with you in this town."

John sat forward. He'd calculated the value of the furs in his head as they had walked down from the citadel. He knew that Garnier would get the better of the deal, but thirty-six bales of fur for two long rifles was daylight robbery.

"My proposal is this, Monsieur Garnier: we'll take two of the long rifles. I want to test fire all four and select the ones that I like best. We will trade half of the thirty-six bales for the rifles, the rest to be paid in silver at a value of two shillings per pelt."

Garnier blinked. His eyes glazed over for a second then he shot back.

"Three-quarters of the bales, the rest in silver."

John came back immediately. "Two-thirds of the bales and the rest in silver at the price per pelt I have stipulated."

Garnier drew a long breath. "Four-fifths or nothing."

John got to his feet.

"Very well, monsieur. We shall remove the pelts and seek other opportunities to trade them." John was taking a risk not only of leaving them with no option to trade their fur but also of making an enemy of this man.

"Stop!" Garnier looked as if he would strangle John.

"Done."

John came back to the table and extended his hand. Garnier looked at him then shook his hand.

"My foreman, Pierre de Launay, will show you where to test fire the rifles. I suggest you do so immediately." John nodded. "I'll have the silver ready for you when you return." Garnier left the building without speaking further.

John sat down and looked at Louis.

"We shall have the rifles and silver also."

"I made the best bargain I could."

"I don't trust the Frenchman."

"You're right. I don't think we should stay in his house any longer."

John got to his feet.

"Let's take a look at the rifles again." John examined each weapon minutely but apart from the cracked stock he could find no flaws. They were the product of superb workmanship, and he looked forward to firing them.

John had completed inspecting the fourth rifle when Pierre de Launay entered the storehouse. He smiled at John and Louis.

"What did you do to make Monsieur Garnier so angry?" He was grinning from ear to ear as he offered them his hand.

"We traded for our fur. In truth, Monsieur Garnier had the better of the trade."

"That may be the case, but he has a long face and a pinched mouth like he has the clap."

Pierre was enjoying himself so much he had to wipe the tears from his eyes. Finally he brought his hilarity under control.

"Monsieur Garnier tells me I am to show you where to test fire these rifles. I have a place in mind that will suit the purpose."

"Do you have powder and shot for the rifles?"

Pierre went to the shelves at the back of the storeroom.

"Take this." He handed John two powder flasks, two bags of lead balls, and a beautifully made wooden box. John put it on the table and undid the latches. The box contained two molds for casting balls, a small iron pot to melt the lead, and a set of tools to maintain and repair the rifles. Each tool was wrapped in an oilcloth and fitted into its own place in the box.

The craftsmanship was excellent, and John felt better about the trade. He put the box in his hunting bag and handed one of the rifles to Louis.

"Wait." Pierre handed John a rifle case made of fine dark leather and another to Louis.

"I don't know if Monsieur Garnier intended these as part of the trade, but they belong with the rifles." John slid the rifle into the case and slung it over his shoulder.

John carried one rifle slung over his shoulder and a second under his arm. Louis and Pierre took one each, and Pierre led them south along the river. They walked for half an hour then turned east to a clearing on the bank of a creek.

Pierre had brought the lid of a small keg to use as a target. He measured out two hundred paces and stood the lid against a stone. They used a fallen tree as a gun rest. John put his hunting bag on the trunk and adjusted the height until he could sit on the ground with the rifle resting level.

John checked the flint and pan on the first rifle and carefully measured the load. He wanted to be sure that he repeated the same steps with each rifle.

"The target is two hundred paces," Pierre said. "Can you hit it at that distance?"

"I don't know. Garnier told me the rifles are accurate to over three hundred paces." Pierre lifted an eyebrow.

"They're fine weapons, but I've never seen anything shoot that far."

John inspected the ball to make sure it was smooth and round before he wrapped it in the linen patch. It was a tight fit, and he had to push hard on the ramrod to seat it.

"I'll fire five times with the first rifle; then you fire five times and we compare. We should try all four rifles then move the target back and do the same again."

"Perhaps we should have fired the rifles before we agreed to the trade?"

John laughed. "It's too late now. Let's see what kind of bargain we have made."

John selected the musket with the cracked stock. He sat on the ground and settled the barrel on his hunting bag and pulled the stock into his shoulder. He placed the sights on the top of the target and squeezed the trigger. There was a sharp crack as the rifle discharged. The stock drove back into his shoulder, but it was nothing compared with the bone-jarring impact of the Brown Bess.

John leapt to his feet and ran to the target. He was astonished to see that he'd missed completely. Louis and Pierre were behind him.

"I don't understand how I could miss entirely." Pierre shook his head. John ran back to the firing position and reloaded.

"Aim low on the target. Don't fire this weapon as if it were a British musket," Pierre said.

John set the sights on the middle of the target, took a slow breath and squeezed the trigger. The bark of the rifle crashed across the clearing and he was on his feet before the smoke had cleared. The barrel top had been knocked flat so he knew he'd struck it. He picked it up and was delighted to see that the ball had struck three inches above centre.

"That's better. The ball doesn't drop as fast as a British musket. Aim lower," Pierre said.

While John reloaded, Pierre and Louis carried several large stones from the creek and built a better base for the target. John's third shot struck close to the second, and by the time he'd fired five shots he was feeling confident. Louis fired his five shots one after another. Each struck the target but closer to the top edge than John's.

They test-fired the other three rifles. There were small differences between them, but each one hit the target. They moved the target back to three hundred paces and fired again, and John was able to hit the target with

440

the first three rifles and missed with the last one. Louis hit the target with the first two, but missed two shots on the third and fourth rifles. John was impressed that they could hit the target at all at that distance.

The barrel top was riddled with holes and of no further use. Pierre counted out four hundred paces to a birch tree on the edge of the clearing and cut a circle of bark out of the tree five feet above the ground.

"That's about the size of a man's head. See if you can hit it."

John settled the first rifle on the hunting bag and took his time to set the shot up. He missed the first two and struck the target low with the third. The fourth and fifth shots struck the upper edge of the target, and as he got to his feet Pierre was grinning.

"I wouldn't have believed it possible if I hadn't seen it with my own eyes."

"I hardly believe it myself." He handed the rifle to Louis. Louis fired five times. Each shot struck above or below the target and one missed. They fired the other rifles, and by the time he got to the third rifle Louis was hitting the target consistently.

It took two hours to test-fire all the rifles. John was elated. He'd never seen a weapon that could hit a target at that range. All four rifles shot well, and John found himself leaning towards the rifle with the cracked stock. He didn't like the idea that it had a flaw, but it struck the target consistently at four hundred paces, and that was more important than a minor crack.

When they had finished they walked over to examine the tree.

"You shoot well."

"I learned to shoot hunting deer in the mountains of Scotland. The landscape is open, so the shot is always long."

"A year with this rifle, and there won't be many who can match you."

John and Louis discussed which rifles to keep and asked Pierre's advice. John wanted the rifle with the cracked stock, and Louis was happy to take one of the others. He fired all three again at two hundred paces, and then three hundred, and decided that the third rifle shot best at two hundred paces. He said that he wouldn't often need to fire farther and took it for his own.

As they walked back to the town John asked Pierre how they'd come into Monsieur Garnier's possession. Pierre told him that Garnier had brought them back from Mont-Royal the previous year. He said that a number of people had expressed interest in purchasing one, but no one was prepared to pay Garnier's price. John had some misgivings about the bargain he'd made, but the trade was agreed to, and he dismissed them from his mind.

Pierre was quiet for a while.

"I must tell you I'm grateful to you and your friend for returning Chantal to the household." He clearly had more to say and John waited.

"I worked for her father, Monsieur Charles. He was a good merchant and a fair man to work for. I was sorry, as many were, when he and Madame Garnier were lost."

John nodded. "How long did you work for Monsieur Charles?"

"More than ten years. I accompanied him on his first journey into the wild." Pierre was quiet, gathering his thoughts. "You must be cautious when you deal with Monsieur Garnier." He looked at John, and his eyes were troubled. "Perhaps I shouldn't speak so plain, but you brought Chantal back to us. I was loyal to her father and owe the same to her."

They walked in silence for some minutes and then John spoke. "I believe that Monsieur Garnier has the better of the bargain we have made, but he seems displeased."

"What you say is true. The fur you brought is good quality. We've not seen such quality yet this season. Monsieur Garnier has the better end of the bargain, but I suspect he had to concede more than he wanted. Keep your wits about you. He's not a man to have as an enemy."

"I'm indebted to you for your counsel, Pierre, and I'll heed it well."

They returned to Garnier's house and replaced two of the rifles in the warehouse. Madam Crevet asked them to wait in the kitchen and a few minutes later Garnier came down the stairs.

He led them to the warehouse and asked Pierre to accompany them to witness the transaction. Garnier went to his desk and took out a sheet of paper and handed it to John.

"I've drawn up a letter that lays out the terms of the trade: thirty-six bales of beaver fur are traded for two Kentucky Long Rifles and 900 shillings in silver paid in coin dated today." John read the letter. His French had improved in the last weeks, but Garnier's handwriting was difficult to make out, and he had to ask for clarification in two places. Garnier tapped his fingers impatiently as John read.

Finally John finished and looked up.

"It is as we agreed, monsieur. May I see the second copy?"

The colour rose in Garnier's face.

"What do you mean? There is no second copy."

"Then am I to presume this is my copy?"

"Why the devil would I make two copies of the agreement?" Garnier was having difficulty holding his temper, but John kept his expression blank.

"Monsieur, my father is one of the largest cattle dealers in Scotland. He taught me from an early age that both parties to a transaction must have copies of the agreement."

A look of surprise crossed Garnier's face. He eyed John suspiciously and changed tack.

"Very well, then. I shall prepare one and you can return for it in a day or two."

"There's no need. We have paper and pen here, I see. I shall prepare it now."

Garnier pursed his lips. "Very well, but don't be long about it." He slid a sheet of paper, quill and ink pot across to John.

John copied the document word for word and took his time to make sure that the language was correct. Finally he sanded the ink, waved it in the air to dry and slid it across the table.

Garnier exploded in anger.

"It's in English."

"Yes, monsieur. Your copy is in French, mine in English. That's fair, I think. I trust your English is better than my French." Garnier stared at him angrily, but John kept his face impassive. Finally Garnier jabbed the pen into the ink pot and dashed off a signature on both copies and threw them across the table. John signed and slid the French copy across to Monsieur Garnier.

Garnier looked at Pierre.

"They have picked two rifles?"

"Yes, monsieur. The other two are back on the wall." Garnier threw a leather pouch on the desk.

"Silver as agreed. You may count it." John opened the pouch and poured the silver pieces out onto the desk and counted them, but he had no way to know the exchange rate between livres and shillings. Garnier watched him closely.

"It's all there, monsieur." John stood and extended his hand. "A fair trade, monsieur." Garnier hesitated then shook John's hand, but his face wore a scowl.

"Pierre will show you out." He turned and walked out of the warehouse.

John looked at Louis and Pierre. Pierre's eyes were big. He held his hands up for silence and closed the door.

"You've made an enemy of Garnier."

John smiled. "I don't think I want him for a friend."

Louis motioned to the door. "I don't trust this man. We shouldn't stay in his house."

John looked at Pierre. "We can't stay here now, my friend."

"Come." Pierre closed up the warehouse and stepped out into the street with them. "Where will you go?"

"We'll find a place to stay in Quebec for some days until we decide what we do next."

"Follow the road south along the river to where the town ends. You'll find Madam Dupuis's inn. She's a friend of mine. Tell her I sent you, and she'll find a room for you." Pierre shook hands with them both.

"Thank you for your help, Pierre. If you have the opportunity to speak with Chantal please explain our sudden departure."

Pierre nodded. "Send my regards to Madame Dupuis," he said.

CHAPTER FORTY

MADAME DUPUIS'S INN WAS A large house on two floors close to the town wall. A woman in her thirties answered John's knock on the door. She was slender and had long black hair and large brown eyes. She was dressed in a black skirt and white blouse that revealed enough white skin to gain John's attention.

"I'm John Wallace, and this is my friend Louis Pictou. Pierre de Launay sent us. He said we might find a room here."

She smiled. "Well, now, John Wallace, if Pierre sent you to me, I must be sure to take care of you. How long do you want to stay?"

"I don't know. We only yesterday arrived in Quebec and need a place to stay while we decide what we shall do next."

Madame Dupuis put her hand to her face and gasped. "Was it you that rescued the Garnier girl from the Iroquois?"

It was John's turn to smile. "Yes, we brought Chantal back to Quebec."

Madame Dupuis took John by the arm. "The whole town's talking about it. You two are heroes in Quebec."

She smiled at Louis and motioned for him to follow. They entered a long hallway with doors opening off both sides, and the smell of baking bread and cooking meat made John's stomach grumble.

"Follow me." Madame Dupuis ran lightly up a set of stairs. She opened a door at the end of the hallway into a small room with two beds set against the walls. There was a row of shelves against one wall; other than that the room was bare.

Madame Dupuis smiled.

"It's one sol for the week, including three meals a day paid in advance."

"We'll stay two days, perhaps longer." John paid for two days. He didn't think it wise to let anyone see he carried a pouch full of silver, so he'd slipped some coins into his tunic before they knocked on the door.

Madame Dupuis smiled and backed out of the door.

"Dinner will be ready shortly. Come downstairs when you're ready to eat."

John set his rifle against the wall, dropped his gear on the floor, and sat on the bed. He put the silver pouch on the bed beside him.

"We must divide the silver." He started to sort the coins into two piles.

"I know little of silver, and I have a fine rifle."

"Half of the money is yours, Louis."

"You understand the language of silver. The merchant would have cheated me, you have my trust, it's enough," Louis said.

Madame Dupuis's food was excellent: beef, potatoes, cabbage, and onions with beer or wine to wash it down. John ate until he thought he would burst. There were six other guests in the house. Madame Dupuis introduced John and Louis as the men who'd rescued Chantal Garnier from the Iroquois, and they were warmly welcomed by all.

Despite the requests from the guests, John declined to describe Chantal's rescue. He didn't think it right to talk about how she had been treated by the Iroquois, and he'd no wish to discuss the fur they'd brought back either. The guests were disappointed, but to his surprise his reticence to speak about their exploits cast him and Louis in the role of reluctant heroes and increased their standing with the group.

The next morning Madame Dupuis gave them a breakfast of bread and cheese with hot tea. She'd taken a liking to them and sat with them while they ate.

"What are your plans now?"

"In truth I do not know. We had made no plans beyond bringing Chantal back to Quebec, although Louis and I had thought that we would try our hand in the fur trade."

446

"Fur is what created this country. There are fortunes to be made if you have the talent and the courage."

John smiled.

"That's what I've been told, but I know little of the business."

"You returned Monsieur Garnier's niece to him. Perhaps he'll be willing to help you. He's one of the most successful merchants in Quebec."

"I believe that Monsieur Garnier's sense of gratitude for Chantal's return stops at the point where money changes hands."

Madame Dupuis smiled. "In Quebec, Monsieur Garnier has a . . . reputation. Perhaps it is for the best."

"When we were at the citadel yesterday to meet with Captain Aubert we met François de La Tour who's also a merchant." Madame Dupuis nodded.

"Monsieur de La Tour is a respected man in Quebec. His enterprise isn't as large as Monsieur Garnier's, but he's successful nonetheless."

"I met François's brother when I was a prisoner in Louisburg."

"What?" Madame Dupuis said." You were in Louisburg?"

One of the maids came to the kitchen door.

"Madame, you must come. The old monsieur who came last night is ill." Madame Dupuis got to her feet.

"We must speak again of Louisburg. There are many in Quebec who had family or friends there." She followed the maid and disappeared up the stairs.

When they finished eating John suggested they visit François de La Tour. He didn't think they would have need of their weapons but neither was he willing to leave them in their room. John sought out Madame Dupuis, and she agreed to lock them in her own rooms till they returned.

The sky was clear and the day promised to be warm as they left the inn and walked along the river to where they had left the canoe. Pierre's men had dragged it out of the water and turned it upside down on the beach by the warehouse. They left it for now, but they would need it to return for the second load of furs.

A man hauling firewood into the town directed them to François's establishment. The compound was some distance beyond the town, close to the river. The main building was built of stone. It had a slate roof, a double set of doors in the centre, and a smaller door at the end. There was also a wooden barn and a boathouse to the west of the main building.

Two men were rolling barrels into the warehouse, and John enquired after François. One of the men went into the warehouse and a moment later François emerged. He waved and called out in pleasure when he saw them.

"John, Louis, I'm pleased that you came." He shook hands with both of them. "Come, we can talk in my office."

François led them to a door at the south end of the building. The office was twenty feet square with a high ceiling and windows looking out to the river. A fireplace was set into the end wall, and a desk stood under the window, stacked high with ledgers and bundles of papers.

François motioned them to take chairs by the desk.

"Make yourselves comfortable." John took a chair opposite François. Louis stood at the window, looking out at the river.

"I'm glad you came. The news that my brother is well has lifted a burden from my mind, and I was hoping we could speak further of the time you spent with him in Louisburg."

"I'm happy to do so." Louis went to explore the compound and left them to talk.

They talked for two hours. John told François how he had met Justinian, the conditions in the prison, the sickness in the town and of how Louis's brother had died. François was interested in everything John could tell him about Justinian, and how the people were faring under the British. He asked John to retell how he and Louis had escaped and made their way through the wilderness to Louis's village.

The more he spoke with François, the more John liked him. He was intelligent. He spoke plainly, and he felt he could trust him.

At one point John felt that there was nothing more to tell and held up his hands. "My head is beginning to ache. I think there's little more to tell, but perhaps we can speak again another day."

François laughed. "I fear I'm exhausting you, but it's a great solace to me to know that my brother is alive and well. What you've told me has given me peace of mind, and I thank you for it."

François fetched a bottle of wine and two glasses from the shelf and poured a glass each for them.

"Now tell me of your dealings with Monsieur Garnier." The wine was excellent, and John drank before he replied.

"We traded our furs to Monsieur Garnier in exchange for two Kentucky Long Rifles that Louis and I wanted, and 900 shillings in silver coin."

François calculated for a moment.

"I don't have a sense of the quality of your fur nor the value of the weapons you mentioned, but I'm afraid that Monsieur Garnier got the better of the bargain."

John nodded. "You're right, François. I understood that when I made the trade, but it would've been difficult not to trade with him, given that he is Chantal's uncle."

"You have the right of it. It would be better not to make an enemy of Garnier."

François poured more wine.

"I fear that I've made an enemy of him anyway. At the very least he will not be my friend." John described how the transaction had unfolded. François's eyes went wide in surprise; then he burst out laughing.

"You made him sign an agreement in English? His blood will boil for weeks."

"As I've said, I don't think that Monsieur Garnier will be keen to do business with us again, even though he got the best of the bargain."

François sat back.

"That may be the case, but you have other friends now in Quebec. I'll be happy to trade with you and Louis if your future expeditions bear fruit." John smiled.

"That may be possible sooner than you think."

François lifted an eyebrow.

"When we freed Chantal from the Iroquois, we took two canoe loads of fur. We didn't know how we would be received in Quebec, and it seemed wise to keep one load in reserve."

François slapped his knee and laughed.

"John Wallace, you continue to surprise me. And is this second canoe of fur of the same quality as the first?"

"We haven't inspected the fur. We thought it best not to disturb the bales. The canoe is the same size, but it contains more bales."

"Are you proposing that we trade for the fur?"

"If you are willing."

François got to his feet.

"I'll be pleased to trade with you, and you'll have a fair price for your goods. I assume that the second canoe is someplace safe. How long would it take you to bring the fur to Quebec?"

"Four or five days."

François paced back and forth.

"The first ship of the season is due to arrive from France within the month. This has been a poor season and prices will be strong. It would be best to complete our transaction before the ship arrives."

John took a sip of wine.

"We can leave right away. We'll need to secure some supplies, food, powder, and we must make some shot for the rifles, but that can be done quickly."

François sat down again.

"Bring your canoe here where it'll be safe. I have a smaller canoe you can use, and you'll travel more quickly. And I'll provide the provisions you'll need for the journey."

"I'll speak with Louis. If we make our preparations tomorrow, we can leave the following day."

François looked out of the window.

"It's known in the town that you brought many bales of fur with you. People may be curious if they see you leaving so soon."

"We'll leave after dark tomorrow and be well up river before anyone knows we are gone."

François nodded. "When you return, plan to arrive after dark. We'll unload the fur and no one will be the wiser."

John got to his feet. "We'll return tomorrow to make our preparations."

John and Louis discussed the plan as they walked back to the inn, and Louis agreed it would be wise to keep their departure secret. No doubt there were people in Quebec who would be happy to rob them or kill them for a canoe load of fur.

They spent the afternoon practicing with their rifles at different distances. John was delighted. He was becoming more comfortable with the weapon, and he could hit a target at four hundred paces consistently. Louis was less consistent at that range, but at two hundred paces he was faster on the target than John.

By the end of the afternoon they were down to their last flask of powder. John's shoulder was aching and his stomach reminded him they'd not eaten since the morning. They cleaned and oiled the rifles and left them in their room while they ate dinner. Later John told Madame Dupuis that they would be gone for a few days, but he paid for the full week.

The next morning they left before first light and paddled the canoe to François's compound. François said he would have the canoe hauled out of the water later in the day, and he led them to his office, where they shared a breakfast of cheese and bread.

"I've brought you supplies of dried meat, cheese, and bread—enough for a week's travel."

"That'll be more than enough. I doubt we'll be gone more than four days."

François led them to the boathouse to inspect the canoe he was to lend them. It was fifteen feet long and almost new.

"It'll be easier to paddle against the current than the cargo canoe."

"We'll launch it after dark. The fewer people who see you leave, the better."

François showed them a small forge at the back of the boathouse and gave them six bars of lead to make balls for their rifles and antimony to harden them. The molds for the long rifles only cast two balls at a time, so it was a slow process. They worked all morning and made over a hundred balls. John cleaned and polished each ball and wrapped it in cloth ready to be loaded. He put some in his hunting bag and stored the rest with their other supplies.

John also made thirty balls for the pistol, and he cleaned and oiled the weapon. There was a stone wheel for sharpening tools in the boathouse and Louis sharpened their tomahawks and reworked the edge on John's cutlass. By the middle of the afternoon they were ready. They agreed they would return in four days after dark, and if they ran into difficulties they would wait until the following night.

After dark they put the canoe in the water and pushed silently into the current. There was no moon, and in moments they were lost in the darkness. Louis had recovered from his injury and took his position in the stern. The river was wide and deep for many miles upstream, and there was little danger of striking a gravel bar, but John kept his eyes sharp for other dangers.

They paddled through the night, stopping once to eat, and put into the east shore at first light. They pulled the canoe out of the water and made camp in the forest. They slept till after midday and after they'd eaten, John sat watching the river. He tried to get a sense of where they were, but they had descended the river in darkness, and he didn't recognize any landmarks.

The second night they passed Trois-Rivières, hugging the east bank of the river. John didn't think they could be seen but caution had become second nature to him. As the light began to grow John started to recognize the landscape. He guessed they were only a few hours from the river, so they pushed on through the morning. It was almost midday when they turned into the river and beached the canoe in the inlet where they'd hidden the furs.

They hurried along the inlet and were relieved to find the canoe and the furs undisturbed. They hauled the canoe to the river, tied both vessels together and waited for darkness. They set off as soon as it was dark towing the small canoe. The cargo canoe felt clumsy, but John drove hard, determined to make their rendezvous with François two nights hence.

The canoe was slow and by the middle of the second night John knew it would take another night to reach Quebec. They put into a creek on the east bank and spent an hour camouflaging the canoes before they made camp. On the third night a quarter moon rose, giving them light to navigate by, but the night was well advanced before they saw the lights of Quebec.

They held the canoe in the middle of the river, and Louis didn't turn into the shore until they were past the town.

"There." John pointed to a single light. François had agreed he'd show a single lantern in the boathouse. As they crept in to the shore, John made out the shape of François's compound. The light came towards them and a moment later François called out.

"Come straight in." François held the lantern up, so they could see his face.

The bow of the canoe touched the gravel, and John stepped out and dragged it up the beach and shook hands with François.

"Well met, my friends. I was beginning to wonder what had happened to you."

"The canoe is heavier than I thought."

"You're here now. Let's get the fur unloaded and the canoes out of the water before daylight."

It took them two hours to unload the furs and drag the canoes behind the boathouse, and then François led them to his office.

"There are several hours of darkness left. Get some sleep, and we'll examine the fur in the morning. I'll secure it in the warehouse until we're ready." They laid their sleeping rolls out in François's office, and John was asleep in moments.

John awoke to find himself alone in the office and daylight streaming through the window. He packed up his sleeping roll and went outside. Louis was in the boathouse, putting an edge on his tomahawk.

"Shall we see what François has to say about the fur?"

François was in the warehouse, stacking barrels with two of his men. He waved and led them to a door at the south end of the warehouse. John found himself in a room fifteen feet deep that ran the width of the warehouse. At the east end there were barrels of powder stacked against the wall and a dozen muskets. Wooden shelves ran along the end wall holding everything from bolts of cloth to cooking utensils.

The west side of the room was given over to fur. A row of bales was stacked along the wall and there were a few individual hides on stretching frames. François pointed to the bales.

"On a good year this wall would be stacked four high with fur."

"It's the same with the other traders?"

François nodded.

"Why is this so?"

"I don't know. There could be sickness in the interior or conflict between the native groups. There are many things that could be the cause."

John looked at the row of bales.

"This is less than half of what you would normally see?"

"It's one third of what I would see in a good year. I suspect this is why Monsieur Garnier agreed to trade with you."

A large table dominated the west end of the room, and their bales of fur were stacked next to it.

"Let's see what you have to trade, my friends." François lifted the first bale onto the table.

"I count forty-four bales?" John nodded agreement.

"Forty-four bales, it is. No wonder the canoe was heavy." François cut the binding, unpacked the furs, and spread them out on the table in a similar fashion to Monsieur Garnier.

François sorted the furs into different sizes, examining each one carefully. He flexed the skin gently and ran his fingers over the hide, almost caressing it. He worked quickly, and John watched everything, trying to understand what he was looking for and how he evaluated the hides.

When he'd finished, he leaned his elbows on the table and looked at John and Louis.

"These are excellent furs. I haven't seen this quality for some years, and I wonder how the Iroquois came by them. The fur is thick and rich. It must have come from far to the north."

"I don't know. Perhaps Chantal can tell more about their origin."

François intertwined his fingers.

"If the rest of the bales are of equal quality . . ." He was lost in thought for a moment. "The Iroquois lands were trapped out many years ago. Now they act as middle men between the interior people and the British. It may be they've gained access to an area that hasn't been trapped before."

It took François the rest of the day to unpack and inspect the remaining bales. When he had finished, he covered the furs with a canvas sheet, and they went to his office to talk. François brought three glasses and a bottle of wine, and they sat at his desk. François started to make notes on a sheet of paper, creating a column of figures down the left side of the page. He worked steadily for some minutes and seemed satisfied with the result.

François looked up.

"This is the best fur I've seen for several years. I would like to think about it further, but I would be willing to offer you a figure of three shillings per pelt for the forty-four bales."

John couldn't help but express surprise.

"That's a great deal of money." He added the number up in his head. "That's more than Monsieur Garnier paid us."

"You have high-quality fur."

John looked at Louis. "I think François is an honest man. We should agree to his price."

John looked at François. "We accept your offer. It's good to deal with an honest man."

François reached across the table and shook hands with both of them. "I'll have the silver for you tomorrow morning."

"I need to speak with Louis further about the silver, but if you're agreeable, we could make an agreement for you to hold a portion of the money for us. It's not wise to carry such a sum of money with us."

"I'll hold the money if you wish. We can make a written agreement that states the sum and how long I'm to hold it for you."

François set the paper aside and sipped his wine.

"Do you recall if Chantal spoke of where the Iroquois had found the fur?"

"She said only that it came from far to the north. She may have more knowledge of this, but there wasn't time to discuss it."

"As I said, it's possible the Iroquois have come on an area that hasn't been trapped before. If that is the case, there could be much wealth there."

John took Father Jean-Louis's map from his hunting bag and spread it on the desk. François was immediately intrigued and got to his feet to examine it in more detail.

"This is finely crafted. How did you come by it?"

"I took it from the priest's cabin after the British attack at Shubenacadie." John traced his finger to a point on the map. "This is where we encountered the Iroquois."

François shook his head.

"That area was trapped out many years ago. He ran his finger along the St. Lawrence to Mont-Royal, and then followed the course of another river to the west. "This is the traditional land route to Hudson's Bay." He ran his finger around the bay. "The fur you brought must come from here where the cold is extreme."

John leaned over the map.

"How did the furs get from so far north to where we encountered the Iroquois?"

"The Hudson's Bay Company claims exclusive rights to trade for fur in this area." François put his finger on the southern shoreline of Hudson's Bay. "The Company built a line of forts along the bay here. The people from the interior bring their furs to the trading posts to exchange them for the type of goods you see here." He pointed to the shelves and boxes stacked against the wall.

John stood up.

"How could the Iroquois have come by the furs?"

"They may have traded with one of the tribes from the northern part of the bay, but it would be unusual for them to travel so far north. It's more likely they captured them before they reached a trading post."

John came back to the map. "The natives bring their furs here to trade." He touched the southern shore of the bay.

François nodded.

"Would it be possible to travel to this region to trade with the northern people in their own villages?"

François smiled. "You're a man after my own heart, John Wallace. I've often thought there would be much to be gained from such a venture."

"Has it been done before?"

"A few have tried, but it's difficult to travel to this region, and the tribes may be hostile. The main difficulty is bringing the furs back without the knowledge of the Hudson's Bay staff or the Iroquois."

François sank into his chair and sipped his wine.

"The person who was most successful in penetrating to the northern part of Hudson's Bay was Charles Garnier, Chantal's father."

John looked at him in surprise. "Chantal spoke of her travels with her parents."

"Could she tell us more of the region?"

John frowned. "I don't know. It seemed to throw up painful memories for her."

François nodded but didn't pursue it. John stepped back from the table. "We'll return tomorrow, then."

John requested that Madame Dupuis give them dinner. They'd not eaten since the night before, and John didn't want to answer questions from the other guests about where they'd been for almost a week. He could see that Madame Dupuis was curious, but she didn't query them. Louis went to bed after they had eaten, but John sat outside on the porch, sipping Madame Dupuis's wine, and let his mind run on until exhaustion overcame him, and he sought his bed.

The next day they left their rifles with Madame Dupuis and set off for the town. They walked for hours, exploring the streets and watching the people go about their affairs. François had told them there were over five thousand people in Quebec. It was a bustling town and everyone seemed to be possessed of a sense of urgency and purpose that was catching.

They visited a haberdashery that Madame Dupuis had recommended. John bought two pairs of breaches, three linen shirts and a wool coat that fell below his knees. He also bought a pair of black hunting boots and three pairs of wool socks. He was reluctant to part with his old boots. They had been a present from his uncle, but they were worn beyond repair. Louis bought two pairs of breeches and also bought new boots, but he preferred to keep his deerskin tunic.

When they returned to the inn, John enquired about the possibility of taking a bath, and Madame Dupuis directed one of the maids to prepare the bath house.

"Some of our guests have formed the habit of bathing. We're happy to accommodate their wishes, although I don't hold with bathing more than a few times a year myself." Louis declined to join him, and John spent an hour scrubbing the dirt out of his skin and combing the tangles out of his hair. Madame Dupuis loaned him a mirror, and he trimmed his hair and beard.

The next morning before going to meet François, John went to pick up his new boots from the haberdashery. The owner had sent them to a cobbler to have them heeled with steel studs. The owner of the haberdashery had promised to have them ready first thing in the morning. John was pleased with them and left his old boots at the haberdashery.

They walked south towards the town gate, turned onto the main street, and came face-to-face with Chantal and her aunt. John was astonished at the change in her. She was wearing a green dress and a white blouse, with a red scarf around her neck. Her hair had been brushed till it shone, and she wore it pulled forward over one shoulder and fixed with a silver clasp. She glowed with health and well-being, and she carried herself with the same natural grace he'd first seen in the wilderness.

John came to a halt. Chantal didn't recognize him for a moment, and then she smiled. It transformed her face and her eyes sparkled with colour.

"Chantal," John said, "it's good to see you. I hope that you're well?" Her features became neutral again.

"I'm well, but much has changed." There was something wistful in her voice, but she went on quickly. "I hope you were able to make a good trade for the fur. My uncle seemed pleased with himself, but I must tell you that he doesn't speak well of you."

John laughed.

"Your uncle got the better part of the bargain, but I'm not displeased with the outcome."

"What of the second load of fur?" Chantal pitched her voice low.

"We traded it to François de La Tour, the brother of one of the men I met when I was imprisoned in Louisburg."

She nodded. "You've done well for being in Quebec so short a time."

Madame Garnier coughed and stepped forward. "I'm pleased to see you looking well and prosperous, young man."

"Thank you, Madame Garnier. You are most kind."

"We must get on now. We have much to do this morning, so I will bid you good day." She took Chantal's arm and set off along the street.

John watched as they made their way up the hill, Madame Garnier's matronly form dwarfing Chantal's slender figure. Something about the image struck John as unnatural. He couldn't identify what it was, but he found it vaguely disturbing. After a moment they turned onto the street leading to Monsieur Garnier's house.

John turned to Louis. "We should go."

John struggled with confusing emotions. It was a shock to see Chantal, who seemed out of place in Quebec, in a town. She wore her fine clothes as if born to it, but she carried the same intensity that had first drawn him to her. He was lost in his thoughts and was surprised when he heard François hail them from the door of his office.

They sat at the desk, and François slid several sheets of paper across to John and Louis.

"I've drawn up an agreement based on our discussion yesterday. The document lists the bales of fur, the number and quality of the pelts. At the bottom the total value of all forty four bales is noted."

John studied the document, and then explained it to Louis. "This is what we discussed yesterday."

"And you are agreeable to the terms?"

"Yes, we are agreed."

François signed both copies of the document and slid them across the desk.

"This is a substantive sum of money. We can live on this for several seasons if we choose."

François nodded. "You've done well for ones so young."

John smiled.

"We've also been fortunate." He put his hands on the table. "And we still have silver from the transaction with Monsieur Garnier. We have no need for more at the moment, so it would be better if you hold the money for us."

"I'll draw up a note stating the amount I'm holding for you. I'll have it ready tomorrow."

They shook hands on the transaction. It was near midday and François brought bread and cheese to the table and red wine to wash it down. He leaned on one elbow.

"Have you thought about what you'll do now?"

"Our main purpose was to return Chantal to her family. In truth Louis and I have not discussed what to do next. When we left Shubenacadie, we had thought to seek our future in the fur trade."

"You've made a good start, and you have friends in Quebec. That's also important."

John looked around at the shelves stacked with merchandise.

"Where do you get the goods to trade?"

"They're sent from France each year. Our ship is expected within the next two weeks, and I have much work to do to get ready."

"How long does the ship stay in Quebec?"

"A week, perhaps two, depending on the weather and how much cargo there is to unload." François smiled. "I'm hoping the ship will bring a letter from my brother. He may even be on board."

John was struck by an idea.

"Do passengers travel between Quebec and France?"

"There are always merchants and soldiers travelling to and from France." John's mind raced, and François put his hand on his arm.

"You're thinking you could return to Scotland?" John looked at him in confusion and an unexpected sense of dread rose up in him.

"It's what I've been striving for since the day I was taken prisoner, but now it seems so long ago. So much has happened."

John got to his feet and went to the window.

"The fishermen say the winter has been hard this year. There have been many storms. I think the ship will be late this year," François said.

John's head was pounding.

"When I was put on the ship for America the crew stopped me from jumping overboard, and when I was a prisoner in Louisburg my only thought was how I could find my way back to Scotland." He came and sat down. "Now when I have the ability to return to my homeland, I'm filled with confusion and dread."

The moments passed slowly; then François gripped John's forearm.

"There's time to consider your future. There are many ships that travel to France."

John nodded. "I must think on this and speak with my friend Louis."

"Our ship won't arrive for a week at least, perhaps longer. Take the canoe and explore the river, hunt with your new rifle." The prospect of exploring made John feel better at once.

"It's good advice." They took their leave of François. He had a year's worth of shipping documents to prepare. They agreed to meet the next morning to sign the note for the silver.

John was lost in thought as they made their way back to the inn, and Madame Dupuis met them in the hallway.

"There's fish soup and fresh bread in the kitchen if you have an appetite." She laughed. "I haven't known you not to have an appetite."

"We'll live up to our reputation," John said.

The cook presented them each with a large bowl of soup and a platter of fresh bread, and after a few minutes Louis put down his spoon.

"What troubles you, my friend?"

John looked up. "We've done well trading, and we have much silver."

Louis nodded. "Why does this trouble you?"

"It's not the silver that troubles me." John looked away for a moment. "I'm faced with a dilemma." He looked at Louis. "Since I was made a prisoner and put on the ship I've been fighting to return to my own land."

"I don't understand."

"When François's ship arrives, I can travel on the ship to France and make my way back to Scotland from there."

Louis eyes became troubled.

"You are my friend. If it is your wish to return to your own land, I must honour your decision. But know this: this land had taken you to its heart. I do not think it will easily let you go."

John buried his face in his hands and rested his elbows on the table. When he looked up, one of Louis's rare smiles lit his face. He so delighted in the transformation that he burst out laughing and slapped Louis on the shoulder.

"François suggested we take the small canoe and explore the river. What do you say to that?"

"It will be good to be in the wild and to be moving again."

CHAPTER FORTY ONE

THEY LEFT THE NEXT MORNING and once they were on their way, John began to enjoy the freedom of the river and the wilderness. They paddled downriver for two days, camping on the bank the first night. On the second day they came to the Saguenay River running to the north. François had told them it was one of the old routes to the interior that had been trapped out years ago. He said the people who lived in the upper reaches of the river still brought fur to Quebec but guarded the trade closely.

The tide had an effect on the river, but John had the sense that they were still a long way from the sea. The river was half a mile across and steep hills rose from each bank forested with pine and birch.

They travelled upriver for four days. On the fourth day they camped early and set up targets to practice with their rifles. John was delighted with the weapon. He could consistently hit a target less than twelve inches in diameter at four hundred paces. He climbed the hill above the inlet and practiced firing downhill, learning to allow for the fall of the ball. Then he cut a target out on a tree two hundred feet above the inlet and worked on firing uphill. This was more difficult, but he practiced it hour after hour until he could hit the target at three hundred paces.

Louis had taken the canoe and his fishing line out into the river, and when John came back to camp, Louis was roasting a huge fish on the fire. John hadn't seen this type of fish before; the meat was white and it was delicious.

They continued into the inlet until they came to a lake. John had hoped to encounter the people of the region, but apart from a long-deserted village, they found no signs of habitation. John wanted to explore the lake, but it would have taken many weeks, and he had to be content with exploring the shore for a day.

On the eighth day they turned back for Quebec. John had fallen into the rhythm of the journey, and it had calmed him. Returning to Scotland was always in the back of his mind, and he knew he would have to come to terms with it at some point.

They were moving from first light till dark, stopping only to eat at midday, and in four days they were back on the St. Lawrence. They camped on the east bank of the river. John remembered the place, and he was sure they would reach Quebec the following day. After they had eaten he sat by the fire, and as darkness began to fall he was overcome by a feeling of melancholy. It was as if a band of steel was squeezing his chest, and it became difficult to breathe. He felt he should speak with Louis, but his mouth was dry, and he couldn't find the words.

John wrapped himself in his bedroll. He lay on his back and watched the stars moving across the sky until sleep found him. His dreams were haunted by fearful images and a wolf's howl filled his mind, a fearful sound like a lost soul wailing in the night. He jolted awake. Cold sweat was running down his face and his scalp was pulled tight across his head. This creature had claimed a place in his heart. For him the wolf would always be the soul of the wilderness and that sound, its savage lament.

Louis was sitting across the fire watching him.

"He's alone and he's afraid. My father used to say he makes that sound when he knows he will die." John shuddered and looked into the fire for a long time; then he looked at Louis.

"I cannot leave this land, Louis. It is a part of me now, and it's where I belong."

Louis met his eye, but he didn't speak as if he'd known this would be the outcome. John stared into the fire, lost in a waking dream, and when the light began to grow in the east, he knew that the wolf would not howl again.

They were on the river at first light. The water was dead flat, rolling out before them like polished stone. Mist clung to the riverbanks, cloaking the forest in white, fading slowly away as the night gave up the ghost to the coming day. The sun rose over the hills, turning the river to silver, bright with the promise of a new day, and John's spirits rose with it.

They pushed on, stopping only to eat at midday. John recognized many landmarks now, and there were dwellings and farms dotted along the shore. He knew they were within striking distance of the town, but the current was stronger than he'd thought. It was late in the day when they came in sight of Quebec, and it was getting dark when they reached François's compound.

As they beached the canoe below the warehouse, John saw two new ships lying at anchor off the town. Night was coming, and he knew he would have to contain his curiosity until the morning.

They dragged the canoe out of the water and carried it to the boathouse. François's office was locked, so they took their gear and made their way to the town. Madame Dupuis had kept their room for them, and the maid let them in and gave them beef stew and bread to eat. John lay awake long into the night. Now that he had decided to stay, it felt as natural as breathing, and his mind ran to the future and what it might hold.

In the morning they went down to the river to see the ships and hear what news they'd brought. Both ships were anchored off the beach, bows facing into the current. They were larger and more robustly constructed than the others John had seen in the river.

The largest ship was over two hundred feet long. It looked like a new vessel. The hull was painted black with white piping along the deck rail and windows. The hatches had been removed and men were swarming over her deck, and barrels and boxes were being lowered to lighters along both sides. Half a dozen men stood talking on the bridge. John thought he recognized François amongst them, but it was too far to be sure.

The second ship was smaller and older. It sat low in the water and moved sluggishly at its anchor. There was hectic activity around it, and John counted six barges offloading cargo.

Three lighters were drawn up on the shore and gangs of men struggled to load boxes, barrels, bales of cloth, furniture, and an endless variety of goods and merchandise onto a line of wagons and carts. Men were shouting and hurling insults. John was astonished at the noise and expected violence to break out at any moment.

John found it all fascinating, and they spent the morning watching. It seemed as if half the town had come to see the ships and watch the drama unfold. He knew it was an important event for the town. The ships not only brought goods and merchandise but news from France and letters from family and friends; everyone wanted to be a part of it.

The following day they sought out François, but he was already on board the larger ship, meeting with his agent from France. René, the foreman, told them it was always this way when their ship came into Quebec. François would spend the first two or three days working through the inventory of trade goods. Over the next week René and his men would unload the cargo and ensure their fur was safely loaded.

The following day François sent a note to the inn, asking John and Louis to meet him at his office early in the morning. When they arrived, François was in the warehouse talking to René, and he came and shook hands with them both.

"Come to my office. I have bread and cheese we can eat while we talk." François's eyes were red. He looked as if he hadn't slept for days, but he was in good spirits.

"I have good news. I received a letter from my brother, Justinian. He's in Bordeaux, sent there from Louisburg in the fall of last year."

"That's excellent news."

"Justinian will stay in Bordeaux for the present, and will act as our agent for the coming year, and he will return to Quebec the following year. In his letter he tells that the market for fur is strong. There have been two bad years in a row now and prices are rising."

François was beaming with pleasure and could barely contain himself long enough to eat his cheese and bread.

"In his letter Justinian has asked me to expand our trade in fur, and he's increased the inventory of trade goods." John started to speak, but François went on. "He mentioned you, John and Louis, in his letter. He speaks highly of you and hopes you made good your escape. He was put on the ship four days after your escape from the prison, so he has no knowledge of your fate."

John laughed. "I'm pleased to hear this. I liked Justinian from when I first met him, and he saved us from being caught during our escape."

The ship will carry my letter to him when it leaves in a few days. I think he'll find it hardly credible not only that you made your way to Quebec, but that we also completed a transaction that was highly satisfactory to both of us."

François frowned. "On another matter, my friend, I've spoken with the captain of the Mercoeur, and he's willing to convey you to Bordeaux. From there Justinian will be able to arrange passage for you to Scotland."

John put his hands on the table. "I've decided to stay in Quebec. My life is here now."

François jumped up from the table and gripped John's hand.

"That is good news indeed, my friend, and Quebec will be the better for it."

John was quiet for a moment; then he looked at François. "How will you find more fur to trade?"

François set his cup down. "I've been busy with the ship's inventory and the news from Justinian. I haven't turned my mind to it yet, but it won't be easy. As I said, the past two years are the worst that I have ever seen."

John tore a piece of bread from the loaf and waved it at François. "Perhaps I could propose a plan that would benefit all three of us."

François stopped chewing and lifted an eyebrow. "What do you have in mind?"

John spread his fingers. "I have listened carefully to what you said about how fur is traded, and I believe that if we could trade with the northern people in their own territories, there may be much to be gained."

François burst out laughing. "I swear that we must be distantly related, John Wallace."

John held up his hands. "There's more."

François's eyes were filled with humour and he nodded. "Go on my friend."

"Louis and I have accumulated a sum of money that you're holding for us. I propose that we form a partnership to trade for fur in the north country. Louis and I will be quarter partners, and you will be half. We'll jointly fund the venture and take any profit on the same basis. I think it's too late to mount a full expedition this year, but I propose we carry out an exploratory venture before the summer is over. We can take trade goods and seek to make contact with people in the north who might trade with us."

François looked from John to Louis and back again.

"It's a bold idea, and I am wholeheartedly in favour of it. I'll need two days to complete my business with the Mercoeur; then I'm free to work on the plans with you."

John nodded.

"When does the ship leave?"

"It'll leave three days hence at first light, all being well."

"I would like to write a letter to my family. Do you think that Justinian would be willing to send it on to my family's home in Crieff?"

"I'll have my last meeting with Monsieur Amyot the day after tomorrow. If you can have the letter ready by then, René will see that I get it. I will ask Monsieur Amyot to deliver it to Justinian. There are many ships that visit Bordeaux. He'll find one that will carry it to Scotland."

François got to his feet.

"I must go. There's much to be done before the Mercoeur sails. Let's meet here in three days to plan the expedition. In the meantime I'll write a partnership agreement based on what we've discussed this morning."

John got to his feet, and they shook hands.

"We're agreed." John smiled. Now that he'd decided to stay in Quebec, he felt as if a load had been lifted from his mind.

"One more thing," François said. "You should plan to leave no later than ten days from today. You will only be able to travel for a few months before the snow begins to fall, so there is no time to lose."

John and Louis had discussed the expedition on their last day on the river, and they were both pleased with the outcome.

"I've long wanted to travel to the far country," Louis said. "It is a good journey to make."

"If we can make a pact with the people in the north, I believe we will prosper."

"It's good to have money to buy powder and shot, but for me the journey is of more value than the silver," Louis said.

John smiled to himself.

"I think you may be the wiser of the two of us, Louis, but if all goes to plan, we'll make the journey and earn the silver."

John made a list of the things they would need. To keep the weight down, they would take only their weapons, cooking utensils, and food for two weeks, and live off the land as they travelled. John reasoned that if they took only a sample of the trade goods, they could take the small canoe. They would travel faster, and it would be easier to portage.

The next day they went to François's compound. John helped Louis replace a section of the skin on the canoe where it had worn thin from the gravel bars. When they were finished, they walked to the town. John wanted to buy another shirt from the haberdashery. He also wanted to buy a belt that could accommodate his pistol. Louis didn't see the point in buying more things they would have to carry, but he went along anyway.

Monsieur Lamaire, the owner, greeted them warmly. They'd spent a goodly sum of money on their last visit, and he was keen to make them comfortable. Monsieur Lamaire said he had a shirt available, and that he had a belt that would suit John's needs.

"The belt's in my storeroom. If you will wait a few moments I'll fetch it."

"That's fine. In the meantime I'll try on the shirt," John said.

Monsieur Lamaire set off to the back of the building, but a moment later John heard him greet another customer.

"Good morning, Madame Garnier. It's nice to see you again."

John saw Madame Garnier enter the haberdashery and Chantal was a few steps behind. Madame Garnier frowned when she saw John, but a look of surprise crossed Chantal's face, and she nodded politely.

Monsieur Lamaire stepped forward to greet them.

"Please come this way, Madame Garnier. Madame Lamaire will be pleased to assist you." Madame Garnier glanced at John as Monsieur Lamaire ushered her to the far end of the haberdashery.

Chantal was wearing a dark blue dress. Black shoes peeped out from under the hem, and she carried a shawl over her arm.

"It's good to see you, Chantal."

She stepped closer. "Thank you, I hope that all is well with you."

"Indeed, things have progressed well." He glanced at Madame Garnier to make sure she was out of earshot. "We traded the second canoe load of fur to François de La Tour." The shadow of a smile crossed her face.

"I'm glad. It means that you've made a start in Quebec."

Chantal glanced over her shoulder and something in the way she looked at Madame Garnier made him uneasy.

"Is everything well with you, Chantal?"

She inclined her head. "I'm well enough, but what of you? What will you do now?"

It was clear she didn't want to speak about herself, and John didn't press her.

"The fur we took from the Iroquois was excellent quality. François believes it comes from a region that hasn't been trapped before in the place they call Hudson's Bay. Louis and I have formed a partnership with François to explore the area and to seek opportunities to trade with the people of the region."

Chantal nodded. "The fur came from the land of the Mistassini people to the north of the place you call Hudson's Bay."

John felt a thrill of excitement run through him. "How do you know—" he began.

Madame Garnier interrupted, calling out, "Come, Chantal, we must be about our business." Chantal glanced at her, then back at John.

"I wish you success, John Wallace. When do you leave?"

"We leave in three days. We will follow the St. Lawrence north, then take the river they call the Ottawa. Beyond that I don't know." Madame Garnier hustled Chantal out. She looked over her shoulder in the doorway; then she was gone.

John was left with an uneasy feeling. He didn't understand why Madame Garnier would behave in such a manner, and Chantal seemed different from when he'd seen her a few weeks ago. His train of thought was interrupted when Monsieur Lamaire returned.

"I think this will suit your purposes admirably, monsieur." He handed John a leather belt with a pocket that would hold the pistol.

"This will work well, monsieur," John said, and he paid in silver.

The meeting with Chantal and Madame Garnier stuck in John's mind. He was preoccupied with it at dinner and lay awake thinking about it before he slept. The next day they met with François to plan the expedition and John pushed the incident to the back of his mind.

They used the priest's map as their working document, and they agreed on what John had described to Chantal. They would follow the St. Lawrence south beyond Mont-Royal. François cautioned them to be careful when they came into the vicinity of Trois-Rivières and Mont-Royal and advised them to bypass both towns. There were many who would see a canoe load of trade goods as too good an opportunity to let pass.

Beyond Mont-Royal they would follow the Ottawa River west and seek a route north to Hudson's Bay. François was able to describe the Ottawa River region, but beyond they would have to find their own way. They calculated that they could travel north for two months before they would be forced to return to Quebec. If they stayed longer, they could be trapped for the winter. The hope was that they would have enough time to reach Hudson's Bay and make contact with the natives in the area.

François suggested they take a broad sample of the trade goods such as axes, knives, cooking utensils, and fish hooks. Blankets and other cloth materials would be too bulky to transport and less valued than metal tools. They loaded the canoe, and John and Louis took it on the river after dark to test it. John was pleased with the canoe's balance, and he was confident it could carry more weight if needed.

The next morning François showed John the partnership agreement he'd drafted. John read it to Louis, and he agreed it was as they had discussed. John signed the document and added a note that he was signing on Louis's behalf.

By the time they were done it was close to midday. They went over their plans once more but could think of nothing left undone and concluded they were ready to depart. They agreed to meet the following day an hour before first light.

The next morning John and Louis were at François's compound before dawn. They carried the canoe down to the beach and were making their way back when François called out to them from the warehouse.

François lit three lanterns, creating a pool of light around the pile of trade goods and equipment on the warehouse floor.

"Did you sleep well, my friends?"

"Louis slept like a baby, but I hardly slept at all."

"I'm not going on this expedition, and I was up half the night trying to think of anything we had missed," François said.

"Perhaps you should come with us, François."

"Unfortunately, my affairs keep me in Quebec, but it's my wish to see the north country one day. Perhaps I will accompany you on the spring expedition."

They loaded the canoe and pushed it into the water. Louis thought it was down at the bow. They moved some of the cargo farther back, but it took several attempts until Louis was satisfied.

When they finished, they walked up to the warehouse to check nothing had been left behind, and John saw the first feathers of light in the sky. The floor of the warehouse was clear, and they stood for a moment wondering how to say farewell.

John could see the dark bulk of the ships in the distance and lanterns hanging from the bow and stern of each vessel. He looked at François.

"Have you concluded all of your business with the agent?"

"It's done for another year. The Mercoeur sails before midday."

John started to speak, but Louis put his hand on his shoulder and lifted his chin towards the town. John was astonished to see Chantal walk into the pool of light around the warehouse door. She wore a buckskin dress, she had moccasins on her feet, and a hunting knife hung from her leather belt. She wore a woolen coat over the dress that fell below her knees and she carried a sleeping roll slung over one shoulder and a hunting bag like John's on the other.

She stopped and nodded to Louis and François then looked at John.

"When last we spoke you told me that you planned to make a journey to the north country to trade for fur. I have come to ask if I may join you."

John was so astonished, it was some moments before he could speak. He glanced at Louis and François. Louis's face was blank, but François eyes were bright with amusement.

"Why would you want to go back to the wilds again? You only recently escaped captivity." John stammered the words out. "Your uncle and aunt would be furious if we take you with us."

"My uncle may have concerns that I'm gone, but my aunt less so, I think."

John looked at François, but he held up his hands defensively.

"Your uncle will say we kidnapped you and will send soldiers to bring you back." Chantal looked at François then back at John.

"Shortly after you brought me back to Quebec my uncle took me to his office to speak with me in private. He told me that he'd taken me into his home, fed and clothed me, and that he was making provisions for my future, and he made it clear he expected me to show him my gratitude." François drew a harsh breath, and the amusement was gone from his eyes.

After a moment Chantal went on.

"My uncle told me that as I'd been the slave and plaything of the Iroquois, I should find little difficulty fulfilling his desires."

"What . . . ?" John burst out.

Chantal held up her hand.

"I wouldn't let him touch me, which made him furious. Eventually Madame Garnier realized what was happening and accused me of trying to seduce her husband."

François slammed his fist into his palm.

"I've always known Garnier was a rogue, but I wouldn't have thought he would stoop to this."

"The merchant is not an honourable man. Why do you want to go with us?" Louis said.

Chantal looked at Louis.

"Madame Garnier made it clear that I'm no longer welcome in her household. She told me that I must leave, or she will have me put out of the house."

A jumble of emotions welled up in John, and he blurted out, "Why would you want to come with us into the wilderness and danger?"

Chantal looked at John with unblinking intensity.

"You did not try to take advantage of me and treated me like a human being, and I have nowhere else to go." John started to speak, but Chantal went on. "I may be of value to your expedition. I heard the Iroquois tell how they took the fur from the Mistassini people. I travelled in their lands with my parents for two seasons. I remember something of the route to reach their lands, and I learned to speak their language from the children of the villages we visited."

John's mind was spinning, but he couldn't deny the thrill of pleasure he felt at the thought of Chantal travelling with them. He glanced at François. He lifted an eyebrow and smiled.

He looked at Louis, and he inclined his head. "The girl will be valuable. Neither of us can speak the language of the northern tribes, and they may remember her and look on us as friends. She should travel with us."

John was still confounded by what he felt, but he turned to Chantal and said, "You are welcome to join our expedition."

"I'm grateful," she said, and John saw the tension go out of her.

"What of food and supplies?" François said.

"We have enough for now," John said, "and we'll live off the land for the better part of the journey anyway."

François clapped his hands. "It's time to begin."

On the beach François shook hands with them and wished them bon voyage.

He took John's hand last. "Much success, my friend. I think it will prove to be an eventful journey for you." His eyes were filled with laughter. John didn't understand his amusement, but there was no time to pursue it. He shook his hand and told him to expect them when the snow fell.

John took his position at the bow. Chantal had made a place for herself in the middle of the canoe, and Louis pushed off. The light was growing fast, but the mist rising off the river hid them from prying eyes. They pushed across the river until the ships were between them and the town; then they turned south for Mont-Royal and the wilderness beyond.

CHAPTER FORTY-TWO

WHEN SCOTT MARCHED OUT OF Boston he had sixty-five men under his command, including Sergeant Crammer and the men he'd brought from Scotland. Scott rode King, and the troops marched in double file, followed by two wagons carrying their supplies and equipment. Scott had sent word to Swatana to meet them north of Albany at Lake Champlain.

Scott was anxious to reach the French territories to set their plans in motion. Soon it would be evident that Elisabeth was with child, and the sooner they married, the better it would be for both of them. The men grumbled at the pace, but he kept the column moving from first light to sunset.

At the end of the second day Lieutenant Paine spoke to Scott outside his tent.

"Captain Scott, I think you're driving the men too hard. They're exhausted and can barely stand by the end of the march," Scott barked at him.

"They're soldiers, Lieutenant, not school boys. Do you believe the French will be swayed to mercy because our troops are fatigued?"

Lieutenant Paine blanched at the vehemence of Scott's response.

"Captain, the men will be in no condition to fight if we keep going at this pace." Scott stepped closer to Paine.

"Lieutenant, you would do better to display fortitude and determination than come whining to me that the men have sore feet. We'll speak of this no further, Lieutenant. You are dismissed." The camp had gone quiet, and all eyes were on Scott and Paine. The lieutenant saluted and strode away, red-faced with anger and humiliation.

Six days later they marched into Albany. A Lieutenant Pencutt from Major Munroe's command met the column outside the town. The lieutenant informed Scott his men were to camp on the Hudson River two miles north of the town. He would bring Scott and the other officers to an inn at Albany, where they would be lodged during their stay. Scott left Lieutenant Paine and Sergeant Crammer to get the men settled and set off for Albany with the lieutenant.

The town of Albany stretched out along the west bank of the Hudson River, and once again Scott was impressed by the quality of the buildings, and the sense of wealth and prosperity in the town. There was much activity along the river. Wharves and warehouses had been constructed to the north of the town, and men were busy unloading vessels.

The British Army at Albany was based at Fort Frederick. The fort stood on a hill to the west of the town. It was constructed of stone, built as a square with rounded corners with the main gate in the east wall.

Inside the fort, buildings stood on three sides of the parade ground and Pencutt pointed out the barracks, officers' quarters, administration building and stables. He said two hundred troops were stationed in the fort. The junior officers stayed in rooming houses, and Major Munroe and the senior officers owned houses in the town. A groom took their horses and Pencutt led Scott to the administration building on the east side of the parade ground.

A sentry came to attention as they approached, and they stepped into the entrance hall.

"If you'll wait here, Captain, I'll inform the major that you've arrived." Pencutt strode away, boots clicking on the wooden floor, and Scott looked around him. The building was a typical army design, utilitarian with no frills, but the building materials were high-quality. Simple as it was it had been an expensive building to construct.

Scott's thoughts were interrupted by Pencutt's return.

"Major Munroe will see you now, sir."

Monroe's office was as plain as the rest of the building. A fireplace was set into one wall, a desk under the window and bookcases on the other two walls. The floor was bare boards polished to a high shine. The only concession to comfort was an oriental rug in front of the fireplace.

Munroe was in his forties. He was of medium height, narrow-shouldered and growing a paunch. He had a narrow face and greying hair, and his eyes were deeply set, giving his face a grave appearance. He came forward and extended his hand when Scott entered.

"Captain Scott, welcome to Albany." He had two rotten teeth on the left side of his mouth and Scott tried not to stare at them.

Monroe went to the desk and motioned Scott to a seat.

"Captain Scott, I'm pleased you've arrived ahead of schedule. Tensions between Britain and the French are high. Our political masters have conveyed their need to demonstrate British authority to the French, so I want to be in the field as soon as possible."

"When do you anticipate leaving?"

"We march the day after tomorrow. I trust that won't be a problem, Captain?"

"We'll be ready, Major."

Monroe smiled, showing his blackened teeth.

"Captain, I understand you are recently arrived in New England and haven't seen action yet. Things are different from Europe. The land is vast, and the natives are still essentially savages."

Monroe would have gone on, but Scott interrupted him. "I spent the previous winter in Annapolis Royal, where I saw action against the natives. I also have a group of Iroquois scouts who will be joining us north of Albany. I believe that I'm prepared for whatever we may encounter."

Monroe got to his feet.

"Very well, Captain, Lieutenant Pencutt will see you have all you need. I will hold a briefing here tomorrow morning at nine o'clock sharp. You'll meet the other officers and will receive your orders for the campaign."

Monroe shook his hand. Scott nodded but didn't speak as he took his leave. Lieutenant Pencutt was waiting in the hall.

"Would you like me to show you your quarters now, sir?"

"Later. First we'll go to the camp and ensure that everything is in readiness for the campaign."

There were sixty or seventy tents set up along the riverbank and over two hundred men were camped there. Scott found his men at the north end of the camp. He saw Lieutenant Paine on the riverbank and motioned him over and dismounted.

"We march for the French border the day after tomorrow, Lieutenant. I want the men ready to move at first light."

"Yes, Captain. Two powder barrels let in water and will need to be replaced." Scott looked at Lieutenant Pencutt.

"See that the powder's replaced today and add two more barrels as a precaution against further damages."

Lieutenant Pencutt led Scott over the bridge and north along the west bank. The New Cross Inn stood on the riverbank half a mile from the bridge. It was a stone building on two floors with stables at the rear. A groom took Scott's horse.

"Will you be taking part in the campaign, Lieutenant?"

"Yes, Captain. I'm looking forward to it."

"Very well, we will speak again after the briefing in the morning."

Scott passed a comfortable night at the inn and ate a good breakfast before he set off for army headquarters. A soldier took his horse when he arrived and the orderly came to his feet when Scott entered the administration building.

"This way, Captain. The briefing will be held in the general staff room."

Scott followed the orderly to a bare room fifty feet by fifty. Four rows of chairs had been set up facing the front and a map table stood under the window.

"You may take a seat anywhere, Captain."

Scott placed his coat on the seat at the end of the front row and stood at the window, watching as the town came to life. A few minutes later Major Monroe entered, followed by Lieutenant Pencutt and four other junior officers. Monroe nodded to Scott and went to the front of the room and set a pile of documents on the table. He motioned to Lieutenant Pencutt.

"Spread the maps out, Lieutenant."

Monroe came over to Scott. "I trust you found the inn comfortable, Captain?"

"Yes, Major. Thank you."

"Excellent. I wanted to warn you in advance: Captain Wathen who was to lead one of the main thrusts of the campaign, has been taken ill and, in his absence, I'm assigning you to lead the west flank."

Scott was surprised, but kept his features neutral. "I hadn't expected to play such a prominent role in the campaign, Major."

"There's nothing else for it, Captain. There are no other officers who have sufficient experience."

"I'm gratified to have been chosen, given that you have little knowledge of my career."

"I'm well advised of your career, Captain, and I believe you are capable of carrying this responsibility."

Scott felt a knot in his gut. The only way Monroe could know his history was if dispatches had accompanied the column without his knowledge. Lieutenant Paine's face flashed into his mind, but he was careful not to show any reaction.

Scott inclined his head. "I'll do my best to live up to your expectations, Major."

"Thank you, Captain. As you've not been active in the border region before, I believe it would be valuable to have someone in your command that has knowledge of the region."

"I do not—"

Monroe cut him off. "Captain Scott, I think it would be best if you accommodate my wishes in this."

The heat rose in Scott's face, and he bit back hot words. "As you wish, Major."

Monroe's expression relaxed. "Excellent, Captain," Monroe said and returned to the front of the room.

A few minutes later he called the meeting to order. He introduced Scott and Captain Alderley, who would be leading the east flank, and came to the point.

"Gentlemen, we're at war with France, and as you know, there's an unspoken understanding that hostilities are not to extend to British and French territories. Be that as it may, we are charged with patrolling the French border and demonstrating our resolve to defend British territory should the need arise."

Monroe locked his hands behind his back and paced.

"The purpose of this campaign is, as I have stated, and nothing further. This is not a prelude to an invasion. Currently, we have neither the arms nor manpower for such an undertaking."

Monroe looked around the room.

"Let me be clear. We will defend ourselves, if necessary, but we will not attack the French or provoke them to attack us. There will be no infringement on French territory, destruction of military fortifications or killing of French citizens. I will take failure to respect this order most seriously." The room fell silent, and few met Monroe's gaze.

After a moment he went on.

"Very well, gentlemen, please gather round the map table."

The map was similar to the one that Elisabeth had given Scott but less detailed. Monroe placed a pointer on the east side of a series of lakes running up to the border.

"I will lead the main body of troops up the east side of Lake Champlain. You may be aware that Captain Wathen has been taken ill." There was some murmuring around the table, but Monroe went on. "Captain Scott will lead the advance along the west shore." All eyes turned to Scott, and he looked back dispassionately.

Monroe went on to describe the route. They would follow the Hudson River north, turn west to Lake George, north again to the head of the lake, and cross the portage at Ticonderoga to Lake Champlain. As the French had reinforced Fort Frederick in the lower part of the lake, they would bypass the fort and proceed up both sides of the lake and converge at the French border. From there they would proceed west, probing along the border to determine the strength of French forces.

Monroe looked up. "Make no mistake, gentlemen. There will be contact with the French, and there may be fighting, but our job is to force the French to deploy troops to the border and keep them from being deployed elsewhere. It is not to provoke an all-out attack."

Monroe told them they were to remain active in the region as long as the weather permitted, and they would be resupplied from Albany as needed. He looked around the table.

"We will recommence these activities in the spring." A collective groan went around the room, and Monroe slapped his hand on the table. "You are soldiers of the Crown, and I expect each of you to act according to your duty. That will be all. I will see you at first light."

As the meeting broke up Major Monroe waved Scott to him. "Captain Scott, this is Lieutenant Watkins. He'll be assigned to your patrol. Lieutenant

Watkins has experience of the area and will be able to provide you with intelligence on the terrain, et cetera."

Watkins was in his early fifties, a squat solid man with heavy arms and a protruding stomach. He had a square face and a drinker's nose. Scott had seen this type of battle-hardened soldier many times but normally amongst the enlisted men. It was unusual to find a lieutenant of his age. Scott knew he was Monroe's spy and would be reporting back to him on his activities.

"Be at the encampment at first light, ready to travel," Scott said, and Watkins saluted and walked away.

"Captain, I trust that I have made my expectations for the campaign clear?" Monroe said.

"Yes, Major. I understand what's expected of me."

"Very well, Captain. I will see you in the morning."

Scott was at the river at first light. The men were formed up in rows of threes along the bank. Lieutenant Paine jogged up and saluted.

"The men are ready to embark." Fifty boats had been assembled to carry the men up river. The boats were heavily built double-ended craft about twenty-five feet in length; each had six sets of oars and a few had masts and could carry sail.

Scott saw Lieutenant Watkins approaching. He had a pack on his back and carried a musket in his right hand. Scott's stomach soured at the thought of Monroe's agent in his midst, but there was nothing he could do about it.

As Watkins saluted, he addressed Lieutenant Paine. "This is Lieutenant Watkins. Major Monroe has assigned him to our company."

Paine shook hands with him. "Welcome, Lieutenant."

Scott noted that Lieutenant Paine didn't show surprise at the late addition to their complement. He looked hard at him and the lieutenant fidgeted under his gaze.

Scott curbed his temper. There would be time to deal with these two later. He addressed himself to Lieutenant Watkins. "Embark the men and keep the boats together."

"Yes, Captain."

Scott turned to Lieutenant Paine. "Send Sergeant Crammer to me."

"Yes, Captain."

A few moments later Crammer came jogging along the riverbank.

"Sergeant, requisition one of those boats and get our provisions and baggage on board."

"Yes, Captain." Crammer turned to go, but Scott stopped him.

"Make sure the troopers who came from Scotland are in the boat."

"What of Lieutenant Paine?"

"Lieutenant Paine can fend for himself."

Crammer's mouth turned up in a grin.

There was no orderly plan to embark the troops and Scott watched as they milled about in confusion. The sergeants barked orders and pushed the troops back from the river, trying to maintain order. A few minutes later a keelboat pulled up to where he waited and Sergeant Crammer jumped ashore.

"Ready when you are, Captain."

The troopers saluted Scott as he climbed aboard. He recognized five men from his original command at the oars as he took his seat in the stern. A few minutes later Crammer and another trooper came down the embankment with Scott's baggage.

"Push off, Sergeant."

They pulled away from the bank and held position in the middle of the river while the remaining troops embarked and they finally got underway.

Scott saw Monroe in the stern of the lead keelboat as the flotilla formed up. His boat was lightly burdened and pulled ahead. The flotilla went ashore at midday to eat and Scott noted that the embarkation process improved with practice.

Scott didn't see Lieutenants Paine or Watkins until the next morning when he caught sight of them making their way through the camp. Lieutenant Watkins's face was blank, but Paine was nervous. He had the look of a delinquent schoolboy about to face the headmaster.

Scott looked from one to the other. "Gentlemen, it's your duty to report your activities to your commanding officer at the end of each day. Why have you failed to do this?"

Lieutenant Paine glanced nervously at Scott but held his tongue.

Lieutenant Watkins coughed into his hand. "Begging your pardon, Captain. By the time we disembarked and made camp we thought it best to wait until first light to report."

Scott stepped close to Watkins, and contempt for this man with his dull eyes and bland insubordination boiled up in him. "I don't give a devil's curse what you or your immature colleague thought, Lieutenant. I don't expect you to think. I expect you to do your duty."

"Begging your pardon, Captain. It won't happen again."

Scott glared at Watkins. "You'll report to me before we break camp each morning and after making camp each evening. If you find that inconvenient, I'll have you broken down to sergeant's stripes where you belong."

Watkins's jaw tightened. Scott saw a flash of emotion in his eyes and he pressed forward.

"Do you understand me, Lieutenant? You will respond to me." There was raw anger in Watkins eyes, and his breath whistled through his teeth. Silence hung in the air for a long moment, and Watkins squared his shoulders.

"Yes, Captain Scott. I understand your orders."

Scott stepped back. "Very well, Lieutenant. Dismissed."

Watkins backed away and Paine hurried after him.

By the end of the second day the troops had become accustomed to handling the boats, and the flotilla was making better progress. The country they passed through was lush. The banks of the river were forested with oak and birch and the land rolled away, rising to low hills in the distance. The sheer scale of the land was hard to grasp and Scott could only guess at its potential. There was opportunity here and he resolved to discuss how to exploit it with Elisabeth.

In the early evening they reached a set of rapids that made further progress impossible, and the flotilla made camp on the east bank. When Paine and Watkins made their report, there was little to tell, apart from one man with a festering leg wound who had been sent back to Albany.

The following day they left the river and marched for Lake George twenty miles to the north. The trail wound its way torturously through the forest, and it was late when they reached the south shore of the lake and made camp.

There were only three keelboats available at Lake George, and Major Monroe reserved these for his personal use. The rest of the column would use birch bark canoes, and a collection of these ranging from fifteen to twenty-five feet in length had been assembled. Sergeant Crammer secured two twenty-foot canoes for their group.

Scott was skeptical of these flimsy vessels, but as the morning progressed, he began to change his opinion. The canoes were light and floated high on the water, and once the troopers learned how to paddle them, they proved faster and easier to manoeuvre than the keelboats.

Lake George was long and narrow with hills rising steeply on both sides. The water was dark blue in colour and cold even in the height of summer. Scott scooped it up in his hands, and it tasted sweet and slightly tart.

It took two days to reach the place the natives called Ticonderoga at the head of the lake. It took all of the following day to portage the canoes, supplies, and equipment the four miles to Lake Champlain. Swatana and twenty of his Iroquois warriors were camped at the lake waiting for them.

The following day they were on the lake at first light. The clouds were scudding across the sky, and they fought a headwind for most of the morning. At midday they put ashore to rest and eat, but the wind held steady, and they made slow progress for the rest of the day. Towards the end of the afternoon the wind almost brought the flotilla to a standstill, and Major Monroe called an early halt.

They put into the eastern shore and made camp, and Monroe sent word for all officers to report to him. Monroe led the group down to the lakeshore and stood with his hands clasped behind his back.

"Tomorrow we'll be in striking distance of Fort Frederick. The fort guards the narrows that give access to the northern part of the lake. There we'll split our force into two groups and advance up both sides of the lake. I will proceed with the main force up the east side of the lake. Captain Scott will lead a detachment of twenty men and the Iroquois scouts along the west side of the lake."

Monroe scratched his chin.

"Our initial goal was to bypass the fort and probe the upper reaches of the lake. We have since received information that the French intend to reinforce the fort. Captain Scott will send the Iroquois to scout the fort and assess its strength, and if it can be bypassed. Even a limited incursion will alarm the French sufficiently for our purposes, but we can't risk our main force being trapped in the northern part of the lake." Monroe looked around the group. "Are there any questions, gentlemen?"

A murmur arose from the officers but no questions came forward. Monroe nodded, contented.

"Very well, dismissed."

Monroe motioned to Scott to follow him along the lakeshore.

"Captain, I received the intelligence regarding the French reinforcements just prior to the meeting. There was no time to advise you of the change of plan." Scott wasn't convinced, but he held his peace. "I want you to send the Iroquois to reconnoitre the fort. You'll follow up and report back to me. If the French are in the area in force, I need to know about it immediately."

"Very well, Major. I'll dispatch the Iroquois at once and will follow with a complement of picked men after dark."

Monroe nodded. "One more thing, Captain: Lieutenant Paine will accompany me. With twenty men you have no need of two lieutenants."

Scott was suspicious. "With twenty men I can manage with a sergeant. Lieutenant Watkins would be better deployed to support your larger group."

Monroe's lips tightened. "I'll be the judge of that, Captain."

"With so small a company, I'll be hard-pressed to find duties to assign Lieutenant Watkins."

The colour was rising in Monroe's face. "I have assigned Lieutenant Watkins to your company, Captain. That's an order. Do you have anything further to say on the matter, Captain?"

"As you wish, Major."

"You're dismissed, Captain."

Scott was furious, and he walked along the lakeshore until he had his temper under control. He was sure Major Coxe had sent a report on him to Monroe. He didn't know what Monroe was trying to accomplish, but he wouldn't give him an excuse to act against him.

Scott sent Sergeant Crammer to fetch Swatana, and when they returned, he told Crammer to stay. Scott asked Swatana to send warriors to scout the fort and told him they would follow in the canoes and meet them after dark. Swatana agreed and went off to find his warriors.

Scott turned to Crammer. "Pick the troopers who came with us from Scotland and any others you trust and have two canoes ready to depart at nightfall."

"Yes, Captain." Scott held up his hand.

"Make sure there are provisions for two weeks on board."

Crammer's eyes narrowed. "Powder and shot?"

"As much as we can carry."

"Yes, Captain." Crammer saluted and hurried away along the beach.

Scott set out as darkness was falling. He had ten men plus Sergeant Crammer and Lieutenant Watkins in two canoes. Swatana and six of his warriors were in their own canoe. Lieutenant Watkins had wanted to know why the canoes were so heavily laden, but Scott ignored him. Swatana and the Iroquois knew the area well and had arranged to rendezvous with the scouts a mile from the fort.

The canoes were swallowed up by the night. Scott could barely see the dark outline of Swatana's canoe, and they stayed close lest they lose them in the dark. Scott lost track of time, but they must have paddled for an hour before he realized they were nearing the shore. When their canoe touched the shore, two warriors emerged from the darkness and pulled it up the beach. Scott was astonished that the Iroquois found their way to the rendezvous point in almost total darkness. Such skill was enviable, but it made him wary of relying too much on them.

Swatana's canoe had already landed, and he was waiting for Scott on the beach. A quarter moon was rising, and Scott could see his outline against the lake.

"The fort is there." Swatana pointed to the north.

"Show me." Scott spoke over his shoulder. "Sergeant Crammer." Crammer fell in beside him. Lieutenant Watkins stepped up beside him, and Scott held up his hand.

"Lieutenant Watkins, you'll remain here and guard the canoes." Watkins frowned, but Scott moved off before he could respond.

Swatana led Scott and Crammer into the trees, moving parallel to the lake. Swatana made no sound as he moved, but Scott and Crammer made heavy going of it, tripping over roots and debris on the forest floor. Swatana was unhappy about the noise they made and he led them along the shoreline where there was light enough for them to see where they placed their feet.

They approached from the south and Scott could make out the shape of the fort and the height of the walls, but couldn't tell what state of repair it was in. There were torches burning on the walls and much background light from inside the fort. The gate was open and Scott could see men moving about inside the compound.

Scott whispered to Swatana. "What did your warriors see before darkness fell?"

"There are many French. They have just arrived, and they carried many boxes into the fort."

"How many men?"

"They don't know, perhaps as many as Major Monroe has."

Cleary the fort had been recently reinforced. Scott watched for half an hour, but there was nothing else to be seen, and they crept back into the trees and made their way back along the lakeshore.

When they reached the canoes, Scott called Lieutenant Watkins and Sergeant Crammer together.

"Lieutenant, you will send a man back to report to Major Monroe that the fort has been reinforced. It's too dark to estimate the French strength but it's significant."

Scott turned to Swatana. "Swatana, will you send one of your warriors to guide the trooper through the forest."

Watkins interjected. "Begging your pardon, Captain, but the canoes will be faster than travelling on foot. Wouldn't it be better to report directly to Major Monroe yourself?"

Scott turned to Watkins. "We'll not be returning to the camp, Lieutenant, so you will send a man to report to the major."

Watkins stiffened. "I don't understand, Captain. Our orders were to reconnoitre the fort and report back to Major Monroe."

Scott glanced at Crammer, and the sergeant moved closer to Watkins.

"Major Monroe spoke of a limited incursion into the northern part of the lake as desirable. The French are not long arrived. We'll slip past the fort in the dark and make a sortie into the northern arm of the lake."

"Begging your pardon, Captain Scott, but I don't believe Major Monroe would approve of such an action . . ."

"Quiet," Scott barked. "I don't care to hear what you believe Major Monroe would not approve of. I'm in command, and you will obey my orders."

Watkins took a step back and then another. "Captain, I believe your orders contravene the directive from our commanding officer, and I can't take part in the sortie you propose."

Scott lost his temper. "Lieutenant, you're relieved of your command. Sergeant Crammer, put Lieutenant Watkins in one of the canoes and send two men to take him back to the main camp."

"Yes, Captain. Come with me, Lieutenant."

Watkins sidestepped Crammer. "Captain, I must advise you that I'll report your actions directly to Major Monroe."

"Report them to the devil himself if you please, but you may tell Major Monroe this. One of the objectives of this expedition is to penetrate the northern arm of the lake. The opportunity exists if we act tonight. Tomorrow will be too late. This is called taking the initiative, Lieutenant, not running with your tail between your legs to report every five minutes. Bold action is what's expected of an officer. You may report that I am taking the initiative in the field as is my duty."

Scott could see the muscles in Watkins's face working. He was perplexed and uncertain of himself. He started to speak twice and stopped. Scott motioned to Crammer. The sergeant took Watkins's arm, and he allowed himself to be led away.

Scott spoke quietly to Crammer. "Load the supplies into one canoe and pick the men we keep with us carefully."

Ten minutes later Crammer returned. "We put the lieutenant and three troopers in the canoe. The supplies have been offloaded"

"Three troopers, Sergeant?"

"They were close with Lieutenant Watkins, Captain. The remaining men came with us from Britain."

"Very well, Sergeant, make ready to depart."

Swatana stood to one side. Scott motioned to him and walked a few steps along the beach.

"Can we slip past the fort in the dark into the upper part of the lake?"

"It will be a simple matter. The French don't patrol the lake at night."

"We'll leave immediately," Scott said.

They kept close to the east bank as they worked their way up to the narrows. The fort was half a mile away. Torches burned every fifty feet on the walls and fires had been lit between the fort and the lakeshore. Scott could hear voices calling out in French, and he cautioned the men to make no sound that would betray their presence.

They lost sight of the Iroquois in the darkness, and Scott sensed the tension in his men as they crawled through the narrows. As they came level with the fort, the wind died and every splash or clunk of a paddle on the hull seemed to be magnified. Scott signalled to stop paddling, and the canoe glided forward on its own momentum. Another hundred feet and the narrows opened up. Scott let out a sigh of relief and gave the order to paddle.

They followed the shoreline for some time; then a canoe glided out of the darkness and Swatana came level with Scott. "We should cross to the west side of the lake. The French do not go there."

"Very well, lead on." Swatana's canoe glided silently forward, and Scott's canoe fell in behind them.

The continued for an hour and then turned northwest, and the clouds cleared enough for Scott to find the North Star and confirm their heading. It was another two hours before he saw the outline of the shore emerge from the darkness. Swatana's canoe slowed, and they came up beside it.

"We will camp there." Swatana pointed into the darkness to the north. "We can make a fire and will not be seen."

"Very well." Scott had reservations about depending on the Iroquois, but for the present he had no other choice.

For the next five days Scott kept the canoes moving from first light till dark, allowing only a short break at midday to eat. The men were tiring, but they knew complaining would bring a swift response from Sergeant Crammer's fists. The Iroquois showed no signs of fatigue.

On the fifth night they camped on an island in the middle of the lake. It was heavily treed and covered with thick undergrowth. The only sounds Scott heard were the birds calling in the woods and the water lapping on the shore, and he had the sense that no man had set foot in this place before.

The next morning Scott delayed their departure until it was fully light, so he could study the map Elisabeth had given him. The lake was larger than he'd thought, and he corrected the scale and the location of the narrows. He was determined to trace their route and record any information that would be valuable to his venture.

The Iroquois camped apart from Scott's men. Scott sent Crammer to find Swatana and a short time later he and two warriors came along the shore. Swatana held his hand palm up.

Scott spread the map on the ground and Swatana squatted down and studied it curiously.

"I've seen this paper before. It's an image of the land." Scott pointed to the island. "I think we're on this island."

Swatana looked closer but didn't reply.

Scott traced the lake with his finger. "French territory begins here."

Swatana nodded.

"Have you travelled in the French territories?"

Swatana shrugged. "The Iroquois go where they please."

Scott pointed to the St. Lawrence River and followed it to the Ottawa River. "Have you travelled on these rivers?"

Swatana sat back on his haunches. "The French call this river the St. Lawrence. The other river flows from the land of the Ottawa people."

Scott pointed to the Ottawa River. "Can you guide me to this river?"

Swatana's eyes narrowed. "Why do you want to travel to the land of the Ottawa?" There was open suspicion in his voice.

Scott wasn't accustomed to being questioned by a scout. Another time he would have had the man flogged for impertinence, but he needed Swatana's cooperation, and he kept his temper under tight control.

"Britain is at war with France. The French could attack us from here." He put his finger on Mont-Royal and ran it along to the Ottawa River. "Part of our mission is to calculate French strength in this region."

Swatana was silent for a long moment. "The French will kill you if you trespass on their lands."

"We're soldiers. We don't fear the French."

Swatana remained silent, and Scott knew he had to get past his doubts. "The French don't trade for fur with the Iroquois. Is this true?"

"The French are our enemies, as they are yours."

Scott swept his hand over the map. "One day Britain will drive the French from these lands then all fur will be traded to the British alone."

Swatana looked at Scott sharply. "When will the British attack the French?"

Scott shook his head. "I don't know. First we must win the war across the great sea."

"If the British drive the French away, there will be much fur for the Iroquois to trade."

"That's possible, but I know nothing of the fur trade."

Swatana ran his finger along the river at the north end of the lake. "We must follow the river north, and then we travel overland and cross the big river to reach the Ottawa. The mouth of the river is close to the French town they call Mont-Royal. The French must not know of our presence."

Scott nodded. "We'll speak of it again when we reach the head of the lake."

It was two days till they entered the river at the north end of the lake. The river narrowed quickly, and they had to drag the canoes over gravel bars and shallows, and by the end of the third day the river was less than two hundred feet across.

After they had made camp Swatana came to speak with Scott. "From here we go overland to the river the French call St. Lawrence. We will leave at first light."

"How far are we from the French?"

"The place the French call Mont-Royal is two days travel to the northwest."

The next morning after they concealed the canoes in the woods, Scott asked Swatana to show him where they were on the map.

Swatana ran his finger along the river at the north end of Lake Champlain. "This is the river." He moved his finger west to the St. Lawrence. "We march to this place north of the cataract."

Scott tapped Mont-Royal with his finger. "It's close to Mont-Royal. There's a chance we will encounter the French."

Swatana shrugged. "The French are in the forest and on the rivers." He ran his finger down the east side of the river. "This is the old portage. This is where we will come to the river.

"We will need canoes to cross the St. Lawrence and enter the Ottawa River," Scott said.

Swatana nodded. "It may cost some scalps, but canoes can always be found."

Scott folded away the map. "Killing will draw attention to us."

"I promised my warriors scalps."

"Do not endanger our mission for the sake of your blood lust."

Swatana made a cutting motion with his hand. "When it is time, our tomahawks will be red," he said and strode away across the camp.

Scott had Crammer divide up the equipment amongst the men. Each man carried food, cooking utensils and their personal gear. They also had their muskets, powder, shot, and a bayonet. Scott carried his personal belongings, a pistol and sabre, in contrast to the Iroquois who lived off the land and carried only a sleeping roll and their weapons. Scott took a compass bearing and marked their location on the map before they set off.

Two Iroquois scouted ahead of the group. The others marched at the head of the column. They moved with an easy swinging gait and Scott's men had to step out to keep up with them. They followed a game trail along the river for two miles and then turned west and Scott took another compass bearing and made a mental note to add to the map at the end of the day.

After some hours the trail petered out, and they had to make their way through the forest. They stopped at midday to eat and late in the day they found a game trail going west and increased their pace. Scott's back ached from the pack and his feet hurt. He hadn't been on a march like this in months, and it would be days before he became accustomed to it.

When they made camp, Swatana came to speak with Scott.

"Tomorrow we will reach the big river. I don't know this trail, but I think we are close to the French town."

Scott hadn't expected to reach the St. Lawrence so soon. "The French must not know of our presence."

"My warriors will scout ahead and find a safe trail."

Scott had the men up at first light and as they prepared for the march he thought of what had happened since he left Boston. He had defied his commanding officer's orders and entered French territory. There was no going back; he would have to resign his commission, but it meant little to him now, and he dismissed it. He thought of how his life had changed since he had met Elisabeth Lockhart. Scott had long carried bitterness in his heart and, if he was honest, sorrow also, but since he'd known Elisabeth, he'd begun to realize it did not always have to be so. This journey had made it clear, and despite the difficulties that lay ahead, he felt a sense of excitement for what the future held.

Late in the afternoon Swatana's scouts returned, and Swatana came to Scott. "The river is a short distance ahead. The trail forks upstream and downstream at the portage."

"Did your warriors see the French?"

"The portage is not much used since the French built a road on the east bank."

"Lead on," Scott said.

An hour later they reached the fork in the trail, and Scott called a halt to speak with Swatana.

"Send warriors upstream to scout the portage. Tell them to find canoes if they can. The others will accompany us to the downstream end of the portage. I want to see the town they call Mont-Royal," Scott said.

CHAPTER FORTY THREE

IN THE MIDDLE OF THE morning they put the canoe into the east bank of the river and Chantal walked into the forest.

"The canoe isn't balanced," Louis said. "I'll shift the cargo."

John took his rifle and sat against a tree to keep watch. He started in surprise as Chantal stepped close to him. Her ability to move quietly was uncanny. He was sure it exceeded Louis's gift for stealth. She sank down and curled her legs under her.

"I am grateful that you allowed me to accompany you."

"You bring much that's valuable. You know part of the route and you speak the languages of the natives we hope to trade with."

A thought occurred to him and he leapt to his feet.

"Wait." He retrieved the map case from the canoe and unfolded the map.

"It is beautiful," Chantal said. She took one end of the map, and they held it between them. John put his finger on the St. Lawrence upstream from Quebec.

"We are somewhere here."

Chantal studied the map then shifted her weight and traced the Ottawa River with her finger. John was acutely aware of her. He could smell the scent of her body, and a thrill ran through him as her leg brushed against his. He felt the heat begin to rise in his neck, and he shuffled back.

John brushed a patch of ground clear, and they spread the map out on the ground. Chantal traced the Ottawa River to the west.

"I think this is where my father turned to the north. We followed a small river, and then we walked for many days."

"Will you be able to recognize the river again?"

"It's long ago, but I think I'll know it. We stopped at a village of the Ottawa People two days' journey to the west of the St. Lawrence. She put her finger on a small river.

"I think it's here or close by."

John studied the map not wanting to look at her. "I don't know how far it is to this place, but I think it will take us some weeks to reach it."

Chantal nodded. She started to speak, but Louis came up the beach and she fell silent.

"The canoe's ready." He squatted and down and John pointed out the river Chantal had identified.

Louis looked at the map for a long time then nodded to Chantal. "It is many days' travel. We must push hard if we're to make the journey before winter."

John got to his feet. "Then let's go."

Louis had redistributed the supplies and equipment and made a better place for Chantal to sit, and John noted that the canoe took less effort to paddle and to turn. They kept going until late in the evening and camped on the east bank. The current was stronger than John had anticipated, and he estimated they wouldn't reach Trois-Rivières until late the following day. They decided to bypass the town, not wanting to draw unwanted attention to themselves.

Chantal got to her feet, and John watched her as she disappeared into the forest. When he turned back Louis was looking at him.

"You should take the girl to share your sleeping roll." John felt his face flush. Louis spoke his thoughts plainly. It was a characteristic he valued, but in this case he found it too personal for comfort.

John hesitated.

"It's not our way to take a girl . . . woman, against her will."

Louis shook his head. "The girl won't resist."

John began to feel guilty discussing Chantal when she wasn't there.

"It's more complicated than that." He was struggling to find the words to say what he felt.

"There's much that I don't understand about your people," Louis said. "You make difficulties where there are none." Louis smiled with rare warmth, and John couldn't help but smile in return.

They were on the river at first light. The sky had clouded over in the night, and the wind had picked up, and by mid-morning it brought a thunderstorm. The rain fell in sheets, and they took shelter in a creek on the east bank. They pulled the canoe out of the water and turned it over to protect the powder and other perishables and took shelter under a pine tree.

The storm lasted for two hours, and it was after midday before they were back on the river. There were still several hours of daylight left when John saw a creek joining the river from the east and he pointed.

"We should camp and dry our things." The creek was wide, and they followed it for quarter of a mile before a gravel bar stopped them, and they made camp.

Late the following day they reached Trois-Rivières. There were dozens of fishing boats pulled up on the riverbank, and two sailing barks anchored off the town. The fort dominated the town. The palisade was built of logs driven into the ground, stretching for three or four hundred feet. John could see the roofs of buildings peeking up above the wall and, from the chimney smoke, he guessed the houses were packed tightly together. The main gate was open and there was a constant flow of people and wagons coming and going. No one took any notice of them. They pressed on and the activity on the river petered out after a few miles.

The following day they reached the river they'd followed from the lake of the Iroquois. They camped in the inlet, but this time they built a fire to cook and keep warm. They were better armed now, and John was less concerned they would find danger on this part of the river.

Three days later they reached Mont-Royal. First John smelt wood smoke on the breeze and half an hour later he saw a pall of smoke in the sky. The river split into two channels around an island close to the east bank, and the current increased, making them work hard to make headway. Finally they came around a turn to the south, and the town came in sight.

Mont-Royal sat on the west bank of the river. The town was surrounded by a stone wall twenty feet in height. John estimated the town extended for two miles along the river and ran west towards the hill that gave it its name.

There were four gates in the east wall, and there was a constant stream of people and wagons coming and going.

John could see church spires and the roofs of houses above the wall. The buildings were built of stone, and there were several large buildings he thought might be the town hall or governor's residence. Outside the wall wooden houses and farm buildings were scattered along the shore in both directions. John was astonished at the size of the town, and the sense of vitality it exuded, and even at a distance he could sense its energy.

Backed by warehouses and lumber yards, wharves and piers lined the riverbank for a mile. Half a dozen ships were tied up at the wharves or anchored in the river. A lighter was tied to one of the ships, and the crew was swaying a huge water cask out of the hold. There was a buzz of activity along the waterfront as men offloaded cargo onto wagons waiting on the dock.

Louis kept them close to the east bank and continued past Mont-Royal. The current was strong, but once they were past the town it eased. South of the town the river opened out into a basin two miles across. The east bank was heavily forested, but John saw farms scattered along the shore where the trees had been cleared.

They paddled into the basin and studied the town again.

"It's larger than I had expected," John said.

"I was here with my parents, but it doesn't seem familiar to me," Chantal said.

John pointed to a hill to the east of the town. "That must be Mont-Royal, the mountain it's named for. I'd like to climb it and see the town from the top."

John looked at Louis. "What do you think, Louis?"

Louis shaded his eyes. "I've never seen anything like it. I could not make my home in such a place."

John was curious to explore the town, but he knew it could prove dangerous. "We should find a place to make camp," he said.

There was little current in the basin, but there was a wind from the south, and it took them an hour to reach the eastern bank. The riverbank was sparsely populated, but they continued south, wanting to stay well away from habitation.

At the far end of the basin a creek entered the river from the east, and John motioned for Louis to bring them closer.

"This may be the place François spoke of, where the portage around the cataract begins."

They put ashore in the creek. The forest had been cleared back from the water for some distance, and they saw the remains of old campsites all along the shore.

John stepped ashore, and they pulled the canoe up the beach. "There's the start of the portage." He pointed to a break in the trees along the beach.

"This route is not much used, I think," Louis said. "François told me that since the road was built on the west bank, the portage has fallen into disuse."

They explored the beach, and it was clear no one had camped here for some time. "Too exposed," John said.

They put the canoe back in the water and pushed into the creek until they found a clearing that suited their purposes. As they waited for the water to boil for their leaf tea, John looked towards the town. "Should we visit Mont-Royal tomorrow?"

"You would like to see this town, I think," Chantal said.

"I've not seen the like since I left Scotland. I do not believe I saw its equal there."

Louis stirred leaves into the pot. "You must visit the town if you wish. I will guard our supplies."

John frowned. "I don't think it's wise for us to be separated." He turned to Chantal. "What do you think?"

"If there's a reason to go to Mont-Royal we should go. I don't believe that just to see it is reason enough."

John sighed. "You have the right of it, both of you." It didn't make sense, but John felt drawn to Mont-Royal.

Chantal was watching him. "You can see Mont-Royal another day," she said.

"Then tomorrow we make the portage and start for the Ottawa River," John said.

"It will take most of the day to make the portage." Louis poured the tea into their cups. "We must scout the route at first light."

"Then we should sleep. Tomorrow will be a hard day." John sipped his tea quietly, but his eyes were on Mont-Royal.

CHAPTER FORTY FOUR

JOHN AWOKE TO FIND CHANTAL heating water for tea and Louis not in camp. As he packed up his sleeping roll, Louis came into camp carrying the water canteens, and they sat by the fire and drank their tea as the day grew around them.

"It'll take most of the day to make the portage," John said and Louis nodded.

"We must scout the portage and find a place to camp above the rapids," Louis said.

They concealed the canoe and supplies in the forest. Louis took the lead. John didn't expect to encounter danger this close to Mont-Royal but caution had become a habit with them. The portage ran through the forest, sometimes close enough to hear the roar of the rapids. The trail had been little used, and in places it was overgrown, and they had to force their way through.

The trail ended at a clearing on the riverbank just above the rapids. Apart from where the trail cut through, the clearing was totally overgrown. John saw deer tracks on the trail, but there were no other signs of activity.

John pointed to a trail on the south side of the clearing.

"We should see where it goes." Louis nodded and trotted across the clearing into the trees. John and Chantal followed fifty feet behind. The trail followed the riverbank for a few hundred yards then turned into the forest and narrowed to where they had to move in single file. John estimated they'd covered less than a mile when they emerged onto the bank of a river coming from the east.

The river was fifty feet across, and the banks were heavily treed with branches hanging low over the water. Louis went to a patch of open ground downstream.

"We can load the canoe at the top of the portage and bring it into the river," Louis said. John could see where the river joined the St. Lawrence a few hundred yards downstream.

"It'll do fine." And he looked at Chantal.

"We make camp here tonight and cross to the Ottawa River tomorrow. Do you agree?"

Chantal looked at him thoughtfully. "I agree."

It took most of the day to carry the canoe and their gear to the top of the portage and by the time they were done John's back was aching and his stomach was growling. They launched the canoe and followed the bank upstream.

As they turned into the mouth of the river Chantal pointed to the west.

"There is the Ottawa River." John couldn't see anything that looked like the mouth of a river.

"I don't see it."

"It's an island; the river flows around it." John still didn't see what she meant, but he was sure they would find out tomorrow.

They beached the canoe, and John started to unload their gear, but Louis touched his shoulder.

"We should sweep the trail." John didn't think there was danger near, but it was their habit to make sure no one was following them. He looked at Chantal.

"I will make the fire," she said over her shoulder. John buckled on his ammunition belt and slid the pistol into its loop. On impulse he slung the cutlass over his shoulder and picked up his rifle.

Louis set off and John fell in thirty feet behind him. Louis stopped at the clearing, and John slid into the bush. They watched for long minutes, seeking signs of movement. Finally Louis stepped onto the trail and trotted into the clearing. John waited rifle at the ready, and when Louis reached the other side he ran smoothly across.

Louis loped away and in a quarter of an hour they were at the downstream end of the portage. They searched the campsite for signs they had been followed, but Louis shook his head and lifted his chin towards the portage trail.

Louis ran back across the open ground and waited for John to join him at the trailhead. John pointed to the river.

"I want to see the rapids. It won't take long." John turned off the trail and pushed his way through the trees to the river. The river was almost a mile across at this point and an island prevented them from seeing the west bank.

It was a spectacular sight: the water between the east bank and the island was a boiling mass of standing waves and torturous currents. It would be impossible for any vessel to make its way upstream against this. François had told him that the natives ran the rapids in their canoes. He doubted that he had the skill to do the same.

The roar of the water was deafening, and Louis put his mouth to John's ear. "It's enough. We should go."

John nodded.

They came back to the trail two hundred feet above the clearing. John turned south, but Louis grasped his arm and pulled him down. He put the side of his hand across his mouth for silence and cocked his head; then John heard it: voices coming from the clearing at the bottom of the portage.

They crept to where they could see across the open ground. John saw a group of men standing by a trail that came in from the east. Four were natives. He was sure they were Iroquois and, to his astonishment, two men were wearing British uniforms. His eye was drawn to one of them. He was a head taller than the rest and broad shouldered. There was something familiar about him that made his nerves tingle.

If these men were here, there might be others. John thought of Chantal alone at the camp, and he touched Louis's arm and mouthed, "We must get back to the camp."

They inched their way back into the trees, and John got to his feet, but he froze as the memory came back to him. It was the sergeant he'd fought in his uncle's croft in Glen Coe.

John started to move back towards the clearing. Louis touched his arm and John put his mouth to his ear. "It's the sergeant I fought in my uncle's home. He's one of the soldiers that murdered your people."

Louis's eyes narrowed, and he stared across the clearing. When John looked again he saw the sergeant salute a man dressed in a dark blue uniform. He moved towards the river and the sergeant fell in behind him.

John sucked in his breath, and Louis looked at him. He knew this man. His skin was darkened by the sun, but he would know that arrogant swagger anywhere. The image of his uncle choking to death flashed into his mind. For a moment anger blinded him, and it was all he could do not to rush across the clearing. He knew it would be certain death and his anger changed to cold determination.

As Scott walked towards the river John was calculating the range, and he slid his rifle in front of him and started to lift it to his shoulder.

Louis pushed the barrel down and leaned close. "They are too many."

John whispered, "It's Scott. He hung my uncle and slaughtered your people."

Louis looked hard at the soldiers. "If you shoot him, we'll be overrun." He didn't say John shouldn't fire. He simply stated that they would be killed if he did.

Louis spoke again. "If the Iroquois take the girl, they will torture her for escaping." Cold fear twisted John's gut. Scott was two hundred feet away, and he knew he could hit him at this distance, but he shook his head.

"There will be another time." Louis gripped John's arm. "We'll hunt him to his death."

They crept back into the forest and Louis led them in a circle back to the trail upstream from the clearing. Then Louis leapt away with John close behind.

John's mind was fixed on reaching the camp. Louis had the right of it. If the Iroquois took Chantal, they wouldn't kill her. She was too valuable as a slave, but they would punish her fearfully. Louis slowed as they approached the top of the portage, and they searched the clearing for danger.

Louis nodded, and they ran hard for the trail on the south side of the clearing. John knew they hadn't waited long enough, and he braced himself for the impact of a musket ball, but none came and he breathed again when they were back in the trees.

The sun was beginning to go down and John strained to see ahead. They were close to the camp when Louis stopped and held up his hand. John stopped and listened. The forest was silent; not even a bird sang and John felt a tingle of alarm run along his spine.

Louis cocked his head and looked at John; then he heard it: a girl crying out. The sound was distorted by the trees, but John recognized Chantal's voice. Panic seized him, and he rushed forward, but Louis caught his arm and leaned close. "Quietly."

John was overwhelmed by the need to reach Chantal, but he forced himself to stop and nodded to Louis.

Louis moved almost silently. John couldn't match his skill, but he had learned much from him, and he knew he would not be easily heard. The minutes dragged by, but finally John recognized a turn in the trail close to the camp. He heard Chantal's voice ring through the forest, and he was astonished when he realized that she was calling out in French trying to warn him.

John saw the river through the trees and a moment later he smelt wood smoke. Louis left the trail and moved directly towards the clearing. John followed; tension squeezed his chest, but he forced himself to place his feet carefully and make no sound.

Finally John saw the camp. Their sleeping rolls and gear were scattered around the campsite. Downstream to their right several men were shouting, and John recognized the dialect as Iroquois. Then Chantal cried out in pain. John turned towards her, but Louis put his hand on his shoulder and backed away from the camp. They moved in a half circle and came back to the river fifty feet downstream. As his view opened up, John's gut tightened. Six Iroquois warriors were standing on the riverbank. They were armed with tomahawks and knives, and John counted three muskets.

Two Iroquois held Chantal by the arms. She was struggling fiercely, but they held her easily. The third warrior had laid his weapons down and was removing his leggings. Chantal lashed out trying to kick him in the groin, and he jumped back in alarm, much to the amusement of the other warriors. One of the Iroquois tore her dress off her shoulder revealing her breast, white as alabaster where the sun hadn't touched it. The Iroquois roared their approval and called out encouragement to their half-naked brother.

Anger burned in John till he thought his chest would burst. Louis touched his arm, pointed to the warriors on the left and tapped his chest and lifted his chin towards the Iroquois holding Chantal. John nodded. He slid the pistol out of his belt and put his hunting bag on top of it to cover the sound while he cocked the hammers then set it on the ground. He did the same with the rifle and nodded to Louis.

John brought the rifle up, and he took slow breaths to calm himself. He aimed at the warrior holding Chantal's left arm; the others were moving too much, and he needed to be sure of a kill. He knew that Louis would wait for his signal, and he placed the sight in the centre of the warrior's chest and squeezed the trigger.

The report of the rifle shattered the quiet of the forest. Louis fired so quickly after him it was impossible to distinguish between them. John was blinded by the powder burn, but he was certain that he had hit his man clean. He dropped the rifle, grabbed the pistol, and charged onto the riverbank.

"A Wallace, a Wallace." Without thinking, he gave the battle cry of his clan.

The powder smoke was still clearing when John burst onto the riverbank. The warrior he had fired at was lying on the grass, a red gash in his chest. Louis was charging the other warriors, tomahawk in hand. The second warrior holding Chantal looked around, his face frozen in shock. The third warrior reacted instantly. He let out a cry of rage and turned, half-naked, and rushed at John. His cry brought the other Iroquois out of his stupor. He let go of Chantal and charged behind his brother.

John ran at the Iroquois and, at the last moment, put his head down and slammed his left shoulder into his attacker's chest, driving him back. The impact almost stunned him, but John gritted his teeth and heaved the warrior back, crashing into the man behind him. John drove the barrel of the pistol into the Iroquois's stomach and pulled both triggers.

The discharge was absorbed by the warrior's body, but John's arm was numbed by the double recoil. The Iroquois dropped like a stone and the warrior behind him stood staring at the bloody mess where his stomach had been. He let out a wail of agony and collapsed, trying to staunch the flow of blood with his hands.

Chantal screamed a warning, and John turned to see a warrior charging at him. He was heavier than John with a broad chest and powerful arms. He swung a tomahawk in his right hand and screamed a war cry as he came on. John reacted without thinking. He dug his heals in and launched himself at the warrior. He was taken off guard and tried to change the swing of his tomahawk, but he was slow. John blocked his right arm, and slammed the pistol into his groin and he grunted in pain and doubled over.

John took a half step back, but the Iroquois straightened up, swinging the tomahawk backhanded. John staggered back, trying to keep his balance and the pistol dropped from his numbed fingers. The Iroquois charged forward and slammed into him, knocking him off his feet. John twisted to the right, breaking his fall with his arm, but the warrior's weight drove him to the ground.

John hardened his body, but his fall had almost stunned him. The Iroquois swung his tomahawk down at John's head. John managed to block his arm, but it was a powerful stroke, and it carried through and struck him a glancing blow on the temple.

John's head slammed into the ground, and the world spun. He grabbed the Iroquois's wrist with his left hand as he fought to stay conscious. The warrior tried to break his grip, but John held on doggedly. Blood ran into his left eye and his mouth. The bitter taste of the blood galvanized him. He let go of the warrior's wrist, grabbed his hair with both hands, and lunged up and slammed his forehead into his face. John felt the warrior's nose crack, and he reared back roaring in pain.

John heaved with all his strength and twisted to the side reaching for his dirk. His hand closed on the handle, but the Iroquois drove him down again, knocking the wind out of him and trapping his arm beneath him. John's chest heaved, gasping for air, and the warrior threw the tomahawk back to strike.

John saw a hand grasp the Iroquois's wrist and a slender arm encircle his neck and a cry of desperation came from Chantal as she threw herself backwards. The warrior's weight was lifted off John's chest. He tore the dirk from its scabbard, and drove the blade in below his ribs. The Iroquois grunted in pain and grabbed Chantal's arm. He almost broke her hold on him, but John drove the dirk in again and again, and he fell back trapping Chantal beneath him. John rolled to his knees and drove the dirk into his chest.

The Iroquois went limp. John rolled the body over, and Chantal wriggled out from under. John looked around. Three Iroquois were down; two were dead and a third was curled up in a ball, clutching his stomach. Louis was on his hands and knees, gasping for breath. John pushed himself up but the world swayed around him and he staggered, reeling with nausea.

Chantal slid her arm around his waist.

"You're hurt. Let me see the wound."

John shook his head. "Louis is injured. Help him."

John stumbled over to Louis with Chantal supporting him. He went down on one knee and Chantal helped Louis to a sitting position. Louis's right eye was swollen shut and blood was oozing from his right shoulder.

"Let me see the shoulder." He pulled Louis's jerkin back and sucked his breath through his teeth. There was a wide gash on Louis's shoulder between his arm and his chest.

John looked at Chantal.

"Help me." He put his arms under Louis's chest and lifted. Chantal took his feet, and they half dragged half carried him to the camp and sat him against a fallen tree. John leaned against the tree as a wave of nausea swept over him.

When John came to his senses Chantal was cleaning the blood from Louis's wound with a strip of cloth torn from her sleeping roll.

"The wound must be sewn shut."

"There's no time. There are British soldiers and more Iroquois at the portage. They'll have heard the gunfire." Chantal's eyes flashed with alarm. She held the cloth against the wound to staunch the bleeding and John cut a strip from her sleeping roll and bound it tight.

John got to his feet, dizziness swept over him and the world went black. When he opened his eyes again, a searing pain shot through his head. He was disorientated but, after a moment, realized he was sitting on the ground with his back against the tree. Louis was a few feet away watching him.

John felt something cold on his face and knew that Chantal was beside him. She was using a wet cloth to clean the blood from his face and head. She sat back on her heels.

"I'm glad you've come back to us." She looked at him almost fiercely. There was some intense emotion behind her eyes that he couldn't fathom, and after a moment she spoke quietly.

"Lean your head back."

Chantal poured water onto his face and washed the blood from his eye.

"How long was I unconscious?"

"It's been some time."

John started to get up.

"Wait, I must bind the wound."

"There's no time."

She ignored him and started to wrap a cloth around his head. "The wound will open and blind you again."

John let her finish then got to his feet. It felt as if his head had been split open, and the world began to spin, but he forced himself to concentrate.

"We must get Louis to the canoe. The British will be coming."

"Louis can you walk?" Louis tried to get to his feet. The canoe was a hundred feet downstream from the camp, and John and Chantal supported him as they struggled along the beach.

John helped Louis to sit in the bottom of the canoe with his back against the cross brace. Louis gripped his arm.

"The Iroquois will come. We must leave."

"I know." John slid the canoe into the water with only the bow resting on the beach and hurried back to the camp, reeling with nausea.

Flies were buzzing around the bodies of the Iroquois as John picked up the pistol and wiped the dirt off. He retrieved the rifles from the underbrush and turned back to the camp. He went ten steps and froze listening. A moment later it came again: a man shouting. It was a long way away, but he was shouting in English.

John broke into a run fighting back the nausea. He knew that if he could hear the British, then the Iroquois were closer. Chantal had bundled their gear into the sleeping rolls and had one under each arm.

"We have to go. Give me one." She handed John one of the rolls and he fell in behind her. His head was pounding and there was a stabbing pain behind his left eye but he forced himself on.

John looked over his shoulder nervously. There was no pursuit yet, but he knew they didn't have much time. Chantal dropped the sleeping roll into the canoe.

"I will push off," she called. John threw the sleeping roll into the canoe and splashed into the river. Louis took the rifles with his good arm, and Chantal was already pushing off as he climbed into the stern.

They back-paddled away from the beach, and John brought the canoe around. He dug his paddle in and Chantal fell in time with him driving for the mouth of the river. John looked back. There was no sign of the Iroquois, but they wouldn't be safe until they were clear of the river and out of musket range. John's stomach heaved and he scooped a handful of water onto his face. Chantal looked back at him. He nodded and she went back to paddling.

John willed the canoe forward, but time seemed to slow as they approached the mouth of the river. Finally they cleared the gravel bar and John brought the canoe around, angling out into the St. Lawrence.

Louis pointed with his left arm.

"There." John turned to see four Iroquois running towards the mouth of the river. There was a flash of colour at the treeline, and he saw five men in red uniforms come out of the forest.

John turned around. Chantal was looking back. She glanced at him then dug her paddle in, and John fell to putting all his strength into it. A moment later two musket shots rang out, and there was a splash twenty feet to the right. John didn't see the second ball fall.

John heard shouting in English, and he looked back. Four men were running along the riverbank. Three wore British uniforms; the fourth was Iroquois. They stopped on the beach between the river and the St. Lawrence. One man turned to the side and extended his arm towards them. John was perplexed until he realized he was holding a telescope. He knew it was Scott, and he stared back, hating him.

When they were well away from the shore Chantal pointed southwest.

"We should go to the south side of the island. I think the current is less there."

"Save your strength," John said. "It's three miles to that headland."

John was startled when three musket shots rang out behind them. The riverbank was half a mile behind them, but he could see the red uniforms at the river mouth, and the powder smoke floating away on the breeze. They were looking upstream. John followed their line of sight and swore under his breath. Half a mile away two canoes were paddling for the mouth of the river.

John spun around. Chantal had seen them, too.

"They fired to attract them."

"They must have sent scouts to find canoes."

"They couldn't have known we were here. Why would they want canoes? Where are they going?"

John shook his head.

"I don't know, but Scott is here, and I have business with that man." Chantal looked at the shore then back at John.

"We must not let them catch us on the river."

"They will be faster than us. We must make the most of our lead. Push hard," Chantal said.

They were in the middle of the river when the wind came up from the south almost bringing them to a standstill. John looked back. The two canoes were already putting out from the mouth of the river. They were a mile behind, but John knew the Iroquois would eat up the gap between them. They had to reach the western shore before they came up with them.

John pushed and Chantal put all her strength into paddling. The Iroquois were coming on fast, and he looked to the western shore and back at the Iroquois, trying to gauge how fast they were closing. He was confident they would reach the shore before the Iroquois overtook them but they wouldn't be far behind.

As they approached the western shore the wind increased and John kept his head down and paddled for all he was worth, not even looking back. Finally they struggled around the eastern end of a headland and the wind dropped.

John started to turn towards the shore but Chantal called, "That's an island; the Ottawa River runs around it on both sides. The western shore is there." She pointed over the bows.

"I see it."

John held steady until they were a quarter of a mile from the shore then turned west into the Ottawa River.

"There." Louis pointed. A spit of land ran out from the shore where the St. Lawrence and Ottawa Rivers met. Beyond the point, a creek joined the Ottawa River from the south. The creek was three hundred feet across and heavily treed on both banks.

John drove the canoe straight in hoping there wouldn't be a gravel bar, and they slid under the shadow of the trees. He kept on for a hundred yards then put the canoe onto the west bank. Chantal dragged the canoe up the beach, and John helped Louis ashore.

"Take only the weapons and a little food." Louis held his right arm against his chest but he could walk. John and Chantal carried their sleeping rolls and weapons, and they made their way up the bank of the creek into the forest.

John turned back towards the mouth of the creek.

"We have to slow the British down." Louis and Chantal followed without a word, and he worked his way to the mouth of the creek and pushed through the underbrush to where they could see the river. John was astonished at how much distance the Iroquois had made up. They were less than half a mile from the mouth of the creek. He moved farther north to where the creek and the Ottawa River met and crouched behind a downed pine tree close to the shore.

Louis came up on one side and Chantal the other.

"We have a clear shot across the mouth of the creek. We can take two, perhaps three."

"You must do it. I can't shoot." John looked at Chantal.

"It'll be dark in an hour. If we can kill or wound some of them perhaps we can escape in the dark."

"Shoot the Iroquois if you can," Chantal said. "They will lose heart if one of their number is killed."

John loaded the rifles and both barrels of the pistol and placed his hunting bag on the tree as a rest and sighted along the barrel. He would have a clear field of fire as the canoes entered the creek. He had time for two shots, but he didn't think he could reload in time for a third.

They sat in silence watching the canoes come on. John was calculating the distance, trying to pick his best shot. The wind had died down and the creek was flat calm. He wouldn't have to allow for the wind blowing the ball off target, but it would be a hard shot to judge; shooting over water always made it more difficult.

As the canoes came closer John picked out the individuals in each vessel. There were four men in each canoe. He recognized the big sergeant in the second canoe, wielding his paddle like a child's toy. He couldn't make out the face of the man ahead of him, but it had to be Scott. If his canoe came up beside the leading vessel, he would try a shot.

John waited until the first canoe entered the creek then brought his rifle to bear. He glanced at Louis and Chantal but both had their eyes fixed on the canoes. The first canoe was four hundred yards out and coming on quickly. The second canoe began to pull level with it. He heard a voice calling out and both canoes turned towards the west side of the creek straight for where they were hiding.

John experienced a moment of panic, fearing that they'd been spotted, but Louis touched his arm.

"They fear an ambush." John kept his eyes on the target and didn't answer. The creek was three hundred feet across at the mouth but narrowed quickly. The canoes were already in range but John waited.

John's nerves were jittery and his hands were shaking. He kept his eyes on the canoes, took a long breath, let it out slowly and lined up on the first canoe. He put the sight on the Iroquois in the stern of the first canoe and waited for the distance to close. Two hundred feet from the beach the canoe started to turn towards the shore. John shifted his aim to the Iroquois in the bow and drew a breath, waiting as the canoe turned to face them.

John placed the sight in the middle of the Iroquois's chest, let his breath out slowly, and squeezed the trigger. The rifle cracked and he was blinded by the powder burn, but certain he had hit the Iroquois. Chantal took the rifle and handed him Louis's weapon and he brought it to bear. As the smoke cleared he saw that the Iroquois in the first canoe was down and both canoes were turning, trying to get away. John put the sights between the shoulder blades of the Iroquois in the stern of the first canoe and squeezed the trigger.

As the smoke floated away, John saw that his second shot had also struck home. Both canoes were driving towards the opposite bank and, even with two men down, were opening the distance quickly. John felt a touch on his arm and Chantal handed him his rifle.

"It's loaded."

"Well done." Scott's canoe had almost reached the far side of the creek, too far for a sure hit. There were only two paddlers in the second canoe, and it was less than three hundred feet away. One of the Iroquois looked over his shoulder, and John put the sight in the middle of his back and squeezed the trigger. It was an easy shot for his rifle. He saw the ball strike and the warrior slump forward into the bottom of the canoe.

John rolled to his knees and started to reload the rifle. Chantal was working on Louis's rifle. He measured the powder, poured it into the barrel, and tamped it with the ramrod. As he took a ball from his ammunition pouch, Chantal handed him Louis's rifle.

"I'll finish it." John brought the rifle to bear on the other side of the creek. One canoe was already drawn up on the beach and Scott and the other soldiers were gone. The second canoe was twenty feet along the beach and he caught sight of the last Iroquois disappearing into the trees.

John sat back. "I'm sure I hit three."

Louis shifted around to face him. "The first shot struck the Iroquois and carried through and hit the soldier in front of him. I saw him fall."

"Louis is right," Chantal said. "I saw the soldier struck."

"Better than I hoped for."

John looked at the sky.

"The British are hard hit, but they'll keep coming."

"We must find a place we can defend," Louis said.

"We can try for the canoe when it is dark."

"The Iroquois will destroy it and lie in ambush, hoping we'll come."

"Can you move?"

"I can move, but I'll be little use if we have to fight."

John turned to find Chantal's eyes searching his face. Her scrutiny made him uncomfortable but he held her gaze.

"We must find a place where Louis can rest."

"There's only an hour of daylight left. We may be able to slip away in the dark."

"Perhaps we can, but Louis can't travel quickly, and he and I have business with Captain Scott."

They gathered up their gear and slipped into the forest. John had seen a line of hills in the distance that marked the edge of the Ottawa River and he followed the creek, looking for a way out of the valley. It was starting to get dark when John heard the sound of falling water ahead. It grew steadily as they moved upstream till they entered a clearing where the creek ran over a rock face and dropped six feet into a pool. The pool took up the whole clearing apart from a strip of open ground to the side of the waterfall. Two pines had fallen on the creek bank, one over the waterfall.

John searched the clearing for danger. Chantal put her hand on his arm and spoke quietly.

"We should rest." John glanced at Louis. He was swaying on his feet and he nodded.

"Behind the fallen trees." The trees formed a barrier on two sides and backed onto the waterfall. It was as defendable a position as they would find.

John helped Louis to sit against the rock face.

"Let me look at your shoulder." Louis nodded but didn't answer. The wound had pulled open and was bleeding freely. The bandage was caked in dry blood and John cut it away with his dirk and squeezed the wound until it stopped bleeding.

Chantal soaked a cloth in the creek and washed the blood from the wound, then tore a strip from her sleeping roll to form a bandage. John's hands were shaking and Chantal put her hand on his arm.

"I'll do it. You must rest."

John sat against the tree and watched Chantal bind Louis's shoulder. Even though they were in danger, she showed no sign of distress, bandaging Louis's wound with quick deft movements. She confused and perplexed him and he despaired of understanding her, but he was drawn to her and even exhaustion didn't diminish his desire for her.

Chantal spread Louis's sleeping roll out and helped him lower himself onto it, and he lay still and closed his eyes.

Chantal sat close to John.

"He's lost a lot of blood, but I don't think the wound has done any permanent damage."

"Let him sleep. He'll need his strength soon enough." John got to his feet and picked up his rifle.

"I'll scout the trail." He slid the pistol out of his belt and handed it to Chantal. "Do you know how to use it?"

"I can shoot it. The rifle, too, if I must."

John slid over the tree and trotted along the creek bank. His body ached, and the pain behind his eye had returned, but he knew it would be folly not to scout the trail. He retraced their route for a mile, stopping to watch and listen before he was satisfied they weren't being followed.

By the time John reached the camp it was almost completely dark. He walked openly. He knew Chantal would be watching and he didn't want her to mistake him for an Iroquois. He climbed over the tree trunk and slid onto the ground and rested his head against the tree. Chantal sat by Louis with the pistol on her lap. She was cutting pemmican into thin strips, and she handed him a piece.

"You must eat."

John tried to remember when he'd last eaten. He couldn't bring it to mind and put it down to the blow on the head. The moon hadn't risen and it was almost completely dark. Chantal sat against the rock face. John could only see her outline and the gleam of her teeth as she ate. Louis's breathing was the loudest sound in the camp.

After he had eaten John felt better. His body ached. The pain behind his eye had eased, but he realized he was becoming drowsy and shook himself awake. He stood up and stretched then crouched down behind the tree, looking out into the darkness.

A few moments later Chantal came and knelt beside him.

"What will we do in the morning?" John was intensely aware of her. He ached to touch her, but he knew it would shatter her trust in him. "How do we escape from here?"

John drew a breath to give him time to compose him thoughts.

"We must take a canoe, ours or one from the Iroquois before first light."

It was totally dark but John was aware that Chantal had turned towards him.

"It will be difficult to get past the Iroquois."

"Louis is not strong enough to outrun them. I think it's better to try for the canoe."

Chantal was quiet; then John heard her move.

"I'll watch. You must rest." John was reluctant to sleep when there was danger near, but he felt Chantal's hand on his arm.

"I'll wake you when the moon rises."

"Very well." He was exhausted but he felt a sense of intimacy with Chantal for the first time, and he regretted its loss more than he needed sleep.

John wrapped himself in his sleeping roll and lay back staring into the blackness. Images ran through his head like a waking dream that would not stop until exhaustion finally overcame him and he slept.

CHAPTER FORTY FIVE

SCOTT PACED THE BANK OF the creek. He was beside himself with anger. They'd been in the middle of the creek well beyond musket range. How could they have been hit at that distance? Two Iroquois were dead, and Swatana had been struck in the neck. It was a killing wound but for now he was still breathing. One of his troopers had taken a ball in the chest. There was blood on his lips and Scott knew he wouldn't last the night.

Scott went to where they had taken the wounded. Swatana was sitting on the ground, his back against a tree. He'd been struck above his collarbone. He was holding a bloody cloth over the wound, and the other Iroquois sat by him, despair on his face.

Scott went down on one knee and spoke to the Iroquois warrior.

"You must track the men who did this to your chief." The warrior shook his head.

"The sun is almost down. I can't track them in the dark." Scott looked at the sky.

"There's still light. One of them is wounded, and they can't have gone far." The Iroquois shook his head.

"My chief is injured, and I must tend to him."

Scott's frustration boiled over, and he shouted, "I order you to track these men down tonight." The Iroquois's face remained impassive, but he didn't move. Scott started to get to his feet, but Swatana put his hand on his arm.

"He knows I won't live. He will not leave until I die."

Scott got to his feet and strode to the bank of the creek.

"Sergeant Crammer." Crammer came at the double.

"Sergeant, send the remaining trooper to bring more men across the river." Crammer hesitated.

"Begging your pardon, Captain, but it'll be dark shortly. They may not be able to find their way back to this creek."

"Do as I say, Sergeant," Scott shouted in Crammer's face. The sergeant flinched and stepped back.

"Right away, Captain."

Scott began to pace. He had been shocked when he recognized the boy through his telescope earlier. The boy had ruined his career, caused him to be banished from his homeland, and his need for revenge nearly consumed him. Yet, somewhere in his mind a hesitation began to take route; a silent doubt that he couldn't articulate was eating away his resolve. It was a new sensation for Scott. It made him feel weak, and he thrust it from his mind in distaste.

Sergeant Crammer came to report that the trooper had taken a canoe and set off across the river.

"Should I light a fire to guide them to us, Captain?"

"I think not, Sergeant. The boy is likely long gone, but there's no need to make targets of ourselves."

"Yes, Captain." Crammer saluted and faded back into the darkness.

Scott wrapped his great coat around his shoulders and sat with his back to a tree. His mind was too agitated to sleep, but he could try to get some rest. He didn't mark the passage of time, but at one point he saw the moon had risen. He watched its yellow glow move over the surface of the river and in spite of his state of mind his head dropped onto his chest, and he fell into a troubled sleep.

Scott jolted awake to find himself lying on his side, and got to his feet, feeling disorientated. He steadied himself against the tree. The moon had gone down, so he must have slept for hours. The sky had clouded over. The forest was in darkness with only a glimmer of light reflected from the river.

Scott felt his way to the creek and washed the sleep from his eyes and worked his way along the shore till he picked out the shape of the canoe pulled up on the beach. There was no sign of the second canoe. Either the trooper hadn't been able to find his way back to the creek, or he had decided to stay on the other shore. He would deal with his failure or disobedience later.

Scott started up the beach when he heard Crammer's voice.

"Captain Scott, sir, is that you?"

"Yes, Sergeant, the trooper hasn't come back with reinforcements, I see."

"No, Captain, I was afraid he would have difficulty convincing the Iroquois to cross the river in the dark."

Scott went to where Swatana lay. The other warrior had constructed a lean-to shelter between two trees. He sat cross-legged on the ground singing to himself and as Scott approached he fell silent. Scott went down on one knee and looked inside.

"Swatana's spirit has departed. It travels now with his ancestors."

"I'm sorry that he has died. He was a strong leader. You must help us find the men who killed him now." The warrior didn't reply, but he got to his feet and Scott stood with him.

"What is your name?"

"I am Onontio, and I will hunt these men."

Scott turned to Crammer.

"Make ready to leave, Sergeant."

"Can the Iroquois track them in the dark?" Scott started to speak, but Onontio interrupted him.

"They will follow the creek. It's the easiest path to travel, and I'll find their trail at first light."

Scott left most of their gear. If the boy eluded them, he wouldn't find him easily again, and the less he carried the better. He took only a pistol and the sabre hanging at his belt.

Crammer carried his musket. He offered a musket to Onontio, but he said he didn't know how to use it, and he needed only his tomahawk to deal with his chief's killers. Onontio led, and they made two attempts to ford the creek before they found a place where it was shallow enough to cross. On the first attempt, Crammer dropped his musket in the creek, and Scott cursed his carelessness. They would have to wait till it was light to reload, and it would cost them time.

On the west bank of the creek Onontio turned to Scott.

"I will lead thirty paces. You must move quietly. Sound carries far in the forest." Scott could only see Onontio's outline in the dark.

"Lead on."

CHAPTER FORTY SIX

JOHN WAS ROUSED FROM SLEEP by movement close by. His eyes flew open and he reached for his cutlass. Then he felt something touch his shoulder and Chantal whispered, "It's me, Chantal." John froze as his hand closed around the hilt of the cutlass.

"What's amiss?"

"All is well, John."

John turned towards her. He couldn't see her, but he sensed her lying close to him. His hand brushed against her, and a thrill ran through him when he realized she was naked. Her hand touched his face.

"Louis sleeps."

John started to speak, but she put her fingers on his lips and put her mouth close to his ear.

"I have been used by the Iroquois. You have seen this." John flinched, but she put her hand on the side of his face. "In the wilderness you could have taken me any time you wished, but you did not."

"I would not . . ." Chantal silenced him with her fingers.

She slid closer until her body lay against his.

"I spent half my life with the Iroquois, and I knew only their ways. They would have named you weak and fearful as did I."

"It is not our way, Chantal."

She moved forward till her face touched his.

"Any coward can take a woman against her will. It takes strength to act as you have done, to show me honour and to give me respect. This I learned in my uncle's house." She caressed his face, her fingers cool against his skin. "You fought for me and fought again when I was in need. Now I give myself to you freely." She held his face in her hands and kissed his mouth. Her lips were soft and the taste of her made him mad.

John was overwhelmed by the emotions that surged in him. His need for her consumed him like fire in his veins, but he had never known a woman's body, and he feared he might fail or disappoint her in some way.

Chantal put her hand on John's chest and slid it inside his shirt. A shiver ran through him and he reached for her. Her body was slender and supple and her skin was cool and soft under his fingers. He slid his hand down her flank, tracing the curve of her hip and the swell of her rump, and she pressed herself against him, her breath hot on his face.

Chantal started to undo the fastenings of John's shirt, and he rolled onto his back, pulling impatiently at his belt and breeches, and Chantal pulled the blanket over them.

He put his mouth close to her ear. "I have never been with a woman."

"It is a natural thing," she said. "It will be good between us." She wrapped her legs around him, pulling him to her. John gasped at the rush of sensation, and she clung to him and cried out, fierce in her passion.

John awoke to find Chantal watching him. She smiled, and it was the most beautiful thing he had ever seen. It warmed his heart and filled him with a sense of belonging that was as natural as breathing.

She touched his face with her fingers. "I began to think you would not wake again."

John put his face in her hair and breathed in the smell of her; then he rolled onto his back and pulled her close. A hint of light was colouring the sky. A thrill of alarm ran through him, and he sat up. "It's almost light. We must go."

Chantal sat up and the blanket slid off her shoulders, leaving her naked. John pulled her to him and kissed her mouth.

John pulled his boots on and dressed hurriedly. Chantal was already dressed and packing up their gear. John heard a sound behind him, and he turned to see Louis looking at him. He knelt beside him. His eyes were clear, but he was tense with pain.

John touched his shoulder. "Can you travel?"

"I can travel, but I have slept too long."

"I'll scout the creek."

"Go quietly. Beware of the Iroquois."

John went to Chantal and knelt. He slid his cutlass onto his back and picked up his rifle.

"You must eat." She held a strip of pemmican.

"I'll eat when I return."

She touched his face with her fingers. "Take care."

John slid over the fallen tree and went down on one knee, holding his breath to listen. He could hear the creek twenty feet away and the rustle of the breeze in the trees. Nothing seemed out of place but doubt lingered in his mind and he waited.

As John started to get to his feet a tiny bird swooped out of the forest and glided away across the creek. The hair on the back of his neck tingled with alarm. There was no bird song, no dawn chorus. John froze as a sound registered in his mind. It was so soft that if it had been in front of him he wouldn't have heard it. It was the sound of moccasins on soft ground. He spun left and brought his rifle around, pulling the hammer to full cock.

The quiet was pierced by a war cry, and John saw an Iroquois warrior emerging from the darkness. He was thirty feet away running flat out, his feet almost silent on the soft ground. John came to his feet and brought the rifle to bear. The Iroquois was still only a dark shape and he aimed for the centre of his body and squeezed the trigger. The crack of the rifle echoed through the forest and the flash from the barrel lit the clearing in an orange light.

John was alarmed at how close the Iroquois had been able to come without being detected, and he knew he wouldn't be alone. He turned and took a step towards the fallen tree and Chantal screamed.

"Down, John."

John threw himself left and something slammed into him, spinning him around. A searing pain shot through his left shoulder and arm and he knew he'd been struck by a musket ball. He dropped the rifle and threw his hands out to break his fall. His left arm was pulsing with pain, but he could still use it. He landed on his left side and rolled to his feet.

John saw a man charging at him along the bank of the creek, tall and broad-shouldered, and even in the dim light he recognized the sergeant he'd fought in his uncle's croft. Crammer was carrying a musket and John saw the glint of the bayonet fixed to the barrel. He was running flat out, his feet pounding on the soft ground; he let out a scream of rage and pointed the bayonet.

John jerked the cutlass from its scabbard. The tree was behind him, the creek to his right, leaving little room to manoeuvre. He let out a yell and launched himself at Crammer. He was outreached by the bayonet but, standing still, he was an easy target. He knew he would only have one chance to deflect the bayonet and he held the cutlass in front of him and concentrated on Crammer.

The crack of a Kentucky Long Rifle barked across the clearing and Crammer was thrown back, turning as he fell. John looked behind him; Chantal stood behind the tree, holding Louis's rifle, powder smoke streaming from the barrel. John was startled by a roar of anger, and was astonished to see Crammer get to his feet, still holding the musket.

Crammer's left shoulder was a bloody mess and his arm hung limp at his side. He staggered a few paces, trying to get his balance, then couched the musket under his arm like a lance and charged at John. He moved with alarming speed and John jumped to his left, barely missing the bayonet.

The sergeant turned, sweeping the musket around at John's head. John took a sliding step inside the reach of the bayonet and blocked it with the cutlass. The impact jarred his wrist, but John threw the musket back and slashed at Crammer's face, opening a wound from his eye to his jaw.

Crammer roared and leapt at John, dropping the musket. He slammed into him, knocking him off balance. He fell backwards and Crammer threw himself on top of him. John dropped the cutlass and twisted, pulling his dirk from its scabbard. Crammer locked his arm around John's neck, reaching for his windpipe.

"I will make an end of you now, boy." Crammer's voice was slurred with pain and blood spattered onto John's face, but even injured, his strength was incredible.

John changed his grip on the dirk and drove it into Crammer's side. Crammer reared back, roaring in pain, and threw himself off John, blood pouring from his side, and rolled away. John got to his knees and threw himself on top of him and drove the dirk into his neck. Blood spurted from the wound, and John struck again and again until Crammer went limp.

John pushed himself off Crammer's body and got to his feet, blood dripping from the dirk. Blood was pulsing in his veins, and his senses were sharpened to a razor's edge. The light was stronger, and he could see every detail of the forest and across the creek. He turned towards the camp, but he caught a flash of colour in the corner of his eye.

Scott was standing on the edge of the clearing. His body was turned to the side, and his right arm extended towards him holding a pistol.

"Finally we come to it," Scott said. "It's been a long chase."

John sucked in his breath. "You owe me a life, Scott, and more for what you've done." He looked at his enemy. Scott's eyes were pale killer blue, and John's hatred all but choked him.

John clenched the dirk in his hand and the blood oozed from his fingers as he prepared to move. Scott's eyes flashed to the right, and he turned and fired the pistol at the camp. As Scott's arm rode up with the recoil, two pistol shots rang out behind him, and John looked back. Chantal was standing behind the tree her arm thrown up from the pistol discharge.

John dropped the dirk, scooped up the cutlass, and charged at Scott. Scott was uninjured, and he threw the pistol down and drew his sabre.

"Perhaps this is better; a pistol shot would be too easy." He started to circle to his left.

John went straight at him bringing the cutlass down in an arch at Scott's face. Scott parried the blow, throwing John's arm to his left. John reversed the blow and struck at Scott's right knee, but he dropped his sabre, parried the blow and came back on riposte cutting at John's face. John leapt back. He stumbled over Crammer's body and only just kept his feet. Scott pressed forward, changing his line of attack and driving John back.

John had learned the basic rules of cut and thrust from his uncle and father, but he'd had little occasion to practice. Scott was a professional soldier, and he parried every cut and slash. He was faster on the riposte and constantly changed tactics, keeping John off balance and driving him back till he was only a few paces from the tree.

Scott feinted left, thrusting for John's hip; then he switched direction and brought the sabre up in an arch to cut at his head. John recognized the feint, and as Scott shifted his balance, he ran straight in at him and thrust for his throat. Scott's eyes flashed with alarm, and he dropped his sabre, taking John's cutlass halfway along its length and leapt back.

The point touched Scott's chest. John saw the red stain form on his tunic, and he launched himself forward. The shriek of steel on steel put his teeth on edge, and he dropped his shoulder and slammed it into Scott, knocking him off balance. Scott was forced to take a step back, and John stepped to the right, cutting at Scott's head. Scott blocked him and trapped their swords between them.

John was finally eye to eye with the man who had hung his uncle, and murdered Louis's entire village. He knew he must kill this man or die trying. He pushed against Scott's blade with all his strength, but he was becoming light-headed. Scott increased the pressure, grunting with the effort, and threw him back.

They faced each other. John's breath was coming in gasps, and his head was spinning, but he kept his eyes fixed on him. Scott lifted his chin.

"You've done me injury, boy. You murdered my nephew and caused me to be banished to this wilderness." Scott's voice was laced with bitterness. He started to speak again, but John overrode him.

"They were raping my cousin," John screamed. "She was no more than a girl. What did you expect me to do, Englishman? Lie down and let them butcher her?"

John saw a flash of emotion in Scott's eyes, but in a heartbeat they turned cold again.

"You hung my uncle. He had no part of killing your nephew, and I'll have your life for it."

Scott sneered at him. "The man was a rebel as are you."

John shouted in Scott's face. "Rebel is a convenient name for anyone you wish to conquer. Were the children you slaughtered in the Mi'kmaq village rebels, Scott? Did hacking them to pieces satisfy your English need to play the master?"

John saw hesitation in Scott's eyes for a second; then his jaw set and he barked, "I'll have done with this now." He sprang at John, striking down from the right faster than John thought possible, and caught him off guard. He threw his cutlass up and parried the blow, but Scott gripped the pommel with his left hand and threw his weight behind it, driving him back.

As he stepped back, John's heel caught on a stone and he stumbled backwards struggling to keep his feet. John crashed into the tree, his elbow struck a broken branch, his hand flew open and the cutlass clattered to the ground.

A cry of rage came out of John, and he threw himself forward, but Scott had his blade at his throat in an instant. John froze. There was murder in Scott's eyes, but John expected no mercy from this man and would give none in return.

"What are you waiting for, Englishman? Killing is what you do best." Scott increased the pressure on the blade till it drew blood, and his eyes bored into John's, and John saw him tense for the final thrust. He gathered himself to deflect the blade, but Scott hesitated. Something changed in his eyes. He stepped back and dropped the blade, keeping his eyes fixed on John.

Scott stood at arm's length, watching him; then John saw a flash of movement on his left. Scott saw it and looked to his right. Louis was charging at Scott, his tomahawk in his left hand and a knife in his right, held close against his stomach. He was ten feet away and covered the distance in two strides. Scott brought his sabre up, but he was slow. Louis swept his tomahawk in a circle, throwing the blade to the side. He turned inside Scott's guard and drove the knife up under his chin.

Scott stiffened and his eyes went wide. He looked at John then crumpled to the ground. John stared at Scott. Blood was pumping from his neck, but his eyes were staring at the sky. The blood flow slowed until he finally lay still. John couldn't tear his eyes away. The man who had caused such misery and grief in his life was dead, but he felt no sense of justice done. Instead a wave of anger gripped him that he'd been denied his vengeance.

John felt a kind of madness take hold of him and a scream came out of him. "He was mine to kill. It was my revenge to take."

Louis was doubled over, holding his right arm against his chest. He straightened up and looked at John. His face was twisted with pain, but his eyes were clear, and he shook his head. John felt as if his blood was boiling in his veins and his hands clenched into fists.

Chantal stepped in front of him. She put her hands on his chest and looked into his face.

"You feel you have been cheated of your revenge, but this man slaughtered Louis's whole village. He had the right to revenge himself on the Englishman. Louis is your friend, John."

John stared at her as if she was speaking a language he didn't understand; then, as quickly as it had come, his anger vanished. He put his hand over hers and let his breath out slowly, and with it went the bitterness that had poisoned his heart for so long.

John went to Louis and put his hand on his shoulder.

"I'm sorry for my anger, my friend. You have avenged both of our families." Louis looked at John for a long moment; then his face creased in a smile. It was so long since he had seen Louis smile that he laughed. Louis grasped John's arm.

"We are as brothers, John. It will always be so."

"It will always be so, my friend," he said.

John felt Chantal touch his arm. "Let me see your shoulder."

Chantal helped him to pull his shirt off and examined the wound. "The ball gouged the flesh on your shoulder and struck the bone, but I don't think it's broken." Chantal washed the wound and bound it up with a piece of cloth.

"We must go. More Iroquois will come." Chantal helped him pull his shirt on and examined Louis's wound.

John picked up his rifle and wiped the blood off his dirk and they gathered up their sleeping rolls and gear. Chantal tied Louis's shoulder up, and he seemed to be in less pain. John and Chantal shared the baggage between them, and Louis carried only his rifle in his left hand.

John walked over to where Scott lay and looked down at the body. His eyes stared at the sky, cold and lifeless. Chantal came and stood beside him.

"Why did he hesitate?"

John shook his head.

"I don't know."

"I don't understand what drives such a man."

"Nor do I, but he is dead, and it does not matter now."

John looked at Scott's lifeless features, and realized he couldn't summon the hatred he had long carried for this man.

He turned to Louis. "Lead on, my friend."

Louis led them upstream, and at the edge of the clearing, John looked back. Scott's body lay still, his dead eyes staring at the sky, Crammer close by. These men had changed the direction of his life, and their malice had haunted his dreams. Now it seemed that with their deaths a chapter in his life had closed. As he walked into the forest he felt the past melt away, and he turned his mind to the next chapter, which would be of his own making.

They followed the creek for several miles until the ground began to rise and made their way around the side of a cone-shaped hill. There were no trees or undergrowth on the hill, leaving half a mile of open ground on the top.

John pointed. "Take us to the top."

"We shouldn't show ourselves in the open," Louis said.

"I want to see the river and where we've come from."

Louis looked at him skeptically, but headed for the summit. They emerged onto a meadow of soft grass, and it took them half an hour to climb to the hill. At the summit John looked back at a breathtaking sight. The St. Lawrence River was to the east. The valley spread out below them forested in deepest green. The Ottawa River was to the north flowing east to join the St. Lawrence. To the west the land ran away into the distance, line after line of hills as far as the eye could see.

John looked at Louis. "What is in your heart, my friend? Where does the trail lead?"

Louis looked to the horizon then back to John. "We started a journey together, and there are many miles yet to travel." Louis's face broke into a smile.

John saw the man who had become his friend in Louisburg, and laughed with him, happy that a warm heart beat within his breast.

John turned to Chantal. "What is your wish, Chantal, now that we are free of the past? What future will you choose?"

Chantal took his hand and twined her fingers in his. "I go where you go now. It is my wish that we never be parted."

John brought her hand to his lips and looked at her face. Her eyes were the colour of the sky, and they shone with tenderness and love. "We shall not be parted, then, as long as we live," he said.

John looked out over the valley below them. The sun had risen over the eastern hills. It turned the St. Lawrence River to the colour of molten lead, and cut a shining path through the land, streaming away into the north and on to the sea. It seemed to John that the river was part of his life now, as if its lifeblood was mingled with his, and he felt at peace.

"Let us begin, then," he said. And they turned again to the west and the vast green land that lay before them.

AUTHOR'S NOTE

THE CHARACTERS IN THIS NOVEL are entirely fictional. In the interests of authenticity, I have chosen names that are consistent with the period, geographical region, and cultural background of each individual. Many of the locations where the story takes place are real and still exist today. In order to maintain momentum in the storyline, I have taken some liberties with locations and the distances between towns and villages, et cetera.